BOY TOY

NOVELS BY MICHAEL CRAFT

Rehearsing

The Mark Manning Series

Flight Dreams
Eye Contact
Body Language
Name Games
Boy Toy

www.michaelcraft.com

BOY TOY

Michael Craft

ST. MARTIN'S MINOTAUR
NEW YORK

www.minotaurbooks.com

Library of Congress Cataloging-in-Publication Data

Craft, Michael.
    Boy toy / Michael Craft.—1st ed.
        p. cm.—(The Mark Manning series)
    ISBN 0-312-26917-X
    1. Manning, Mark (Fictitious character)—Fiction. 2. Guardian and ward—Fiction. 3. Amateur theater—Fiction. 4. Teenage boys—Fiction. 5. Wisconsin—Fiction. 6. Gay men—Fiction. I. Title.

PS3553.R215 B69 2001
813'.54—dc21

                                                                2001019162

First Edition: June 2001

10 9 8 7 6 5 4 3 2 1

Cette fois,
en anglais:
For Leon

Acknowledgments

The author wishes to thank Paul Boyer, Ray Cebula, Richard Hawkins, Judy Rossow, Nancy Simpson, and Rick Smoke for their generous assistance with various plot details. A special note of gratitude is offered to Keith Kahla and Mitchell Waters, whose efforts have advanced this series in print.

Contents

PART ONE

Teen Play

WORLD PREMIERE

Dumont Players' new production should prove 'utterly mah-velous'

By GLEE SAVAGE
Trends Editor, Dumont Daily Register

Aug. 1, DUMONT WI—Excitement abounds among the Dumont Players Guild as the amateur theater company prepares to mount the premiere production of *Teen Play*. The original script was written by local radio personality Denny Diggins, who also directs the show. Opening night is this Friday, curtain at 8:00 P.M., with six performances running over two weekends at the historic Dumont Playhouse.

The play's plot is highly self-reflective, centering on a conflict between two teenage actors involved in the production of an original play, itself titled *Teen Play*. Said Diggins, "It's an unusual conceit, one truly meant to challenge its audience. What I intend to deliver," he added in a tone well known to longtime radio listeners, "is an utterly *mah*-velous evening of theater."

The roles of both playwright and director are new to the flamboyant Diggins, who has aired the often controversial *Denny Diggins' Dumont Digest* for nearly 20 years.

Asked about the motivation to try his hand at theater, he explained simply, "It was time to broaden my oeuvre."

The young cast of *Teen Play* is headlined by two accomplished high school actors. Jason Thrush, 17, will enter his senior year at Unity High this fall with three years of acting experience in eight productions. Thad Quatrain, also 17, attends Dumont Central, where the acting bug bit him just this past year. Both young men are double-cast in the production, playing the leading role of Ryan in alternating performances. Jason Thrush will star as Ryan in Friday night's premiere.

This reporter had the opportunity to watch a recent rehearsal at the Dumont Playhouse, downtown on First Avenue. Without telling too much, suffice it to say that the two-act play does deliver on its author's promise. Friday night, petty rivalries will set the stage for murder when the baring of dark secrets leads to grim revenge. Don't miss it. ❏

Wednesday, August 1

RYAN. *Turn, crossing to Down Left window.* (*flippantly*) Not that it really matters, Dawson. Not tonight. It's only *community* theater. *Pick up football from desk.*

DAWSON. *Rise, following.* (*from behind*) And what's *that* supposed to mean?

RYAN. *Turn to him. Pause.* It means, there's a world beyond Podunk. *Gesture toward dark sky outside of window.* There are bigger things ahead. *Cross to Center, twiddling football in hands.* (*thinking aloud*) For some of us.

DAWSON. (*laughing*) Lighten up, Ryan. We're *kids*, for God's sake. And I *thought* we were friends. This isn't a contest.

RYAN. Everything's a contest, pal. *Throw football to Dawson, hard.*

DAWSON. *Fumble ball. Cross one step toward Center.* No, Ryan. It's a play, not a contest. We open soon, and we're in it together, all of us. We're a team.

RYAN. Good teams win. And winning teams have winning players. (*smugly*) Some are better than others.

DAWSON. *Step nearer.* (*getting angry*) Okay, "pal." You're better than the rest of us—you're the best. *Step face-to-face.* Is *that* what you need to hear?

RYAN. (*grunting*) Not from you. *Shove Dawson, palms to chest.*

DAWSON. (*with resolve*) Watch it. It's not cool to treat a friend that way. And if that friend happens to be your understudy—well, don't be stupid.

RYAN. (*slyly, quietly*) Don't *you* be stupid, Dawson. I know all about that "little incident" over spring break. *Poke Dawson's chest with finger.* Not something we'd care to spread around, right?

DAWSON. (*hatefully*) Why, you . . . *Lunge at Ryan.*

RYAN. *Trip Dawson.* Don't make me laugh, you pathetic . . . *Tumble together to the floor.*

(*Sound Cue 7: Desk phone rings, continues throughout.*)

RYAN AND DAWSON. *Tussle. Ad-lib epithets. Roll together against Right Center end table, upsetting lamp. After lamp CRASHES:*

(*Lighting Cue 11: Room partially darkens.*)

RYAN. *Pin Dawson to floor.* Tonight, or opening night, or any night, don't ever forget this. Don't ever forget who's on top. *Tense pause. Release Dawson.*

DAWSON. *Rise, brushing self with hands. Cross to Up Right doorway. Pause, looking back.* (*bitterly*) Keep it up, Ryan, and you may not live till opening night. Remember, I'll be waiting in the wings. *Exit.*

RYAN. *Laugh, sprawling on floor, as:*

(*Lighting Cue 12: Quick fade to black.*)

(*Sound Cue 8: Phone rings LOUD one last time in darkness. Then silence.*)

"Mah-velous!" proclaimed Denny Diggins, clapping, breaking the theatrical spell. Rising from the dim pool of light that spilled from his makeshift director's table in the fifth row of seats, he called to the control booth, "Houselights, please!" As he ambled to the center aisle, the rest of the cast and crew gathered near the front of the stage, applauding the two young actors for their performance of the fight scene that concluded act one.

Though the boys had made the scene look easy and natural, I knew that it had taken weeks of work—part of June and all of July—every movement carefully choreographed and rehearsed. I gladly added to the applause. Dawson, the kid who made the final threat, was played by Thad Quatrain, my seventeen-year-old ward. Two winters ago, when I moved to Wisconsin as the new owner and publisher of the *Dumont Daily Register*, Thad's mother, a wealthy cousin of mine, died unexpectedly, leaving Thad in my care. Technically, he and I are second cousins, but we think of each other as nephew and uncle. In our day-to-day lives, we dispense with the specifics of kinship and simply call each other Thad and Mark.

My full name, by the way, is Mark Quatrain Manning. I'm forty-three, a reporter by training who made waves in Chicago as an investigative journalist. My acclaim stemmed from a succession of high-profile stories that I reported for the prestigious *Chicago Journal*. What's more, I am gay—a distinction that I refused to hide when I myself discovered it nearly four years ago, at the height of my career and at the brink of middle age.

"Mark! Neil!" said Thad as he leapt from the stage and bounded up the aisle. I was sitting in the back row of seats with Neil Waite, a thirty-five-year-old architect, the man in my life. Rising from our seats in the otherwise empty auditorium, I noted the curious and distinct smells of the historic theater: dust and mold, the fresh lumber and paint of the newly finished set, an electrical transformer somewhere that should have been scrapped long ago. "Well," Thad asked through a grin as he approached us, "what'd you think?"

Neil was first into the aisle and swept Thad into a big sloppy hug. "It really pulled together, didn't it? And *you* were worried! The scene looked great, Thad."

"Thanks!" Then Thad suddenly backed out of their hug. "Sorry, Neil—I didn't mean to stink you up. I'm sweating like crazy."

We all were. For Thad, the physical demands of the fight scene had soaked him with perspiration, but for the rest of us, the heat alone was sufficient to keep us damp and feverish. August in central Wisconsin could be brutal, and though the old theater was air-conditioned, the amateur troupe could barely afford to run the lights. For rehearsals, the auditorium was cooled to a level just shy of tolerable.

My turn to hug the kid. "Hey, don't sweat the sweat—we won't melt." And I clapped my arms around him, a gesture that echoed Neil's. "You're really getting *good*, Thad. We're proud of you. Thanks for inviting us tonight."

I'd never seen him rehearse, and indeed, the whole theater thing was something of a mystery to me. Less than a year ago, when Thad had begun his junior year at Dumont Central High, he was still adjusting to his new life with "two dads," showing little interest in school. He needed *some* sort of involvement to snap him out of an adolescent funk that sometimes had a rebellious edge, so Neil encouraged him to audition for a play. Thad took Neil's advice and discovered talents that had lain dormant. The bug, as they say, bit, and he appeared in all three plays at school that year, each time mastering more challenging roles. Come summer, he was loath to let the long, hot months pass without honing his newfound craft. Again it was Neil who suggested the remedy—community theater. And it was Neil, throughout, who coached Thad in the lore and taboos of the art of Thespis; it was Neil who spent patient hours helping Thad memorize lines; it was Neil who knew exactly how to quell Thad's doubts and butterflies. I could only look on with awed amusement as Neil helped effectuate this transformation of our inherited child, once sullen, now so gung ho.

So when Thad invited Neil and me to attend his dress rehearsal that night, I jumped at the chance. I wanted to get a firsthand look at this magic, this discipline found so addictive by those who "tread the boards." What I saw, though, was simply work—rigorous work—and its rewards seemed elusive at best that muggy night. But I could tell from Thad's sprightly banter, from the energy I felt through his touch, that his mind's eye had locked on a future brimming with the boundless promise known only to youth.

(Never could I have guessed that tragedy was brewing.)

"Now remember," he was saying, "on Saturday we switch roles. I'll star as Ryan, with Jason playing the smaller role of Dawson."

"Which means," said Neil, "you both have to learn the other half of the fight."

"We've got it nailed," Thad assured us. "Jason and I rehearsed the reverse casting last night, and it was every bit as good as tonight. In fact," he added with a nudge, "*better*," meaning, of course, that he preferred playing the leading role.

"People! People!" called Denny Diggins from the front of the stage, clapping for attention, sounding downright schoolmarmish. "Listen up. Act one looked fabulous tonight. I have a few notes, as usual"—he brandished his clipboard—"but I'll save those for the end. Take a fifteen-minute break, relax, try to cool off, then onward with act two. Remember, people: focus. We've got a great show on our hands." Hopping from the edge of the stage, looking decidedly unathletic, even foppish, Denny signaled that he needed to talk with someone nearby, a nice-looking man who was not in the cast—a crew member, I presumed.

Some of the company wandered to the lobby in search of soda. Others gathered in clumps of conversation or lent a hand at a long work-table where volunteers folded and collated program books. A Latino boy sat by himself in a front-row seat, reviewing his script. Jason Thrush, Thad's colead, who had just played Ryan in the fight scene, remained center stage, sitting on the floor, indiscreetly blowing his nose into a wadded handkerchief while chatting with some other kids who had joined him there. Among them were Kwynn Wyman, a classmate and friend of Thad's whom I'd met at the house, and another girl, conspicuously pretty (the word *nubile* sprang to mind), whose eyes suggested an interest in Jason that went beyond the teamlike camaraderie of fellow cast members.

A few observations about Jason Thrush are in order. Though I'd heard the name often during the rehearsal period of *Teen Play*, I'd never seen him till that night, and then from the back of the auditorium. I knew that he was Thad's age, seventeen, and on the basis of a short feature that had appeared in that morning's *Register*, I knew that he'd been involved with theater a few years longer than Thad. Jason's surname was familiar—a local industry bore the name Thrush, so I assumed his family to be moneyed. But because he and Thad went to different schools, I knew nothing more about him.

I did know this: physically, Jason Thrush was a knockout. Face, body, bearing, you name it—he was classically handsome and athletically butch, though not brutishly muscular, lacking only a smile, a real smile. Something about him seemed hard or distant. Perhaps he was distracted by the summer cold he was nursing. More likely, he was just stuck-up, looking down with disdain upon a world less beautiful and privileged than himself.

Objectively, Jason was better looking than Thad. Don't get me wrong. Almost anyone would agree that Thad too was an attractive young man—he'd had his own share of luck in the gene pool. What's more, he'd grown out of his adolescent gawkiness, and his theatrical pursuits had refined both his movement and his speech. He was pleasant, intelligent, and hardworking.

On a purely cosmetic or superficial level, though, Jason Thrush took the prize, hands down, and I could understand why he'd been chosen to play the starring role in Friday's premiere. I didn't know if the play's director had justified this decision based on Jason's greater acting experience, or if lots had been drawn, or if coins were tossed. Regardless of how the casting was arrived at, it made sense to me—in spite of my prejudices resting loyally with Thad, in spite of Thad's gut-deep desire to star in the opening, now two nights away.

"Hey," said Thad, "since we've got a few minutes, I want you to meet some people." He started leading us down the aisle toward the activity near the stage.

"Are you *sure?*" asked Neil, laughing. "We're just a couple of old farts."

I knew what he was really asking: Wasn't Thad embarrassed to have his teenage friends see him dragging around his "parents," parents who happened to be a same-sex couple? Such a setup was pretty rare any-where. In heartland Dumont, it was unique—and a tad controversial.

Thad stopped in his tracks, turning back to us. "Are you kidding?" His tone was reprimanding, but the emotion underlying it was pure affection. "I *enjoy* showing you off. Come on." And he continued down the aisle.

Neil and I followed, sharing a melting glance that confirmed his knees had weakened, as mine had. He squeezed my shoulder and whis-pered into my ear, "How'd we ever get so lucky?"

I shrugged. I laughed. How else could I answer?

"Mr. Diggins?" said Thad, approaching his director. "You've met my family, haven't you? Mark Manning and Neil Waite."

Denny Diggins turned from the conversation he had just finished with the good-looking crew guy. Denny's big smile was forced and toothy; the too deep chestnut hue of his hair vainly covered gray. "Of course, Thad. So very good to see you gentlemen again." He reached to shake our hands limply, greeting us in turn: "Neil. Mahk." Though Wisconsin-born forty-some years ago, closer to fifty, he claimed to have studied abroad at some point in his youth (a little research of my own had revealed that college took him no farther than Madison), and he spoke with an affected, vaguely Continental accent. So I was "Mahk."

Neil had encountered Denny from time to time that summer, recruited into parental tasks of running various production errands, so they were chummy enough. My own history with Denny, though, stretched back a few months further and was considerably less cordial.

His radio program, *Denny Diggins' Dumont Digest,* was something of a local institution. The afternoon interviews drew a respectable audi-ence, leading Denny to claim bragging rights as the town's only *other* dependable news source—the primary source being the *Dumont Daily Register.* Denny never missed an on-air opportunity to trash my paper, at times questioning my journalistic integrity. His pompous and out-landish claims of superior professional standards were nothing short of libelous. Indeed, I had considered suing this self-inflated fruitcake more than once. On the calming advice of a lawyer friend, I had done nothing, realizing that Denny would relish a juicy, public controversy with me. My best response was no response. Why dignify his nonsense by wasting my time with it?

This decidedly tense relationship would change, though, when Denny wrote his play and convinced the Dumont Players Guild to mount its premiere production, with Denny himself as director. His casting needs included two strong teenage leads. Imagine his dismay when auditions revealed that one of the most accomplished young actors in town was Thad Quatrain, foster child of the dreaded Mahk Manning. Denny needed Thad to help assure the success of his debut as a playwright, and naturally, I wanted Thad to enjoy the opportunity and excel at it. So Denny and I entered a period of strained truce. Thad was largely unaware of the bad blood between Denny and me, and in fairness, Denny was good to Thad, whose talents continued to blossom, even under the tutelage of an eccentric director.

Neil was saying, "We can't wait for this weekend, Denny. We'll be bringing a crowd. Looks like you're ready."

I added, "It's been a long haul, but it was obviously worth it. Thad talks of little else these days. I can see why—great job tonight." Though the compliments felt like shards of glass in my throat, they were sincere enough.

"*Thank* you, Mahk," Denny gushed. "I had no *idea* what I was biting off when I began this venture." He whisked a silk hankie from somewhere—it must have been tucked up a sleeve—and began mopping his brow, bemoaning the heat, the work, the lack of proper funding for the arts, and on and on. As he yammered, I noticed something. There near the stage, a distinctive new scent had joined the smells of dust, lumber, and paint that I'd whiffed from the back row of seats. It was sweet and flowery, with a hint of pine, vaguely familiar. Had Denny doused himself with too much aftershave for the hot night? "But all the effort," he concluded, "has indeed paid off. Just a few technical glitches to resolve, and the show, I daresay, will be *perfect*."

"Which means," added the other man, whose conversation we'd interrupted, "I've got work to do." His good-natured comment seemed to confirm my assumption that he was on the show's crew. He stood about my height, not quite six feet, and seemed about my age, perhaps a few years younger. Due to the heat, he'd worn shorts that night (I wished I'd done the same), showing legs that were nicely toned and well tanned. Though sweating, and apparently beleaguered by Denny's "technical glitches," he displayed an amiable attitude that complemented his pleasant features. I was hoping to be introduced when, to my surprise, he asked through a handsome grin, "How's it going, Neil?"

"Fine, Frank. Though it seems *you've* got your hands full tonight."

"Just the usual last-minute travails of an amateur tech director."

Denny assured us, "The best in the business."

"For the price," added Frank, "which is nothing."

We all laughed. I extended my hand. "I'm Mark Manning."

"Duh," said Neil, slapping his head, "sorry, Mark. I thought you'd met. This is Frank Gelden, the show's technical director. You'll rarely see him down here in the theater—he's usually cramped up in the control booth, working lights and sound." Neil pointed up and back, in the direction of the balcony.

"I enjoy it," Frank explained with a shrug. "Pleased to meet you, Mark."

Thad said, "I've told you about Mr. Gelden before. He's our faculty adviser for Fungus Amongus." Responding to my bewildered stare, Thad amplified, "You know—the mushroom club."

Then he sat at the nearby worktable, joining the playbill assembly line.

"Jeez," I said with a laugh, shaking my head, "I can't keep track anymore." I really couldn't. There'd been a time, barely a year earlier, when Neil and I had fretted that Thad lacked "involvement" and could be headed for trouble. Now he had so many interests, I wondered if he needed to scale back. There was theater, of course—plus cars, photography, and of all things, the school mushroom club. There were doubtless other activities that hadn't even sunk in with me yet. I asked Frank, "You're a teacher, then, at Thad's school?"

"I'm a teacher, yes, but not at Dumont Central. Actually, I'm on the natural-sciences faculty at UW–Woodlands," he told me, referring to the local branch-campus of the University of Wisconsin. "I'm a molecular-biology prof, and mycology has always been a special interest, so I volunteered to advise Central's mushroom-hunting club. They're a great group of kids, the Fungus Amongus."

Looking up from his program-stuffing, Thad informed me from the corner of his mouth, "Mycology is the study of mushrooms."

I mussed his hair, telling him, "I figured." Turning to Frank, I said,

"Between your volunteer work at Central and your volunteer work for the Players Guild, how do you find time for teaching?"

"I'm off all summer, and when things do get frantic, well—Cynthia and I have no kids of our own, and I like being able to help. It's fulfilling."

In a nutshell, Frank Gelden struck me as a nice guy. Interesting too. I removed from a pocket the pet fountain pen I always carry, an antique Montblanc, and made a note to mention Frank to my features editor, Glee Savage. She might want to work up a story on him. Local readers can't get enough of those homey, feel-good profiles.

"How *is* Cynthia?" asked Neil. "Could you let her know that when she gets back to town, I'll have a revised set of drawings for her?"

Something clicked. I interrupted, "You mean Cynthia Dunne-Gelden?" She was a recent architectural client of Neil's, a businesswoman planning a sizable addition to her country home. I'd wondered how Neil knew so much about Frank's involvement with the theater group, since Neil's own involvement was tangential at best. The house project explained everything: Neil knew Frank through Cynthia.

Neil proceeded to detail for me exactly what I'd just figured out. While nodding to these presumed revelations, I had the opportunity to get a closer look at Frank, intending to inspect his legs again, to study their lustrous nap of sun-bleached hair, but my eyes locked on his wedding ring. Oddly, this tangible symbol of "where he stood" came as something of a relief. More often than not, upon meeting an attractive man, I was content to presume him gay until my wishful, groundless theory was contradicted by reality. I would then mourn the loss of yet another potential addition to the brotherhood. In Frank's case, though, I was glad to set this speculation aside from the outset. Frank's life had already touched both Thad's and Neil's, so I prudently nipped any prurient notions then and there, before they had an opportunity to root in the fertile loam of my imagination.

"I'll phone her later tonight," Frank said of his wife. "She'll be delighted to hear about the blueprints—she's been itching to break ground."

"Denny?" asked a woman as she stepped into our circle of conversation. She carried a pile of clothes and a long, ratty wig. "I've made all the changes to Tommy's costume. Got a moment to check him out before act two?"

"Of course, Joyce. Anything for you, my dear." Then Denny remembered his manners. "Oh. You already know Neil Waite, but I don't believe you've met Thad's, uh . . ." He gestured toward me, whirling his hand vacantly, unsure what to call me.

"Uncle," I supplied the missing word, taking only minor offense at Denny's hesitation. "My pleasure, Joyce. I'm Mark Manning."

She offered her hand, after extracting it with some difficulty from the bundle she carried. "I thought so," she said, "from your pictures. My name's Joyce Winkler, costume mistress extraordinaire." She puffed herself up with comic pride, then blew a stray lock of hair from her sweat-shiny forehead.

Neil told me, "Joyce is also Nicole's mom." Drawing a blank look from me, he elaborated, "Nicole is in the cast. She's up there with Jason and Kwynn." His glance led my eyes to the stage.

Jason Thrush still sat center stage, talking with two girls as other kids milled about. I knew Kwynn Wyman, Thad's friend, so I assumed Nicole Winkler was the other girl, the pretty one I'd noticed doting on Jason. She was still at it. Though she chattered vacantly while preening her luxuriant gold tresses, her hungry eyes betrayed an obsession with the hunky young actor. I had sensed this from the back of the theater; now, at closer range, Nicole's lewd daydreams were embarrassingly obvious.

Her mom was explaining, "Theater has always been Nicole's thing, not mine. But she's been through some . . . 'rough spots' lately, and she's off to college this fall, and, well, I thought it was time to do a bit of bonding. So here I am, 'sharing her interests.'" Joyce laughed at the pile of clothes in her hands, at the self-imposed drudgery she'd taken on. "And the worst part was juggling schedules with my *real* job. I owe people night shifts for a year now."

Denny told us, "Joyce is a lab technician at the hospital."

"I don't know squat about sewing, but duty called, so here I am. Fortunately, most of the 'costumes' are just street clothes."

"It's a contemporary drama," Denny reminded us through pursed lips, "requiring little by way of *constructed* costuming."

"Except"—Joyce hefted the wig, robe, and whatnot in her arms—"the Old Man. I've pricked my fingers to the bone building the one costume that spends the least amount of time onstage. Let's nab Tommy," she told Denny, "and see if this sucker *finally* fits."

"Dear, sweet, put-upon Joyce," Denny told her, "I am at your command." And with a regal flourish befitting a Louis, he led her away from us, approaching the smallish Latino boy who sat alone, studying his script.

"I'd better get busy myself," Frank told us. "There are a couple of complicated cross-fades in act two that just haven't been working. Of course, it would help if we had some decent equipment—every circuit is already overloaded, and most of those dimmers are on their last legs."

I sniffed. "I thought I smelled something electrical."

He laughed. "Don't worry. I'll get things patched together. We'll survive the two-weekend run." He turned to bound up the aisle toward the balcony, then paused, telling us, "Break a leg in act two, Thad. Good to see you again, Neil. And great to meet you, Mark."

We echoed his friendly sentiments, and he was gone—eaten, it seemed, by the shadows of the old theater. "Nice guy," I told the others. It was an offhand comment, conversational filler, not intended to carry any subtext, but as I said it, his wedding ring glinted in my mind's eye.

"Mr. Gelden's the best," Thad agreed, rising from the table with a pile of finished programs. "All the kids in Fungus Amongus really like him. And he's worked harder on *Teen Play* than most of the cast." Thad jogged the stack of programs on the table, then crouched to place them in a corrugated box.

Neil told me, "Cynthia has suggested more than once that the four of us should get together—a double date."

I laughed. "Fine with me."

"Wow," said Thad, jerking his head toward the brightly lit apron of the stage, "you'd never know Tommy in that getup." Joyce and Denny fussed with the kid's costume, which made him look like a hermit, an ancient troll, replete with a wig and beard in the style of a scruffy Jesus. Thad was right—Tommy's costume totally disguised the boy within.

Confused, I said, "Denny called *Teen Play* a 'contemporary drama.' What's up with Tommy? He looks like an extra from some Bible epic."

Showing me a program, pointing to a line near the bottom of the cast, Thad explained, "Tommy Morales plays the Old Man, a bit part in act two. He pops into a scene that's sort of a dream, speaks a few words of wisdom, then vanishes."

"Oh." I didn't get it.

Thad continued, "Tommy is also the understudy for Dawson, the role I'm rehearsing tonight. Since Jason and I are double-cast as both Ryan *and* Dawson, either of us could take over the leading role of Ryan if the other couldn't go on for some reason. Tommy would then step into the role of Dawson."

"Ahhh." Now I did get it. "That's why Tommy had his nose buried in the script—the Old Man doesn't take much study, but Dawson does."

"Right. He's learning Dawson's lines. And if he ever needs to *play* Dawson, he can still play the Old Man as well because the two characters are never onstage together. No one would recognize Tommy beneath that beard anyway."

With a grunt of approval, I told Thad, "I'm impressed. Denny has all the bases covered." Laughing, I added with comic foreboding, "Should disaster strike."

I have always scoffed at superstition, but there are doubtless those who will chide me for tempting fate with my glib tone. (In retrospect, I concede that my smug humor may have been brash, for tragedy did indeed prove to be looming. Still, I am reasonably certain that the impending calamity was rooted not in my offhand cockiness, but in the premeditated scheming of a killer.)

"Mica," said Thad brightly to a girl who strolled past, in front of the stage, "I didn't know you were here tonight."

She stopped, turning to eye Thad with a blank expression that barely acknowledged his existence. Her features were pretty, if hard. Her fingernails (the word *talons* sprang to mind) were lacquered black. Her gleaming black hair was long and straight, chopped severely above a pert butt clad in a stretchy, black miniskirt that pushed the envelope of modesty—though modesty was clearly a concept that had never crossed her radar. She was of course pencil-thin. She told Thad dryly, "I didn't think to report my presence. If you *really* need to know, I'm just keeping an eye on baby brother." She smiled so faintly, it must have hurt.

Neil whispered in my ear, "I think that's Mica Thrush, Jason's older sister."

"What a fright," I whispered back. She and Thad were talking about something; she was asking how long the rehearsal would last.

With a low chortle Neil said, "Jason and Mica—typical spoiled rich kids."

"Hey," I reminded him, "Thad Quatrain is a 'rich kid.'" By now, Jason had noticed his sister in the auditorium and, from the stage, joined the conversation with Thad and her.

"Yes," Neil conceded, "but Thad's hardly 'typical.'"

"Of *course* not," I agreed, mocking blind parental pride. "He's *ours*."

Exactly what happened next is not clear to me, as I was still gabbing with Neil, but at some point I became aware that Thad's conversation with Jason had grown agitated, even heated. Other people's chatter was quelled by this, and everyone in the theater, cast and crew alike, turned to listen.

Jason now rose from where he was sitting and stepped to the edge of the stage, stuffing his handkerchief in his jeans. He paused, looked Thad in the eye, and told him through a sarcastic smirk, "I see you brought your two daddies tonight. Are they proud of their boy toy?"

His words had the predictable effect—all present were stunned silent. The sheer bigotry of Jason's attack, delivered with such bald arrogance, was meant not only to degrade Neil and me, but worse, to question the nature of our relationship to Thad and, in doing so, to hurt and humiliate him. As intended, Jason's words did hurt Thad. I could see it in the boy's face, in the way his body seemed instantly drained of energy, of life.

I wanted to rush to Thad's defense, but anything I might have said would be perceived as a defense of *myself*. Oddly, I felt no urge to mount a counterattack against Jason's adolescent homophobia. Rather, it was his mean-spirited bravado, his jock-boy swagger, that tempted me to forgo eloquence and simply slap the shit out of him.

Weighing all this, I felt paralyzed, wondering why the hell Denny Diggins didn't do something, or at least *say* something. After all, he was in charge here—he had the authority and responsibility to maintain a semblance of decorum among his troupe. But silence reigned.

Finally, when someone did speak, it was Thad. The color had returned to his face, and I was delighted to read the intent in his grin. He had wisely decided to brush off Jason's attack by trivializing it, as it deserved. He would respond to the words of an ignorant bully by bullying back, but with humor. Paraphrasing the closing words of act one, Thad said, "Keep it up, Jason, and you may not live till opening night. Remember, I'll be waiting in the wings."

A ripple of laughter and a chorus of *ooh*'s drifted through the theater, lightening the tension.

But Jason wouldn't let it rest. "*Ooh*," he said, picking up on the feigned fear voiced by the others and tossing it back at them. "I'm quakin', Thad. I'm shakin' in my boots." In a girlish voice, he asked the heavens, "However will I sleep tonight?" Then, focusing again on Thad, he said, "That's a pretty lame threat, coming from *you*, boy toy."

This elicited another round of *ooh*'s from the crowd.

But it was Kwynn Wyman, Thad's friend who'd been yakking onstage with Jason during the break, who spoke next. She sauntered downstage next to him, paused, and in the hot glare of the floodlights, snorted loudly, smelling him. She said, "That's a pretty lame comment, coming from *you*, Jason—considering that cheap perfume you're wearing."

Others nearby waved their hands and held their noses, confirming that it was Jason who'd overdone it with the aftershave that night. And Kwynn's description of it was dead-on—the flowery scent was anything but manly. Jason's sister, Mica, dropped her steely composure and was the first to burst into laughter, quickly followed by others. Neil and I allowed ourselves a hearty chuckle, but Thad restrained himself, choosing instead to bead Jason with a quietly amused, unflinching stare of victory.

"Now, people, people!" scolded Denny, at last coming to life, rapping his hands. "Enough of this 'teen play.' We've got *work* to do, people! Places, everyone. Act two." He turned, calling up to the control booth, "Frank? One minute till blackout."

The cast rushed to take their positions onstage. The crew disappeared behind the scenes. Denny returned to his director's table in the fifth row. Neil and I chose seats near the middle of the auditorium. As the houselights began a slow fade, I mused about the petty skirmish we'd just witnessed—Jason's slur, Thad's threat, Kwynn's comeback. They all seemed so . . . well, so *juvenile*, so inconsequential.

(Or so I thought. I hadn't a clue that little Tommy Morales would soon be called upon to save the show.)

Thursday, August 2

Following a night of rain, the next day dawned hot and muggy. Sunrise consisted of a searing whiteness that slid upward through a blinding haze.

The house on Prairie Street, built for my uncle Edwin's family in the years before air-conditioning was common, was designed to combat the dog days with broad, overhanging eaves shading long rows of shallow windows. A year ago, during my first summer in the house, I learned that while these features were deemed ingenious a half century ago, they didn't begin to match the comfort-pumping power of several thousand BTUs. So the lovely old home was invisibly modernized with a high-efficiency air conditioner that I was assured "could frost a church." An expensive retrofit of concealed ducts now blew bone-chilling relief from the high corners of every room. The house was sealed tight on that torrid August morn, and though birds greeted the day from surrounding treetops, I wasn't even tempted to crack a window and hear their song. So much for fresh air.

"Going for a run?" Neil had asked me earlier, when we'd kissed, thrown back the covers, and swung our feet to the floor, rising from opposite sides of the bed.

I hesitated. A run with Neil was never drudgery; the mere sight of him in motion was its own reward (ah, the joy of aerobics). He too got a certain charge from our mutual workouts in the park, which were frequently topped off at home by a more languid form of exercise. "Uh, the heat"—I waffled—"not today. Sorry, kiddo."

A bit later, around seven-thirty, when I arrived downstairs for break-fast, having showered and dressed for a busy day at the *Register*, I was alone in the kitchen. Neil was still out running. Thad was still in bed; he would sleep till noon if undisturbed. Barb, our live-in housekeeper, hired a half year ago in late January, didn't seem to be around either. Coffee was freshly made though—bubbles still floated on the surface near the top of the glass pot. Morning papers were set out with a platter of pastries and bagels.

I poured coffee into an outsize *Chicago Journal* mug (old habits die hard), sat at the table, and opened the *Register*, skimming the front page. There had been no overnight changes to the layout I'd approved at yesterday's late-afternoon editorial meeting—the world, it seemed, was as quiet as the house.

"Christ, it's hot already!" said Neil, rattling the back door open, then closing it behind him with a thud.

I grinned. "Told you so." Raising my cup, I offered, "Hot coffee?"

He answered by throwing at me the white gym towel he carried, damp with his sweat. Bare-chested, he'd taken off his T-shirt before leaving the house, hanging it on a coat hook near the door. He now grabbed the shirt and started blotting himself with it. The indoor air felt suddenly icy against his wet skin—his nipples were erect.

"Here," I said with a laugh, getting up, "let me swab you down. Keep the shirt dry—you'll need it."

We met in the middle of the room, where I took the T-shirt from his hands, set it on the counter, and began drying him with the towel. He could easily have done this himself, but he understood that I *wanted* to perform this duty—it was a labor of love. So he stood passively, watch-ing without speaking as I worked my way down his body, starting with his hair, his neck, then his chest, where I paused to warm his nipples with my tongue. Had anyone walked into the room, we'd have pre-sented a tableau at once erotic and ridiculous: he, the architect returned from a run, standing buffed, sweaty, and near naked in the kitchen, wearing only silvery nylon shorts, cracked white-leather cross-training shoes, skimpy ankle socks; and I, the freshly groomed publisher of a small-town newspaper, hunkering before him in a crisp white shirt, jaunty yellow-and-gray-striped tie, perfectly creased gabardine slacks, spit-polished cordovan oxfords.

Like a wet, fleshy tether, my tongue bridged the gap of this unlikely union, this spontaneous melding of animal and intellect. The taste of him shot past the essence of coffee that lingered in my mouth. On the surface of his skin, salt drawn from his body excited my senses and made me want more of him. Squatting lower, I reached behind him to mop his back, stopping at the waistband of his shorts. Then I dried his legs, working up from the ankles, again stopping at his shorts. Nuzzling his crotch with my chin, I felt the warm lump of his erection, moist against my face. Looking upward, glancing past the contours of his chest, I asked, "Where's Barb?"

"It's Thursday—farmers' market this morning." He traced both index fingers over the tops of my ears. "She was headed for the park while I was coming back."

That would keep her busy for the few minutes I needed, so I pulled down his shorts and helped work them past his shoes. His penis bobbed blindly for me in the cool air, but I resisted the temptation to provide its warm target. Instead, I slid the towel between his legs and finished the job of drying him, first his testicles, then his butt. The course nap of the terry cloth aroused Neil all the more, so on an impulse, I drew the towel between his legs again, holding its opposite ends taut, in front and behind. Lifting, I began pulling the towel back and forth, sliding it first up his crack, then up past his testicles, again and again, as if flossing his groin.

At first Neil laughed. Then he moaned. Then he fell silent as he widened his stance, squeaking his treaded soles on the kitchen floor. Crouching a bit, he rocked his hips, countering the direction of the towel, riding out a fantasy that I could not envision but was happy to stimulate. He looked down at his penis, by now painfully engorged, then stared into my eyes, woozy and amazed, mutely begging me to finish what I had started.

It wouldn't take long. Guiding the head of his cock along my tongue toward my throat, I was unprepared for its heat, its rocklike rigidity, its sheer size. I had sampled his arousal countless times, but this was unprecedented, a happy new plateau, so to speak. While nursing this bit of manly wonder that had taken root in my mouth, I whipped the towel one last time through Neil's cheeks, its million tiny terry fingers teasing a million tiny naughty nerves. In the same instant, his rocking stopped, he tensed, and then—rapture. He grabbed my hair, I grabbed his buttocks, and together we drained him of the sort of ball-busting, mind-bending orgasm rarely enjoyed by men old enough to vote. (The onset of adulthood has its other rewards, such as drinking, travel, and discretionary income.)

Neil, remember, is pushing middle age, and I'm already there. What's more, this was in the kitchen, on a weekday, with me fully dressed. All in all, I felt pretty damn proud of myself.

"*That* was inventive," Neil told me with a soft laugh, still catching his breath. His words had the grateful ring of sublime understatement.

I stood, pressing his nakedness against my clothing, loving the touch of him. "My pleasure, kiddo."

He finger-combed my hair; I was again office-ready. "Seriously," he said, "that was incredible. Four years together, and it just gets better."

I kissed him deeply, letting him taste a bit of himself in my throat.

He picked up his shorts and stepped into them. "You've raised the bar considerably, Mr. Manning." He tucked himself in with some effort, still showing a considerable bulge. "I owe you one."

"You owe me nothing," I assured him while moving to the sink. Tossing my necktie over a shoulder, I leaned to rinse my mouth with a fistful of water.

"I *mean*," he explained, stepping behind me and pulling my hips to his, "I owe you some equally creative lovemaking."

Intrigued, I asked over my shoulder, "A debt of honor?"

"Precisely. This will take thought and preparation and possibly some scheming. But the debt *will* be repaid." Then he patted my butt, telling me, "I need to run upstairs and put myself together."

"Aww," I pouted, turning to him, "keep me company. Have some coffee." I picked up his T-shirt from the counter and handed it to him.

"Sure." He pulled the shirt over his head, first popping that beautiful shock of mussed hair through the top, then working his sinewy arms through the sleeves. The body of the shirt dropped over his shorts, just concealing the lump.

The back door cracked open. "Any coffee left?"

"Come on in, Doug," I called. "We were just sitting down."

And in strolled Douglas Pierce, sheriff of Dumont County. He had befriended me during the week I moved to town and had since become an important news source for the paper. Over time, his friendship with Neil and me grew warmer, and we entered each other's circle of closest confidence. Letting himself into our kitchen that Thursday after his morning workout (his hair was still wet from showering at the gym),

Pierce repeated a routine we had come to expect and enjoy. As usual, he carried a large, fresh Danish kringle he'd fetched at a downtown bakery, adding it to the other pastries on the table.

"Christ, it's hot," he said, echoing Neil's earlier entry-line while removing his sport coat, draping it over the back of "his" chair. As our chief elected law enforcer, he chose not to wear a uniform, but street clothes, and I'd long admired his skill at assembling a tasteful business wardrobe. He even passed the scrutiny of Neil's design-trained eye. As these observations might suggest, the Dumont County sheriff is gay. Sitting, he took an appreciative look at Neil approaching the table in his nylon shorts—there was a carefree bounce to my partner's step. Dismayed, Pierce asked, "You're not going *running* out there, are you?"

"Finished already. Just the usual four miles." As Neil sat, I joined them at the table with extra cups.

Pierce continued to appraise Neil's attire, observing, "But you look so fresh, so . . . *energized,*" a clear reminder that, at forty-six, he'd risen through his department's ranks as a detective.

Neil and I glanced at each other, each stifling a laugh.

Pierce looked quizzically at each of us, back and forth. "What'd I miss?"

"Nothing," we blurted in unison, feigning innocence but sounding guilty.

Pierce sat back, crossing his arms, shaking his head. "You guys . . ."

Neil leaned forward. "Have some coffee, Doug." And he poured for all of us.

We spoke of the weather (no relief in sight), the food (any form of Danish being preferred over any form of bagel), and the news (not much).

"Yeah," said Pierce, "it's been a quiet summer. Usually, when the weather heats up, things can get a little dicey, but so far so good."

Neil wiped his mouth, laughing. "Come on, Doug. When was the last major crime wave that embattled your department?"

Pierce smiled, swallowing coffee. "Point taken. The mean streets of sleepy little Dumont are hardly an urban war zone. Thank God."

Neil and I nodded our accord. While munching a flaky slice of kringle, though, I wryly noted, "Try putting out a daily paper sometime, and you'll come to appreciate a modicum of mayhem. When the local garden club makes page one"—I tapped the front of that morning's *Register*—"you're in trouble."

"Don't forget," said Neil, "the Dumont Players Guild is mounting a world premiere tomorrow night. *There's* a story—play it up."

"Glee Savage has it covered," I told him. "That story's where it belongs—in features. My news sense tells me that *Teen Play* won't make the front page."

"Not even when your own *kid* is in it?"

"*Especially* when our kid is in it."

"Oh, wow," said Pierce, "I almost forgot—how's Thad doing with the play?"

"Neil and I saw last night's dress rehearsal, and Thad was terrific. I hate to admit it, but Denny Diggins may have a minor hit on his hands."

Neil added, "Thad has really grown into his role—*both* of them, actually. I'm glad he decided to give community theater a try this summer. The school plays have been great for him, but it's important to get beyond that and learn to work with adults on a production."

I nodded. "Thad *has* grown in recent months, and not just as an actor. I was surprised by his maturity last night—especially during the 'incident.' "

That caught Pierce's attention, but before he could ask about it, Neil said, " 'Incident' aside, Thad's maturity was evident all evening. When I used to be involved in theater, a director once told me how every production seems to have its 'pillar'—a cast member who earns the respect of the entire company by setting an example and inspiring the others. Clearly, Thad is that pillar, that leader. Last night during intermission, when he was obviously drained by act one and the fight scene, what did he do? Instead of goofing off with his pals and guzzling Mountain Dew, he chose to squire his 'parents' around, make introductions, and help out stuffing programs."

"That surprised me," I admitted, "not only that Thad was stuffing programs, but that the programs *needed* stuffing. The print shop could have done all the collating and bindery work—for a price, of course. The Players Guild must *really* be strapped to take on grunt work like that." Shaking my head, I uncapped my pen and made a note to write the group a check.

"Back up," said Pierce. "What about the 'incident'?"

Neil and I glanced at each other. Though proud of the way Thad had handled it, we were more embarrassed than angered by Jason Thrush's homophobic crack. But Pierce had asked—and he would be sensitive to our mixed feelings. Neil told him, "Thad's costar sounded a distinctly sour note during intermission." Then Neil related the whole "boy toy" incident, including Thad's threat: "Keep it up, Jason, and you may not live till opening night. Remember, I'll be waiting in the wings."

Pierce seemed surprised, exhaling a soft whistle. "Tough stuff."

"No," I explained, "it was *clever*, Doug. Thad was paraphrasing the last line from act one. He simply substituted Jason's name for the character's name, Ryan."

"Ahhh," said Pierce with a laugh. "Kids."

I agreed. "Just adolescent horseplay. One minute, there's a major blowup; the next, it's forgotten." These words were meant to assure myself as well as Pierce. After all, the grand total of my child-rearing experience barely topped eighteen months.

"Come opening night," said Pierce, "all will be well, I'm sure."

Neil asked him, "You're still going, aren't you?"

"Wouldn't miss it—Friday *and* Saturday. Roxanne is coming up, right?" Pierce was referring to Roxanne Exner, an attorney friend of ours in Chicago. Even after Neil and I moved north, she continued to visit regularly, sometimes making the four-hour drive for business reasons, but usually motivated only by friendship, as was the case that coming weekend.

Neil answered Pierce, "Yes, Rox is driving up on Saturday to see Thad in the starring role. Tomorrow night, Thad plays the smaller role, but it *is* the premiere, so the rest of us had better be there—you, me, Mark, and Barb."

"Where *is* Barb?" asked Pierce, looking around the room as if she might be hiding in a corner.

"Farmers' market," I told him. "She likes to shop early—to find the best stuff, I guess. She's got her hands full getting ready for the cast party here at the house on Saturday night. I offered to get a caterer, but she wouldn't hear of it."

"She's certainly the strong-willed type—a far cry from old Hazel."

We joined him in laughing at this comparison. Hazel Healy had been the Quatrain family's longtime housekeeper, her tenure dating from the birth of the eldest of my three cousins, all of whom she helped rear, including Thad's mother, Suzanne Quatrain. When my uncle Edwin died, Hazel remained in the service of the house's new owners, and when I myself acquired the house on Prairie Street, she helped me settle into it. Though she was efficient, hardworking, and loyal, I did not try to dissuade her from her decision to retire, announced within weeks of my arrival. She was getting frail, after all, and her eyesight was failing. Florida made sense for her. As for me, her retirement made sense because, frankly, I didn't like having her around. She was old, not only in her years, but in her rectitude and her outlook. She was piously Catholic, with a myopic morality and a small-town attitude to match. She was judgmental and stiff, addressing me only as "Mr. Manning" or, worse, "sir."

Barb Bilsten, at forty, was not only younger, but . . . well . . .

Barb Bilsten was walking through the back door at that very moment.

"For God's sake," she whined, juggling several bags of produce, "do you suppose one of you three able-bodied fairies could give me a hand with this crap?" As we all shot to our feet, she continued, "No—don't bother—sorry for asking—I can handle it myself."

Neil sat again, laughing, but Pierce and I foisted our aid upon Barb, each carrying a couple of bags to the counter as she closed the door and removed her sweatband, visor, and a heavy pair of three-hundred-dollar Chanel sunglasses, festooned with gold hardware. She had dressed for the heat in much the same attire as she typically wore around the house—running shoes with baby-blue puffball anklets, baggy white Bermudas, and a pink Lacoste polo shirt worn a tad too tight for her top-heavy endowment. "Christ, it's hot," she announced, slapping her wallet and sungear on the counter.

"So I've heard." I glanced into the shopping bags and saw corn, tomatoes, green beans—the usual summer cornucopia—as well as an array of unnameable, trendy vegetables of exotic extraction. Some were downright grotesque; it was unsettling to think they had grown in Wisconsin soil. "What on earth are you making? We're having a houseful of kids, remember."

"And I suppose you want me feeding them shit? Wait and see—this is delicious and wholesome."

I hate the word *wholesome*. "Maybe we should just order pizza."

"*It's under control,*" she assured me. Case closed.

Pierce asked, "Am I invited?"

"Well, *sure*," Barb, Neil, and I chorused. "Of course, Doug." It hadn't even occurred to us to specifically invite Pierce—our home was always open to him.

"You're part of the extended family, Sheriff," Barb told him, tweaking his ear. She was cooling down. "And besides, we may need you on Saturday. If the little bastards get rowdy, you can legally off'm with your Uzi." She pointed to the small revolver Pierce sometimes carried in a discreet (I daresay tasteful) shoulder holster of burnished tan leather.

We laughed. Barb was just being mouthy—she loved the little bastards. But I was also amused by something else she'd said. She had called us an "extended family," meaning the five of us: Neil, me, Thad, Barb herself, and even Pierce. Funny. None of us were related, except Thad and me, who were only second cousins. Still, the crowd on Prairie Street had indeed taken on the feel and dynamics of a family.

From the table, Neil asked, "Barb, have you had breakfast yet? Join us."

"Thanks. I think I will." As Pierce sat down again, Barb went to the refrigerator and pulled out a can of diet cola, the only liquid other than alcohol that ever passed her lips—I'd bet she brushed her teeth with it. Getting a glass from a cupboard for her, I sat at the table as Barb joined us. She popped the can and filled her glass.

Neil freshened our coffee and passed her the platter of picked-over pastries, offering, "Have some."

She noticed, as I knew she would, that the bagels were untouched. She asked everyone, "What's the matter? You don't like Jew food?"

I would normally bristle at such a comment, but as Barb herself was Jewish, she could say such things with impunity—and often did.

On behalf of all present, I explained, "My disaffection for bagels has nothing to do with their origin. The point is, I just don't like them. They're tough. They're tasteless. And here in the Midwest, where most of us were *not* weaned on them, we've been slow to acquire a yen for them—in spite of the now ubiquitous strip-mall shops that try to make them more palatable while offending purists by stuffing the damn things with blueberries and all manner of whatnot. Ultimately, though, eating a bagel is like trying to eat a sponge." I crossed my arms, resting my case: "They're not doughnuts, Barb, and never will be."

"*Well,*" she sniffed, daintily spreading cream cheese on one of the items in question. "Pardon me, I'm sure." And she broke into laughter.

This insouciant attitude was reflected in the bald pride she took in defying stereotypes. On the morning when she'd first gone shopping for our household, she'd paused at the back door and turned to tell me, "Don't get your hopes up—I *never* haggle over a price." Before leaving, she added, "And I *don't* winter in Miami." I noticed as well that she never peppered her sentences with Yiddish. In fact, Neil once uttered an experimental *Oy!* in her presence, and she promptly threw a dishrag at him.

As for Barb's religious views, which she and I had discussed at length one quiet evening shortly after she came to work for us, they were anything but Orthodox. If she believed in God at all, it was a naturalistic deity, and her Judaism was reduced to a heritage. "I consider myself a cultural Jew," she told me, and I realized that the concept was one that I could borrow. Though I had long ago dismissed the notion of God's existence and therefore scoffed at Christ's purported divinity, I was raised in a family and a society that, by and large, paid lip service to this belief. Doctrines aside, I had absorbed the whole mythology and had become, to paraphrase Barb, "a cultural Christian." There was no point in fighting it—it was part of my self-consciousness. In other words, though I was certain there had never been a "virgin birth" to remove my "stain of original sin," I felt blissfully free to enjoy the trappings and hoo-ha of Christmas. For that matter, so did Barb.

At breakfast that morning, she dropped the topic of bagels and got down to the business of running the household. Between bites she asked, "Are there any bills you want paid, Mark?"

After a slurp of coffee, I answered, "There's a fresh stack on my desk in the den—you know where to find the checkbook." Pierce subtly caught my eye, wrinkling his brow in a curious expression. I told him, "Yes, Doug, Barb has full access to the household accounts. She handles money better than I do."

She added, "MBA from Chicago," meaning the University of Chicago, one of the best business schools anywhere. Then she turned to Pierce, sticking out her tongue, just the tip.

Pierce laughed softly. "Barb, you're one unlikely 'maid.' "

Indeed she was. And after half a year with us, it was easy to forget her background. Though raised in Dumont and schooled in the Midwest, she'd sought her fortune in the pressure cooker of New York finance, struggling up the ladder as a money manager for an investment firm. When I'd first interviewed her, I had, ignorantly, asked if that meant she had been a stockbroker. Appalled by the question, she assured me in no uncertain terms, "I *don't* do retail. My role was essentially that of an analyst, involved with emerging markets." Unfortunately, the bottom had fallen out of those markets, and worse, she had discovered that "ninety-nine percent of my colleagues were pigs, total chauvinist assholes who couldn't see past my tits." So she cashed in her chips, which were considerable, and bailed, returning to her roots in Dumont. She'd had it with business, and though straight, she'd had it with men—at least for a while.

During that first interview, I was up-front about the unconventional nature of our household, and she made it equally clear that the whole setup appealed to her—she was comfortable with gay men, and since she'd never married or had children, she appreciated the opportunity to nurture Thad. I liked her simply because she was the polar opposite of Hazel, a breath of fresh air. At a deeper level, Barb would add even greater diversity to our "family," providing a valuable exposure for Thad as he prepared to leave his white-bread upbringing and stick his toes into the larger world. Clearly, Barb wasn't seeking a lifetime career as a domestic. She didn't need the money—she was "buying time," she admitted, and needed "a situation for a while." She gave me her commitment, though, to remain with us at least until Thad went off to college, a year and a half from the time she was hired. So we shook hands, and she moved in.

Neil got up and took the empty coffeepot to the sink, rinsing it. Returning, he paused by the refrigerator, asking Barb, "More pop?"

She shook her head and drained the last of her glass. "Too much gas. I need to practice later, after you guys leave the house."

Again the quizzical look from Pierce.

Neil returned to the table, telling him, "Her new clarinet—it's a beauty."

Barb nodded proudly, dabbing her lips with a paper napkin. "A genuine Leblanc. Made in France. Opus model, grenadilla body, silver keys—*the* best."

"Six grand," I said, supplying the detail that Pierce wanted to hear.

"Zow!" he said. "I'd think you'd get *gold* keys."

"Actually, they're available, special order." She grimaced. "But that's tacky."

This from the woman who'd had the bumpers of her Range Rover gilded—now *that's* tacky. But when it came to issues of music, the woman did indeed have high standards, and this was an intriguing new piece to the puzzle that was Barb Bilsten. At first blush, she seemed jaded and smart-mouthed to the point of being coarse. It was easy to overlook her deeper intelligence, her analytical precision. As for her family's cultured background and her own refined musical talents—who'd have guessed?

She had previously mentioned her old clarinet, needing a new one, a good one, wanting to take some remedial lessons. I hadn't known she was serious till last week, when she'd arranged to visit the instrument company's American headquarters in the southeast corner of the state. She'd hopped into her Range Rover one morning, driven down to Kenosha, spent a few hours with their resident clarinet guru, and driven back triumphantly with her new Leblanc. Only then did I realize that my own knowledge of classical music (a point of snobbish pride, I confess) paled next to hers.

She was saying, "It's *important* to have music in the house—there's a child under our roof. Haven't you read that music makes you smarter? It's true. They've got these studies now that show how musical training sort of 'hardwires' kids' brains to let them learn *everything* better and faster. I'm hoping Thad'll get interested."

She was right. I couldn't have agreed more. Still: "Thad has so *many* interests."

Neil quipped, "What a difference a year makes."

"It wasn't that long ago," agreed Pierce, "when he didn't even have friends."

Barb nodded meaningfully. "He has plenty of friends now, including a few of the female persuasion."

I shared a smile with Neil. "We've noticed," I said. "Neil and I sat him down for 'the talk' not long ago. I don't mean 'birds and bees'—he knew about the mechanics years ago. No, we talked to him about responsibility in general and safe sex in particular. He'd heard it all before, of course, but he really seemed to appreciate that we cared enough to break the ice and get down to specifics." Swirling the cold coffee in my cup, I recalled the knot in my stomach as we'd broached that conversation.

Neil leaned forward, elbows on the table, to continue the story. "Thad knew exactly what we were driving at—disease and pregnancy—and he addressed our concerns head-on. He actually told us not to worry, explaining that he wasn't really 'dating' yet. But I'm sure it's only a matter of time."

With good-natured skepticism, Barb asked, "What about Miss Kwynn? She's been around the house quite a bit lately."

And again, that questioning look from Pierce. "Who?"

"I think Kwynn Wyman is just a theater pal," I answered. "She's a nice girl too. You should have seen the way she stuck up for Thad last night. When the dating bug does bite, I hope Kwynn's nearby."

"My my," clucked Barb, rising from the table, "so look who's playing matchmaker." Removing a few dishes and her glass, she rinsed them at the sink.

I had no snappy answer to her comment, realizing that it contained a grain of truth.

"Leave your dishes," Barb told us, moving toward the hall. "I'll clean up after I've tapped Mark's checkbook." And she left the kitchen to pay some bills, going to my den at the front of the house.

"Whoa," said Neil, glancing over his shoulder at the clock, "it's nearly eight. I'd better head upstairs and get my act together—I've got a busy day ahead."

Before he could stand, I asked vacantly, "What are you working on?" The reason I asked (I already knew the answer) was simply to keep him sitting there for a few minutes, or even a few more seconds. The mere sight of him was food to me, a source of energy and sustenance. Though I could never get enough, I didn't deserve him at all. During our four years together, I'd had slips of fidelity—in my dreams and in my fantasies and, once, in a cabin in Door County—but the man in my life stayed in my life. He was a successful architect who had first moved his practice from Phoenix to Chicago to be with me. Then, when my professional wanderlust had brought me north to Wisconsin to run my own paper, he had agreed, with only mild complaint, to an arduous "arrangement" of alternating weekends while pursuing his career in the city. I couldn't possibly expect him to chuck the prestige and dazzle of his Chicago firm—to uproot himself again just to be with me—but last autumn he had decided to do exactly that, setting up his own practice right here in Dumont, in a converted storefront on First Avenue little more than a block away from the *Register*'s offices. There in the kitchen, in front of Sheriff Pierce, I reached across the table and took his hands in mine. "What was that project?" A goofy smile betrayed my clumsiness at keeping him in the room.

He smiled back at me, not the least bit goofy. He made no move to draw his hands from mine and, in fact, leaned an inch or so nearer. "The home office, remember? Cynthia Dunne-Gelden?"

"Hey," said Pierce, entering the conversation, "that's a nice place— out there on county highway B, right?" He swirled the last inch of coffee in the glass pot, considered whether he wanted it, then poured it into his cup. No steam rose from the dark, tepid liquid.

Neil let his hands slip from mine, answering Pierce, "That's the one. It *is* a nice place, but it'll soon be even better."

I explained to Pierce, "The wife is some sort of executive who travels a lot and wants to build a freestanding home office near the house." Turning to Neil, I asked, "What does she do?"

"Just . . . *business.*" He shrugged. "She's a vice president for some cell-phone firm based in Green Bay. Lately she's been spending quite a bit of time at the main offices, but mostly she courts and curries bigger clients out this way. Her territory includes Dumont, which is why she decided to settle here. That was eight years ago, when she married Frank."

I asked, "Frank was already here then?"

"Right," said Pierce, having spent most of his life in Dumont. "Frank Gelden was born here. He's about forty, a good five or six years younger than me, so I didn't know him in school, but the family has been around forever. Frank teaches, right?"

Having learned this information only twelve hours earlier, I answered, "He's a molecular-biology prof out at Woodlands. Smart, productive—sounds as if he and Cynthia are a perfect match, though I've never met *her.*"

"You will on Saturday," Neil told me, getting up, carrying his cup and a few dishes to the sink. He paused to stretch a runner's kink from between his shoulders. When it popped, he finished his thought: "She'll be here at the house, at the cast-and-crew party with Frank."

"Great."

"Anybody home?" called a younger voice, Thad's, as he bounded downstairs from his bedroom, shot through the center hall, and appeared in the doorway to the kitchen. "Oh"—he stopped, seeing us—"hi, everybody."

"Well, good *morning,*" I told him, turning in my chair for a good look. He was fully dressed (T-shirt, shorts, hiking shoes), carrying a knapsack and a flat-bottomed wicker basket, looking ready to leave the house. I'd rarely seen him up and at'm before noon when there was no school. I laughed. "Trouble sleeping?"

"It *rained* last night," he announced, beaming.

Neil folded his arms. "We noticed. So what?"

"Good for the corn," Pierce offered lamely—as if any of us cared.

"Good for the *mushrooms*," Thad explained. "Ought to be some great hunting today, so I wanted to get an early start."

I smiled through a cringe. Had he been a half hour earlier, he'd have gotten a real eyeload—Neil and me doing our improvised towel dance there in the middle of the kitchen.

"Morning, hot stuff!" said Barb, returning from the den. Giving Thad a shoulder hug, she asked, "Heading out for fresh fungi? I spotted a few beauties in the park when I was there earlier."

He nodded eagerly, ready to bolt for the door.

She wagged a finger. "Eat first."

He opened his mouth to protest, then spotted the platter on the table. "Bagels!" he chimed, then reached in front of me to grab one.

Barb eyed me with a tight smile, a smug air of conquest. Bending to speak in my ear, she said, "Hook a kid early enough, and he'll eat anything."

I could well recall Thad's first encounter with a bagel, shortly after Barb's arrival. He'd looked at the dense, oily roll with an inquisitive, apprehensive expression, poking at the thing with a fork, as if it had hurtled to the table in flames from Mars. "They're just like doughnuts," Barb had lied to him, "but better." To my surprise, he bought that, and before long, he'd acquired a taste for the things. His maturing palate, though, did not sufficiently expand to include cream cheese, which he still couldn't stomach, so this morning he slathered a half bagel with peanut butter. (In this ongoing rumpus regarding bagels, it goes without saying that lox had yet to be broached.)

Preferring *any* topic to the one that wouldn't die, I said, "Mushrooms in August? I thought they were sort of an autumn thing, like—what are they?—morels."

Thad nearly choked (on his you-know-what). He and Barb looked at each other, bug-eyed, then broke into rude peals of laughter.

I was stunned. Pierce was confused. Neil explained, "I believe the morel is a spring mushroom."

"*Mark*," said Thad when he had regained sufficient composure to speak, "morels grow in *May*. You know, 'May madness'? It's the morel hunt. They're the most prized of edible mushrooms, and *everyone's* after them."

Barb lectured, "But there are delicious species thriving all year long—well, not in winter, of course. But now, for instance, in deep summer, chanterelles and porcini are bustin' out all over." She turned to Thad, "Hey, hot stuff, keep your eyes peeled for black trumpets."

"The mini-chanterelles?" he asked, taking his field guide from the knapsack.

"Right. I could use maybe a pound for one of my party recipes, a favorite—"

"Now *wait* a minute," I interrupted, alarmed. "You mean to tell me you're going to go digging for this stuff in the park, then feed it to a houseful of *guests?*"

"Mark," Neil shushed me, "Barb's a hell of a cook, and Thad's a studious young mycologist—"

"But—"

Thad assured me, "Mr. Gelden's the best. He's an expert. He made sure that *everyone* in Fungus Amongus passed their identification-training sessions. I scored a ninety-four!"

Good God, I thought, what about the other six percent?

Neil told me, "Frank is an intelligent, committed teacher. I'm sure his first priority has been to help the kids distinguish between edible and—"

"Hey," said Barb, as if something had clicked. "Are we talking about *Frank Gelden*—forty years old, kinda geeky?"

We all turned to her. "Well," I stammered, "he's a . . . *biologist.*"

"I'll be *damned*," she said, thumping a palm to her forehead. "Frank and I went to school together, in the same class. God, I haven't seen him in over twenty years. Still the same old nerdy type, huh?"

Neil, Pierce, and I shared a quick, amused glance. Pierce told her, "No, actually, he's, uh . . . he's a rather attractive man."

"Sociable too," I added. "Very pleasant."

"*Frank?* This I gotta see. We all used to think he was—"

"You'll see him Saturday," Neil told her. "He'll be at the party. He's the play's technical director."

Pierce told Thad, "Speaking of the play, I hear you've got a hit on your hands."

"I sure hope so, Sheriff. We've worked real hard on it."

Pierce got up from the table. "One last rehearsal tonight?"

"Nope." Thad stuffed the field guide back into his knapsack, smiling with satisfaction. "Mr. Diggins says we're ready. He gave us tonight off, to rest up for the opening weekend. It'll be nice to stay home for a change—but it'll sure seem strange not being at the theater."

Pierce joked, "Well, at least Jason Thrush will be out of your hair."

Thad's expression visibly soured at the mention of his costar.

Barb told him, "You can help me clean those chanterelles tonight."

"Yeah," he said, brightening, hoisting his knapsack. "I'm off to the park."

"Uh-uh-uh," Neil reminded him. "You've just eaten. What's next?"

"I know, I know," said Thad, sounding put-upon but fully accepting the drill. Stepping to the hall that would lead him upstairs to his bathroom, he quoted Neil, " 'One must respect one's instrument.' "

Pierce looked at me obliquely. Under his breath, he asked, "Huh?"

I explained, "Theater talk for 'brush and gargle.' "

"Ahhh."

Neil said, "It may sound silly, but it's a sensible ounce of prevention. The kids have worked so hard—a sore throat could really screw up the show at this point."

Thad paused in the hall, considering this. Turning back to us with a cheery grin, he noted, "Jason has had that bad cold for quite a few days now. If it gets any worse, he may not be able to play the lead in tomorrow night's premiere. How cool would *that* be?"

And he blasted upstairs for the ritual cleansing of his instrument.

Friday, August 3

B ecause Neil's architecture office is located midway between the *Register* and our favorite local restaurant, the First Avenue Grill, I frequently take a noontime stroll along Dumont's main street, stopping to meet him so we can enjoy lunch together. On Friday, though, he was booked for a long midday meeting out at Quatro Press, the town's largest industry, which was founded by my late uncle, Thad's grandfather, Edwin Quatrain. Because I now sit on Quatro's board of directors, and because the thriving printing plant seems in continual need of expansion, I had no trouble securing for Neil a contract to assist in these matters on a retainer. Though the work has no glamour, Neil takes satisfaction in doing it well. What's more, the money is good—a "bread-and-butter account," he calls it—and the retainer has added considerable security to the iffy period of establishing his practice here.

That Friday, I walked alone to the Grill in my shirtsleeves; it was too hot for a jacket, so I had left my sport coat at the office. I tugged the knot of my tie and unbuttoned my collar, allowing an extra quarter inch of breathing room. Folded under one arm were that day's front sections of both the *Chicago Journal* and the *New York Times*—since I'd be alone at table, I'd use the time to catch up on the *Register*'s "competition."

Ducking into the shade of the Grill's storefront awning and opening the door, I felt a rush of air-conditioning welcome me like a hug. Stepping inside the simple but handsome dining room, I paused to button my collar and adjust my tie.

"Good afternoon, Mr. Manning," said the hostess. "So nice to see you, as always. Your table's ready, of course."

"Thank you, Nancy." Though I'd eaten here nearly every day (some evenings too) since arriving in Dumont, and though the same woman had always greeted me and seated me, I realized that I knew little about her. I knew, for instance, that her name was Nancy Sanderson, that she owned the Grill, and that she had a special love for food, concocting the daily specials, which were always worth trying. Despite this culinary passion, she had a lean build that made her seem tall, but in fact her always perfect hairdo topped out no higher than my eyes. She was older than I, perhaps in her later fifties. Unlike the rest of the staff (most of them buxom Wisconsin women, all uniformed in crisp whites, like nurses of yore), Nancy dressed smartly, but with little pretense of high fashion; that day, she wore a sensible, summery knee-length green skirt with a matching jacket. I had no idea whether she was a Mrs. or a Miss, as the ring on her finger was of ambiguous design. This lack of basic information was due, no doubt, to her reserved manner. Not that she was stiff or cold—in fact she was highly cordial—but the correctness of her bearing and the formality of her inflections kept personal matters at a distance.

Walking me to my usual corner table between the fireplace and the front window overlooking First Avenue, she said, "You might enjoy today's special, a mock chicken Caesar, nice and crisp, perfect for such a hot day."

Sitting, I set my newspapers on the far side of the table and draped the large linen napkin over my lap. "Sounds promising. What's 'mock' about it?"

"I made it with succulent strips of chicken mushrooms, lightly sautéed with wine and shallots, which are then added to the traditional Caesar salad, prepared with freshly coddled egg." With a gentle smile and a slight bow of her head, she added, "If you'll forgive my immodesty, it's quite delicious."

Timidly, I returned her smile. "Chicken mushrooms?"

"I forgot"—she paused for a quiet laugh (which carried a hint of condescension, I felt)—"you're not *from* here, are you, Mr. Manning? You weren't brought up with the traditions of mushrooming that are part of our local heritage. The wooded countryside does indeed seem to yield a special bounty here, and generations of Dumonters have delighted in the hunt's pleasant roving."

Since she'd gotten off track, I asked again, "Chicken mushrooms?"

"That's their common name, of course. They're also known as sulphur shelf, or more correctly, *Laetiporus sulphureus*. Strikingly beautiful, orange-tinted, they grow in overlapping clusters, or 'shelves,' along logs or tree trunks. They fruit most abundantly right now, in the deep of summer. I harvested these myself, just this morning. The texture and flavor are remarkably similar to chicken."

I'd heard the same thing said of rattlesnake, but I assumed Nancy would not appreciate this observation, so I refrained from sharing it. "That sounds wonderful, but I think I'll take a look at the menu first."

"Certainly. I'll send Berta over to take your order in a few minutes. Shall I bring some Lillet while you consider your choice?" She was referring to a pleasant French aperitif stocked at the request of the *Register*'s retired publisher, Barret Logan, also a Grill regular. Since I'd bought his newspaper and taken over his standing lunch reservation, it seemed appropriate to adopt his "usual" as well.

But the hot weather made me wary of alcohol, so I answered, "Thank you, Nancy, not today. Just iced tea, please."

As she bobbed her head and slipped away, I made a show of opening my menu for careful perusal, but I knew the offerings so well that I didn't need to read them—I'd have the steak salad and, depending on what was fresh that day, perhaps some berries for dessert.

Setting the menu aside, I reached for the *Chicago Journal*, pushed my chair back a few inches, and began reading the folded paper, resting it against the table's edge. Skimming the headline story—another Cook County ghost-payroll scandal—I was momentarily drawn into the world of big-city politics that had once consumed my interests but now seemed so remote. With a silent chuckle of surprise, I turned the page, realizing that I didn't miss my old reporting career at all, not even its high profile or busy pace. There were other rewards to enjoy—right here in Dumont—such as the day-to-day pleasures of an ordinary life with Neil, such as the wonders of watching Thad mature into early manhood.

"It was Thad Quatrain," said a nearby voice, breathy and secretive.

My head jerked up from the paper. Had I really heard Thad's name, or had I merely imagined the name popping from my thoughts?

"My *God*," said another lowered voice, another woman, barely able to quell her excitement. "You mean they *fought*? They actually *fought*?"

"They were rolling on the *floor* together," the other assured her, "knocking over *furniture*. Thad *threatened* Jason. The whole rehearsal came to a *standstill*. Denny Diggins could barely maintain *order*."

Unfolding the paper and raising it, I turned, peeking around the edge of my makeshift camouflage. At an adjacent table, two middle-aged ladies lunched, their noses inches apart, each of them pinching icy shrimp tails, gnawed to the husk, plucked from a shared shrimp cock-tail. I recognized neither woman, neither the source nor the listener, and from the confused and faulty account of Wednesday's rehearsal, it was apparent that neither of them had been there. This was mere gos-sip, secondhand at best, embellished and mutated in the retelling.

"Well," said the listener with a low chortle, "it's not surprising. The rivalry between those two boys is practically *legendary*."

"*Everyone* knows," agreed the source, pausing to suck her tail before plunking it onto a saucer already piled high with shrimp debris. Picking a fleck of husk from her lips, she added, "Joyce's story just confirms it."

Aha. She had heard something from Joyce Winkler, whom I had met Wednesday night—the costume lady who had juggled her work sched-ule at the hospital lab in order to do some bonding with her daughter Nicole. The two women at the Grill, I assumed, were other high-schoolers' moms, and news of the "boy toy" incident was now working its way through the gab circuit. I doubted that Joyce had related the incident with the imprecision of the current recounting, and in fact, I couldn't really blame her for passing it along—I'd built a successful career as a reporter doing essentially the same thing. The difference, of course, was that my own "gossip" was always in writing, and what's more, I was fully accountable for the accuracy of my stories.

"The bottom line," said the source, dabbing her mouth, leaving a smear of liver-colored lipstick on her napkin, "was that Thad actually threatened to *kill* Jason. Everyone heard it. In *my* book"—she sat erect, folding the napkin and placing it on the table—"that goes well beyond the bounds of healthy, normal teenage rivalry."

Even with no breaking news on Friday, it was a busy day at the *Register*, with the typical rush to lock up Sunday's extra sections. Adding to this routine tension was a sense of opening-night jitters, absorbed from life with Thad during his year of growing theatrical involvement. As the afternoon wore on, I found myself repeatedly checking my watch, counting down the hours till curtain. I also found myself replaying the troublesome conversation I'd overheard at lunch.

The shrimp woman had a point: though she was fuzzy on the details and circumstances surrounding the "boy toy" incident, perhaps I should have been more alarmed by Thad's threat. Granted, he was merely paraphrasing a line from a play, its context obvious to all present. And granted, he did this to defuse a volatile situation, sloughing off bigotry with humor. Still, Thad was young, and perhaps he needed to hear—specifically, from me—that death threats, however lamely intended or seemingly justified, should be considered off-limits in the resolution of future disputes.

So when I arrived home from the office, I offered to drive Thad to the theater that evening, even though, some months earlier, I'd bought him a seventeenth-birthday car (an efficient Japanese compact, nothing too flashy, but it was new and it was red, giving him sufficient peer status to get his mind off the "car thing" and the "job thing," allowing him to focus on school). He could easily have transported himself to and from the theater that night, as he had done all summer, but I knew he'd gladly accept my offer because, oddly, riding in my car together had come to represent the cement of our relationship, our mutual trust.

Earlier, when Thad's mother had died (traumatizing enough) and he had found himself placed under my guardianship (all the more traumatizing, as he had never even met an openly gay person), he had referred to me, on the day we met, as a "fucking fag." This, needless to say, had created something of a chasm between us, one that neither of us felt inclined to bridge. Ultimately, it was my car, a big black Bavarian V-8, that broke the ice. Though he didn't think much of me or of my imagined bedtime proclivities, Thad couldn't help being impressed by my car, which apparently raised me, in his eyes, just above the threshold of total degeneracy. He let me drive him to lunch one day, and things began to soften—we had our first civil, mature conversation. Later, to his astonishment, I offered to lend him the car for some outing he'd planned with friends, and to my astonishment, he brought it back in one piece, on time, with profuse thanks. To this day, I don't think twice about handing him the keys. All he has to do is ask.

So when I asked if I could drive him to the theater on opening night, he didn't think twice before answering, "Sure, Mark, thanks. Curtain's at eight, but I have a six-thirty call."

Around six-twenty, we hopped into the car, and I backed out of the driveway onto Prairie Street. Glancing over, I asked, "You have . . . everything?"

Through a quizzical smile, he asked, "Like what?"

I shrugged. "Script? Costume? Makeup?" He'd brought nothing.

He explained, "The script is memorized. Everything else is at the theater."

"Just checking." I reached over and mussed his hair. "Good luck to—" I stopped myself. "Break a leg tonight. You'll be great, I'm sure. Neil and I are really proud of you. We'll be counting the minutes till eight— can't wait." I turned onto Park Street, heading toward downtown.

"Actually," he said with a laugh, "I hope you two are *bored* tonight. I mean, you've already seen the show, at Wednesday's dress rehearsal. That was a perfect run-through. Hope it's just as good tonight."

"It's different, though," I insisted, "with a real audience—the collective anticipation, the adrenaline, the mutual feedback."

He caught my gaze for a moment. His smile was flat-out beautiful. "And that's what makes the magic."

We rode in silence for a block or two, passing the park on our right, its waxy foliage still radiant in the hot evening sun. I was thinking about what Thad had said—not only the magic, but Wednesday's rehearsal. He'd opened the door to the very topic I meant to broach.

"Everything's okay with you and Jason, right? That spat at dress rehearsal—it won't affect the performance, will it?"

"Nah," he said, a bit too blithely, "we have our differences, and I'll be glad when he's back at Unity High and I'm back at Central—and I'll *never* forgive him for the way he treated you and Neil—but we'll pull together for the good of the show. Like they say, 'the play's the thing.' "

I quizzed, "Who said that?"

"Shakespeare. *Hamlet.*"

"Which act and scene?"

Thad crossed his arms and gave me a get-real stare. "Don't press your luck, Mark." After a pause, he added, "So, inform me, which act and scene?"

"Haven't a clue." And we shared a laugh. As it waned, I told him, "Not to get 'heavy,' Thad, but that whole confrontation is still sort of bothering me. It was all Jason's fault—I understand that—the kid's a jerk, period. And believe me, you handled it with great maturity by letting the whole thing fizzle and not escalate. But still, you *did* make a threat, and taken out of context—"

"Mark," Thad interrupted me, placing his fingertips on my arm as I drove, "I know. It was dumb. It was *not* cool. I was mad, and I wasn't thinking straight. It seemed clever, so it popped out. I'll apologize to Jason in the green room tonight—in front of everybody."

My mood instantly lightened. Since we were both so clearly in sync on this issue, I allowed myself to violate the exact principle I meant to preach: "Kill him with kindness, eh?" Har har.

Thad flumped back in his seat, laughing loudly, slapping both knees. I myself indulged in a low chortle as I turned onto First Avenue, the downtown's main street.

The Dumont Playhouse was located only a few blocks from the *Register*'s offices. The theater was always touted by the Players Guild as "historic," and indeed, it was nearly a hundred years old, but the place had something of a checkered past. It was originally built as a vaudeville house, with a wide stage, lofty fly space, and some eight hundred seats—easily the largest auditorium in a small town that was growing fast in the heart of paper-mill country. With the advent of talkies and the death of vaudeville, the playhouse was converted to a movie theater, its stage walled over with a screen. Then, in the seventies, when smaller theaters became the trend, the handsome old theater was chopped down its middle, creating two smaller auditoriums with awkwardly angled rows of seats facing half-screens. Finally, when the first "multiplex" opened on the edge of town, the venerable old playhouse closed its doors, presumably for good.

It had sat empty for a couple of years, beginning to deteriorate, when a struggling community-theater group, the Dumont Players Guild, discovered the lure of historic preservation, purchasing the hulk of a building for a song and securing the troupe's first permanent home. Half of the screen was removed, exposing the stage in one of the auditoriums, which alone could seat the group's expected patrons. The other auditorium was used for storage and workspace, the Moorish-themed lobby was spiffed up, and the Dumont Playhouse again opened its doors. The Players soon learned, though, that their new home was no bargain, its upkeep and restoration draining meager coffers all too quickly. But they hung with it, securing private grants and public sympathy as they strove to save the theater—and in doing so, they lent a note of luster and tenacity to the once-fading downtown.

On that Friday night, though the sun would not set for another hour or two, the original ornate marquee outside the playhouse was already ablaze with its chaser lights, announcing the new production that would soon grace the theater's old stage (or at least half of it). The sight of the bright, frenetic sign, though gaudy and dated, actually brought a lump to my throat, and I sensed that it had the same effect on Thad as he stared at it. Driving past, I placed a hand behind his head and gave his neck a squeeze, a silent good-luck wish, a tactile message that I appreciated the commitment he'd made to help bring the theater to life that night.

Clearing my throat, I asked, "Stage door?"

He nodded.

I pulled around the block to the rear of the theater, where a small parking lot accommodated cast and crew. A number of cars had already arrived, and people were milling about—strange, I thought, given the heat. The stage door was shimmed open, and I could glimpse confused activity within. Thad's brows furrowed with wonder as I pulled into the lot and parked. Denny Diggins pranced out from backstage, joining the hubbub, fluttering from group to group, asking questions. Both Thad and I got out of the car as Denny approached us. Before he could speak, my reporter's instincts took over, and I asked, "What's wrong?"

He threw his hands in the air. "Jason's not here."

I glanced at Thad. Thad glanced at his watch. He told Denny, "It's just six-thirty. He's not late yet. There's plenty of time."

Denny wagged his head, palms pressed to his cheeks. "No," he explained through a pucker of frustration, "there's *not* plenty of time. We don't know where he *is*." Denny dropped one hand from his face, raising the other to hold his forehead, as if staving off a migraine. "I've been concerned about his cold, naturally. I spoke to him yesterday, and he said he wasn't feeling any better. So I told him to get plenty of rest, then tried checking on him this afternoon, but couldn't reach him. I've phoned again and again, but can't get past his machine. Something's *wrong.*"

I stepped nearer, telling Denny, "Don't jump to conclusions. He could be anywhere. He's probably on his way here right now." This was truly an unexpected turn of events—not Jason's questionable whereabouts, but my leaping forward to console Denny Diggins, of all people.

He said, "I hope to God you're right, Mahk."

Kwynn Wyman, Thad's friend, had seen us arrive and walked over to meet us. Hearing the last of our conversation, she said, "Please don't worry, Mr. Diggins. I'm sure Jason's fine. But in any event, we're covered, remember. Thad's ready to play Ryan tonight if he needs to."

"And he just may need to," said Denny, looking to the hot-hued heavens with an expression that asked, Why me?

"I'm ready if you need me," Thad assured Denny. "All we can do is wait."

And waiting in the wings, so to speak, was little Tommy Morales—perched on the stairs to the stage door, script in hand, studying the role of Dawson.

Later that evening, a few minutes before eight, Neil and I mingled with the crowd in the theater lobby. Doug Pierce and Barb Bilsten were with us, as planned, and through the bobbing heads I spotted a familiar figure—or rather, her purse.

Glee Savage, the *Register*'s features editor, was a veteran staffer, having been with the paper since her journalism-school graduation some thirty years earlier. She played to the hilt her role as local fashion maven, bringing a much needed dash of pizazz to the streets of our backwaterish little city. Her manner of dress was unpredictable, verging on zany, but a constant feature of her ensembles was the style of purse she always carried. In a word, the purses were big, nearly two feet square—flat carpetbags—collected in a seemingly endless variety of colors and patterns.

Glimpsing such a purse, imprinted with giant green banana leaves, I knew that Glee was on the premises. Though she had come to enjoy the show, she was also working that night, having assigned herself to review the opening. I told my companions, "Let's see if Glee wants to join us. I need to ask her something."

Neil, Pierce, and Barb readily agreed—they would enjoy Glee's company, but more important, they knew what was on my mind. We'd already discussed my earlier encounter with a flustered Denny Diggins in the parking lot, and we wondered if Glee had any news regarding Jason Thrush. Would he perform as scheduled that evening?

I tried catching Glee's attention by waving my program over the heads of the crowd, but she didn't notice, so Barb took charge, emitting a shrill whistle from her teeth. (This involved fingers, lips, and saliva, as well as her teeth—a particularly butch little trick that I have never mastered.) The babble halted momentarily as all heads turned. "Glee!" commanded Barb. "Over here!"

Recognizing us, Glee waved, then moved toward us through the crowd as the hubbub built to its previous level.

"Evening, boss," she told me, arriving in our midst. We all exchanged pleasantries. She asked, "What's up?"

"Care to join us inside? We have an extra ticket or two."

"Sure." Big smile. Big oily red lips.

"For God's sake," said Barb, getting right to the point, "what's the deal with this Jason creep?" She'd heard about the incident at dress rehearsal, but Jason had been "the creep" for several weeks already, since the announcement that he would be starring on opening night.

Glee's look of confusion made it apparent she'd heard nothing.

I explained, "When I brought Thad to the theater earlier, there was some concern about Jason Thrush. He's been ill, I guess, and Denny couldn't reach him this afternoon. There was talk of a possible cast change."

"Really?" Glee arched her brows. "Nothing's been said to *me* about it. The lobby photo display still has Jason centered on the top row."

Pierce flipped through his program book to the cast of characters. "Jason Thrush as Ryan," he confirmed. "No stuffer announcing a change. Hey"—he jerked his head toward the double-doored entrance to the auditorium—"people are starting to go in."

"Great. Everything must be okay," I said, unable to mask a tone of mild disappointment that contradicted my words. "We'd better take our seats."

So the five of us began jostling with the crowd toward the doors to the main aisle. While inching forward, Neil nudged me. "Over there," he said into my ear. "It's Mica Thrush—looking trampy as ever."

I had to laugh, finding Neil's characterization too charitable. She was all in black again, but tonight's outfit was even more revealing—a silky little slip of an evening dress with a backless plunge toward dangerous territory. As she walked, her long, straight hair shifted, brushing the top of her butt crack. People were staring, exactly as she wanted, though she pretended not to notice. I didn't know her age, but she had referred to Jason as her "baby brother," so I guessed she was twenty or so. Eschewing the obvious topic of her perilously bare ass, I told Neil, "Jason must have made it to the theater. Why else would she be here?"

He shrugged, not caring—Mica Thrush was not worth pondering.

Inside, we found our seats and settled in. Thad had secured a prime location for us, about a third of the way back from the stage, on the aisle. Pierce asked for the outer seat, in case he was called away; I sat next to him, with Neil next to me; Barb and Glee took the inner seats.

We chatted quietly, paging through the program, glancing at the ads. The *Register* had, as usual, taken the back cover; Quatro Press, the inside front. Glee snapped open the top edge of her purse and extracted her steno pad, pen, and a petite flashlight, in case she needed to take notes during the performance. Barb and Neil discussed some lingering details of the next night's party—everything was under control.

At three minutes past eight (I checked my watch), the houselights started their slow fade, and the audience instinctively hushed itself. We knew we were moments away from raising the curtain on a brand-new play, a world premiere. Sure, it was a local effort, and chances were Denny Diggins's original script would never be staged again, but still, there was a palpable excitement—the hint of great things to come, the magic, as Thad had called it. And the room grew darker.

But when the houselights reached half-power, they paused.

"Ladies and gentlemen," began a disembodied but familiar voice (Denny's, over a loudspeaker), "the Dumont Players Guild wishes to announce the following cast changes: in tonight's performance, the role of Ryan will be played by Thad Quatrain"—Neil and I discreetly grabbed each other's fingertips in a proud, congratulatory gesture—"and the role of Dawson will be played by Thomas Morales. Thank you."

Predictably, a murmur swept through the crowd as the lights continued their fade to black. Some, surely, were disappointed by the announcement—those who had come to see Jason. Others—like us— were delighted, having preferred to see Thad in the starring role all along. But most were simply surprised and curious: What had happened?

Just before the houselights winked out, I noticed someone stand in the packed auditorium and begin walking up the aisle toward the lobby. There was no mistaking the lean figure, the sultry swagger, the black satin—it was Mica Thrush, heading out of the theater.

The crowd again hushed itself as the room went completely dark. Then, with an audible hum, the stage lights came on, full power, and the scene was set. *Teen Play* had begun. After a few lines of opening dialogue from minor characters, Ryan made his entrance, and to my surprise (Thad's too, I'm sure), the audience erupted with applause, as if cheering the hero, the understudy who was called upon to save the show. I knew, of course, that Thad was thoroughly rehearsed in the role—he would have played Ryan the next night anyway—but this distinction was lost on the crowd as they clapped their approbation and support. Without breaking character, Thad and everyone else onstage momentarily froze in a tableau, waiting for the applause to wane, then continued with their dialogue. I had never heard Thad in better voice. And I had not before seen him in the role of Ryan, which he acted with confidence and authority. If the last-minute casting change threw him at all, it was not the least bit evident.

I quickly dismissed the real-world issues and actions and problems that had led to that moment, allowing myself to slip into the new world being created behind the proscenium. As theater folk would say, I "suspended my disbelief" and bought into the whole fabrication, forgetting that it was Thad up there. As minutes passed, the plot began to twist and thicken. I wondered, really caring, What next?

Pierce, squirming in his seat next to me, broke my theatrical spell as he reached inside his jacket and unclipped the pager from his belt. The gizmo had apparently alerted him with a vibrating signal, and he now strained to see its readout in the dim light of the auditorium. Adding to this distraction, Glee passed her penlight down the row to him, rousing Barb's and Neil's curiosity. Heads in the row behind us turned as well, wondering what we were looking at. At last Pierce managed to position the pager at a legible angle under the narrow beam of light. Nudging my knee with his, he offered me a look at the readout—he was needed at the Thrush residence, the home of the missing actor. Rising from his seat, he headed for the lobby.

Turning to give Neil's arm a squeeze of apology, I rose, following the sheriff out of the theater.

In the lobby, Pierce told me, "It's police business. You stay, Mark. Thad would want you here."

"I know," I conceded, nodding, "but I've got an uneasy feeling that whatever's happening at the Thrushes' might spell trouble for Thad. Please, Doug—I feel I need to be there."

He paused briefly, gathering his thoughts, but was too rushed to argue. "All right," he said, exhaling. "But you won't get in on your own. Ride with me."

The Thrush residence was located in a pricey development of larger homes near the edge of town—a rolling-knolls subdivision peppered with old oaks and the sort of shake-shingled mini-mansions that Neil often derides as "big dumb houses." Some looked like storybook castles, others like Mediterranean villas. A particularly ungainly specimen resembled the Alamo—with a front-loading three-car garage. There were several examples of Disney-French, one of which, at the end of a cul-de-sac, was meant to pass for a cozy countryside stable, but it was just too damn big. The intended ambience was further contradicted by an assembly of police vehicles, hastily parked at jumbled angles, flashers flashing. I had never known exactly where Jason Thrush lived, but clearly, we'd arrived.

It was past eight-thirty, and dusk was slipping toward night. I got out of the car and waited for Pierce to finish on the radio. The conversation was sufficient to tell me what we'd find inside, but not a word was said that explained how it had happened. A sheriff's deputy came out of the house and jogged down the sidewalk to meet us as Pierce got out of the car.

Pierce quickly introduced us—the man in uniform was Jim Johnson, the first officer to arrive on the scene.

"Who called it in?" Pierce asked him.

"The sister. She's a weird one—named Mica."

"Who else is home?"

"Just the father." Johnson didn't need to mention the dozen cops, the crew of evidence technicians—or the coroner.

"Let's have a look," said Pierce, and the three of us walked up to the house.

Though the exterior resembled a stable, the inside leaned, shall we say, toward the opulent—nothing says "welcome home" quite so eloquently as that touch of Versailles. Louis-this, Louis-that, everywhere. Chandeliers, gold hardware, tasseled curtains, the works. Though our mission was grim, I couldn't suppress a wry smile, wondering how Neil would react to this place.

There didn't seem to be anyone around. Pierce asked Johnson, "Where?"

"Upstairs. Bedroom." And he led us up the curved staircase.

The upstairs hall was abuzz with hushed activity. Officers sidled into and out of a brightly lit room that I assumed to be Jason's. Mica was on the far side of the hall, standing speechless next to a seated man who held his head in his hands. I assumed this to be her father, but he seemed far too old.

Pierce stepped to the bedroom door. "Could we have some room, please?" he quietly asked everyone, who filed out to the hall.

I followed Pierce inside. We were not alone. Dr. Vernon Formhals, the county coroner, was present—as was the body of Jason Thrush.

The death of someone young, who has yet to hit his prime, is always a startling event. More than merely mourn the tragedy, we grieve at the loss of *potential*—the victim represents promises unfulfilled and a life unlived. What's more, such death seems such a *waste*, and in Jason's case, this sense of forfeited opportunities was amplified by a perfect physique on the verge of manhood, lost. How easily I forgot my disdain for the living person, which had been home to a mean and arrogant spirit. That spirit had now flown, leaving only its handsome hull.

Jason lay prone on his bed, one leg dropped over the edge, his foot to the floor. He was dressed for a summer day in knit shirt, shorts, and tennis shoes. The bed was neatly made, its pillows unrumpled. He looked as if he had just lain down for a nap. Or had he collapsed there? His face was turned toward us, eyes gently closed, like the frozen portrait of a beautiful sleeping child—but the image was spoiled by a sizable gob of mucus that hung like molten, greenish rubber from his sagging mouth.

"God," I said, stepping close to stare into his blank visage, "what happened?"

Dr. Formhals answered, "No idea."

Pierce asked him, "Natural causes?"

"Can't tell yet." Stretching a fresh pair of white latex gloves over his massive black hands, Formhals explained the obvious need for an autopsy, the various tests they could run, the expected timetable for obtaining results.

As the coroner spoke, I remained at the bedside, crouching to study the body, weighing the mixture of attraction and revulsion I felt. There was no indication of trauma or struggle; Jason simply lay there, dead. Sniffing, I concluded that he could not have been there more than a few hours, as there was no foul hint of decay. Nor had his bowels discharged, perhaps due to the position of his body. In fact, the predominant smell at close range was sweet and flowery—the same "cheap perfume" noted by Kwynn Wyman at Wednesday night's rehearsal. He'd laid it on thick again. Inhaling the fruity scent, I was struck by a vague sensory memory, not from Wednesday, but from long ago. The fragrance was familiar. Had I known someone else who once wore it?

Rising (my knees cracked), I turned to ask the coroner, "Can you estimate the time of death, Vernon?"

He stepped next to me at the bedside. "This is preliminary, of course." He draped his palm over the thickest part of the boy's upper thigh, telling us, "The body is still slightly warm." He poked the leg with his index finger. "The skin still blanches when touched." Then, using both gloved hands, he gently lifted Jason's head and moved it about, observing, "The first signs of rigor are evident in the neck and jaw." Allowing Jason's head to rest again, Formhals paused to pat it, smoothing a still-lustrous lock of hair above an unhearing ear. Turning to us, he continued, "The room had been closed and air-conditioned, a steady seventy-two. The boy probably died between three and four hours ago."

Pierce checked his watch. "Nine now. That would put it between five and six."

Formhals nodded. "Close enough."

I told them, "That explains where Jason was at six-thirty. But Denny Diggins said he'd been trying to phone him all afternoon and could never get past the answering machine."

As Pierce made note of this, I glanced around the room, taking my first real look at it (since entering, I'd been focused, naturally, on the body). Jason's second-floor bedroom was spacious and well furnished, not Frenchy like the rest of the house, but looking like a typical "guy's room"—well, a typical *rich* guy's room. There was a bed, desk, dresser, and a few side chairs, all of matched dark hardwood. The curtains, bed-spread, and a large upholstered chair and ottoman shared the same handsome plaid fabric, very nubby, correctly masculine. The thick beige carpeting was perfectly clean, surely wool. There were lots of framed pictures, two (maybe three) wall mirrors, and an abundance of *stuff*—sports gear, trophies, stereo, television, computer, and on the desk, a telephone, the oversize sort of office phone with extra buttons. In spite of Jason's many possessions, his bedroom had an anonymous, sanitized feeling, like a hotel room.

I didn't see an answering machine, so I reasoned that Denny's calls must have been picked up by voice mail. But why hadn't Jason answered in the first place? Was he there in the bedroom, sick and dying? Or was he simply somewhere else? I realized there was a lot to sort out, and so did Pierce—his face wrinkled in a perplexed scowl as he stood near the bed scratching notes.

"My son was all I had, you know."

We turned as the decrepit-looking man entered the bedroom from the hall, grasping the doorjamb. He wore a conservative business suit and white dress shirt, but no tie or shoes. Pierce crossed the room to assist him to a chair. "My condolences, Mr. Thrush. I'm so sorry."

"You still have me, Daddy," said Mica, appearing in the doorway, still in her Dracula drag. "Don't forget about me." Her expression, as usual, was flat and plastic, as if she wore a mask. She said the words through hard-edged black lips, without apparent emotion. Her tone carried nothing to convince us that she meant to console her father or mourn her brother. If anything, she sounded mildly amused—and terribly bored.

The Thrush patriarch glanced briefly at his daughter, as if staring straight through her into the hallway, as if she didn't exist. Then he turned back to us. Ignoring both the sheriff and the coroner, choosing me, he fixed me in his gaze. Though we'd never met, he explained, "Jason would have followed me in the business, *my* business, the business I founded and nurtured. But now"—he dropped his head backward and laughed at the ceiling—"now it seems the mantle will be passed to Mica."

"Not *yet*, Daddy," she told him, watching me instead of her father. "There's *so* much left for you to accomplish." She didn't mean a word of it, making no attempt to disguise her insincerity.

"May I ask you a few questions, Mr. Thrush?" said Pierce, readying a fresh page of his notebook.

That was my cue—I extracted my own notepad from a jacket pocket and uncapped my Montblanc, hungry for a few facts. I soon learned that Jason's father was Burton Thrush, age fifty-six. He claimed a history of ill health, which explained why he appeared far older than his years, forcing me to wonder if his son's unexpected death would simply be too much for him. His wife had died some years ago; Jason and Mica were their only children. He confirmed that Jason was seventeen, Mica twenty-one.

While Pierce conversed with Thrush, I watched Mica saunter through the room. She brushed within a hair's breadth of Coroner Formhals, pausing to trace her sharp, black fingernail over his strong, black chin and down his throat. She smiled faintly as his eyes widened. He stepped back, giving her a clear path to the bed.

She stood there, beading baby brother with a stare, as if he were holding his breath and they were playing a game. When he didn't move, she began to appear impatient. With hands on hips, she leaned over the bed. As her hair fell forward, her bare back and most of her ass were exposed squarely to Formhals, who gaped in astonishment for a moment before turning away to fidget with something in his medical bag.

Mica leaned closer over her brother, then smiled. She tried blowing in his ear. Getting no response, she proceeded to tickle him, first his neck, then his armpits, then down his sides, groping under his hips.

Burton Thrush, engrossed in grief, didn't even notice.

Pierce had a busy night ahead of him and would not be returning to the theater, so he asked a deputy to drive me back.

Walking through the quiet lobby, I peeked through the doors into the auditorium. I'd been gone for about an hour, and Thad was now onstage with Tommy Morales, playing Ryan and Dawson. Having attended the dress rehearsal, I recognized the scene from act two—I'd missed most of the performance. I recalled that there would be a brief scene shift near the end of the show, when I could slip in without disturbing anyone.

Waiting with the door cracked open, I listened to the dialogue. Thad and Tommy were acting up a storm, not dropping a cue, with the packed audience dead quiet, hanging on every word. The scene soon ended with a momentary blackout. As the audience responded with a polite round of applause (nothing effusive yet, as the play's climax still lay ahead), the houselights came on dimly, signaling a pause while the stage was reset. Opening the door, I returned to my seat.

Neil, Barb, and Glee turned toward me, leaning in their seats, a silent plea for information. But the houselights had already begun to fade, so I replied with an apologetic shrug, raising a finger to my lips. My news would have to wait, which came as something of a relief. For the moment, I was glad to shoo from my mind the recent encounter with Jason's corpse—and his dysfunctional family—replacing that disturbing reality with a few minutes of theatrical distraction.

Unfortunately, I was soon reminded that the last scene of *Teen Play* bore a striking resemblance to the scenario that had just been played out at the Thrush residence. The action resumed onstage:

The rivalry that has been developing between the two main characters, Ryan and Dawson, now climaxes in murder. It is the night when the play within the play is scheduled to open, and Dawson kills Ryan, stepping into the leading role.

Thad and Tommy gave a chilling, realistic performance of the dra-

matic ending, and the audience reacted as intended, momentarily horrified by the ruthless bludgeoning they witnessed. But I was all the more
stunned—not that the staged gore bore any physical similarity to Jason
Thrush's demise, but the circumstances were staggeringly alike. Surely,
I feared, as soon as the news broke that Jason had died that night,
everyone who had seen the play would make the same connection,
wondering if art had imitated life—or vice versa.

Suddenly the room was dark, and the audience burst into applause. I
wasn't even conscious of the play's final moments, but it had ended,
and the crowd loved it. I felt Neil hug my shoulder; Barb leaned over
him to give me a thumbs-up; Glee scribbled notes with a wide, happy
grin. Thad, it seemed, was a triumph. During curtain call, when it was
finally his turn to walk downstage for a bow, cheers rang from the
crowd, and within moments, we were all on our feet. Thad dutifully
waved Denny Diggins to the stage to share the applause, and I had to
admit that our pompous fledgling playwright had delivered on his
promise. Joining the others, I clapped all the louder.

After several curtain calls, my arms ached and my palms stung. At
last the applause faded, and the actors left the stage as the houselights
came on.

"Mark," Glee told me, stretching to shake my hand, "it was *mah*-
velous, wasn't *it?*" We all laughed our agreement. "I'll scamper right
over to the office to write my review—there's just enough time to make
the morning edition."

I then realized that I myself had a deadline to meet. As the only
newsman on the scene when Jason's body was discovered, I'd need to
"switch hats" tonight, stepping out of my publisher's role and back into
that of reporter. Duty called. It was a page-one story—and to think that
only yesterday I'd been bemoaning the lack of local news.

"Actually," I told Glee, "I need to take care of something back at the
paper as well. I'll give you a ride." The *Register*'s offices were only a few
blocks away, and I assumed Glee had walked to the theater, as her
apartment was also downtown.

"Hold on," Neil interrupted. "We've got to see Thad first. He'll be
expecting us backstage. Look"—he pointed to a side door near the
front of the theater—"others are herding back there already."

He was right. We *had* to congratulate Thad—I felt bad enough that
I'd missed most of the performance. Glee and I could spare a few minutes before rushing to our computers. Besides, if we needed more time,

I was in a position to fudge our deadline. After all, presses now rolled at my command. "Thanks for the reminder," I told Neil, giving him a hug. "First things first."

While most of the audience was now jostling toward the lobby, a smaller pack of well-wishers bucked the tide, moving toward the stage. Our party of four, Thad's cheering section, joined this latter group, filing through a narrow door that led to the wings. Amidst the happy chatter that surrounded us, Neil asked me, "What happened? You're obviously itching to write a story. And where's Doug?"

I leaned to whisper a few words to him.

"Oh, no." He looked at me with dismay, fingers to lips.

I wasn't sure if he was simply upset by the news of Jason's untimely demise or if he already grasped its implications. In any event, I'd dashed his high spirits—but he'd asked a direct question, and there was no point in dodging it. Saying nothing more, I found his hand at my side and gave his wrist a squeeze of reassurance as we moved closer to the commotion backstage.

Parents and friends were caught up with the young cast in a giddy, congratulatory swirl. Denny Diggins darted about, accepting the adulation of any who would offer it. Moms tittered, dads blustered, kids yapped and laughed. And through the crowd I spotted Thad's head bobbing, looking for us. "There," I told our group, pointing to him. I waved. Barb whistled.

His head snapped in our direction. Beaming, he worked his way toward us through the friendly mayhem. "Hey!" he called. "What'd you think?" He didn't need to ask—he knew very well that he'd led the cast to a smash opening—but he needed to hear it from us, and we gladly obliged.

Neil met him first. Big hug. "What a night! You did it, Thad."

Barb's turn. "Thataboy, hot stuff!" She gave him a kiss, then playfully boxed his ears. "I hope that Leonardo wimp has some backup plans—'career alternatives,' as they say." She laughed wildly.

"Thanks, Barb!" Then Thad noticed Glee. "Hi, Miss Savage." Aware of her mission that night, he sheepishly asked, *"Well?"*

Big, obvious wink. "You'll have to wait till morning, I'm afraid." Leaning close, she gripped his upper arm, the sleeve smeared with makeup and stage blood. "But I have a hunch you'll get a rave notice."

"He'd *better*," I told her with a laugh. As I spread my arms, Thad stepped into my embrace and I told him, "You have no idea how proud you've made us." I patted his sweaty back, mussed his already tangled hair.

"Thanks, Mark." Then he backed off a few inches. "But did you *like* it?" He smiled, waiting for my routine compliments. "The play, I mean."

After an awkward hesitation (the few seconds felt like minutes of agony), I confessed, "I'm really sorry, Thad, but I *missed* most of the show. Sheriff Pierce and I were called away. But I promise, I'll be here start-to-finish tomorrow night, no matter what."

To my profound relief, he didn't seem to mind. "That's okay"—he cuffed my shoulder—"you and the sheriff, you're busy, important guys." As an afterthought, he asked with idle curiosity, "Where *is* Sheriff Pierce? What happened?"

"*Yeah*," said Barb, elbowing Glee with a sisterly nod, affirming that they were waiting for answers, and now. "What the hell's up with that disappearing act?"

I glanced at Neil. "Thad," I said quietly, focusing on the boy, "something awful has happened. Jason Thrush was found dead in his bedroom this evening."

"Huh?" murmured Thad, Glee, and Barb. "What?" "My God."

Kwynn Wyman had just emerged from the crowd, all smiles, stepping forward to tell Thad something, but he didn't notice. He asked me, "How did he die?"

"We don't know. The sheriff and the coroner are still there with Mr. Thrush, and—"

"What?" said Kwynn, startled by our somber tone. "Mr. Thrush died?"

"No," Thad answered, turning to her. "It's unbelievable, but it was Jason."

Her mouth trembled. Then she blurted, *"Jason's dead?"*

Her words were loud enough to catch the attention of those around us, who instantly dropped their own conversations, turning to listen to ours. I explained to Kwynn, "Jason's sister found him in his bedroom tonight after the play started. We don't know how he died. There were no signs of—"

But there was no point in continuing. Word was out, spreading fast, and the jubilant opening-night clamor was quickly transformed to a chorus of gasps and shrieks. Denny Diggins rushed forward, his face drained of color, demanding to know what had happened. Tommy

Morales tagged behind him with a blank look of alarm, trying to hear what was said. Other cast members gathered around, stricken by the news that one of their own had died so tragically and so young. Then, as if on cue, the whole cavernous space fell silent, except for the sobs.

After a few moments of this instinctive, respectful lull, Nicole Winkler, the pretty one, said through an anguished cry, "I can't believe he's dead! I'll never believe that Jason's gone . . . not really gone."

"Holy shit!" someone said. "It's just like the play."

Someone else: "Yeah. Jason died on opening night."

Another: "Unreal. How could it happen—"

Bitterly, through her tears, Nicole reminded everyone, "Thad *threatened* Jason. And now Jason's dead."

PART TWO

Fairy Rings

CORONER STUMPED

Jason Thrush, popular local teen, found dead of mysterious causes

By CHARLES OAKLAND
Staff Reporter, Dumont Daily Register

Aug. 4, DUMONT WI—Jason Thrush, a popular local student and talented young actor, was found dead yesterday evening at home in his bedroom. He attended Dumont Unity High, where he would have been a senior this fall. He was 17.

Cause of the boy's death is still unknown. He had been suffering from an apparent summer cold, but was otherwise in excellent health. The body bore no signs of trauma or struggle, and the victim had no known history of drug use.

His body was discovered by his sister, Mica Thrush, shortly after eight o'clock last night. Dumont County sheriff Douglas Pierce and coroner Vernon Formhals were both called to the scene. Time of death is estimated between 5:00 and 6:00 P.M. yesterday.

"We are treating this case as a suspicious death," said Pierce. "There was no immediate evidence of foul play, but only an autopsy can reveal whether the young man died of natural causes or not."

Dr. Formhals told the *Register* that routine toxicology tests would be performed, regardless of findings of the physical examination. "In perplexing cases like this," he said, "it can take weeks to find definitive answers."

Jason was preceded in death by his mother, Patricia Thrush, ten years ago. He is survived by his sister, Mica Thrush, 21, and by his father, Burton Thrush, 56, founder of Thrush Typo-Tech, a local print-related industry.

Friends and teachers remember Jason Thrush as a diligent student, aggressive athlete, and accomplished actor. His theatrical experience included roles in eight productions. In an ironic twist, his death occurred on the very evening he was to perform the leading role in *Teen Play*, an original production of the Dumont Players Guild.

Thad Quatrain, another young local actor, was called upon to star in last night's premiere. A review by the *Register*'s Glee Savage appears elsewhere in these pages. ❏

Saturday, August 4

N eil tossed the morning paper onto the table. "Christ, Mark, did you have to drag Thad into the story? It all but points an accusing finger at him, stopping just short of naming him as a suspect."

Turning to Neil from the kitchen counter, I carried two mugs of coffee to the breakfast table, trying to explain, "There was no way to leave Thad out of the story. You heard the suspicious gossip start to snowball at the theater—I'll bet phones were ringing all night. So I deliberately soft-pedaled the circumstances that could suggest Thad's complicity. That's why I didn't assign the story, but wrote it myself."

"Hey," said Barb, stowing something in the refrigerator, closing it with a thud. "I read the paper already. That wasn't *your* story, Mark—there was some other name on it." She crossed her arms accusingly, as if catching me in a fib.

Neil laughed. "Though the story carries Charles Oakland's byline, Mark actually wrote it, Barb."

I explained, "When I took over as the *Register*'s owner and publisher, I knew there'd be times when I'd want to report a good story. If I used my own name, though, my reporting might lack credibility, since readers here have grown used to seeing my name on editorials—in other words, opinion. For factual reporting, then, I simply invented a pen name, Charles Oakland." I slurped some coffee, the day's first. As I'd had a late night, I needed the caffeine.

Not satisfied, Barb eyed me askance, asking, "Isn't that . . . well, *dishonest?*"

"Why?" I asked in return. A note of defensiveness colored my voice. "Writers often use different pen names for different audiences. The point is, I stand behind every word I've written. That story is accurate and unbiased."

"Uh-huh. That's why you 'soft-pedaled the circumstances' regarding your kid."

She had a point. Perhaps I had slightly compromised my journalistic integrity on that issue. And I realized, with considerable surprise, that this stretching of principles didn't bother me in the least. I told both Barb and Neil, "I would do anything in my power to protect Thad."

Barb gave me a wink and a thumbs-up. "Can't argue with that."

Neil stood, leaned to kiss the top of my head, then sat again.

He wore loose, olive-hued cargo shorts, a rumpled white shirt, no shoes yet—Neil looked great in anything. I was in a comfortable old pair of khakis, as I'd be going to the office, but there was no need for a tie on the weekend, so I wore a soft, faded plum-colored polo shirt, the one that Neil always said looked good on me ("It complements your gorgeous green eyes," he put it). Barb wore something like a sweat suit, but it had gold-braided trim.

I asked anyone, "No sign of Doug this morning?" I had a taste for the kringle Pierce usually brought with him—the sugar might provide a needed energy boost.

"It's Saturday," Neil reminded me. "He usually gets a later start at the gym."

"We *all* should have gotten some extra sleep this morning," I said. "After the excitement last night—the premiere *and* Jason's death—I'm feeling sort of whipped. I'll bet Thad won't roll out of bed till one or two." As an afterthought, I added to Barb, "Unless *you* sent him out on another early-morning mushroom hunt."

"Nope," she said matter-of-factly, puttering with something near the stove, "I got all the black trumpets I needed on Thursday. They dried all day yesterday, and today the culinary wizardry happens. Everything's under control."

Neil asked, "Just what is it you're concocting?"

I didn't want to know.

"Nothing fancy," she said with uncharacteristic modesty, banging pans as she pulled them from a cabinet. "Sort of a party dip, a spread for crackers, bread . . . even bagels! You just simmer the black trumpets in a bit of milk, chop them up fine, then sauté them in butter. With a fork, you blend in chives and plenty of cream cheese till it's gooey enough for spreading. Easy. And I *love* serving it. Guests can never figure out what's in it, but lots of folks rave about it."

Right, I thought. They're the lucky ones. The others have perished.

I asked, "Are we all still sure that tonight's party is a good idea?" It wasn't so much the mushrooms as Jason's death that fanned my doubts.

Barb turned to me, one hand to her hip, the other brandishing a wire whisk. "I thought we *decided*. I thought that was the *point* of our discussion last night till God only knows what hour."

Neil raised both hands, a gentle gesture meant to appease both of us. "It's a sticky question, yes, but we did talk it through, all three of us, and we concluded that it would be better *not* to cancel the party. Obviously, Jason's death is shocking and unexpected. But the Players Guild isn't canceling the run of *Teen Play*—'the show must go on'—and contrary to that spirit, canceling the party would only appear grim. Besides, the party's been planned for weeks, a lot of preparation has gone into it, and it'll give the cast and crew an opportunity to meet outside the theater and talk through their feelings about the tragedy. It won't be exactly the festive evening we had planned, but it will be good for the kids." Neil looked from Barb's face to mine. "Right?"

"Right," I conceded. "Plus"—and this was really the strongest argument, I thought, for forging ahead with our plans—"the party will give Thad the opportunity to act as host, show off a bit, and curry favor with his friends."

"Especially those 'friends,' " added Barb, "who seem all too eager to believe that he was somehow involved with Jason's death." She'd pinpointed the core issue, and we fell silent for a moment, lamenting the circumstances that now cast Thad in such a dark light.

It had been a chilling experience backstage the previous night, watching the tide turn so quickly. One minute, Thad was a hero, the unflappable young actor who had just led his troupe to a triumphant opening; the next minute, when news broke of Jason's death, he was seen by some as a scheming, murderous understudy. None of us considered for even an instant that Thad could have any connection to Jason's death, and I had no reason to feel that the official investigation would ever focus on him. I did, however, harbor a nascent fear that Thad could suffer some serious emotional damage from the suspicions of his adolescent peers. It was important to resolve quickly the questions surrounding Jason's death and, in doing so, to restore Thad's good name before smoke implied fire.

"He seemed okay, didn't he, when we talked before bed?" Though I'd been there, and though I'd answered this question to my own satisfaction—repeatedly—I still needed Neil's reassurance.

"He was fine, Mark. If anything, he found the irony of the situation sort of *funny*." Glancing at the clock, Neil added, "He isn't losing any sleep over it."

Though Neil's words were meant to allay my fears, they succeeded in raising a new worry: Was Thad's reaction to Jason's demise too cavalier? Or was his nonchalance merely a cover for deeper feelings that he preferred not to air?

Barb opened the fridge, grabbed a diet cola, and joined us at the table. Popping the can, she said, "Look, guys. Thad'll be fine. He's at an impressionable age, but he's a good kid, with two wonderful dads. He'll pull through this, and so will you." She tasted the soda, then added, "Jason's autopsy will clear everything up, and the whole mess will be history. It could be over by nightfall."

"Thanks, Barb," Neil told her. "I hope you're right."

She snorted. "Of *course* I'm right."

Watching her slug pop from the can, I offered, "Can I get you a glass?"

She dismissed my offer with a flip of her hand. "Just something to wash."

I sighed—not a sigh of exasperation, but resolution. "Well, then, the party's on. There's plenty left to do, I'm sure. How can I help?"

Barb flipped her hand again. "I'm doing food. Neil's doing flowers and all the froufrou stuff. You, Mark, just go to your office, print your papers, and solve your crimes." She stood. "But leave your checkbook."

"Now *there's* a familiar request."

She patted my shoulder. "That's because you do it so well, hon." And she left the room, stepping into her nearby quarters, adjacent to the kitchen.

"Speaking of crimes," said Neil, reluctant to broach the topic, "what do you think? *Was* it a crime?" He rose from the table, got the coffeepot from the counter, and returned to fill our cups.

I sighed—not resolution this time, but frustration. "Good question. I *hope* it wasn't a crime. I hope Jason simply succumbed to some serious, undiagnosed illness, its symptoms having masqueraded as a cold. Right now, I'd bet on natural causes. If there *was* foul play, there was no immediate evidence of it. Besides, I can't imagine who'd have sufficient motive to kill Jason—he was conceited, yes, but hardly diabolical. In any event, this town doesn't need another murder hanging over it."

Pointedly, Neil added, "Neither does our quiet, happy household here on Prairie Street." With a grin, he looked over the edge of his cup at me, then drank.

Sitting back, I drummed my fingers on the newspaper there on the table. Rhetorically, I asked, "What *would* it take to kill a kid, to slay him in his prime? If it *was* murder, it's a particularly loathsome case."

"The classic murder motives," Neil rattled off, "are greed, passion, and revenge. Take your pick."

"Don't forget the motiveless murder—the kill for the thrill—the proverbial 'perfect crime.' "

Neil shuddered. "Let's not go there, okay? I would prefer to believe that we left the psychopaths and criminally insane back in the big, dirty metropolis."

"Chicago's not dirty," I told him in a mock scolding tone.

"Correct. But you *know* what I mean: small-town Wisconsin hardly strikes me as a breeding ground for dementia." Neil raised the mug in both hands to drink from it, but decided he'd had enough, setting it down.

Not quite joking, I suggested, "What about Mica Thrush?"

Not quite laughing, he conceded, "She *is* a weird one."

"Those were the very words used to describe her by Deputy Jim Johnson, first to arrive at the scene last night."

"Plus, she's heavily into 'gothic' chic—black clothes, black lips and nails, the works. Do you suppose Mica has an unnatural fascination with death?"

"Last night she did. You should have seen her toying with the corpse—in the very room where her father was bemoaning the fact that she was now his sole heir."

"Whew." Neil leaned forward, resting on his elbows. "This might be the easiest murder case *we've* ever solved." He laughed.

So did I. "Easy, Watson. As far as we know, there hasn't even *been* a murder."

A loud, shrill squawking noise interrupted us—it sounded like a stricken duck. Then Barb broke into rude guffaws, entering the kitchen with her clarinet mouthpiece poised before her lips. With her other hand, she carried a black leather case, a foot or so long, placing it on the table in front of us.

"That was lovely," I said dryly. "I'm so glad you made the investment in a really *good* instrument."

"Don't get smart. It was worth every penny. I'm just a little rusty and could use a few lessons." She snapped open the case, revealing the various sections of the clarinet, each nested in a velvety, contoured compartment. Unscrewing the metal ligature from the mouthpiece, she removed the reed, then tucked everything back in the case. "But"—her tone had suddenly turned ingratiating—"I could really use someplace to practice, someplace out of the way where I won't bother people."

"How 'bout the cellar," I suggested, managing to keep a straight face.

Neil cuffed me, telling Barb, "Just take one of the spare bedrooms. There's plenty of space upstairs—glad you can make use of it."

It was a good suggestion. The house had been designed for twice the number of its current inhabitants, and the second floor had five bedrooms. (On top of which, literally, was a third-floor great room, a wonderfully mysterious vaulted space that carried rich memories from my childhood.) The largest of the second-floor bedrooms, originally my uncle Edwin's, was now occupied by Neil and me. My aunt Peggy's lovely old room was set up as a permanent guestroom. Thad had one of the smaller rooms, which left two others. One of these was essentially a storeroom now; the other had served as a temporary workroom for Neil before he'd permanently moved his practice and opened the downtown office. Barb was welcome to either of these extra rooms.

"*Thanks*, guys," she told us, using both hands to simultaneously tweak one of my cheeks and one of Neil's—an annoying habit, though well meant. "I can't wait to set up. I'll practice in my spare time, promise, when no one's around."

"Fine," I told her, "but don't worry about bothering us—there's nothing wrong with a little music in the house. When do we get to hear you play something?"

"Maybe never." She splashed both hands in the air. "I'm in serious need of lessons, *remedial* lessons. Where to start?"

Neil asked, "Have you lined up a teacher yet?"

"Well, *no*"—hand to hip—"that's the *point*."

I got up from the table and crossed to the sink to rinse my cup. "This is a little out of my league, but you might want to talk to Whitney Greer."

Barb turned to me with a blank expression. "Who's she?"

"*He*," I corrected her, "is manager of the Dumont Symphony Orchestra."

Barb laughed. "No offense, guys, but he sounds like a hairdresser."

"Ahhh," said Neil, enlightened, "he'll be at the party tonight. That's a great suggestion, Mark. I'll bet he could connect Barb with some fine clarinetists."

"Hold on," said Barb, "I'm still a few steps behind. This is a *theater* party tonight, right? How'd this Whitney guy get in the picture?"

Neil explained, "Both the Dumont Players Guild and the Dumont Symphony are amateur groups, but they need some professional help. Neither organization can afford a full-time manager, so they 'share' Whitney Greer, who serves as executive director of both groups. He has no artistic control, but he—"

"Yeah, yeah," she interrupted, "I get it—the executive director is the paid help who minds the books and generally takes care of stuff. So this 'Mr. Whitney' is the orchestra guy too, huh? Maybe I *should* have a talk with him." She paused, looking suddenly wary. "I forgot about the Dumont Symphony Orchestra—haven't heard them in twenty years. Are they any *good?*"

"Very," I assured her. "Oh, I know—community orchestras are often maligned, and they sometimes deserve it, but the Dumont Symphony is a notch or two above the norm. They're over fifty years old, with a decent endowment, and they've done a valiant job of maintaining professional performance standards. Granted, their season consists of only five or six concerts, but they're good ones. The community orchestra, like the community theater, adds an important dimension to our quality of life here, and—"

"Enough already," she said, bumping me aside so she could load the dishwasher. "I got the picture. Sure, I'll talk to Whitney. Thanks for the tip."

When she had finished in the kitchen, she wiped her hands, retrieved the clarinet case, and headed toward the front hall. "I'll be upstairs. Since Roxanne's coming early, I'd better get her room ready."

"Thanks," we told her, and she was gone.

Neil got up from the table, slung an arm around my waist, and strolled me to the kitchen window, looking out at the backyard, green and still under the hot-white summer sky. Idly, he let his head drop against my shoulder. "It was good of her to change her plans today." The topic had shifted to Roxanne Exner, our Chicago lawyer friend.

I turned my head to smell his hair. "I don't think she *had* any plans, other than driving up to see Thad tonight. When I phoned her late last night and told her everything that had happened, she offered to get an early start today in order to be here by noon. We'll meet with Doug Pierce at my office—unofficially, of course. He took a bit of convincing, but ultimately, Doug's a friend as well as a cop."

"Good thing." Neil stood straight, a curious look crossing his face. "Where's Carl *this* time? It seems we never see him anymore." He was referring to Carl Creighton, an Illinois deputy attorney general. Before Carl had gotten involved in politics two years earlier, he'd been a senior partner at the prestigious Chicago law firm where Roxanne worked— and where she and Carl had met, becoming romantically involved. When Carl had left the practice, he'd promoted Roxanne, and the firm now bore the name Kendall Yoshihara Exner.

I answered Neil, "I assume Carl's down in Springfield again. He's been spending a lot of time there lately."

"Hope it's not a strain on their relationship."

"Well . . ." I hesitated to continue. "She did mention that she needed to talk to us this weekend. Whatever it is, she was less than giddy about it."

"Damn." Neil bit a nail. "Carl's been good for Rox. I've known her since college, and she needs to settle down—emotionally, I mean."

"Surely you're not hinting at the M-word." My tone was facetious, but in fact, neither one of us believed Roxanne would ever marry. She was simply too independent, a quality I found at once admirable and maddening.

Neil reminded me, "After two years of regularly sharing a bed with Carl, Rox still maintains her own apartment. No, marriage isn't her style, but she needs Carl's support, his maturity."

"Don't tell Roxanne that. She's sensitive about their age difference. She doesn't want it looking as if she's 'dating Dad.' "

Neil smirked. "They're twelve years apart—he's only fifty."

I hugged him from behind, resting my head on his shoulder. "I hope you'll be that charitable a few years down the road when *I'm* 'only fifty.' "

He snorted. "Don't count on it."

Then he turned around and kissed me, and I felt like a kid.

Roxanne phoned me from her car that morning to say the weekend traffic out of the city was clogged with vacationers heading north; she was running later than she'd hoped. So we abandoned our plan for a casual lunch at the house, and she would drive directly to the *Register*'s offices for our meeting with Sheriff Pierce.

"Will Lucille be there as well?" she asked.

"She's my managing editor," I reminded her. "The Jason Thrush case could develop into a major story. I hope not, but the paper needs to be prepared. Why do you ask?"

"No reason." She laughed. "See you at two, Mark."

The reason Roxanne had asked about Lucille Haring is that neither woman was the "marrying type." While this would seem to imply that they had a great deal in common, in fact they did not. For Roxanne, wedlock seemed unlikely owing to her sheer independence; Lucy was also the independent sort, but more to the point, she was a lesbian.

They had first crossed paths two years earlier at a party Neil and I had hosted in our Chicago loft. Mixed signals (i.e., Roxanne's new summer haircut, a short-cropped bob) led to faulty assumptions, and Lucy propositioned Roxanne. The misunderstanding was quickly righted, leaving Lucy mortified and Roxanne magnanimously forgiving—which only served to convince the mannish Miss Haring that there was still some shred of hope in her quest for the stylish Miss Exner.

So when I climbed the stairs from the *Register*'s lobby that Saturday afternoon and entered the second-floor newsroom alone, it didn't surprise me that Lucy looked up from the city desk, noting, "Oh. I thought you were bringing Roxanne." The comment was spoken offhandedly, but its undertone was clearly crestfallen.

Suppressing a smile, I told her, "She's on her way, just running late," and I slipped into my office to check my desk.

I found the usual assortment of memos, circulation reports, story proposals, and mail, but nothing needed my attention over the weekend, so I sat back for a moment, surveying the quiet hubbub beyond the glass wall of my outer office. The newsroom was staffed by a skeleton crew that afternoon, as Saturdays are always slow for news, summers sleepier still. For once, I realized, I was not annoyed by this torpor. Both by training and by instinct, I had an itch for action—the point of news-papers, after all, is *news*—but just then I had little taste for the late-breaking or the hard-hitting. So far, Jason Thrush's death, though tragic, was merely "unexplained." There was no assumption of foul play. And I wanted it to stay that way.

These musings were interrupted by the sight of Roxanne, who had just climbed the stairs and was zigzagging toward my office through the maze of newsroom desks, followed by Lucy. Roxanne wore a smart white summer pantsuit that, miraculously, appeared to have survived the long drive without a wrinkle. Lucy also wore pants, as was her habit, but they were drab-colored, of vaguely military styling, which gave her the look of a redheaded Texaco attendant.

I rose from my desk and met them in my outer office, greeting Rox-anne with a kiss. "Rough drive?" I asked.

"Bumper-to-bumper all the way up to Milwaukee. But then it thinned out."

Lucy offered, "Can I get you . . . water or anything?"

Roxanne tendered a wan smile. "I'm fine, thanks."

"Then let's get comfortable," I told them, gesturing that we should sit. The space outside my office had been intended for a secretary, but unlike Barret Logan, the previous publisher, I had not found need for one, relying on the downstairs receptionist for phone duties. So the small anteroom was put to good use as a conference area.

We settled into the upholstered chairs that surrounded a low table. Lucy unloaded an armful of files she'd carried from the newsroom; I unclipped the pen from my pocket and readied a notebook; Roxanne set her gray leather handbag on the floor. I was collecting my thoughts and about to speak when the phone warbled. Having grown used to these interruptions, and having grown tired of running back to my inner office to take the calls, I'd recently had an extension of my line installed here in the conference room. "Excuse me," I told the ladies as I answered the phone on the center table.

"Sorry to bother you, Mr. Manning. It's Connie downstairs. It's time for my break, and I wondered if you're expecting anyone." On week-ends, the lobby doors to the street were kept locked, and visitors needed to be buzzed in.

"Thanks, Connie. The sheriff is coming, but we'll cover for you. Go ahead."

As I hung up the phone, Lucy asked, "Buzzer duty?"

I nodded. "Do you mind?"

"Nah." With a smile, she stood, excused herself, and left for the lobby.

Leaning toward Roxanne, I told her, "Thanks for rushing up here today. The situation with Thad isn't quite a crisis, but the—"

"Mark," she interrupted, leaning forward, mirroring my posture, "as I mentioned on the phone last night, I really think we need to talk. As for Thad, well of *course* I'm more than happy to offer legal advice, moral support, or whatever it takes. Meanwhile, though, I've been dealing with some . . . issues. And you and Neil are really the only guys I care to turn to with this."

Pointedly, I asked, "What about Carl? Or is Carl the, uh, 'issue.' "

Sitting back, she nodded—it was a tiny wobble of the head, barely perceptible, but it spoke volumes.

She didn't seem prepared to offer more, but since she herself had steered our discussion to this topic, I asked, "Where *is* Carl this weekend? We haven't seen him in a while."

Again she nodded. "Springfield, naturally."

I shrugged, minimizing the implications of his absence. "He's a deputy attorney general. It's no surprise that he needs to spend time in the state capital."

"No, Mark"—she wagged a hand—"it's not just the time in Springfield. It's—"

"Wait," I told her, my turn to interrupt. "Here comes Lucy with Doug Pierce. Maybe we should continue this later."

"Thanks, Mark." She smiled. It wasn't clear if she was grateful for the warning or the offer to talk later or both.

I stood as Pierce crossed the newsroom and walked into my office with Lucy. "Hey, Doug," I told him, "thanks for coming over on a Saturday." I shook his hand, but also pulled him close in something of a half hug, a body brush.

He clapped my shoulder (he'd always been much more adept than I at that sort of guy stuff), quipping, "I'm a public servant, Mark. Your wish is my command. Though I must repeat"—his look turned serious—"this meeting strikes me as unorthodox at best." Then, turning to Roxanne, he smiled, bowing his head. "My favorite barrister." And he shook her hand warmly, clasping it with both of his.

"Hi, Doug," Roxanne answered, sounding suddenly chipper, "nice to see you again." Her grin betrayed the lusty interest she'd always had in him, even since the previous autumn, when our speculation was ended and we learned unequivocally that, yes, Pierce was gay. No doubt about it, Roxanne had a habit of falling for gay men (Neil and me, for instance, before she introduced us), which is why both Neil and I had greeted with cautious optimism her evolving relationship with Carl Creighton—the proper, well-bred, divorced, old-school sort of Brooks Brothers legal genius for whom the term *straight* had been invented. If things were now deteriorating between Roxanne and Carl, I shuddered to think how she might react to their failed romance, fearing she might revert to her old self-deceptive (and self-destructive) exploits.

Equally unsettling were the odd cross-dynamics now at work in my outer office. Lesbian Lucy was pining over straight Roxanne, who was off-limits, while Roxanne entertained visions of undressing the openly gay sheriff, also off-limits. Pierce's inscrutable libido was, as always, kept well in check, while I couldn't help wondering (just wondering) if he ever thought of me "that way." The whole setup defined the very notion of sexual tension.

"So," said Pierce, "what have we got?" He, Lucy, and I joined Roxanne, sitting around the table.

I began by summarizing, mainly for Roxanne's benefit, "At a rehearsal last Wednesday, Thad and another young actor, Jason Thrush, got into a verbal pissing match. Jason started it. Thad ended it by paraphrasing a threatening line from the scene they'd just rehearsed—Thad told Jason that he 'may not live till opening night.' Sure enough, last night, Jason didn't make it to the theater, Thad stepped into the leading role, and minutes after Thad's triumphal performance began, Jason's fright case of a sister found Jason at home, dead of unknown causes. Right after the show, as soon as news of Jason's death got out, speculation began to spread that Thad had made good on his promise."

Roxanne looked toward the ceiling, thinking. "So then," she said, "you've got two distinct problems. First, how did Jason die? And second, how do you shift the focus away from Thad?"

"Precisely."

Pierce cautioned, "I need to keep an open mind about this, Mark. That second question is your concern, not mine."

Lucy skipped past that, saying, "The cleanest, most obvious answer to the second question is simply to answer the first. Once it's shown that

Jason died of natural causes, which I assume to be the case, any question of Thad's possible involvement disappears."

I told everyone, "That's exactly how I hope it'll play out, but for Thad's sake, it needs to happen fast. Good God, I *know* Thad didn't kill Jason, and I have no doubt that the facts will exonerate him—eventually. By then, though, some serious damage may be done."

Roxanne didn't understand my concern. "You mean his . . . 'reputation'?"

"No, not at all. Well, sort of. Look, in the last year, Thad has managed to pull himself out of a nasty adolescent funk. Now he's taking school seriously, he's making friends, and he's getting 'into' things—most notably, theater. Suddenly, his newfound friends are turning against him, thinking him capable of murder. That's *bound* to put a crimp in his ego. And if the investigation drifts on inconclusively for a few weeks, as it often does when toxicology is involved, this whole mess will follow Thad back to school—at the start of his senior year, no less." Frustrated, I paused to rub my forehead. With a sigh I concluded, "He just doesn't need this, not now. He's at a vulnerable juncture in his life. I don't want to see him hurt."

I must have sniffled—Pierce leaned over and patted my arm. There there now.

He said, "I want to get this wrapped up as quickly as you do. But you're right, Mark—the investigation of a death that's merely 'suspicious' can indeed drag on because we simply don't know what we're looking for. So you might want to bring your own investigative talents to the fore. My own limited police mission at this point is to determine the cause of Jason's death, which may not go far enough or fast enough to serve *your* mission of clearing Thad of suspicion before the gossip gets out of control."

I must have sniffled again—now Lucy was leaning to pat my other arm, a warm gesture inconsistent with her usual no-nonsense manner, her stiff bearing.

She told me, "I'll do whatever I can, Mark. Depend on me. Besides, this is sure to make a great story. After all, we could *use* a few scorching midsummer headlines, and if, in the process, we also get Thad off the hook, all the better." She sat back in her chair and jogged the pile of manila folders she'd brought from the paper's morgue. "The sheriff's right—we *don't* know what we're looking for, but it's never too early to start digging. I've pulled everything we've got on the Thrush family as well as the Thrush business. There's quite a bit, but I'll study it all, and when I'm through with that, I'll get busy on the computer."

This was the Lucille Haring I'd known, respected, and hired. She was a loyal, dedicated worker, a skilled researcher, and a peerless computer wiz. Her rare bouts of ditsiness erupted only with Roxanne on the scene, and even now, with the object of her desire mere inches away, Lucy was back in control, telling me things I needed to hear.

Not to be upstaged by this outpouring of support, Roxanne rose from her chair and glided around the table, stopping behind me. She placed her hands on my shoulders and told the others, "I've known Mark longer than anyone in this room, and I've never known him to back off from the challenge of righting a wrong. As a reporter, as a man, and now as a father, he's been tireless in the unpuzzling of perplexities, whether petty or dastardly. This I tell you: if foul play has *again* wounded the collective psyche of fair Dumont, Mark Manning will not rest till truth be bared, justice served. To this same end, I pledge the assistance of my own meager skills. Behind him I stand."

Puh-leeze. Screwing my neck, I looked up into her face.

"How was that?" she asked.

"Plastic. Mawkish. Inflated to the point of insincerity."

"Take it or leave it, bud."

Bending my head, I kissed her fingers on my shoulder. "Thanks, Roxanne."

She fluffed the hair on my temples, then stepped back a pace, crossing her arms. All business now, she asked, "Where are we?"

Pierce reviewed the known facts: "Jason Thrush was found dead at home by his sister shortly after eight o'clock last night. Based on the observed condition of the corpse, Vernon Formhals estimated the time of death to be a few hours earlier, between five and six. For the previous several days, Jason had exhibited symptoms that were assumed to indicate a bad summer cold. He was found fully clothed, lying facedown on his bed; we don't know whether he collapsed there or if he had lain down, then died. The body showed no signs of physical trauma, and the room showed no signs of a struggle. How did Jason die? In short, it's a mystery."

Listening to this, Roxanne had returned to her chair. She sat, thinking, teeth pinching her lower lip. She then said, "Logically, we have three possibilities: he died of a bad cold, which seems unlikely; or he died of some other natural cause, possibly an illness with coldlike symptoms; or he was murdered, the victim of foul play, such as poisoning. Have I missed anything?"

Lucy shook her head. "That would seem to cover it." She tapped her pencil on a pad, where she had drawn a grid. With her other hand, she raked her fingers straight back through her short red hair. "Wait," she said, zeroing in on the blank fourth square she had drawn. "Poisoning isn't necessarily foul play—it *could* be accidental."

Pierce and I exchanged a glance, nodding.

"Good point," said Roxanne. "I stand corrected—we have *four* possibilities." She turned to Pierce. "A complete medical-legal autopsy is under way, I presume?"

"Yup. Vernon said he'd get going on the physical examination this morning." Pierce looked at his watch; it was about two-thirty. "The lab work could still take a while—weeks, in fact—but Vernon ought to be through with the grisly stuff. Maybe he has some initial findings." Pierce turned to me, indicating the phone on the table. "Shall I try to catch him?"

"*Sure,*" Roxanne and Lucy answered for me, in unison.

I laughed. "By all means. Go ahead, Doug."

He pulled the phone over to him, lifted the receiver, and punched in the number. A moment later: "Hi, Vernon, it's Doug. Glad I caught you in. Any progress with the Thrush boy?"

Pierce nodded as he listened, reached for a notepad, then reconsidered, telling the coroner, "Vernon, hold on. I'm here with Mark Manning at the *Register*'s offices. We're doing some brainstorming with his editor and a lawyer friend. Do you mind if I switch you to the speakerphone so we can all talk?"

Pierce listened for a moment, then chuckled. He told me, "Vernon says he'll tell you what he knows, but it's off-the-record at this point."

"No problem." I reached across the table and pushed the speaker button.

Pierce hung up the receiver, asking, "Still there, Vernon?"

"Yes, Douglas." Formhals's rich baritone was barely recognizable through the low-fi electronics, sounding like a transmission from the moon.

"Good afternoon, Doctor," I told him. "Thanks for talking to us." I knew that he and Lucy were acquainted, but I couldn't recall if he and Roxanne had met, so I made a proper round of introductions. Then I asked if he could share any findings regarding Jason Thrush.

"Please understand," he told us, "that this is all very preliminary. Results of the external and internal examinations were inconclusive, and further testing, including toxicology, is necessary. At this point, there's very little I can confirm."

Looking up from the notes I was scratching, I asked, "And that would be . . . ?"

"For starters, we can conclude that Jason's time of death was between five and six yesterday, as initially estimated. Further, the *mechanism* of death was respiratory failure, but that doesn't tell you what you need to know—yes, he stopped breathing, but why? There are many conditions and circumstances that could be responsible. As of now, the specific *cause* of death is unknown."

Roxanne asked, "So we're back to square one?"

"Oh, no, not by a long shot. I found several rather conspicuous conditions that provide valuable hints regarding the direction of further testing. Specifically, Jason's body was severely dehydrated, and closing of the throat was noted, as was the presence of copious mucus in the mouth and throat."

I said, "Even *I* noticed the mucus in the mouth."

Pierce added, "It was hard to miss."

"Are you saying," asked Roxanne, "that the kid choked on his own snot?"

There was a pause. The coroner coughed, then said, "In effect, yes."

Pierce said, "So it wasn't 'just a cold.' "

"Actually," said Formhals, "it was. He had a common cold, albeit a bad one. I found no evidence of other medical conditions that would mimic those symptoms. In fact, he was in excellent health."

Lucy made the obvious comment: "Except, he was dead."

"As a doornail," confirmed the coroner (whose sense of humor was dry, at best). "Let me explain. Even though Jason's illness was 'just a cold,' something else apparently exacerbated the symptoms so seriously that he choked, which in turn led to respiratory failure."

"Doctor," I told him, "you have our undivided attention. You referred to 'something else.' Like what?"

He paused before telling us, "Poisoning."

"My God," muttered Lucy.

"Specifically," added Formhals, "mushroom poisoning."

"*Mushrooms?*" said Roxanne, incredulous.

"Uh-oh," said Pierce, catching my eye.

Formhals continued, "It's merely a theory, and there are still several possibilities that need to be explored, but the boy's symptoms—dehydration, closed throat, and copious mucus—do strongly suggest certain types of mushroom poisoning. Of course, the stomach contents still need to be analyzed, so we don't know yet whether the subject ingested mushrooms, and still further testing will be required to detect the presence of particular toxins. Still, there is nothing to indicate whether the *manner* of death was accidental or deliberate. For now, though, the mushroom theory is the best one we have, so . . ."

The coroner was still talking, but I'd tuned out. Pierce was still watching me, and I was worried. It was bad enough that Thad had threatened Jason, but now there was talk of mushroom poisoning, and during the previous school year, Thad had become quite the young expert in this area. I had no doubt of his innocence in Jason's death, but it was clear that Pierce now had one more reason not to let our friendship cloud his objectivity.

Formhals concluded, "I'll try to put a rush on the tests—not sure it'll do any good, though. *Everyone's* in a hurry when the evidence takes a turn toward murder."

The rest of the afternoon was lost to fretting. I returned to the house with Roxanne, and we informed Neil of the coroner's disturbing theory, deciding not to mention it to Thad yet—he had a performance that night, as well as the party afterward, so there was plenty on his mind already.

"Crap," I said to Neil in the bedroom that evening as we dressed to go to the theater. "This mushroom wrinkle is way out of my league. It leaves me feeling so helpless—I mean helpless to help Thad. My knowledge of fungi is nil."

Tying a perfect Windsor with a quick, fluid motion, Neil reminded me, "We have a friend who's a mycologist—at least I do."

I paused midknot, feeling like an idiot. "Of course. Frank Gelden, the adviser to the mushroom club at school—he might be a great resource for pinning down particulars that could exonerate Thad before this whole mess spins out of control. You know Frank far better than I do. Do you think he'd be willing to help?"

"Oh, I think so," Neil answered through a coy grin. "Since I started working on the home-office project with Cynthia, both she and Frank have mentioned several times that they'd like to get to know us better. They'll be here at the party tonight. Let's nab Frank and tell him about the coroner's theory. I don't know if Frank could actually be of help, but if nothing else, I'm sure the mushroom angle would intrigue him."

I nodded. "Worth a try." Sprucing the knot of my tie, I mulled Neil's comment that Frank and his wife were eager to know us. I had not yet met Cynthia, and I had spoken to Frank only once, but he'd surely sparked my interest. The prospect of a budding friendship appealed to me.

Shortly after seven-thirty, I drove Neil and Roxanne to the theater, where Pierce would meet us. Because Barb had already seen Thad play the leading role in Friday's opening, she felt that her time would be better spent on last-minute spiffing for the cast party that night, so she decided to stay home, promising Thad she'd attend the show again the next weekend.

In the car, Neil and I continued to gab about the vexing implications of the coroner's mushroom theory. Neil was in the backseat, and I was at the wheel, with Roxanne sitting next to me in front. During a pause in the conversation, I realized that she hadn't said a word since getting into the car.

"Jeez," I said, turning to her, "I'm sorry, Roxanne. I forgot—there's something you've been wanting to discuss with us."

She patted my leg. "That's okay." Her tone was sincere, though shaded by melancholy. "You guys are concerned about Thad—we all are. My 'little issue' can wait. Maybe we can find some time to talk later tonight."

"Of course," we assured her. "Just say when."

Turning onto First Avenue, I was surprised by the sight of congested traffic down the street in front of the playhouse. I had presumed that the previous night's performance, being the premiere, would draw the biggest crowd—and in fact the theater had been full—but tonight there were far more cars, and a line of people wormed its way from the box office past the next-door antiques store. "Glad we have tickets," I told the others.

After we'd managed to park, I found that the lobby was packed. Grumbling would-be patrons were now being turned away from the ticket booth. For the first time in the Guild's history, the playhouse had completely sold out, not only every seat, but standing room as well. The buzz in the lobby confirmed, as I feared, that this rush of interest in amateur theater had been generated not by Glee Savage's glowing review in that morning's *Register*, but by the news of Jason Thrush's death, by the uncanny life-imitates-art circumstances, and by the knowledge, now common, that Thad Quatrain had threatened the Thrush boy before he died, stepping into the leading role.

Neil and I divvied up our tickets. He and Roxanne would work their way toward the auditorium, escaping the crush of the lobby, while I would remain, waiting for Pierce. After a minute or so of watching the door, I spotted Pierce across the lobby, his head bobbing above the others, apparently in search of us, so I began sidling through the crowd in his direction.

Along the way, I noticed Glee Savage enter the theater, accompanied by Lucille Haring. Glee had originally planned to review both the Friday and Saturday performances because of the double casting. Those plans had now changed, of course, but she had enjoyed the show so much, she was back for another look. Lucy, on the other hand, had not, to my knowledge, planned to attend at all, but with the murder and the potential for developing news, she had decided to see the play out of sheer curiosity; her decision was doubtless bolstered by the assumption that Roxanne would be in the theater that night. With devilish insight, I now understood why Lucy (not, by nature, a party person) had so readily accepted my invitation to the house after the show.

Setting these thoughts aside, I continued through the crowd toward Pierce. Surrounded by a babble of voices, I seemed to hear both everything and nothing that was said. Snatches of conversation, phrases lacking context, words without meaning—the chatter was like aural wallpaper, seamless and unending, a random pattern of hearsay and do-tell, spoken in loud whispers of gossip. Most of it, I was certain, pertained to Thad and Jason, but I tried to assure myself that I was merely being paranoid, imagining my own concerns being bandied about by this cross section of the town's faceless, nameless populace.

Then I actually heard the two names, clearly and unambiguously, spoken by a woman within inches of my ear: ". . . a world of difference between Thad Quatrain and Jason Thrush." I stopped, turned my head, and saw the speaker standing near my side, her back to me, conversing with another woman whom I did not recognize. The speaker seemed familiar, though, even from behind—her proper posture, her measured speech, her perfect, stiff hairdo. She was now speaking of Jason's death in a tone neither hushed nor gossipy. She stated flatly, "What goes around, comes around. Sometimes destiny doles out its own harsh justice." And with that, she offered the other woman a nod of farewell, leaving the distinct impression that she saw no tragedy in Jason's passing. As she moved away, I got a good glimpse of her profile. It was Nancy Sanderson, owner of First Avenue Grill.

Distracted by this encounter, I momentarily lost sight of Pierce in the shifting crowd. Focusing again on my mission, I stood on the balls of my feet, noticed Pierce doing the same, and caught his attention. Holding the tickets over my head, I motioned toward the double doors to the auditorium.

A minute or two later, we greeted each other with a perfunctory handshake, took our programs from the usher, and headed down the aisle toward our seats. I told him, "Strange crowd tonight."

He glanced around. "*Great* crowd tonight."

I hesitated. "I don't know—something tells me they're out for blood."

Arriving at our row, we found the two outer seats left open for us so that Pierce could sit on the aisle; I resolved to sit through the entire show that night, regardless of whatever enticing emergency might lure Pierce away. Neil and Roxanne had taken the inside seats, but between them sat someone else, a woman I'd never met. As Pierce and I slipped in and sat down, Neil told me, "We ran into Cynthia Dunne-Gelden, and we had Barb's extra ticket, so I asked her to join us." Then he introduced us.

"Mark," said Cynthia, stretching across Neil to shake my hand, "at long last, such a pleasure." Her gold bracelets rattled.

I returned her smile. "My pleasure entirely. Neil's told me so many nice things about you." Saying this, I realized that Neil had in fact told me little about the woman, and I was surprised to note that she did not fit the vague mental image I'd drawn of her.

I'd known only that she was a businesswoman, apparently well-off, and married to Frank for eight years. Frank was forty, but I felt that he looked younger than his years; Cynthia seemed older. Though she looked trim and fit, and she dressed beautifully, she was not (to be coldly objective) "pretty." In short, I thought that she and Frank seemed mismatched—but I quickly chided myself for judging them on mere appearances. They were both mature adults when they had married, and it was unfair of me to question their pairing on such superficial grounds. Clearly, I reasoned, their commitment ran deeper than "good looks," and the ring on her finger proved it. Recalling too the ring on Frank's finger, I was ashamed of myself for finding him so attractive, for judging her so unworthy.

Cynthia was saying to me, "I'm *dying* to get acquainted later this evening at the party—thanks, by the way, for inviting us." Then she returned to the conversation she'd already struck up with Roxanne, who sat on her far side.

Neil leaned toward me, fanning his playbill open. "Have you seen this?"

I opened my program and found a new page inserted in the center. There was a general announcement that, for the remainder of the run, the role of Ryan would be played by Thad Quatrain, the role of Dawson by Thomas Morales. The announcement was followed by a short letter, signed by Denny Diggins, informing the audience of the tragic death of Jason Thrush (on the off chance that someone there that night hadn't heard the news yet). Finally, at the bottom of the page, was a solemn, black-bordered box with funereal script, dedicating the entire production of *Teen Play* to the loving memory of Jason Thrush.

More and more, I was getting the uneasy feeling that Thad would have a rough time winning over the audience that night.

And I was right.

When the houselights finally dimmed and the crowd hushed, there was the usual moment of expectancy before the stage lights came on, but the mood of the audience was palpably different from that of the previous night. On Friday, there was a mood of excitement; the crowd was ready for magic. Tonight's audience, like a many-headed beast waiting in the dark, projected a silent anticipation that was both grim and demanding.

With a sudden hum, the stage lights were at full power, and the play began. After a few lines of opening dialogue from minor characters, Thad entered as Ryan. If he was expecting the same round of spontaneous applause that had greeted his entrance on opening night, he was surely disappointed—not a sound came from the audience, not even a cough, not even a squeak from the old seats. Hurdling this cold welcome with aplomb, Thad plunged onward into the scene.

Several pages into the script, Tommy Morales made his entrance as

Dawson, the smaller of the two leading roles. For the first time, the audience came to life, greeting Tommy as they had greeted Thad the night before. The characters onstage knew how to handle it—they froze in tableau until the applause began to wane, then carried on with the scene as if nothing had happened. But something *had* happened, of course, something profound. The crowd, by some mysterious, fickle, collective logic, had bestowed star status on Tommy. Were they *punishing* Thad? Had they already judged him responsible for Jason's death? Had they decided to shun Thad?

Those were the vibes they seemed to be sending, a silent message that Thad decoded with ease. Before my eyes, his performance began to deteriorate. His vocal projection flagged, his words lacked the dual sparks of life and realism, and at one point, he even flubbed a line (a first in his year of acting), which further shook his confidence.

In contrast, Tommy's performance soared. He played the smaller role of Dawson with all the insight and maturity that Thad had shown in the same role at Wednesday's rehearsal. Though Tommy had stepped into the role on Friday and played it only once, he now performed it with the confidence that arises from weeks of rehearsal. In spite of the agonies I felt for Thad, I was genuinely impressed by the skills of his younger counterpart.

When intermission at last mercifully arrived, I breathed a sigh of relief. Though Thad's performance was clearly "off," he'd made it through the first half, and I hoped the brief break would give him the opportunity to collect his thoughts, focus on his role, and reignite his dramatic passion for the rigors of act two.

"It was *wonderful*," said Cynthia Dunne-Gelden, leaning from her seat.

Roxanne seconded, "Thad's stealing the show, all right."

They were both sincere in their compliments, but neither had seen the previous night's performance, so they couldn't appreciate how far Thad had slipped. "Actually," I told them, "Thad seems a bit . . . tired tonight. I'm sure things'll pick up after intermission."

Pierce and Neil nodded their agreement, but offered no further comments.

The rest of the row got up, excusing themselves for a stretch in the lobby, but I remained alone in my seat, claiming fatigue—true enough, but more to the point, I had no appetite for the jabber I'd encounter out there. Real or imagined, all the buzz would be Tommy-this and Tommy-that; references to Thad would be gloating and disparaging.

Just who, I wondered, *is* this Thomas Morales? Thumbing through the program, I found the cast members' profiles. He was listed last, since his assigned character, the Old Man, was the play's smallest role. Under his name, a parenthetical line also noted that he was understudy for the role of Dawson. His blurb was brief. I learned that he was sixteen, a year younger than Thad, attending the same school, Dumont Central, where Tommy had appeared in every play for the past two years. The credits all struck me as minor roles, and I assumed this was due to his height, which was a few inches on the short side, or perhaps the leading roles routinely went to upperclassmen—I wasn't sure. *Teen Play* was his first production outside of school. He thanked the Dumont Players Guild; the show's director, Denny Diggins; his high school director, Mrs. Osborne; his mother and father; his four siblings; and God.

I'd never met Tommy, though I'd seen all that fussing with his Old Man costume at Wednesday's rehearsal. I couldn't recall that Thad had ever spoken of him, and though they'd been in school plays together, I'd simply never noticed Tommy, confirming my hunch that his roles had been small. Watching the first half of his performance tonight, I had no reason to think he was anything other than "just a good kid," and his printed litany of thanks seemed to bear out this conclusion. On top of which, his face had a certain innocence, a boyishness. Indeed, his darker skin and delicate features made him look downright beatific, like a little Latin cherub. Still, he had just trounced my own kid in act one—I decided I didn't like him.

Act two did nothing to soften my prejudice.

Thad's performance remained at low ebb, but the audience had ceased to notice—all eyes were now on Tommy. He acted his little heart out, playing not one role, but two (Dawson and the Old Man). During the final encounter, the bloody bludgeoning in which Dawson kills Ryan, the audience roared its approval as Tommy slew Thad. The previous night, the crowd had witnessed this climactic scene in silent, breathless horror, but tonight they got a kick out of it, venting their hostilities as if at a century-old melodrama. They all but threw vegetables.

It was the curtain call, however, that frosted the theatrical cake. The audience was having a great time, applauding and whistling as the actors came onstage for their bows, working their way up from the smallest roles to the leads. When there were two spaces left, center stage, where Dawson and Ryan would bow, there was a long (dramatic) pause—*where the hell was Dawson?* The audience continued clapping uncertainly, then out hobbled the Old Man in full costume, one of the quickest changes I'd ever witnessed. When the Old Man *finally* made his way to downstage center (milking every feeble step), he bowed as if his back would break, then, on the upswing, whipped the wig and beard from his face, revealing (*oh, my God!*) that it was none other than Dawson—little Tommy Morales, there in the flesh! The audience ate up this shameless grandstanding, as if everyone were taken by complete surprise, as if no one had even glanced at a program. They *loved* it. They were on their feet, clapping their hands raw, shouting themselves hoarse.

After what seemed a full minute of this brouhaha, Ryan (the star, remember, my nephew Thad) wandered out for his bow, doomed to an anticlimactic reception. Though the audience remained standing (only because it was time to leave), the level of hysteria instantly dropped, leaving polite applause. Thad bowed for the scraps that were offered, but before he'd even risen, the stage lights winked out. A moment later, when the cast had disappeared, the houselights rose.

Chatter broke out all around, but I wasn't listening. Purses snapped, keys rattled, people were moving into the aisle. Neil gave me a nudge. "We'd better get going," he told me, affecting an upbeat tone, trying to mask his own disappointment. "Our guests will be arriving at the house."

I nodded without comment, stepping with Pierce into the aisle, my eyes still focused on the empty stage. Then an obvious thought crossed my mind:

Tommy Morales owed tonight's triumph to the death of Jason Thrush.

A mixed crowd of kids and adults would descend upon the house on Prairie Street for the cast-and-crew party. By the time I arrived home with Neil and Roxanne, early arrivals were streaming up the sidewalk from the street; others, earlier still, were already inside, as evidenced by the blur of silhouettes passing by the windows.

"I need a drink," I told my companions as we climbed the back stairs and crossed the porch.

"I'll second that," said Neil, who had found Thad's disastrous performance even more upsetting than I had.

Pausing at the kitchen door, Roxanne asked warily, "Isn't this a *kids'* party?" She was questioning the presence of alcohol, which she herself had forsworn—with good reason.

While sensitive to the issue, Neil was in no mood to slog through this particular night without booze. Entering the house, he explained, "There'll be plenty of adults around, crew as well as parents. Most of *them* will want to drink, and they can help keep an eye on things. As an extra precaution, adults will serve themselves here in the kitchen, under Barb's menacing gaze; the kiddy bar is in the dining room with the food."

As he said this, Barb let out a shrill whistle. *"Hey, you—out, you little delinquents!"* And a pair of inquisitive kids backed out of the kitchen, laughing.

"Evening, Barb," I said dryly. "Everything under control?"

"Yeah"—she snapped her fingers—"no problem." Then: "What's *wrong* with you guys? Somebody die?"

Neil answered with a half laugh, "You mean it shows? Thad didn't do so well tonight. The audience was hostile. Frankly, I think we *should* have canceled the party—things could get weird." He stretched his shoulders, grimacing.

"Nah," Barb assured him, stepping behind to knead the kink from his neck, "the party will be good for all of you, even Thad. He's the big man tonight."

She was right. The whole point of tonight's festivities was to let Thad shine—I just hoped the party's tone would in fact be "festive." Looking about, I realized that everything was in order, even the bar, so I helped myself to some Japanese vodka, pouring stiff shots over ice for both Neil and me. Neil sliced an orange peel, twisting slivers of it over our glasses, the finishing touch for "our usual." Roxanne helped herself to mineral water, opting for some orange peel as well. Tasting it, she nodded her approval. Neil and I exchanged a silent toast, then drank. The evening looked a measure better already.

The main crush of guests had begun to arrive, with repeated rings of the doorbell, which were answered by anyone nearby. Bracing myself, I told the others, "Time to mingle." Roxanne stayed behind with Barb for the moment, but Neil and I ventured forth from the safety of the kitchen.

Thad had arrived from the theater, still looking sweaty from a quick shower, but exhilarated. With Kwynn Wyman at his side, he'd managed to leave the horrors of the performance behind. Someone turned up the music in the living room, and to my relief, the whole house took on a party atmosphere. The kids had discovered Barb's lavish spread of food in the dining room, descending on it like a throng of refugees—they were even wolfing the black-trumpet spread (after having heard the coroner's mushroom theory that afternoon, you couldn't have paid me to touch it, let alone eat it). Spotting me standing there staring at the goo, Thad came over and sampled it, swiping from the bowl with a finger.

I put a hand on his shoulder. "Tough crowd tonight, eh?"

He rolled his eyes. "You just never know. Every audience is different. I was sorry it didn't turn out better for Roxanne, though."

"She loved it."

Tommy Morales popped up to the table.

"Hey," said Thad, "try this, Tommy. Black trumpets—I picked them yesterday, and Barb made the spread. It's great." He was blissfully ignorant of the cream cheese he was eating.

"Yeah?" Tommy's eyes sparkled (he had a beautiful face, I'll hand him that). He tried the spread on a piece of warm, crusty bread. "Wow. They're right at their peak. Where'd you find them?"

"As if I'd tell!"

Both boys laughed, fellow devotees of the hunt, it seemed. What surprised me, though, was that neither said a word about that night's performance—there wasn't a hint of animosity over what had happened. Maybe I'd been imagining their rivalry, suckered by the realism of their acting. I still had a lot to learn about the theater world.

Leaving them to their black trumpets, I found Roxanne in the center hall, chatting with Sheriff Pierce, Glee Savage, and Lucille Haring, who'd all arrived together. Glee was explaining to the others that Thad had been much better the night before, that the mood of the audience had soured.

I butted in. "Thad just shrugged it off. He says every audience is different."

Glee clutched her enormous purse. "I wish I could be that resilient."

We all agreed that kids were a mystery, even though we'd all been there ourselves. As we continued to compare notes, the front door kept opening with each new arrival.

Denny Diggins walked in, looking a bit shaken by the odd turn his show had taken that night. Putting our past animosities aside, I stepped over to him, observing, "You seem to be in need of alcohol."

"Thank you, Mahk." He fluttered his eyelids. "That would be *mah-velous.*"

And I steered him toward the kitchen.

Our guests seemed to be finding everything, and everyone already knew each other, so my hostly duties were minimal. I didn't see Neil about, and Roxanne was still gabbing with her group, so I felt free to wander and observe.

The house had never looked better. Both Barb and Neil had out-done themselves in their weeklong efforts to make sure Thad would shine as lord of our manor that night. In addition to the bounty of Barb's buffet (which seemed to be available at every turn, not only in the dining room), Neil had cleverly decorated the entire first floor, combining seasonal wildflowers and branches with theatrical-themed items (masks, megaphones, oversize marquee letters, even a clunky old spotlight fixture that anchored the centerpiece of the main table). The kids loved it, the parents were suitably wowed, and for the moment, at least, no one was openly voicing the belief that my nephew was a cal-culating killer—on balance, not a bad night.

Still, Jason's mysterious death was *the* hot topic of conversation that evening. Drifting from room to room, I kept an eye on my guests' needs and, more important, an ear on their chatter. Huddled on chairs or sprawled on the floor, clumps of kids gossiped and squealed about Jason's demise. Even though the coroner had not yet ruled out natural causes, everyone now giddily assumed that Jason had been murdered, and there was no shortage of theories as to whodunit or why. I noted as well that, among the troupe of young actors, there was no lack of drama in the scenarios discussed. Suspicion fingered everyone that night.

"Jason was a quarterback at Unity," said one of Thad's classmates from Central High. "I don't know his teammates, but I'll just *bet* there was some fierce rivalry there—and practice starts in a couple of weeks."

"What about that coach?" asked someone else. "You know, the young one, the assistant. They had some big run-in at the end of last season. I heard that he tried to throw Jason off the team, but his rich old dad paid someone off."

Yet another: "Nah, the team needed him. Maybe they didn't *like* Jason, but I doubt if they'd just . . . *kill* him."

"Mr. Quimby would've," said someone from Unity.

"Who?"

"The driver's ed teacher. He had a real . . . 'problem' with Jason."

"What driver's ed teacher doesn't have 'problems'?" asked another, cracking everyone up.

"Hold on," said a girl. "What about that old guy we've noticed hanging around the theater? Someone said he stinks."

"That derelict? The stranger with a beard?"

While they debated the pros and cons of the deadly derelict, I couldn't help thinking of the Old Man, the minor role played by a heavily costumed Tommy Morales. At dress rehearsal, Thad had mentioned, "You'd never know Tommy in that getup." Had Tommy perhaps put disguises to more sinister use?

Now Thad told the group, "Here's an idea: What if Jason wasn't murdered, but died of fright or something? I mean, opening night, and he was *already* sick—he could have just keeled over."

Thad's suggestion, which struck me as no less likely than others that had been floated, was met with a conspicuous, awkward silence. Finally, someone said, "That's pretty far-fetched, Thad. Jason was an experienced actor. He wouldn't just 'die of fright.' " Others were quick to join in dismissing Thad's idea, and their collective skepticism spoke volumes: many of those present did indeed wonder if Thad had something to hide.

Turning away from the group, I noticed Lucille Haring standing alone near the front door and intended to ask her if she'd found anything of interest in the *Register*'s files on the Thrush family, but someone tapped my shoulder.

"Mr. Manning? Do you have a second?" It was Thad's friend Kwynn. I smiled and was about to say something, but she signaled with a turn of her head that we should move away from the circle of young actors. What's more, I read in her features a clear look of concern.

"What is it, Kwynn?"

When we had moved into the front hall, away from the group's glances, she said, "I'm worried about Thad, Mr. Manning."

Unsure where she was heading, I suggested, "His performance was a bit off tonight, but I think he's just tired."

"Not that." Her face wrinkled. Reluctantly, she explained, "It's Jason's death. Thad won't admit it, but it's really getting to him—I can tell."

"It was a shock to everyone, of course."

"But it's worse for Thad, Mr. Manning. You see, a lot of people seem to think that Thad . . . well, this is hard to say, but they think that Thad actually had something to do with it, which is crazy. Nobody's said it to his face, as far as I know, but it's obvious what they're thinking, and Thad knows it too. I can sense it in his mood. He's different."

My features must have fallen while I listened to her words, which confirmed my fears, because suddenly she was eyeing *me* with a look of deep concern. "I didn't mean to upset you, Mr. Manning. I'm sorry if—"

"No, Kwynn"—I mustered a smile and a soft laugh—"don't apologize. I'm glad you shared this with me. Keep an eye on him, okay? We'll pull him through it."

"*Sure* we will," she said, mirroring my smile. "We'll *both* keep on eye on him. He'll be fine. Won't he?"

I nodded, perhaps convincing her, if not myself.

She returned to her friends, and a moment later, I noticed that she was sitting next to Thad, joining in the fun, embroiled in the whodunit. It was nothing more than adolescent gossip, first whispered in clusters about other kids there at the party, then dismissed in gales of laughter—their way of "dealing with it," I guess.

At the height of all this morbid humor, a particularly hearty outburst was nipped short by the sudden appearance of Mica Thrush, a late arrival. Blushed faces told me that I wasn't the only one whose suspicions had been aroused by the vampirish Miss Thrush. She whisked through the front door, slamming it behind her, commanding silence. When all heads turned, she explained to everyone, "I've come to represent the memory of my dear—*late*—little brother." A momentary smile bent her oily, black lips, then she sauntered to the buffet table and found a radish, which she would graze on all night, chewing it with tiny, rodentlike nibbles.

"Correct me if I'm wrong," said Lucille Haring, sidling up to me, "but that must be the bereaved Mica."

With a grin I asked my editor, "However did you guess?"

"According to my research, Jason had just one sister, Mica. She'd be . . . oh, twenty-one now, I believe."

"I was meaning to ask you about the *Register's* files. Anything of interest?"

"The Thrushes are a prominent Dumont family, so there was plenty of material, but little of interest—other than the frightening Miss Mica."

After a tantalizing pause, I cocked my head as if to ask, Well . . . ?

Lucy explained, "Four years ago, during her junior year at Unity High, Mica Thrush was expelled from school. She was taking biology, with a first-period lab session. One morning, claiming she'd done it 'for extra credit,' she brought in and unveiled for the class a neighbor's cat that she had freshly vivisected—it was still warm."

"Good Lord."

"The incident traumatized many of her classmates. Some refused to set foot in the lab again; others couldn't sleep; most of them ended up in some form of counseling or therapy. She'd pulled sick pranks before, but this was the last straw for school administrators. Neither her father's loot nor his influence could get them to reverse the expulsion."

"Then what? Off to a good, expensive—remote—Swiss school?"

Lucy shook her head. "Nope. She simply never finished. One of her classmates was quoted, saying that Mica had pulled the stunt specifically to get out of school, that she'd wanted to drop out for years. As far as I know, she's lived at home since."

"My," I mused, eyeing the subject of our discourse, "such a treasure."

"As for the rest of the family, our files contain little of note—business stories on Burton Thrush, sports stories on Jason, and a few clips on Jason's theatrical pursuits at school. There's nothing, however, that even remotely suggests a motive for the boy's death."

I thanked Lucy for the information, and she wandered into the crowd, ostensibly to get some food, but presumably to seek out Roxanne.

Another late arrival was Frank Gelden, accompanied by his wife, Cynthia. Neil and I greeted them at the door. Frank apologized, "I'm usually the last one out of the theater, making sure everything is shut down. Did we miss much?"

Before we could answer, Cynthia told us, "I really should have accepted your offer to drive me to the house. I hate being late—it's sort of a fixation. I didn't realize Frank had so many duties after the show."

"Such," he lamented, "are the manifold responsibilities of the volunteer tech director," but his tone wasn't serious.

Dispensing with chitchat, I told them, "The bar's in the kitchen. Let's get you something." And I began leading them down the hall.

"Actually," said Cynthia, stopping, "I don't care for anything just yet." She turned to Neil. "But if you don't mind, I've been *dying* to see that third-story great room you've told me so much about."

Neil nodded, smiling. He told me, "The stand-alone home office I've been designing for Cynthia was inspired by our own lofty attic room. If you'll excuse us, I'd like to show it to her."

"Sure," Frank and I told them. "Enjoy yourselves."

And they started up the wide stairway to the third floor of the house.

Frank turned to me. "Cynthia loves working with Neil. He's been great."

"Believe me, Neil appreciates the opportunity to work on something 'tasty'—something other than another factory addition." We laughed.

"Uh," Frank reminded me, "how about that drink?"

I jerked my head toward the back of the hall and led him toward the kitchen. On the way, Roxanne caught my attention with a finger wag, so I told Frank to go ahead—I'd join him in a minute.

Stepping over to Roxanne, I asked, "Having a good time?"

She smiled, sipping from an icy glass of La Croix. "I am, actually." Her voice was barely audible over the din in the hall.

"We still need to 'talk,' don't we?"

"We do—you, Neil, and I. But, uh"—she covered an ear with her free hand—"this doesn't seem to be the time or the place."

"Besides, Neil's upstairs talking shop with Cynthia right now. I promise, after the party, the three of us can all sit down and get serious."

She grinned. "Not *too* serious. I just need a bit of counseling."

"What are friends for, counselor?"

"Thanks, Mark." She leaned and kissed my cheek. "Later."

"Later." I returned her kiss, then took my leave.

Arriving in the kitchen, I felt an instant sense of calm—the room was far quieter than the front of the house, and I looked forward to refilling the glass I'd long emptied. Several parents mingled with Frank at the room's center island, set up as the bar. Joining them, I asked, "Finding everything you need, Frank?"

He hoisted his glass, freshly filled—its sparkling amber color suggested Scotch and soda. "Everything I need."

"*Frank?*" said Barb, turning from the far side of the room, where she'd just popped a trayload of something into the oven. "Frank *Gelden?* Is that *you?*"

He gave her a blank stare as she moved toward us. Then: "Good God, not Barbara Bilsten, class of seventy—"

"Finish that sentence," she interrupted, "and you're dead meat." We all laughed. "I must say, the years have been good to you. You look *great*." Eyeing him up and down, she shook her head in astonishment. On Thursday morning, she'd described him as a geek in high school; she didn't seem to find him at all geeky now, and her leer confirmed it. "You're a different man, Frank."

"People change," he explained with a shrug. Tentatively, he added, "It's still Barb *Bilsten?*"

With a nod, she verified that she had not married.

"So, uh"—he whirled a hand in the air—"what have you been *doing* all these years? I haven't seen you around."

She gave a quick history of her high-power career as an East Coast money manager, dismissing the whole experience with a flick of her hand. "I'm much better off back here in Dumont, at least for a while. And what about *you*, Frank? I hear you're teaching a mushroom class or something." She rolled her eyes. "What's *that* all about?"

With a mild laugh, he straightened out the details for her: molecular-biology professor at Woodlands, faculty adviser to Fungus Amongus at Thad's school, technical director for the Dumont Players Guild.

"Gee," she said, "that's a plateful—doesn't leave time for much of a social life."

Was it my imagination, or did her tone now carry the ring of flirtation? Uh-oh.

And right on cue, in walked Neil with Frank's wife.

"Neil, Cynthia!" said Frank. "You'll never believe this—what a coincidence. Barb Bilsten and I went to high school together and haven't seen each other in at least twenty years. Small world, huh?"

Cynthia smiled, but looked confused. "You're both *from* here, right?"

Barb shook her hand. "That's right, Cindy—my pleasure, by the way. See, Frank called it a coincidence tonight because I've been *gone* for twenty years. I hit sort of a midlife career crisis, if you know what I mean."

"Do I ever." Cynthia winked. "Fortunately, mine hasn't hit yet. Only a matter of time, though." She and Barb laughed, bonding, doing the sisterhood thing.

Neil interjected, "Come on now, Cynthia. You're nowhere near hitting the skids—good thing too, since you'll soon be writing checks for an extraordinarily handsome home office."

"Ohhh," said Barb, enlightened, "*you're* Neil's client." She pulled

Cynthia aside, but only a few inches, confiding in a loud whisper meant to be overheard, "You really should be charging *him*, you know. He's nuts about that project."

"So is Frank. Planning's half the fun, and we're having a ball."

Barb froze, looking stupefied—she'd connected the dots. "We?"

Frank laughed, taking Cynthia's hand. "Sorry, Barb. I guess we weren't clear. Yes, man and wife—eight long years."

"Eight *wonderful* years," Cynthia corrected him.

He pecked his wife's lips.

Barb seemed at a loss to grasp their words. "You mean you're . . . *married?*"

Neil patted her back. "Sorry, Barb. Better luck next time."

We all laughed, and Barb self-effacingly joined in, but I got the impression she was genuinely flummoxed by this encounter—within a few short minutes, she'd both found and "lost" Frank. I, in turn, was intrigued by her reaction. When she had come to work at the house, she told me she'd sworn off men for a while. Was she now reconsidering that stance? Wherever her head was at, I had to admit, Frank would be a prize.

"Oh, Barb," said Neil brightly, "there's someone I want you to meet." Was he trying to set her up already—some sort of consolation prize?

Barb gave him a questioning stare.

"Look who's here." Neil waved over to us a man who had just entered the kitchen for a drink. I didn't know him, but his face was familiar. Neil said, "This is Whitney Greer, executive director of both the Players Guild and the Dumont Symphony." Of course—his photo was in the *Register* from time to time, and his mug smiled from page two of every program book.

Neil made the complete round of introductions. Frank already knew Whitney from his theater work, but neither Barb nor I had met him. Cynthia spoke as if she knew him, but I think she was faking it, feeling that she *should* know him.

Barb's mood instantly brightened as her focus shifted from Frank to her clarinet. "I'm so very pleased to meet you, Mr. Greer," she told him, her manner uncharacteristically deferential. "If you have a few moments, there's something I'd like to discuss with you."

Before Greer could respond, Neil said, "Actually, there's something *we* need to discuss," referring to the Geldens, me, and himself. I assumed he was steering us toward the coroner's mushroom theory.

"Maybe we could all freshen our drinks and try to find someplace quiet."

"My den," I suggested.

"Delightful," agreed Cynthia.

So while Barb cornered Whitney Greer to quiz him about the prospects of remedial clarinet lessons, I poured a glass of good chardonnay for Cynthia, topped off the rest of our drinks, and led our group out of the kitchen, into the noisy hall.

Heading toward the front of the house, we encountered Thad with a clump of other kids that included Tommy Morales.

"That really sucks," said one of them, his tone commiserative.

"*Tell* me," said Tommy. "It's like fate or whatever. I'd do *anything* to make theater 'happen' for me—I figure it's the surest way out of here. Now this."

"What would it cost to fix?" asked Thad.

"Way more than I've got," said Tommy. "I planned on working this summer, but I wanted to be in the play too. I couldn't do both, so I had to give up the job."

As we stopped to listen, Frank asked, "What's wrong?"

Hangdog, Tommy looked up to tell us, "My car. It's just a beater, but it gets me around—at least it *did*. Today the transmission went. Guess I'm scr—" He rephrased, "Guess I'm skunked."

Frank smiled. "Tell you what. Your place isn't far out of my way. Why don't I just swing by and give you a lift for the rest of the run?"

"*Would* you?" asked Tommy, looking much relieved. "That would be *great*. Thanks, Mr. Gelden."

"Then I'll pick you up at twelve-thirty tomorrow for the matinee. Do you need a ride home tonight?"

"It's covered, thanks. But tomorrow would be great. Really—I appreciate it."

As we four adults continued toward the den, I told Frank, "You struck me as a hell of a nice guy last Wednesday when we met, and you just proved I was right."

He shook his head, looking a bit bashful, which made him all the more endearing. "With kids that age," he said, "wheels are *everything*. Tommy comes from a large family of modest means—his wreck of a car won't be in working order soon. So he's stuck bumming rides, considered particularly humiliating among his peers. He doesn't need such a pointless source of anxiety during the play. Why *wouldn't* I help out?"

Cynthia tugged his earlobe, telling us, "God, I *love* this guy."

Frank blushed. Pretending not to notice, I slung an arm around Neil's waist and opened the door to the den.

My uncle Edwin's den, now my own domain, was intentionally kept off-limits to the party that night. Located in a front corner of the house, just off the entry hall, the room would have been a logical target for revelers in search of somewhere to talk and eat, away from the crowd, but this was *my* space, and I didn't want it invaded by strangers. The huge old mahogany partners desk, flanked by matching leather chairs, was laden with paperwork I'd left in progress, as well as my calendar, assorted sentimental curios, and a few framed pictures—personal stuff—it was nobody else's business. So I'd left the room closed, dark, and unwelcoming. Our guests got the message, and my turf had not been violated.

Entering with Neil and the Geldens, switching on the lights, I was struck again by the room's uncommon beauty, a handsome quality, distinctly masculine. Even the air felt good—while the rest of the house had begun to warm up with the party, my sequestered bailiwick felt cool and fresh.

"Oh, *my*," said Cynthia as she stepped inside, "what a charming little retreat."

In truth, it wasn't all that little. The oversize desk occupied only a corner of the room. The remainder of the space, on the opposite side of the door, was used as a sitting area with a comfortable chesterfield suite of tufted-leather furniture facing a fireplace. The unique mantel and surround were architect-designed in the same Prairie School style as the house. Though the hearth was now screened and dark for the summer months, it provided an inviting focal point that seemed to stimulate conversation and camaraderie. Instinctively, the four of us settled around the cocktail table, facing an imaginary fire.

"Well," said Frank, "at long last—we can all get to know each other."

Neil had mentioned earlier that the Geldens seemed eager to make our acquaintance, couple to couple, and now I felt glad to know them—we fell easily in sync, with a promising rapport. These optimistic thoughts were tainted, though, by the troubling circumstances that had prompted Neil and me to pull the Geldens aside that night.

When I sensed a lull in our small talk, I got to the point, shifting from banter to business. With a soft laugh I observed, "There's a certain topic we seem to be talking *around* tonight."

Frank nodded, tracing a finger around the rim of his glass. "Jason's death has been here in the room with us all along—like a pink elephant lolling on your desk."

"And everyone was reluctant to mention it," said Neil, setting his drink aside.

Cynthia sipped her wine, then set her glass on the table near Neil's. "I'm aware of the general situation, of course, but I'm not as close to it as any of you are. Forgive me if this question seems insensitive, but am I correct that the circumstances have led some to see Thad in a bad light?"

Neil assured her, "The question isn't at all insensitive, Cynthia. We're beyond the point of denial—yes, there are some who suspect Thad of involvement in Jason's death." He summarized the "boy toy" incident at dress rehearsal, ending with Thad's paraphrased threat from the script. "Now some people are wondering if Thad made good on his threat."

"But that's ridiculous," said Frank. "That's just *kids* talking. I heard the threat, and Jason clearly provoked it. This is mere circumstance."

I cleared my throat. "Unfortunately, the circumstances got stickier this afternoon." Frank and Cynthia exchanged an apprehensive glance. "Sheriff Pierce and I spoke to the coroner, who'd just completed his initial examination of the Thrush boy."

Though I did not intend to tantalize my listeners with this narrative, Frank had inched to the edge of his seat. *"And . . . ?"*

I paused. "And we may need your help."

Frank and Cynthia again exchanged a glance, but now they were simply confused. Frank turned to me, saying, "Of *course*, Mark, I'd do anything to help Thad. But how?"

I told the Geldens what I'd learned: "Dr. Formhals has so far determined that Jason died of respiratory failure, which in turn was caused by something that severely complicated the symptoms of his cold. Formhals stressed that this is speculative, and it does not necessarily point to foul play, but he called it his 'best theory.' He thinks that Jason may have died from mushroom poisoning."

"Good Lord," said Cynthia, reflexively raising a hand to her throat.

Though visibly shaken, Frank tried to remain analytical. "Do you mean that the mushrooms themselves were lethal, or did they have a deadly effect because of Jason's cold?"

"The latter, I think, but I'm not sure. Formhals himself was just starting to piece this together. Jason's stomach contents still need to be analyzed, and then they'll run tests for specific toxins. It could take a while."

"And meanwhile," said Frank, nodding his understanding, "suspicion could continue to mount against Thad."

Neil answered, "Exactly. We hardly need to tell *you* that Thad's knowledge of mushrooms is fairly impressive."

"*Very* impressive," Frank corrected him. "He's an astute student and an avid enthusiast. That would normally be a high compliment, but under the circumstances . . ."

"Which is why we're turning to you, Frank," I told him. "Hell, I don't know a jot about mycology, but you're an expert, and to be perfectly honest, we're desperate to stay one step ahead of the coroner—and the sheriff."

"Say no more," said Frank with a smile, raising his hands in a comforting gesture as he sat back in his chair. "As you can well imagine, you've piqued my interest—not only at a professional level, but at a very personal level. Cynthia and I are proud to count you and Neil as *friends.* If I can, I'd like to help you trash the coroner's theory and put Thad in the clear." Frowning, he added, "Come to think of it, this tends to cast suspicion on just about anyone in Fungus Amongus."

I had to laugh. "Sorry to say it, but I've always felt that mushrooming has some decidedly creepy overtones."

Neil smirked, shushing me, then turned to Frank. "Seriously, we appreciate your offer to help. It goes without saying that Mark and I are also proud to count you and Cynthia as friends."

Cynthia clutched Neil's forearm. "And at the moment, you and Mark are 'friends in need.' Don't worry. Soon, we'll all look back and laugh at these developments."

Daring to feel a bit of optimism, I leaned forward in my chair, asking Frank, "Any initial reaction to the coroner's theory?"

"There are at least five thousand species of mushrooms growing in the United States. Of these, perhaps a hundred are poisonous, causing reactions that range from mere indigestion to death. Because the symptoms of mushroom poisoning can be easily confused with those of other illnesses, we don't really know how many Americans die from mushrooms each year, but the number is probably in the range of a hundred to a thousand. Most victims are amateur hunters who should have spent more time studying their field guides."

I asked, "What about instances of actual murder by mushroom poisoning?"

Frank shook his head. "Very rare. A would-be killer could never predict with certainty the effect of particular mushrooms on an intended victim. Poisonous mushrooms—'toadstools'—would make a chancy murder weapon at best."

Neil reached for the cocktail he'd set aside and drank a goodly slug. He told us, "I feel better already."

Frank raised a hand in mild admonition. "Even though mushroom poisoning strikes me as unlikely, the coroner has called it his 'best theory.' He's based that on *something*, some particular results of his examination that we simply aren't privy to. Anyway"—he grinned—"I could use a refresher in Toadstool Pathology 101, so let me do a bit of research and pin down some facts. It may take me a day or two, but once I'm up to speed, let's regroup and figure out what's next."

On instinct, the four of us lifted our drinks and exchanged a silent toast.

"I know," said Cynthia, fingering the stem of her wineglass, "let's do dinner at the house. We've been *dying* to get together with you two, and now we have the perfect excuse to entertain."

"Not that we need an 'excuse,' " Frank added.

"Actually," Neil told Cynthia, "the timing works out perfectly. You and I ought to go over the final plans for your home office. I'm ready when you are."

Frank asked her, "What's your schedule next week, hon?"

"Same as last week—Tuesday through Friday, I'll be in Green Bay. So Monday evening would be good." She asked Frank, "Is two days enough time for your toadstool refresher?"

He assured us, "I work best with a deadline."

"Mark?" Neil asked. "Shall we call it a date?"

I smiled. "It's a date."

Sunday, August 5

When Neil awoke the next morning and suggested that we go for a run together, I didn't think twice about answering, "Sure, great idea." Either the heat was letting up, or I was getting used to it. Though dawn was already an hour past, it was Sunday, so the house was still quiet when we left through the front door and took off at a trot down Prairie Street.

Neil laughed, his voice blending with the chatter of birds and with the sound of our shoes on the pavement. He turned to me and said, "Even *Barb* was still in bed."

"How could you tell?"

"She hadn't made coffee—at least I couldn't smell it. Deductive reasoning, pal."

"Actually, I believe that's *inductive*."

"Oh." He was normally a stickler for such distinctions, but it seemed he couldn't care less about this one. I interpreted his nonchalance as a sign that he'd slept well, that he'd put aside, at least for now, the vexing developments of last week.

"Barb should sleep all day," I said. "She really knocked herself out last night—I don't know *when* she finished cleaning up."

"I told her we'd all pitch in if she'd leave it till morning. Not her style, I guess."

"Good." We laughed while turning the corner at Park Street, moving along our regular route. As usual, I simply enjoyed the sight of Neil at my side, and I let him pull a half pace ahead of me so I could get a better look. As usual, he wore nylon shorts; mine were cotton. Neither of us wore shirts.

We soon left the street, following a steep, shady path that led us through a bank of trees at the park's perimeter. As the path leveled off and we entered a clearing, I asked, "When did Roxanne go to bed?"

"Didn't notice. It must have been late. Why?"

Running at a comfortable pace now, I told him, "Earlier in the evening, she mentioned again that she wanted to 'talk' to us. We planned to sit down after the party, but things got late, and I forgot about it."

"God"—Neil shook his head, an awkward feat while running—"I forgot too. There's obviously something important on her mind. Hope she doesn't think we're neglecting her."

"I hope she doesn't think *Carl's* neglecting her, but that's the impression she gave me yesterday at the office."

"Once we get back," Neil said with resolve, "we'll give her all the time she needs."

Our conversation lapsed as we entered the long middle portion of our run. I like to think of that phase of our workouts as "the cruise." Between the warm-up and the cooldown, it's the extended period of serious exercise, burning calories at a steady, elevated rate. The challenge at this stage is not performance, but endurance, and I've always marveled at the trancelike momentum of a runner's "second wind," which masks pain as pleasure.

Neil understood this as well. He'd learned this secret of the cruise long before he knew me, and indeed, this common knowledge was one of the things that would bond us when we met. The first time we ran together, on a mountainside road near his home in Phoenix four Christmases ago (it seems like another life, on another planet), the rigors of running took on an erotic edge for both of us. That same morning, I first made love to a man. It was the morning when Neil truly entered my life, entered me, and changed the world as I knew it. No wonder, then, that our runs became an earthy ritual, a shared fetish that sometimes roiled our passions, sounding an overture to sex.

On this August morning, though, my thoughts were more sublime than lusty. The man I loved was there at my side as we ran through a pristine world inhabited by us alone—a piney Eden shared only with benign little creatures, some furry, some feathered, but no snakes.

"Rest?" asked Neil. We had looped three times through the park's valley floor, logging some four miles. Ahead lay the lagoon. A pavilion near the water's edge had a broad porch with benches where we often relaxed in summer or warmed ourselves in winter. A pair of ducks splashed near the bank of a tiny island, just big enough to ground a willow.

I replied with a nod, and we veered from the path, slowing our pace to a jog, then a walk, as we approached the shelter. During our run, the bright day had grown hotter, and we were both now drenched with sweat. Having not worn shirts or carried towels, we had nothing we could use to blot ourselves, so we trudged up to the porch, dripping.

Choosing the center bench, which faced a perfectly framed view of the lagoon and the leafy slopes of the hills beyond, we sat and rested. Despite the heat of the day, we had settled mere inches apart, and we instinctively touched knees. Flexing the muscles of my calf, I felt Neil do the same, and I thrilled at the grinding of his ankle against my sock—simple pleasures.

I had not yet told him about my conversation with Kwynn at the party—that she had confirmed my fear that Thad was badly shaken by the mounting suspicion of his friends—but this serene moment was not the time to burden Neil.

After a minute or two, our breathing eased. "So," said Neil, "what did you think of the Geldens?" The question may have seemed out-of-the-blue, but in fact, the Geldens had crossed my own mind more than once that morning.

"Cynthia's not quite what I expected, but I do like her. And Frank's great."

Neil squinted. "What did you expect? Cynthia, I mean."

"I'm not sure. Having just met Frank on Wednesday, I didn't know him well enough to expect *anything* about his wife." I hesitated. "But I thought she'd be prettier. And younger."

Neil mulled my words for a few seconds. "Cynthia's intelligent, sophisticated, and really quite charming—she has plenty to offer."

"Absolutely," I agreed at once. "Once I got to know her, I could see that."

Neil nodded. "But still, she's not what you expected. Hmm. I met Cynthia first at my office, then Frank a few meetings later. Now that you mention it, *he* wasn't what I expected."

"You were pleasantly surprised?"

Neil grinned. "And how." He rubbed his leg suggestively against mine.

Laughing, I patted his inner thigh, brushing his crotch with the edge of my hand. Aware that I was starting something we couldn't finish, I removed my hand from his leg and languidly crossed my arms. "I will say this: they both seemed to take a genuine interest in Thad's predicament."

"I told you before: they seem to have a genuine interest in *us.*"

Considering this for a moment, I admitted, "I'd like to get to know *them* better too. It would . . . round us out."

Neil swung his face toward mine. "I beg your pardon."

"Think about it. Since our move to Dumont, by and large, the town has 'accepted' us. Sure, we've made friends, but most of them are either coworkers or gay—or both—which is fine. It wouldn't hurt us, though, to count at least one straight, married, *normal* local couple among our social circle."

Neil snorted. "In other words, we could broaden our horizons."

I shrugged. "Precisely."

He ran a hand through my wet hair, flicking the sweat from his fingers. "We could all go to PTA meetings together."

I reminded him, "Not with the Geldens. They're childless; until recently, so were we. They're affluent and worldly; forgive my immodesty, but so are we. When you think about it, we've got quite a bit in common."

"You needn't convince *me.* She's a good client, he's easy on the eyes, and they're both decent people—a great couple, period. What's more, they've taken the initiative to seek out our friendship. Why *not* reciprocate?"

"No reason whatever. I'm looking forward to having dinner with them tomorrow night. We should bring something nice."

The two of us thought about this in silence, gazing at the lagoon. Then we looked each other in the eye, saying in unison, "Wine." Not very original, perhaps, but we knew we could compensate for the predictability of our gift by liberating an unexpected, impressive vintage from our cellar.

I stood. "Ready?"

Neil nodded, stood, and stretched.

"Are we running back? Or walking?"

A sheepish look of indecision crossed his face. He didn't want to be the one to shy away from exercise.

So I saved him the angst. "It's getting hot. We've already had a good workout. Let's walk."

He didn't protest, and we strolled off at a leisurely pace, rounding the lagoon and returning to the path that led us through the vast, grassy field of the park's floor. Without a word, we approached the wooded hillside and climbed the ravine, emerging into civilization—the quiet streets of Dumont.

During our entire time in the park, we had encountered not even one other person, which struck me as odd. The midsummer Sunday should have been a prime date for picnics, I told myself, but still, the day was young, the heat already intense—the whole town, it seemed, had made a collective decision to hunker indoors this morning. I smiled. Churches would have a rough time meeting their quota this week.

"I've been giving it a lot of thought."

Neil's words broke my train of thought, but I was certain I hadn't missed some earlier snatch of conversation. With a chuckle, I asked, "What?" We were just turning off Park Street onto Prairie.

He paused. With a twitch of his brows, he answered, "My debt of honor."

Ahhh. It had been three days since I'd wowed him in the kitchen. With the troubling events that had transpired since then, I'd forgotten his pledge to outdo my inventiveness. With renewed interest, I asked, "Payback time?"

"We need to discuss some options."

"Now? Here?"

"No, at home." His pace grew brisker as we covered the remaining block or so, and I didn't lag behind. Heat be damned.

Arriving at the house, we entered through the front door. (Smelling coffee, I induced that Barb had risen.) The cool indoor air shocked my damp, sun-bit skin as we crossed the hall to the stairway. Upstairs, we made a quick turn into the large, handsome bedroom that had once been my uncle Edwin's. It was more of a suite than a bedroom, including its own bathroom, dressing room, and a screened, private sunporch beyond a wall of French doors.

Closing the hall door behind us, I asked, "You wanted to discuss something?"

Neil sat on a bench at the foot of the bed and began unlacing his shoes.

"Wait," I said before he could answer. "Let me." Crossing the room, I sat before him on the floor. Removing his shoes, I kissed each of his knees and stroked the muscles of his calves. Feeling blessed, I paused to worship him (it was Sunday, after all). When this transcendental moment had passed, I raised my head and looked into his eyes. "I don't deserve you."

"Sure you do," he said glibly, leaning forward to bestow a peck on my forehead. "What's more, you deserve some significant, creative pay-back." He stood.

His nylon running shorts were about level with my eyes, and I observed, with a measure of disappointment, that he was not aroused. As long as I was sitting on the floor, I removed my own shoes, setting them next to his, soles touching. "So," I said, "you've been considering some 'options'?"

"I have." He stepped out of his shorts and shrugged into a light cotton robe, cinching its belt. His tone turned unexpectedly serious as he told me, "You taught me something valuable, Mark."

Not understanding him, I stood. Touching his shoulders, I asked, "What do you mean?"

He took my own robe and helped me into it as I slipped out of my damp shorts. Warming my chest with his hands, he asked, "Got a minute to talk?"

"*Of course.*"

He jerked his head toward the sunporch, and I followed as he opened one of the glass-paned doors and stepped out to the comfortable aerie with its white wicker furniture and floor-to-ceiling screens. Since air-conditioning the house, we hadn't used this room often, which now struck me as a waste. Neil had found a wonderful retro-style oilcloth splashed with an oversize pattern of palms and tropical flowers; the furniture was uphol-stered with it, and the big windows were swagged with it, creating the impression of a garden in the treetops. From this lofty vantage point, a pleasant confusion arose: Was the room indoors or out? Even though the space was open and airy, commanding a view of the landscaped back lawn, it was also secluded and private, with no sight lines to other windows.

The main group of wicker furniture consisted of a sofa and two arm-chairs gathered around a long, cushioned bench that could double as a coffee table, with trays for this purpose. Neil set these trays aside and sat on the bench, patting the slick oilcloth cushion, inviting me to join him. Shoulder to shoulder, we looked out through the trees, through the dapple of shifting shade and light. Though painted white, the room felt and smelled green.

"You taught me something valuable," he repeated.

I nodded, listening.

"During the years we've been together, our love has grown and our commitment has deepened, but at times I've gotten the feeling that our passion has waned—"

I opened my mouth to protest, to reassure him, but he put a finger to my lips.

"Don't misunderstand me. During the course of any relationship, it's inevitable: at some point, the honeymoon is over, and what's left is the rest of your life, your *shared* life together. Commitment replaces infatuation. It's natural. For some couples, it proves to be a dangerous hurdle, but for us, I think, it was simply 'the next step.' We've grown well together. And I look forward to growing old with you, Mark." He took my hand.

"So do I, kiddo. But you're only thirty-five, and I'm not *ready* to grow old yet."

He smiled. "Good. That's my point. What you taught me Thursday morning is that we don't *have* to let go of the passion—not yet. In my memory and my fantasies, our 'old days' of hot sex have always lingered, sometimes with a certain note of longing. But the other day, in the kitchen, you managed to top anything from our past. Did you plan it, every move of it?"

"No," I assured him with a laugh. "It just happened. It just felt right."

"*I'll* tell the world."

I nodded, reliving the pride I'd felt at the moment of his orgasm. "I noticed that you seemed to enjoy yourself."

"It was way beyond enjoyment." He nuzzled my shoulder. "It was ecstasy."

"It was for me too—knowing I could reach you that deeply."

"And that's what made it *love*making. It was truly 'physical love,' not just sex."

I took his chin in my hand. "It was time to recapture that."

He nodded, kissing my fingers. "The security and comfort of our relationship had stolen some of its fire. Then *zap*, there you were, holding the match." He stood, looking outdoors for a few seconds, before turning to tell me, "When I announced my debt of honor that morning, there was an element of humor to the challenge I set for myself."

"Why not? Sex or love—separately or in tandem—*should* be fun."

He smiled. "You're a wise, wise man, Mark Manning. And over the days that have passed since incurring my debt of honor, I've arrived at a wisdom of my own. I've come to understand that I truly do owe you the passion of our past. What's more, after considerable thought, I'm confident that I can meet this challenge." He crossed his arms, grinning.

I lolled on the bench, propping myself on one elbow. "You've captured my interest—*and* my attention. Where are you headed with this?"

Neil paced the length of the room, lecturing, "I asked myself aloud, 'What would Mark like? What would *really* do the job for him?' Numerous possibilities came to mind. Maybe a trip alone together, the classic second honeymoon. But that seemed too 'planned'—the moment we arrived, the pressure would be on."

With a grimace, I concurred, "Performance anxiety."

"Right. Who needs it? So then I thought, What if I confront him with the prospect of sex—"

"Lovemaking," I corrected him.

He rephrased, "What if I confront him with the prospect of lovemaking somewhere unexpected? Somewhere off-limits, even dangerous?"

I sat up again. Warily, I asked, "Like where?"

"Like . . . one of our offices."

I shook my head. "Performance anxiety."

"Right. I knew that wouldn't fly. Besides, having already *told* you about it, I could never really *surprise* you with it."

"Surprise, then, is a necessary element of the formula?" Our discussion was getting a tad academic. Facetiously, I wondered if I ought to take notes.

"Well, *yes*," he explained, as if tutoring a naive pupil. "On Thursday morning, had you told me, 'When you return from your run, Neil, meet me in the kitchen, and if no one interrupts us, I'll pop your load with a gym towel'—well, I doubt if the whole experience would have had the same impact."

I conceded, "You raise a valid point . . ."

"So, yes, the element of surprise is crucial."

"Which means, you can tell me nothing?"

"I can tell you plenty." He sat next to me. "But I can't tell you everything."

I ticked off, "No trips, no office sex, no performance anxiety. Hmm. Where does that leave us?"

He tapped his noggin. "Massage."

My brows arched. "*That's* intriguing."

His brows arched. "I thought it might punch your buttons."

"Okay, what *about* massage?"

He weighed his words. "It involves a fantasy experience with an erotic masseur."

I couldn't help smiling. "You certainly *have* punched my buttons." From what he'd told me, I assumed he'd arranged something with a service, possibly from Milwaukee or even Chicago. Some beefy guy (or guys) had been screened, approved, and hired to travel north to pleasure me (or us) in inventive ways with highly trained manipulative skills. I was already aroused, just imagining the possibilities, the configurations, the logistics. "Are the plans made yet?"

He rose. "They are." And he moved to the French doors.

Trying to stall his departure, I pleaded, "Tell me more."

Before slipping back into the bedroom for his morning shower, he said, "Who, where, and when—those are the elements of surprise."

He paused to smile, and then he was gone.

Showered, dressed, and at last ready for the day, Neil and I went downstairs together and entered the kitchen. It was around nine o'clock.

Barb and Roxanne were both slumped at the kitchen table. Barb gulped a Diet Coke; Roxanne sipped coffee. Barb chomped on a bagel; Roxanne was slabbing one with cream cheese. Neither woman was looking her best that morning, so I refrained from commenting on their breakfast.

"Morning, ladies," I cheerioed from the doorway.

"Hi, Rox. Morning, Barb," said Neil, his greetings overlapping mine.

They both turned to look at us, bleary-eyed. I could understand Barb's fatigue—she was up late cleaning after the party had ended—but Roxanne's lassitude had me stumped.

Stepping to the counter to pour coffee for Neil and me, I blabbed, "Wonderful job last night, Barb. I heard nothing but raves all evening."

"Did you notice what disappeared first? My black-trumpet spread." Barb winked at Roxanne, as if proving a point.

Roxanne obliged, "It was fabulous," but her voice carried little enthusiasm. If I hadn't known better, I'd assume she'd been drinking. I'd never seen her so haggard during her sober years, but then, I rarely saw her this early in the day.

Sitting at the table, Neil asked, "What's wrong, Rox? I didn't notice when you slipped away to bed. Was it late?"

"No, actually." With the fingers of one hand, she tried to do something with her hair, but her efforts proved insufficient. "I was tired all day, so I went upstairs well before midnight. Then I couldn't sleep."

Carrying the two mugs of coffee to the table, I joined the others. "Sorry if we kept you up. I should have done something about the music."

"No, Mark. It wasn't that. I've had a lot on my mind."

"And you've been *trying* to talk to us about it." Again I apologized, "Sorry."

Neil said, "If you're in the mood, we're all ears."

Roxanne and Barb glanced at each other, giving the clear impression that they'd just covered the topic that was still a point of speculation to Neil and me. Awkwardly, Barb rose from the table, saying, "I have some things to do upstairs. Need to set up my music room."

"Oh?" said Neil. "Sounds as if you had a productive conversation with Whitney Greer last night."

"Very." Barb threw her Coke can into the trash, placed her glass in the sink. "He gave me the names of two fine clarinetists who might be willing to take me on as a student. I want to brush up a bit, though, before auditioning for either of them." She ducked into her quarters adjacent to the kitchen, still talking, loudly. "It's time to set up for practice and get to work." She emerged from her room with her clarinet case, a music stand, and an armload of sheet music. "So if you'll excuse me, I'll just . . ." And she sidled out through the hall, headed for the stairs.

Neil and I looked at each other. I said, "That was abrupt."

Neil turned to Roxanne, telling her, "I got the impression she was anxious to leave." He grinned. "Have the ladies already discussed a certain hot topic?"

"Duh." Roxanne rolled her eyes. "Yes."

Both Neil and I scraped our chairs an inch closer to the table. I paused, looking at Roxanne with a warm smile. "Come on now. What's the problem?"

She gripped her coffee with both hands. "It's not exactly a problem. It's . . . It's . . ."

Neil asked, "It's Carl?"

She nodded.

Neil and I exchanged a knowing glance. I told her, "Look, Roxanne, I know you haven't been seeing Carl as much as you'd like lately—we'd *all* like to see more of him. But his office has responsibilities, and if he needs to spend time in Springfield, well, that's part of the package. He's not *ignoring* you; he's just doing his job. I'm sure he'd prefer to spend much more time with you, but—"

"*Of course* he would," she interrupted. "That's the whole point." She looked at me as if to ask, What are you driving at?

I was now a bit confused myself. Tentatively, I suggested, "If his Springfield duties are keeping you apart, and if you both recognize the problem, there must be some sort of solution—"

"Oh, there is."

Neil laughed uncertainly. "Then you're not talking about . . . splitting?"

"God *no*," said Roxanne, also laughing. "I must've been sending the wrong signals. Carl and I aren't talking about splitting—we're talking about *moving in* together." She nodded, once, as if putting a period on her statement, then lifted her cup and sipped some coffee.

This was not at all what Neil and I had expected. Further, this failed to explain why Roxanne had seemed so stressed. I said, "That's terrific news, Roxanne. Are there any definite plans yet?"

"I gave notice on my lease last week. Come September, the moving vans roll, and my life will be transported in boxes to Carl's home on the North Shore." As an afterthought, she explained, "His place is far bigger than mine."

"Fabulous!" we told her. "Wonderful!" Our words served as verbal pats on the back, and she responded with a smug, proud little grin.

Neil frowned. "What am I missing, Rox? You came up here in a tizzy, needing to discuss 'issues,' but everything sounds ducky. What's the problem?"

She paused, pushed her coffee aside, and leaned forward on her elbows. "The *problem* is that I know Carl too well. This moving-in business didn't happen quickly—it took us two years. It was debated and calculated, but ultimately inevitable. It was a big step."

I shrugged. "Great. So?"

Neil touched my arm. "I think I get it. Rox has an uneasy feeling that the *next* step may be inevitable as well." He turned to her. "Am I right?"

She slowly wobbled her head—neither an affirmative nod nor a negative shake. She repeated, "I know Carl too well."

Growing exasperated, I said, "All right, I'll say it: we're talking about the M-word." No one missed the irony in my reluctance to say the actual word.

Roxanne breathed a tiny sigh—it sounded like a whimper. She scraped some cream cheese from her partially eaten bagel and licked it from her fingernail.

From upstairs, I heard a few experimental notes tooted on Barb's clarinet.

Neil said, "Pardon the cliché, Rox, but it takes two to tango. If there's a wedding in the works, it won't be entirely Carl's doing."

"I *know* that." She flicked a ratted lock of hair from her forehead, leaving a trace of cream cheese on her eyebrow. "What scares me is this: I think I want it as badly, as deeply, as he does. If he . . . 'pops the question,' I doubt that I'll be able to say no."

"Then just say yes," I told her, suggesting the obvious.

In the pause that followed, Barb began practicing scales—slowly, but with measured precision. The distant notes wafted down the stairs and through the hall with rich sonority and glasslike purity.

"It's the commitment," Roxanne told us, trying to remain calm and analytical. "Living with the guy is one thing, but giving him *my life* is another."

Neil reminded her, "You don't *have* to do it at all."

Barb's scales became more fluid and agile, picking up speed.

"*Arrghh.*" Roxanne stood. "I know. The decisions are mine. I'm not being forced. And in fact, Carl has been remarkably patient, not the least bit pushy, no pressure at all."

Smiling, I told her, "You want this so bad, you don't even recognize yourself."

"I *know.*" She dropped into her chair again. Through a pout, she said, "This isn't *me*. What happened to strong-willed, independent me? I'm turning into this . . . *mate* or something, and I don't like it."

"You love it," Neil told her.

She muttered, "Maybe I do." From her tone, you'd have thought she'd been sentenced to death.

The sounds from Barb's clarinet began to take the shape of a melody, played quietly at first, hesitantly, with a misblown note here and there. Slowly, the sweet phrases began to connect in longer and longer lines, suggesting the structure of a longer work that was familiar but forgotten. In a word, Barb's music was haunting. Though still in its fumbling, nascent stages of practice, it already displayed both its player's control and its own primitive beauty.

Neil and Roxanne's conversation had taken a new turn. Roxanne answered him, "I don't think so. Why?"

"Well, as long as Carl doesn't have to be in Springfield next weekend, why don't you bring him up here? Use Thad's play as an excuse—Carl should see it. Not that Carl needs an excuse to visit, but maybe, if the mood struck, we could all have a heart-to-heart about your plans."

"Group therapy?"

Neil laughed. "Something like that."

She nodded. "Let me think about it."

The phone rang—a startling sound on that still Sunday morning, an odd time, really, for anyone to call. Perhaps it was Pierce or Lucy, with news. Or even Carl, checking on Roxanne. I didn't want the noise to disturb Barb's practice or Thad's sleep, so I quickly pushed my chair from the table, rose, stepped to the counter, and picked up the receiver before the second ring. "Hello?"

There was a pause. Sensing trouble, I asked, "Yes . . . ?"

"Let me talk to boy toy," said a girlish falsetto, a vocal disguise at once ridiculous and effective. The voice added, "Killer boy toy!" Then, with an eerie laugh, the line went dead.

Gingerly, I replaced the receiver, as if handling something foul.

It was apparent from their cautious expressions that both Neil and Roxanne, watching from the table, could guess the gist of what had happened. Neil muttered, "Uh-oh."

I repeated what had been said, mimicking the voice, then told them, "It could have been anyone—man, woman, or child—anyone who was at the theater last Wednesday night. Or anyone who heard about it."

Rox observed, "Sounds typically adolescent to me."

Neil said, "I don't suppose the caller ID solves this little mystery."

Shaking my head, I tapped the gizmo. "Pay phone."

"Naturally."

The fun and games had now truly begun.

By unspoken consensus, it would be a quiet day. The party—to say nothing of Jason's death and now an ugly, anonymous phone call—had sapped all of us. Thad had a twelve-thirty call for his two-o'clock matinee, so the shank of his Sunday was shot, and he slept all morning. Roxanne had no plans for that afternoon, as she would not be driving back to Chicago till the next morning, so she offered (to our amazement) to help Barb in the preparation of an early supper for the household. Both Neil and I planned to spend a bit of time at our offices that afternoon; he wanted to put some finishing touches on Cynthia Dunne-Gelden's building plans, while I just wanted to keep an eye on things at the paper.

I offered to drive Thad to the theater on my way downtown to the *Register*, so around twelve-twenty, we got into the car together and pulled away from the house. He didn't exhibit the high energy that typically animated his speech and manner prior to a performance. In fact, he was quiet.

"Tired?"

"Yeah. Guess so." He didn't even look at me.

"Expecting a good crowd today?"

He turned. "Sundays can really be dead, but I bet we'll sell out again."

With a soft laugh, I told him, "I'm sure you'll give it your best, regardless."

He paused before asking, "Regardless of what?"

"The size of the audience, that's all." He must have thought that I had meant "regardless of their hostility," and I probably had.

"Mark?" he said, shaking his head. "I really sucked last night."

"No, Thad." I reached over and patted his arm. "It wasn't that bad. There was some strange chemistry in the audience—it wasn't your fault. You've always told me that audiences are unpredictable, and, hey, last night you proved it. Or *they* did. In spite of everything, though, you were the consummate pro, a real hero."

"*Tommy* was the hero," he reminded me, managing a laugh.

Unable to argue his point, I simply reassured him, "A flash in the pan."

We rode onward in silence, and I knew—on the basis of my own instincts, already confirmed by Kwynn Wyman—that the suspicions of Thad's peers had really started to eat at him. Before Saturday's performance, Thad had laughed off the whispered accusations that he'd made good on his threat to kill Jason, but now he showed traces of the sullen personality that had been so troubling to Neil and me when Thad's life had unexpectedly merged with ours. We'd worked hard to prop up his esteem and ignite productive interests, but all that progress was suddenly threatened—our "happy kid" was at the brink of a crisis. What's more, I feared that these preoccupations could take a toll on his performance in the play that day, now only ninety minutes away. Would his command of his role continue to deteriorate, as it had last night?

"Thad," I said tentatively, "I hope you won't let these . . . circumstances get to you. It'll all blow over."

He turned to me with a quizzical look. " 'Circumstances'?"

Forced to be explicit, I told him, "Jason's death. It seems a few of your friends have the crazy idea that Jason died as the result of your threat on Wednesday night."

"Oh"—he laughed, trying to put *me* at ease—"they're just goofing off."

"Of course they are. Sheriff Pierce will have this cleared up right away."

"Sure, I know that." He waved off my concern, putting up a good act.

Pulling into the parking lot behind the theater, I routinely told him, "Break a leg today. Show 'em who's boss."

"Thanks, Mark."

"Need a ride home after the show?"

"Nah. Some of us might go out—not sure. I'll get home okay."

I turned the car around near the stage door and stopped. Thad got out of the car and greeted a pack of kids who were waiting outside, less than eager to spend the sunny afternoon in a dark theater. Thad received a smattering of heys and thanks—the party was deemed a success, I gathered. Kwynn caught my eye and flashed me a feeble, uncertain smile, then rushed over and gave Thad a friendly kiss on his cheek. Others moved away from him, though, regrouping on the far side of the stage door. Was it my imagination, or was the troupe dividing into factions of Thad's supporters and detractors?

Mulling this, I noticed another car pull into the lot, parking in a nearby space. With the sun glaring on its windows, I couldn't see who was inside. But then the doors opened and out stepped Frank Gelden and his passenger, Tommy Morales, whose car had broken down. Frank had already spotted me, and he hailed me with a wave and a smile. As I got out of my car, I watched Tommy make his way through the kids in the parking lot. I wondered if he had clearly allied himself with either of the factions, but apparently not—he went directly into the theater and disappeared in the backstage darkness.

Frank and I met midway between our cars, shaking hands. He wore shorts, looking good. The afternoon heat was sweltering; the asphalt of the parking lot felt gummy under my shoes. I told him, "Hope they've managed to cool down that old theater for the afternoon."

"I'm not counting on it." He laughed, fanning the cuffed ends of his baggy shorts. "I'm just anxious to get the show behind us today and take a few days off."

"I thought you theater folk *loved* this grind."

With a sheepish shrug, he admitted, "For me, the fun is in the rehearsal, the preparation, the buildup. Once the show is running—well, that's just *work*."

"And then, when it's over, you miss it."

"Right! There's nothing rational about it, Mark. Oh, by the way"—he clapped a huge, strong hand on my shoulder—"great party last night. Cynthia and I had a blast. And we're looking forward to tomorrow evening with you and Neil."

"So are we, and really, we can't thank you enough for taking an interest in Thad's predicament—the mushroom angle."

Widening his stance, he removed his hand from my shoulder and parked both palms on his hips. Nodding, he told me, "I've started my research already. I hit the books as soon as we got home last night and stayed up reading way too late." He laughed, stifling a yawn, which seemed too well-timed to be genuine.

I smiled. "Did you learn anything?"

"Nothing conclusive yet." His face wrinkled. "But . . . well, let's just say that the coroner's mushroom theory may not be so half-baked after all."

Instinctively, I frowned.

"Sorry, Mark. I know that's not what you were hoping for. Still, I've barely scratched the surface of all this, and I have no reason to think that it points to Thad. I intend to sort through everything at home tonight after the play. Tomorrow, I'll do some Internet research and, if necessary, hit the library. I promise, though, I'll have more complete information by tomorrow at eight."

"That means, I presume, cocktails at eight?"

He nodded. "Be there."

He clapped my shoulder (his hands, I again noticed, were enormous, muscular, and beautifully veined), then he trotted across the parking lot to the stage door, where he gathered the straggling cast members and shooed them inside.

With a thud, the big metal door closed behind them.

A few minutes later, I arrived at the *Register*'s offices, parked in my space near the rear lobby entrance, and let myself in with my key—on Sundays, no one was on buzzer duty. Crossing the lobby and climbing the stairs to the newsroom, I felt comfortably at home and in command.

Not that I have ever struggled with issues of "control," but there was an undeniable satisfaction in standing at the helm of this little ship of journalism, knowing not only that I owned it, but that I was up to the task. Indeed, some had scoffed that I was overqualified when I'd hatched my scheme to leave Chicago for Dumont. Disproving their contention, I quickly discovered that my skills as a reporter had simply not prepared me for my duties as a publisher. There was plenty to learn. And in time, I learned it.

What I felt, then, as I entered the newsroom, was something of a *paternal* satisfaction—I was guide, steward, and provider, not just a boss. Even the air here seemed alive, humming with mild activity, carrying a whiff of ink (at least in my imagination, as the actual printing plant was housed in separate quarters, nearby but not adjacent to the offices).

I greeted the weekend crew as I strolled between their desks toward my office along the opposite wall. The editor working the city slot looked up from his computer terminal. "Oh—hi, Mark." He stopped typing. "Did Lucille find you? Something from the coroner."

"Thanks," I told him, already halfway to her office.

Lucille Haring saw me coming and met me in the aisle. "I think you'll like this," she said, waving a fax. "Your office?"

"Sure." I led her through my outer office, opened the inner door, then stepped inside. Sitting behind my desk, I asked, "What's up?"

She sat opposite me, sliding the paper onto the desk. As I skimmed over it, she read from her own notes, telling me, "Coroner Formhals has issued a follow-up report, saying that analysis of Jason's stomach contents did not reveal the presence of ingested mushrooms. His final report, however, is still pending the results of toxicology tests."

She'd summarized well. I slid the paper away and sat back in my chair, thinking. I smiled. "No mushrooms in Jason's stomach—that seems to debunk the mushroom theory, therefore casting suspicion away from Thad, right?"

"That's the way I read it," she agreed, scratching the coppery stubble behind her ear. She frowned.

"What's wrong?"

"If the mushroom theory is out the window, why is the final report still pending?"

I shrugged. "Toxicology. That's routine with suspicious deaths, right?"

She nodded, but looked puzzled.

I shook my head, as if to clear my thinking. "I admit, I'm confused by the biology involved here. If there were no mushrooms in Jason's stomach, what *could* the toxicology tests reveal? Is Formhals now looking for something else?"

She suggested the obvious: "Ask him."

"No"—I smiled—"*you* ask him. Phone him, set up an interview, and run him through the whole mumbo jumbo. After yesterday's conference call, my underlying concern for Thad would be transparent if I questioned Formhals myself."

"No problem," said Lucy, jotting a few notes, "I'll get right on it and try to reach him. Chances are, though, I won't be able to see him till tomorrow."

"Keep me posted."

She nodded, gathered her notes, and left.

I had started keeping my own file on the case, which I now retrieved from the credenza behind my desk. Opening it, I added the copy of the coroner's follow-up report, and uncapping my Montblanc, I scratched a few marginal notes, mostly questions. Clearly, this latest development would be of interest to Frank Gelden in his exploration of the mushroom angle, but he was now busy at the theater—I would phone him that evening with the update.

Meanwhile, I decided to phone Sheriff Pierce. Saturday night had been a late one for all of us, and he hadn't made his routine stop at the house this morning after his workout. He'd probably slept late for a change, possibly skipping the workout as well. I wasn't sure whether to try reaching him at home or at his office, but I opted for the office, and he picked up the phone on the first ring.

"Hi, Doug. Slow start today?"

"Thanks to *you*. Hey, Mark—great party."

When we'd exhausted a few more pleasantries, I asked, "Have you seen the coroner's latest report?"

"Yeah. Right here in front of me. Still inconclusive."

"I was hoping that Formhals might have some quick answers that would wrap this thing up, but it's not playing out that way. Where do we—" I stopped myself, rephrasing, "Where do you go from here?"

"*I*"—he emphasized the pronoun—"thought I'd go over to the theater this afternoon for a backstage visit. After the show, I want to talk to the cast, run them through some basic questions."

Hesitating, I asked, "This will include Thad, I suppose?"

Pierce's tone was matter-of-fact. "Well, sure. Like it or not, Mark, Thad is a part of this. I'm not saying I think he was involved, but objectively speaking, it's plausible. The sooner I get some routine questioning out of the way, the better for everyone."

This was not what I wanted to hear. "I think I should be there, Doug."

"No, Mark. You'd only heighten the tension, and I want to keep it low-key. Remember, there's no evidence of foul play yet, so there's no official police investigation yet. We're still at the 'inquiry' stage. I simply intend to gather some background on Jason and his relationships with the rest of the theater crowd. As for Thad, if I can pin down his whereabouts during the days and hours leading up to Jason's death, all the better."

Grimly, I observed, "That sounds a lot like an alibi."

"Call it what you will. If it puts Thad in the clear, then this whole mess is finished—at least from his perspective—leaving me to tangle with the DA, who's taken an inordinate interest in this case."

Pierce was right, of course. He was doing his job, and he knew how to do it. As for me, I was acting not only like an inquisitive journalist, but like a fretting parent as well—the last thing he needed.

"Hey," he said, his tone more personal and placating, "I'm scheduled for a follow-up visit to the Thrush residence tomorrow morning. With the death a few days old, everyone might have a fresh perspective."

"I could use a fresh perspective myself."

"Then why don't you ride out there with me after breakfast?"

I paused. "Thanks, Doug."

"For what?"

"Your friendship. And your kringle."

"Raspberry tomorrow?"

"Perfect."

Monday, August 6

Monday morning, Pierce delivered the promised pastry after his early workout, and life felt back on schedule at the house on Prairie Street. Neil was ready for the office, Barb was ready to tackle laundry, and Roxanne was ready to drive south, intending to return on Friday or Saturday with Carl. Thad was still asleep, exhausted by the first three performances of *Teen Play*.

Sunday evening, he hadn't said much about the matinee or about Pierce's backstage visit with the cast. What's more, Thad had arrived home looking like hell, with a scrape on his forehead and cuts on a hand and an elbow, which he dismissed as the result of a vigorous but clumsy rendition of the fight scene concluding act one. None of us pressed him to elaborate, though I was itching for details.

Let him sleep, I thought the next morning. Slumber protected him from the predicament that had mounted over the weekend, and while he slept, I could take action to help him. Pierce and I were returning to the scene of Jason's death. With clear heads—and our combined investigative skills—perhaps we could begin to make sense of the perplexing case.

"Care to drive?" asked Pierce as we left the house by the kitchen door. Since the Thrush residence was located some distance from downtown, there was no point in taking both cars. The sheriff's souped-up, county-issued sedan was fast but spartan, so the decision to ride in style was reached with minimal discussion.

"Sure."

A break in the weather was promised for later that day, but the morning was sultry. Humidity hung over the town like a bright fog. Traveling along the highway toward the city line, we spoke over the drone of my car's air conditioner.

"Thad hasn't said anything," I told Pierce, "and neither have you. What happened at the theater yesterday? Any developments?"

He heaved a sigh. "Nothing conclusive, I'm afraid. I talked to the kids and got their take on Jason, but no one really seemed to open up—they weren't about to 'dis' their fallen fellow cast member. They portrayed him as smart and affable, maybe a bit arrogant because of his family's circumstances, but generally they paid tribute to him as an all-round popular guy."

"Makes sense, I guess."

"Yeah," agreed Pierce with a note of derision, "they were only too eager to overlook that fracas with his teammates."

I instinctively slowed the car as I turned to ask, "Huh? Did I miss something?"

Pierce palmed his forehead. "Sorry, Mark, I wasn't thinking. I assumed you knew about it, but the incident took place about two years ago, just *before* you moved to town. It was in the fall. One night, Jason and some of his football buddies got drunk, then got hungry, went out, and tore up a restaurant. Quite the scandal, though Burton—Papa Thrush—did everything in his power to hush it up."

"Unbelievable." I shook my head. "Burton managed to keep it out of the *Register*. Lucy did a complete morgue search on the Thrush family, and we never ran a word about it. I learned after my arrival in Dumont that Barret Logan, the paper's previous publisher, was prone to spike a story if it reflected poorly on the town's 'better' families—including the Quatrains."

With a shrug, Pierce observed, "Those were different times; Barret and Burton were from a different generation, one of 'gentlemen's understandings' and such."

Pondering this, I nearly forgot my reason for broaching this discussion. "And what about Thad? How'd he do with your 'routine questioning'?"

Pierce paused. "Fine. Just fine."

I gave him a confused glance, needing more.

"Thad accounted very well for his whereabouts during the latter part of last week. He was usually rehearsing or palling around with Kwynn or at home, which is all easily verified. Unfortunately"—Pierce hesitated—"there's no way to corroborate the story of his whereabouts during the seemingly crucial period of Friday afternoon. He said he was out of the house, on his own."

I was afraid to ask, "Doing what?"

Pierce nodded. "Mushrooming."

"Great. Peachy."

The sheriff acknowledged, "So it didn't turn out exactly the way I'd hoped. Still, I'm damn glad I happened to be at the theater."

Befuddled, I asked, *"Why?"*

He rubbed his chin. "I guess Thad didn't tell you about it."

"Now what?"

"Thad left the theater shortly before I did, and when I went out to the parking lot, he was in trouble. A pack of Jason's friends, four or five of his Unity High teammates—the same crowd involved in the 'scandal'—had ganged up on Thad and intended to do some serious harm. They already had him on the asphalt, and they were shouting about Jason. I intervened, of course, and set them straight. Thad laughed it off, so I sent the others home with a firm warning."

With my head spinning—I really should have pulled over—I asked, "Are they still a threat?"

Pierce hedged. "I doubt it. They've already made their point. And they certainly didn't expect to encounter *me* while they were doing it. They know that I know how to find them."

This was scant solace. I told Pierce about Sunday's anonymous phone call, then we both fell silent, mulling Thad's worsening predicament.

Turning onto the road that led to the Thrushes' chichi subdivision, I tried to clear my head and focus on the business at hand. "Jason's father, what do you know about him?"

"For starters, he's fifty-six, and he's not in good health."

"I noticed. I'd have guessed his age to be twenty years older."

Pierce explained, "Burton Thrush has had a rough run of luck, both physical and emotional. His wife's death really threw him. I think that's what started his downhill slide."

"How'd she die?"

"Car accident. Ten years ago. Totally unexpected. One day at the office, he got the phone call. Patricia was dead—and his life had changed."

"Just what *is* his business? I know he founded Thrush Typo-Tech—something to do with printing?"

"Right. Burton founded the company sometime during the seventies. They produced an innovative line of phototypesetting equipment, which profitably served the Quatrain family's Quatro Press, among many other large printing firms." Pierce turned to me. "You probably know more about the technology than I do, Mark."

I nodded, staring ahead as I drove. "Funny. When you said 'photo-typesetting,' it crossed my mind that I hadn't heard the term in a while. There was a day, though, when it was state-of-the-art, largely replacing Linotype when the industry switched from hot type to cold."

"You've lost me."

"I won't bore you with the particulars, but in a nutshell, phototypesetting was computer-driven, while Linotype was essentially mechanical. Computer technology continued to evolve, and phototypesetting—which involved touchy equipment and finicky chemistry—was soon replaced by laser typesetting and now direct-to-plate technology. I didn't realize there was still a market for phototypesetting."

"Actually," said Pierce, "there isn't. Even though the technology has never been clear to me, I've understood for some years that Thrush's business has been floundering. Typo-Tech had its heyday at the time it was founded, but Thrush's equipment soon became obsolete. He's struggled to play catch-up ever since, and the company has been on the verge of bankruptcy more than once."

"Ouch. Judging from that house, he's accustomed to a fairly lavish lifestyle." As I said this, we turned off the road, into the wooded development of tacky minicastles.

"Burton's pretty shrewd," Pierce assured me. "You can bet that he's taken steps to safeguard his personal assets. The family's financial situation has remained secure, but the business could collapse anytime."

I tisked. "I've known entrepreneurs before. If Thrush thinks like most company founders, he tends to confuse his own identity with that of his business. To lose the business would be akin to death."

"Plus, he's had emergency bypass surgery twice. A host of complications has robbed him of the middle-age vigor he now needs."

Pulling into the Thrushes' cul-de-sac, I summarized, "He's lost his wife, his health, probably his business, and now his golden boy of a son—to mysterious causes. That should be enough to put *any* man under. I'm surprised he can handle it."

"I'm not at all sure he can, Mark. This isn't over yet."

I braked the car in front of the cutesy country mansion and checked my blazer pockets for pen and pad. Opening the door, I flinched at the assault of steamy August air. Pierce and I walked up the sidewalk together, following its gratuitous twists and turns—a supposedly charming touch intended to accommodate landscape features that had never been installed.

Before we reached the house, I noticed the rustle of curtains—from *two* windows, one downstairs near the front door, the other upstairs, where a figure in black peeped through the glass. Our arrival had been noted.

Pierce rang the bell, and before his finger had left the button, the door cracked open. "Good morning, Burton," said Pierce. "Thanks for making time for us."

The door opened wider. Burton Thrush clung to the knob as though he might fall. He hadn't dressed—he wore slippers, pajama bottoms, and a bulky bathrobe to protect against the air-conditioned chill. Though shaved and groomed, his pale complexion and dour expression made him look wraithlike. Eyeing me on the stoop, Thrush demanded of Pierce, "What's *he* doing here?"

"Mark Manning is trying to help."

"*Help?* I've heard everything, you know—there's good reason to suspect that his own flesh and blood, Thad Quatrain, is responsible for killing my Jason."

I would have rebutted this, but Pierce beat me to it: "Now, Burton, we have no proof that Jason died of unnatural causes, and aside from a childish spat between the two boys, there's little to link Thad Quatrain to this tragedy. Mark is a friend of mine; he's an honorable man and a skilled investigative journalist."

I jumped in: "But I'm not here hounding for news, Mr. Thrush. I simply want to see the mystery of your son's death solved. I'm certain that the truth will exonerate my nephew."

With a weary wag of his head, Thrush stood aside to admit us. Closing the door behind us, he said, "I do want this wrapped up, you know." The words had a strangely impatient tone, at odds with his grieving.

Pierce told him, "Dr. Formhals knows the urgency of issuing a final report. We all have reason to want this wrapped up."

Thrush led us into the living room, collapsing into a big, ugly chair with tapestry-like upholstery and heavy wooden legs and arms—it looked like something pilfered from a monastery. "Formhals needs to get his ass in gear," Thrush yapped.

"The required tests take time," Pierce told him flatly, losing interest in assuaging the grump. The sheriff sat uncertainly on the front edge of a frilly white sofa.

I joined him, sitting on the next cushion. I said to Thrush, "The need for the autopsy is regrettable—the very idea is understandably difficult for the family. But the purpose of the procedure is to find the truth. Why would you want to rush it?"

"So I can *bury* him," Thrush answered, bug-eyed.

I heard a laugh, a quiet outburst that was quickly stifled. Glancing over my shoulder toward the front hall, I caught a flash of black disappearing beyond the arched doorway to the room.

"Mica!" said Thrush. "Stop lurking."

She sauntered into the living room. "Sorry, Daddy. I didn't know you had company." We all knew she was lying; I myself had seen her in one of the upstairs windows, watching our arrival. She had sneaked downstairs to eavesdrop. Her father's word choice was apt—she was indeed "lurking."

Thrush told her, "The sheriff and his friend aren't convinced that Jason was the victim of foul play." He snorted. So did Mica.

Pierce reminded him, "I *said* that we have no proof. That's why we're here."

Thrush snorted again. "And what do you think you'll find?"

Pierce shook his head. "I have no idea. But we need to begin somewhere."

"Returning to the scene of the crime, eh?"

"We don't know if there *was* a crime." Pierce was getting annoyed.

Mica piped in, "Make the men hurry up, Daddy."

Listening to her baby talk, I had to remind myself that she was twenty-one. I asked, "And what's *your* interest in speeding this along?"

Mica strolled behind her father and spindled a lock of his hair around her finger. "Daddy needs his insurance money."

Pierce and I shared a glance.

Thrush batted away his daughter's hand. "It's not a question of need."

"But there is an insurance policy?" asked Pierce.

"Of *course*," said Thrush, as if addressing an idiot. "That's just sound financial planning. Jason was to be my successor at Typo-Tech. I've lost more than a son; I've lost the future of my business. Surely, you'll agree, that's worth *something*."

Pierce hesitated. "May I ask how much?"

Thrush sneered. A finger of drool escaped from the bent corner of his mouth; he wiped it with the back of his hand. "It's none of your business, but I'm sure you have ways to ferret out any confidential information that suits your whims, so I'll tell you: ten million dollars."

Pierce's brows arched. "That's a nice round figure."

Mica giggled.

Though I'd have no trouble remembering these details, I reflexively opened my notebook and uncapped my pen, asking, "And the claim can't be settled until the coroner rules on the manner of death?"

Thrush gave me a steely nod.

"Well, then," said Pierce, "it seems we all have our reasons for wanting to get to the bottom of this. Perhaps if we stopped sparring with each other, the investigation could be expedited." He stood. "If you have no objection, Burton, we'd like to visit Jason's bedroom."

Thrush flicked his hand, a smug gesture of permission and dismissal.

As I rose, Mica offered, "I'll take the men upstairs," and she led us through the hall to the stairway.

"We know the way," Pierce told her.

But she wouldn't take the hint. "The cops made sort of a mess," she said, leading us up, "but after the doctor took Jason away, things calmed down. Now everything's back *just* the way it was. Except Jason, of course." Her lips parted in a weak smile as she exhaled her breathy little laugh—she sounded like a dog panting.

Arriving in the upstairs hall outside Jason's room, we found the door closed, and though Mica had insisted on escorting us, she made no move to open it. "Excuse me," said Pierce, moving past her, gripping the knob, and swinging the door wide.

Following Pierce inside, exactly as I had on Friday evening, an eerie sense of déjà vu washed over me. The eeriness was compounded by an obvious difference: the corpse was missing from the bed. In my mind's eye, though, I saw Jason clearly. No doubt about it, he was one handsome young man. The vision of him sprawled there would have been enticing had it not been for the tragic circumstances—and the gob of mucus hanging from his mouth.

Mica had finally entered the room, and Pierce asked her, "That phone has more than one line, right?"

She glanced at her brother's desk. "Four," she said, nodding. "Maybe only three. Daddy works at home a lot. The extra lines are for the business."

Pierce glanced at me. "That complicates things with Ma Bell. They can generate computer records of every call in and out, but since this isn't a murder investigation, they'll take their time."

I asked Mica, "Were you at home Friday afternoon?"

"Most of the time. I think so."

"The play director, Denny Diggins, told us he tried phoning Jason repeatedly that afternoon, leaving messages."

She grinned, suppressing a laugh.

"Did you notice a lot of phone calls that day? Did you find the messages?"

She shrugged. "The phone rings a lot. There may have been messages for Jason, but we wouldn't have saved them. I mean—he's dead."

Pierce sighed. "Maybe we can recover the voice mail. I'm not sure what it would prove, though."

I agreed, "We're fishing. We're looking for any connection to Jason that could suggest a motive for foul play. He was a popular guy—in recent weeks, he may have spoken by phone to hundreds of people."

Again I noticed the abundance of *stuff* in Jason's room—sports stuff, stereo stuff, computer stuff, and framed photos. I opened a closet door and found more of the same. Stuff was piled on shelving and on the floor. His wardrobe was extensive for a high school student. Hooks on the inside of the door held a leather varsity jacket and a cardigan-style letter sweater.

Pierce was asking Mica about Jason's athletic activity, taking copious notes, but I felt he was on the wrong track, and besides, the topic didn't much interest me. So I studied the room at my leisure.

Closing the closet door, I moved to the dresser. Its top was cluttered with more stuff—trophies, brush and comb, a dish for change, a model car, more framed photos, as well as unframed snapshots that were wedged around the mirror. Some of the pictures were of Jason alone. In others he posed with groups of guys, perhaps teammates, all frolicsome and butch; the photos could have been clipped from the pages of an Abercrombie & Fitch catalog.

Leaning close to examine these photos (some of his friends were truly worth studying), I was distracted by a familiar scent. I thought of Neil. A wrinkle of curiosity pinched my brow, then my nose led my gaze to the bottle. There amidst the clutter on Jason's dresser was a bottle of Vetiver, a pricey French men's cologne long used by Neil. I not only recognized the bottle, but I'd know the smell anywhere—a distinctively crisp, woody, masculine scent.

This brought to mind another scent, the fruity, flowery fragrance I'd noted on Jason's body Friday night. Kwynn Wyman had noticed it Wednesday as well, at dress rehearsal, when she accused Jason of wearing "cheap perfume." It wasn't Vetiver—no one could possibly confuse the two fragrances.

So what was it? I searched the top of Jason's dresser, but I saw no cologne other than the Vetiver; there were no other bottles, flasks, or atomizers. What's more, the Vetiver was two-thirds empty, so Jason clearly used it; the bottle was not merely some unwanted gift displayed on his dresser. I recalled thinking at Wednesday's rehearsal that Denny Diggins, then Jason, had oversplashed the aftershave that night. Was the fruity scent perhaps exactly that—not cologne, but aftershave?

"Where's Jason's bathroom?" I asked Mica, interrupting Pierce's questions.

She pointed to the door, which I had assumed was another closet.

Pierce followed as I crossed the bedroom, opened the door, and entered the bath. "What are you looking for?" he asked.

"Aftershave. Just a hunch."

But my hunch didn't pay off. Searching the countertop, drawers, and cabinets near the sink, it didn't even seem that Jason, at seventeen, had been shaving daily; his only razor was a like-new electric, doubtless a coming-of-age birthday gift. Among all the usual toiletries, I found no second scent. In fact, I found a fresh bottle of Vetiver, still in its cellophane-wrapped, forest-green box. I also found a box of condoms, half-used, no cellophane.

Returning with Pierce to the bedroom, we found that Burton Thrush had joined his daughter there. Climbing the stairs must have been taxing—he looked worse than he had earlier. "Well," he wheezed, "what's the verdict?"

Pierce told him, "Nothing yet, I'm afraid."

Thrush wheezed again, but this time it carried a note of derision.

Pulling out my pad and reviewing the notes I'd made, I glanced about the room again. "Mr. Thrush, can you help me with a few questions?"

"Get on with it," he snapped. "My time is valuable."

Valuable indeed, I mused. He seemed to be living from breath to breath.

I asked him, "Do you happen to know if your son used any fragrances other than Vetiver, perhaps an aftershave?"

He looked at me as if I were out of my mind. "How the *hell* would I—" His answer was interrupted by a coughing jag.

"Mica?" I asked.

She shrugged stupidly.

I returned my attention to her father. "Did Jason date much?"

With a touch of defensiveness, he answered, "Well, *yes*."

"And whom did he date?" (There's nothing quite so off-putting as the pedantic use of the objective case when one intends to seize control of a discussion.)

"There were . . . *lots*," Thrush sputtered. "Jason was an athlete and a scholar. On top of which, he was blessed with rugged good looks. He dated many girls." With haughty composure, Thrush added, "I daresay Jason had the pick of the crop."

From behind me, I heard Mica's tiny dog-pant of a laugh. I also heard Pierce click his pen for some notes.

"What has me stumped," I told Thrush, scratching behind an ear, "is all these photos. Your son had many friends, obviously, but there are no girls in these pictures. Jason was still young; I thought maybe he hadn't started dating yet. That's the only reason I ask." Actually, the reason I asked was that I'd found his stash of condoms. Clearly, the kid was sexually active. Either that, or he was uncommonly tidy when it came to masturbation.

Thrush wearily explained, "I told you: Jason was an athlete. He counted all his teammates among his friends. The pictures reflect that."

"That makes sense," I conceded, striking a question from my notes. Still . . . what about those condoms? "Can you recall the names of his girlfriends?"

Again that spooky little laugh slipped out of Mica.

Thrush started counting on his fingers, but couldn't seem to come up with any names. Then something clicked; he tapped his noggin. "Nicole Winkler, that was her name. They were quite thick, you know—quite thick." He attempted, without success, to twine two fingers as a demonstration of how close they were. "In fact, Nicole was homecoming royalty with Jason at last fall's big dance. They made a splendid couple—splendid. I'm sure you'll find the photo here some-where."

I'd studied all the photos and seen nothing of Nicole. If Jason ever had such a picture, it was stuck in a drawer, not framed in tribute to a magical evening.

"If you have any doubts," continued Thrush, "just ask the pretty Miss Winkler. They were truly smitten."

I made a note of it, but had already observed and concluded that Nicole was "smitten." Unfortunately, I couldn't ask Jason if the feeling was mutual.

"Mr. Thrush," I said, closing my notebook, "I never knew Jason, and it seems that I still don't. In the three days since his death, I've thought about him a lot, but he's an enigma to me. How would you describe him to a total stranger? How would you describe your relationship?"

"He was my *son*," Thrush reminded me, as if I were dim-witted. "What more need I tell you? He was my only son, the heir to my busi-ness. He was to carry on the family name. In recent years, I've had lit-tle else to live for. I'd hoped to see him through high school, then college, so I could hand over the reins."

Thrush paused, resting his back against the wall, looking as if he might drop. "As a child," he continued, letting his vacant eyes drift across the ceiling, "Jason was one of those *special* boys—everyone loved him, the mere sight of him. When his mother died, he was braver than I was, and he was only six or so. It was a joy, such a joy, to watch him grow out of childhood and approach maturity. There was nothing he couldn't do or couldn't conquer."

Thrush paused again, turning his head against the wall, locking his eyes on mine. "I suppose you know that he viewed your nephew, the Quatrain boy, as his rival. Even though they went to different schools, Jason saw your boy as the only other one who measured up, at least in terms of theater, for whatever *that's* worth. Ironic, isn't it, that this asi-nine little play should bring them together and pit them against each other, head-to-head. And now, of course, my Jason is dead. He was to be the father of my grandchildren."

Mica told him, "I can still give you grandchildren, Daddy."

Thrush shot her a sidelong, wild-eyed glance. The notion of Mica procreating had seemingly never crossed his mind, and he was now aghast (as I was) to consider the grim possibility.

I had no other questions for Thrush, and neither did Pierce, so we thanked him for his cooperation (a diplomatic nicety, baldly insincere) and excused ourselves. Thrush remained in Jason's room, looking at the empty bed as we stepped into the hall and descended the stairs.

Mica followed us. Pierce and I didn't speak, feeling uncomfortably tailed.

At the front door, we turned to thank her, but she said nothing. Glancing over her shoulder, she slipped out the door with us and followed us to the street. Her behavior was downright weird—was she drugging? By the time we arrived at my car, I was sufficiently rattled by her presence that I was tempted to jump behind the wheel and floor it. Besides, it was hot. Time to go. But Pierce paused before opening his door and asked Mica, "Do you . . . need something?"

She looked Pierce in the eye, then me, then Pierce again. Through a slit of a smile, she told him, "Jason didn't date."

I was suddenly in no hurry to leave. I asked, "What do you mean, Mica? Your father said he dated *lots* of girls."

"Daddy liked to *think* that, but Jason liked boys."

I glanced at Pierce with blank surprise. Mica's assertion was intriguing, to say the least, but I wasn't sure if I believed it, considering the source.

Pierce asked her, "Jason was gay? What makes you think that?"

"I just know, that's all. He'd say things; I'd hear things. And despite what Daddy says, Jason couldn't *stand* that Nicole bitch—she drove him nuts."

I asked, "Did Jason have boyfriends?"

"He had *sex* with boys—quite a few, if that's what you mean."

That was precisely what I'd meant. "Anyone in particular? Was there one boy he got together with most often?"

"Was there someone special?" added Pierce.

Mica nodded coyly. "Oh, yes. But he's not a boy. He's much older. And he and Jason were on the outs—I could tell. I heard Jason fighting with him on the phone."

"*Who?*" Pierce and I asked together.

"Isn't it obvious?" She panted her anemic little laugh, then turned away from us, walking up the sidewalk to the house. When she got to the door, she stopped and looked back.

With a fey flick of her wrist, she told us, "Have a *mah*-velous day, gentlemen."

And she disappeared inside the house.

Shortly before noon, I left the *Register* to walk the block to Neil's office. Emerging from the newspaper's lobby onto First Avenue, I noticed at once that the weather had changed. It was still hot, but the humidity had dropped. The summer sky had turned from white to blue, with a cheery midday sun hanging high overhead. A mild breeze had picked up—a meteorological fillip. For the first time in weeks, it was actually a pleasant day. I didn't even bother to loosen my tie.

Strolling through the noon rush along Dumont's main street, I laughed aloud at the contrast between this "urban" scene and the one I had left in Chicago. The big city had ample allure, of course, and there was genuine glamour to the lakefront neighborhoods where I had lived and worked. Still, life in small-town Wisconsin offered its own rewards, and I enjoyed to the fullest Dumont's quieter pace and simpler plea-sures. Was I discovering some deeper meaning to long-held notions of success and growth and ambition? Or was I simply getting old? Even *that* dreaded question, I noticed wryly, didn't seem to bother me.

What bothered me, in spite of these blithe musings, was the web of circumstances surrounding the death of Jason Thrush, a web that grew more tangled every day, a web that threatened another young man whose happiness and future now rested with my ability to protect him from the darker side of life in Dumont, where "reputation" was lifeblood, where gossip could kill.

NEIL M. WAITE, A.I.A. The discreet sign on the storefront snapped my momentary funk and had me grinning like a kid on a date. One of the greatest rewards of my reinvented life on the moraines of Middle Amer-ica was my ability to amble a few hundred yards at lunchtime, open the door (as I was now doing), and pop in on the only man who mattered.

"Hi," said Neil, looking up from his worktable. Pocketing a pair of reading glasses, he asked, "How was your morning?"

"It had its moments." Closing the door behind me, I crossed the small office and met him in a loose embrace. "You look great today, as usual." I sniffed his neck. "Smell nice too." Just checking—he had indeed worn his Vetiver, and it was indeed the same fragrance stored in two bottles in Jason's suite. It was *not* the fruity scent I'd smelled in the theater or noticed on Jason's corpse.

Leaning back on his draftsman's stool, he asked, "Did you go to the Thrush house, as planned?"

"We did," I assured him, parking my butt on a file cabinet. As I began recounting the visit, I observed Neil's work space, taking comfort in its tidy permanence.

Neil had decided to move his practice to Dumont only nine months earlier, but he was clearly entrenched here now, and busy as well. Though he ran essentially a one-man shop, he had recently taken on a part-time apprentice, a college student, to help with some of the bigger projects. Today, though, he worked alone in his studio, which had proved to be the perfect use for a handsome old First Avenue storefront that had sat vacant for a few years. Everything was now painted white, with gray trim and nubby charcoal carpeting. New suspended light fixtures gave the space a trendy, postmodern feel. The big display windows on either side of the door were shuttered to eye height, with diagonal stripes of light pouring in between the vanes and from the bare glass above. The floor space was divided equally between its clerical and design functions, with the usual furnishings and equipment for each— desk, basic business computer, file cabinets, conference table, phone, and fax for the office; drafting table, taborets, engineering computer, plotter, flat files, and sample racks for the studio. It was Neil's domain, and he ruled it well, looking every bit the prosperous local architect in his crisp plaid shirt, knit cotton necktie, and pleated worsted slacks.

He asked, "So Jason's dad had a monster insurance policy, eh?"

"Ten million."

"*There's* a motive if you need one." Using a long-handled horsehair brush, he whisked eraser grit from a large floor plan on his drafting table.

"The charming Mica stood to gain as well," I reminded him. "Daddy's sick, and she's now the sole heir. Plus, she's *weird*, Neil. She literally lurked."

Neil laughed. " 'Lurked'?"

"I swear to God—peeking from behind curtains, sneaking down the stairs, eavesdropping around corners—she *lurked*. You'd expect no less from someone who'd vivisected their neighbor's cat."

"*What?*"

I filled Neil in. "Then, when Pierce and I left, Mica skittered out to the car with us and dropped a bombshell." I grinned, hoping to tantalize Neil, knowing he'd enjoy the next part.

He set a few drafting tools aside. "Well . . . ?"

"Get this: Mica told us that her brother, Jason, didn't date. I found this unlikely because I'd seen a well-depleted stock of condoms in his bathroom. Then she told us that Jason preferred boys."

"No way."

"She said she was certain. I just don't know whether to believe her."

"Yow—that *would* be a whole new angle."

"But that's not the half of it. The plot, as they say, thickens. Not only was Jason gay, according to Mica, but he'd also been having an extended affair with someone older, and they were recently on the outs."

"Another possible motive."

"Possible," I agreed. "And here's the most enticing part: Mica didn't exactly say it, but she strongly implied that the other man was none other than"—I paused for effect—"Denny Diggins."

Neil's jaw dropped. "Good God. It sounds crazy, but it sort of fits. I've never been sure, but I *assume* Denny is gay—"

"Who wouldn't?"

"—and he obviously likes being around kids, or he wouldn't have written and directed *Teen Play*. What's more, he cast Jason as the opening-night lead. I admit, the whole setup is conceivable."

I stood. "But why—and how—would Denny kill Jason on Friday night? We don't even know yet if Jason *was* killed, but if he was, and if Denny was somehow motivated to do it, why would he threaten the success of his own play by killing off the star on opening night? That doesn't fit. Does it?"

Neil thought, shook his head. "No. Unless we don't have the whole picture."

"*That's* a safe bet." I laughed. "This whole new angle is based on nothing more than the unsubstantiated claim of Mica Thrush. She's as wacky as they come, not what I'd call a dependable source in the first place. Second, she herself stood to gain from her brother's death, and frankly, that whole family is so dysfunctional, I wouldn't be a bit surprised if either Mica *or* Burton murdered the kid."

"Then where did Mica come up with the Denny Diggins angle? Did she pull it out of thin air?"

I snapped my fingers. "That's exactly what she did. Minutes earlier, up in Jason's bedroom, Pierce had asked her about the phone system there, mentioning that Denny had repeatedly tried calling Jason on Friday, leaving several voice messages. That could easily have inspired her to spin the story about a relationship with Denny. Thanks for the insight, Neil."

"My pleasure," he said, removing masking tape from the corners of the plan on his drafting table. He paused. "Still, it's an intriguing notion: Jason Thrush was gay. It's all the more intriguing to think that he was into older men." Neil twitched his brows. "Talk about ironic."

I gave him a quizzical look.

He explained, "The rivalry between Jason and Thad first became apparent to us at dress rehearsal, when Jason accused Thad of being our boy toy. It would be the height of irony if Jason, the accuser himself, was in fact the boy toy."

"Gee." I nodded. "I hadn't thought of that. If Mica's story is true, Jason's put-down of Thad was not only unconscionable, but supremely hypocritical—accusing someone else of being what he hated in himself."

"Heavy, man." Neil's tone was facetious. Then he paused, getting serious. "You know, from the moment it happened, Jason's 'boy toy' comment struck me as sort of . . . *off* somehow."

I nodded slowly, sensing Neil's logic.

He continued, "Think about it: Would a straight guy, supposedly a young, homophobic het jock, use a term like *boy toy?* It's so . . . Madonna. The expression just strikes me as intrinsically gay, like *fag hag.* Where would Jason pick up such argot—if not from the inside?"

Neil had raised an intriguing point. Perhaps I was being too hasty in my eagerness to dismiss Mica's claim that her brother was gay. Recalling all those framed photos of Jason palling and horsing with his Abercrombie crowd, it was easy to imagine what was making him smile.

"Yeah," I admitted, "Doug and I had better take another look at this. We simply weren't willing to take Mica at her word. But who knows?"

"There," said Neil, adding the plan he'd just finished to a stack of other blueprints, preparing to roll them up. "Ready for lunch?"

"Not so fast." I grinned. "What are you working on?"

With hand on hip, he told me, "It's about time—I thought you'd never ask."

Stepping behind him, I said, "Show me something beautiful, kiddo."

"The conference table is better for spreading things out." Bundling the plans under an arm, he led me to the front of his office, where four chairs surrounded a generously large table. Light from one of the display windows filled the whole area.

Neil fanned out the plans, making sure he had them in the correct order. The sheets measured perhaps two feet by three, not actually blueprints, as in the old days of ammonia-stenched diazotypes, but blackline prints, essentially large photocopies of his original drawings. Neil was also adept at computer drafting, which could spit out prints from a plotter, but he preferred traditional methods for residential work. "These are my plans for the addition to the Geldens' country home."

"I should have guessed. Big presentation tonight at dinner?"

"No harm in mixing a bit of business with pleasure." Then he walked me through the plans.

The first sheet was a site plan showing the boundaries of the entire property and the relationship of the existing house to the new construction, the road, and the neighbors. "Wow"—I said—"I had no idea the place was so rambling—what I'd call an 'estate.' "

Neil nodded. "It's five acres. Wooded, secluded, a lovely setting." With a grin, he told me, "The house ain't bad, either." He flipped the page, revealing a closer view of the house plan in relation to the new building. The new part was shown in far greater detail, but even the existing house showed all of its rooms—it was impressively sprawling. "It's a solid four thousand square feet, all on one floor. Lots of fieldstone, timbers, and other natural materials. Reminds me of a lodge in New Hampshire. It was built some thirty years ago, and Cynthia bought it from the original owners around the time she married Frank."

"Frank married well," I observed dryly. "Did you draw elevations?"

"Not of the main house, but I did a nice perspective rendering of the new building, shown in relation to the existing house. Here we go." He slid a drawing out from the bottom of the pile.

"It's *gorgeous*, Neil. Suitable for framing."

He leaned next to me and hugged my waist. "Many clients *do* frame the renderings. I admit, this is one of my better ones."

The drawing instantly conveyed his entire aesthetic concept for the new quarters. Since he had described the project as a "home office" for Cynthia, I had envisioned something rather meager in scale—like a weatherproofed hut in the backyard. But this was lavish and whimsical, truly a "design statement," as Neil might call it. For starters, the new building was two stories high, capped by a sort of lookout porch. It reminded me of a huge gazebo; on the drawing, Neil had labeled it PAVILION. The charming old main house lolled in the background, separated from the new pavilion by a boardwalk that cut through a garden and crossed an expanse of turf. The new structure rose from a cluster of trees as if it had grown there; the building materials, the same used for the main house, gave the pavilion the look of a natural addition to the landscape. In terms of mood, an element of fantasy permeated the entire design.

"Has she seen it yet?"

"Just sketches. But she loved the idea."

"God, I don't blame her." I shook my head. "That's a lot of office though."

Neil jabbed me with his elbow. "It's not *all* office. As long as we were at it, we added a few nice . . . touches." He flipped back to the floor plans.

Cynthia's work space was on the second floor of the new building. It had its own bathroom, a galley kitchen, and a large sitting room as well. An open stairwell rose from the ground level and went up to the roof terrace. I noticed that the entire ground floor of the pavilion was simply labeled SPA. A smaller area of the existing house was also labeled SPA. I tapped the word on the drawing. "What's that?"

"Their adult playroom." He smiled. "The existing house has a nicely equipped spa—sauna, whirlpool, workout area. Cynthia calls it their 'own private world.' It's not just for show; they actually use it and enjoy it together. So the new building will include a larger spa, designed from the ground up, all state-of-the-art."

My brows arched. "Sounds wonderfully sybaritic."

"It will be. Cynthia wants indoor *and* outdoor splash pools, total privacy for nude sunbathing, even a 'meditation garden.' " He pointed out these features on the plan. "She has the wish list; I make it happen." He riffled through the remaining plans—working drawings and details of cabinets, trim, plumbing, wiring, even custom-designed tile patterns.

Looking at all this, I was amazed anew at Neil's talents. "Cynthia is one lucky woman. Clearly, she's found the right man."

He stepped back, asking skeptically, "Are you referring to me—or Frank?"

I laughed. "You, of course. But Frank's not bad either."

Satisfied with my response, he nodded while rolling the plans into a bundle, securing them with fat rubber bands.

"Thanks for the preview. I've been looking forward to this evening, but I had no idea their place was so posh. Having seen it on paper, now I'm *really* eager to pay a little visit and see the place for myself."

"Our purpose," Neil reminded me, "is to discuss some of the finer points of mushroom poisoning."

"Yes"—I conceded—"a dinner with a purpose."

"First things first though. Are you ready for lunch?"

"Starved."

A few minutes later, we had left Neil's office and walked the remaining block to First Avenue Grill. Passing the windows of the restaurant on our way to the front door, I could see through the reflections in the glass that the crowd within was on the thin side. "Why is that?" I wondered aloud. "Restaurants never seem to do very well on Mondays."

Neil shrugged. "Maybe it's just the decent weather today. People would rather be outdoors."

"But they still have to *eat*. What do they do—go to the park and forage for nuts?"

He laughed, swinging the door open for me.

Entering the Grill together, we were greeted at once by Nancy Sanderson. "Mr. Manning, Mr. Waite, so nice to see you. Your table's ready, of course."

While leading us across the room, she paused to tell us, "By the way, congratulations on your nephew Thad's performance with the Dumont Players this past weekend. Do extend my best wishes to him." She smiled brightly—an effusive expression not typically allowed by her polite, restrained manner.

I thanked her, adding, "I thought I saw you in the lobby on Saturday night."

"I was there," she affirmed, nodding. "And I couldn't have been more impressed. Thad is such a *talented* young man."

"Yes, he is," I agreed, though I couldn't imagine how she had come to that conclusion on the basis of Saturday's performance—Thad wasn't running on all eight cylinders that night.

Neil thanked her on Thad's behalf.

"I'm sure you're very, very proud of him." She beamed.

"We are," we told her.

But I was doubly confused. Not only did I find her praise of Saturday's performance unwarranted (was she just being polite?), but even more perplexing was her uncharacteristic mood—I had never seen her so upbeat and chipper. What's more, it seemed odd that she made no mention of Jason Thrush's untimely death, and I clearly recalled overhearing her sour comment on that topic Saturday night: "What goes around, comes around." It almost gave the impression that she was glad Jason was dead.

As I pondered this unlikely possibility, Nancy took us to our table, where Neil and I sat. Settling in, unfurling my napkin, I noticed the front door open. Sheriff Pierce walked in with Dr. Formhals, the county coroner. Directing Neil's attention to the door with a nod, I asked him, "Do you mind if they join us? Might be informative. Sorry to intrude on 'our' time though."

With a wink, he reminded me, "We see *plenty* of each other. Ask them over."

Nancy told us, "I'd be happy to extend your invitation." With a bob of her head—not quite a bow—she slipped away to greet the new arrivals.

Pierce listened, then looked in our direction with a wave and a smile. He and Formhals began moving toward our table. Nancy followed with the extra menus.

We stood, greeting them, and the four of us were soon clustered around the linen-draped table. Neil and I sat across from each other, as before, with Pierce and Formhals now between us. Nancy excused herself to seat another group of patrons who'd just arrived.

Formhals laughed his low, soft chuckle. "It seems we've been running into each other with uncanny regularity, Mark. It's a pleasure, of course."

With a weak grin, I said, "I wish I could say the same, Vernon." I tried to explain, "Circumstances . . ."

He laughed heartily now. "I *know*, Mark, I know—the coroner isn't most people's idea of 'good company.'" He sat back, smiling.

Pierce told me, "I understand Lucille Haring has an interview with Vernon this afternoon."

"Right after lunch," Formhals added. "I'll walk back to the *Register*'s offices with you, if you don't mind, Mark."

"Not at all, Doctor; I'd be honored. I knew Lucy planned to call you, but I didn't know when you were meeting."

Neil entered the conversation, asking anyone, "Some new development?"

I answered, "Not that I know of."

Formhals shook his head. "No, your editor simply wanted some clarification on the preliminary report I issued yesterday afternoon."

I had of course asked Lucy to interview him because if I did so myself, he would correctly assume my motive to be protection of Thad, not news-gathering. I told him, "The *Register* hasn't printed anything regarding your mushroom theory yet. When we discussed it by phone on Saturday, it seemed speculative at best. Then, on Sunday, your report left me confused."

He leaned forward on his elbows. "Then *ask* me, Mark." He smiled.

As long as he had opened the door, I was tempted to take a few notes, but I felt he might remain more candid if I left this discussion off-the-record. I recapped, "On the basis of Jason's symptoms, you told us on Saturday that you suspected mushroom poisoning. In yesterday's report, you said that analysis of Jason's stomach contents did not reveal the presence of mushrooms. But you drew no conclusions from this, awaiting the results of toxicology tests."

"That's absolutely correct." He nodded.

Neil gave me a look that asked, So . . . ?

"So," I continued, "if there were no mushrooms in Jason's stomach, what could the toxicology tests reveal? Are you now exploring some other angle?"

He shook his head. "Mushroom poisoning is still my best theory. Had I actually *found* the mushrooms, that would have cinched it. It didn't work out that way, so it now remains for toxicology to prove or disprove the theory."

Pierce asked the question I'd been trying to ask: "If there weren't mushrooms in Jason's stomach, doesn't *that* disprove the theory?"

Again the coroner shook his head. "Some mushroom toxins are slow-acting. The mushrooms themselves could have been ingested and passed through the intestines days earlier, leaving the toxins to do their work."

Neil nodded, taking an analytical interest in this unappetizing discussion. He asked, "What about vomit?"

"The subject had not recently vomited. His throat was clogged with mucus, remember, but there was no residue of regurgitation."

"Now then," said Nancy, reappearing at our table, "let me tell you about today's special."

We all turned to her with sheepish smiles, as if caught in the midst of a lewd discussion. Though I was no longer hungry, I tried to look interested.

"I'm particularly proud of this recipe—it's so fresh and so seasonal." She clasped her hands together and instinctively ran her tongue, once, across her upper lip. "I call it king bolete thermidor."

Neil arched a brow. "Sounds interesting. What's in it?"

"King boletes, of course—*Boletus edulis*, more popularly known as porcini."

"Ah." I should have guessed. "Mushrooms."

"The king bolete is, for mushroom hunters, one of summer's richest rewards. Highly prized by gourmets, the handsome, smooth-capped bolete is large, firm, and meaty. Yesterday afternoon, I discovered a bounty of these choice edibles in a small pine grove not far from my home. After a bit of experimentation, I hit upon a thermidor recipe that complements their bacony flavor and succulent aroma *perfectly*—if you'll pardon my immodesty." She cast her gaze downward.

The four of us exchanged a glance.

"Thank you, Nancy," I told her. "That's tempting, but I think we'll need a few more minutes with the menu."

Later that afternoon, I was at work in my office at the *Register*, poring over an ever thicker file of notes and research regarding the circumstances of Jason Thrush's death. A rap on the doorjamb interrupted my thoughts.

"I'm finished with Coroner Formhals," Lucy told me from the doorway.

I waved her in. "Anything beyond what he told me at lunch?"

She shook her head, sitting across from me at my desk. Reading from a steno pad, she recounted their entire interview. The bottom line was the same: the coroner's best theory was still mushroom poisoning, and it would remain so until disproven by toxicology.

Looking up from her notes, she saw that my attention had returned to the file on my desk. "Still with me?"

With a soft laugh, I said, "Sorry, Lucy. It's just that the forensics seem stalled for now—at least till Formhals gets those test results. Since lunch, I've been preoccupied with a new angle."

"Oh? Care to share it?" She sat back, wedging a bright yellow pencil between her ear and a short shock of her bright red hair. She twitched her head inquisitively. For a moment, I saw her as an exotic bird.

Blinking this image from my mind, I asked, "Care to do a bit of digging?"

Her grin confirmed her readiness. Though I'd taught her the ropes of journalism here on the job in Dumont, she'd arrived with formidable research skills, and more often than not, it was I who now depended on *her*, not vice versa. She asked, "Who's our subject?"

"Nancy Sanderson. I know nothing about the woman, except that she owns First Avenue Grill and, like half the town, seems mushroom-crazed. But who *is* she? And what's behind her apparent animosity toward Jason Thrush?"

A glint of interest. "Animosity?"

I recounted Nancy's harsh comment about Jason that I'd overheard in the theater lobby. "Then today, at lunch, she was all giddy and gabbing about Thad in the play, without even mentioning Jason's death, which at least merits lip service, regardless of how she felt about him. Her behavior, in a word, seems suspicious."

Lucy made a note. "I'll get right on it. Anything else?"

"Nope. Not right now."

She stood. "Then I'll leave you with your thoughts." And she did.

My thoughts led me back to my file, which in turn led me back to that morning's visit to the Thrush house. I picked up the phone, dialed the sheriff's department, identified myself, and asked for Doug Pierce.

Within moments, he answered, "Hi, Mark. You just caught me. What's up?"

"That whole encounter with Mica Thrush this morning—I told Neil about her contention that Jason was gay, and after we talked about it, Neil seemed to think she might be on the level."

"If it's true, it's an intriguing wrinkle, to say the least."

"What do you think of the Denny Diggins angle?"

He reminded me, "I have no firm reason to think that Jason Thrush died of anything but natural causes."

I paused. "I hope you're right."

"Even if toxicology should point to foul play, I see no point in tipping our hand to Diggins and putting him on early alert."

"You're right. There's no urgency, at least with regard to Denny. If Jason was murdered, and if Denny did it, he'd be unlikely to bolt out of town during the run of his own play—he's too egotistical. He'll stay put through the weekend."

Having said that, I felt that I'd just set a deadline for the investigation. Certainly, we didn't want to lose sight of Denny Diggins, but more important, I feared that the second weekend of *Teen Play* could be devastating for Thad if suspicion still hung over him.

It was time to wrap this up. But how?

Upstairs on Prairie Street, Neil and I spiffed for our evening at the Geldens'. Neil had suggested that our dinner date warranted a second shave and shower, so we gabbed while tending to these ablutions in the white-tile bath adjoining our bedroom. Rinsing his razor, Neil asked, "Did you hear from Roxanne today?"

"We said our good-byes in the kitchen; I was on my way out, and she had just come down for coffee. Nothing since then." I was a step ahead of Neil, brushing my still-damp hair. Peering sidelong into the mirror, I examined the creep of silver through my temples. To my surprise, I liked the look of it.

He laughed softly—*carefully*—while shaving his chin. "I half expected her to phone from the car. She seemed so distraught over the whole move-in business."

I paused. Looking him in the eye (in the mirror, that is), I told him, "I'll bet she was just worried about *our* reaction. She needed some reassurance that we wouldn't think less of her for . . . for giving away a part of herself."

He stopped shaving. "You mean, giving herself to another man? Were we supposed to be jealous?"

I shrugged. "Maybe. The three of us have had some 'romantic dynamics' at work over the years, but I doubt if she feels we're in any way threatened by Carl. When I said that she'd be giving away a part of herself, I was referring to her edge, her independence."

"Don't count on it!"

I laughed, explaining, "In our eyes, 'she' will suddenly become 'they.' "

Neil nodded. "True enough. We won't think *less* of her, though."

I repeated, "She needed some reassurance."

He rinsed his face. "Did we handle it all right?"

"Think so. Hope so." I was finished at the sink. We were both shower-naked. I asked, "This isn't dressy tonight, is it?"

He eyed me askance. "You can't go like *that*." With a grin, he continued, "Cynthia said, 'Just us, just casual, just friends at home,' or words to that effect." He dabbed on some Vetiver, and the scent seemed amplified in the steamy confines of the bathroom.

"Khakis, then?"

"What else?"

While dressing in the bedroom, my thoughts began to focus on the evening ahead. "Not to dampen tonight's festivities, but I'm really curious to find out what Frank learned about mushroom poisoning. I can't imagine there's any sort of scenario that would point to Thad."

Neil pulled a soft yellow knit shirt over his head and smoothed the collar. "Even if Jason was deliberately poisoned with mushrooms—murdered—Thad's interest in mycology is no indictment. Mushrooming is an uncommonly popular pastime in Dumont. Seems goofy to me, but *lots* of people here have that specialized knowledge."

"Including"—I looked up from buckling my watch band—"every kid in town who's been a member of Fungus Amongus."

Neil arched a brow. "Is Thad still home? Let's ask who else is in the club."

I shook my head. "He left an hour ago, going over to Kwynn's, I think."

"Frank can fill us in. We'll just have to wait till—"

"*I* know"—finger snap. "Thad's yearbook. What's it called? *Central Times.*"

Neil said, "I know where he keeps them—the bookcase next to his dresser."

And we left the bedroom together, headed for Thad's room across the hall, near the back of the house.

His door was wide open, so we had no qualms about entering. During the time we'd lived in the same house, I was amazed to watch the transformation of Thad's quarters. In the beginning, his room was little more than a spartan cell, reflecting a tenant with few interests and low self-esteem. He was innately neat, and that didn't change, but as he blossomed—as a student, as an actor, as a *person*—so did his lair. I was struck now by how different this space was from the bedroom occupied by Jason Thrush, which had seemed as sterile as a hotel room. Thad's room had character. Books, magazines, and CDs abounded. Clippings and posters covered the walls. Stacks of play programs and scripts shared space on his cramped but well-organized desk. And a new stack I noticed—college catalogs—made me catch my breath. Was there really only a year left?

My eyes drifted to the window, where I noticed an array of mush-rooms that had been collected, jarred, and labeled for study, lined up on the sill. I hadn't seen them at first, as they were obscured by the foliage of a large potted schefflera. Taking a closer look, I had to chuckle. To my untutored eye, all the mushrooms looked essentially alike—earthy, gray, and rubbery—with the exception of one variety that was down-right pretty, with reddish caps, spotted white.

"Here we are," said Neil, picking up three volumes of *Central Times*. Checking the contents page of the most recent edition, he mumbled, "Clubs," and flipped to the back of the book.

I stepped close as he turned the pages. Band Boosters. Chess Chums. Debate. Friends of French. Aha—Fungus Amongus.

"Good *grief*," said Neil, gawking at the large photo. "There must be thirty members—I had no idea." Front and center was Frank Gelden, faculty adviser, wearing a handsome smile and a bush jacket. Neil tapped his finger on a face in the front row. "There's Thad."

Otherwise, the members of the mushroom club were just faces in a crowd. I'd need to read the long caption to see if there were any famil-iar names. As I began to do this, though, from the corner of my eye, a face behind Thad—directly behind him—caught my attention.

Neil saw it too. "Hey, it's Tommy Morales."

"I'll be damned—the understudy who got lucky. Chances are, Tommy knows as much about mushrooms as Thad does."

"He's a year younger," Neil reminded me.

"But Thad's been in the club for only a year."

"True . . ."

"Read through the caption, Neil. You know Thad's theater crowd better than I do. Are there any other members of Fungus Amongus who are also involved with the Players Guild?"

He took a moment to peruse the long lines of small type.

Looking up, he told me, "Not a one."

Driving out of town on county highway B, we agreed that it was a per-fect evening for our informal soirée at the Geldens'. It was a few min-utes before eight; night would not fall for another hour, but the sun had swung low in a clear sky that bled from indigo to copper.

"Their driveway is just ahead," Neil told me. "There, on the left."

A generic rural mailbox marked the entrance, giving no clue to the lavish grounds that lay within, well hidden from the road. "This really *is* an estate," I said, recalling the comment I'd made earlier that day in Neil's office. "The money in the family must be Cynthia's. Biology professors at extension campuses aren't *that* well paid."

"Definitely. She's the big breadwinner. The building project is entirely hers—and she writes all the checks."

As the house came into view around a turn of the drive, I told Neil, "Glad we brought some decent wine." Having seen the plans earlier, I knew the house would be big, and I'd gotten a sense of its style from the perspective drawing of the new pavilion. Still, I was unprepared for its overall beauty and the impact of its setting. This was *not* the sort of nouveau-riche residence so often derided by Neil as a "big dumb house." Though indeed large, it was, in a word, charming. Neil had said it reminded him of a lodge in New Hampshire, and the description was apt—from its sloping fieldstone chimneys to its timbered bay windows. The whole house lay nestled (there is no other word but *nestled* to describe the spatial relationship) in a verdant clearing framed by oaks, punctuated by pines. The driveway swung into a large, brick-paved parking court, fenced by a low wall of mature, waxy boxwood, pruned with precision. I had never found much appeal to the notion of "country living," but if I were ever tempted to try roughing it, it would be here.

I braked the car, cut the engine, and grabbed the two bottles of wine; Neil grabbed his roll of architectural drawings. As we got out of the car, warm evening air carried the heavy scent of pine, which wafted with birdsong on a mild breeze. Loose pea gravel from between the bricks grated under our shoes as we approached the front door of the house.

Before we reached the porch, the door swung open and both Frank and Cynthia stepped out to greet us. "Welcome," said one of them. "Glad you could come," said the other.

"Beautiful evening," said one of us. "Thanks for having us," said the other.

Cynthia tapped her watch. "Right on the button—we like that."

As we met on the porch, there was an awkward moment of hesitation, then the four of us dove in for a round of hugs. Neil and Cynthia kissed, which didn't surprise me, as I'd seen them do it on Saturday night, but till then I'd never known Frank to offer anything more affectionate than a prolonged handshake. Tonight, it was all hugs and back pats, and I enjoyed without guilt the brief feeling of his arms around me, his chin on my shoulder.

"Hey," he said, recognizing the label of the bottles I carried, *"Pavillon Rouge.* One of our favorites—a superb second pressing of the Château Margaux."

If he meant to impress me, he did. I was doubly glad we'd brought a good year, as he doubtless knew the hierarchy of vintages. "We guessed you'd prefer red," I told him. "Don't feel obligated to serve it though." As I handed him the bottles, I added, "A gift for your cellar."

Cynthia chimed, "Of *course* we'll serve it. A perfect choice—we haven't uncorked anything yet." She turned to Neil. "And I see what *you've* brought. I'm *dying* to get a look at those plans."

Frank took charge. "Cocktails first," he commanded, then led us all inside.

I was prepared to be wowed, and the interior of the house did not disappoint. In keeping with the home's "country" style, the furnishings and decorating were tastefully laid-back and comfortable, but not the least bit cutesy or primitive—no butter churns, rifle racks, cow-themed ceramics, straw wreaths, or other Martha Stewart touches. Rather, an easy palette of neutrals dominated the living room, with plump, over-stuffed furniture upholstered in soft stripes and solids. Handsome, mis-matched rugs lay scattered about the wide-plank floor, while the lofty, beamed ceiling disappeared beneath a crisp whitewash, lending an overall impression of unfussy elegance. A row of French doors along the back wall of the living room looked out upon an expansive green space; if I recalled correctly, this would be the site of Neil's pavilion.

Frank played bartender. His Scotch and Cynthia's chardonnay were already poured. "Correct me if I'm wrong," he told Neil and me, "but you guys drink vodka, right?" Without flinching, he added, "Straight?"

Neil told him, "Vodka, yes; straight, yes; but plenty of ice. Do you happen to have an orange?"

"Not usually," Frank answered, grinning, "but I noticed the color of your twist on Saturday." And he produced, as if by magic, an orange from behind his back.

We laughed. I told him, "You're an exceptionally accommodating host."

Cynthia agreed, "He *does* know how to entertain. This doll even cooks!"

He said, "Look who's talking. Cynthia herself is a marvelous cook."

Under her breath, she rejoined, "Guess who taught me."

Within a minute, the zesting of the orange had been performed and we all had a drink in our hands. Cynthia lifted her glass: "To a most promising friendship."

We all seconded, then drank.

"Actually," said Frank, "Cynthia and I really do look forward to knowing you better. I just hope our, uh . . . 'marital circumstances' aren't too square for you."

"Are you kidding?" quipped Neil. "Mark and I could use a few more straight friends—it broadens our horizons." And we indulged in one of the many hearty rounds of laughter that would mark the evening.

Not long after the first drinks were finished, Cynthia reminded Neil, "I'm *dying* to see those plans."

I told her, "I got a preview before lunch today. Neil's never done better work. He's lucky to have a such a client."

"*I'm* the lucky one," she insisted.

Neil told her, "I don't know if I can stand all this flattery. Mark's right though—I think you're going to love the plans." He turned to me. "I need to discuss a few budget details with Cynthia, and since we're still reasonably sober, this might be the best time. Maybe Frank could show you the house."

That sounded just dandy, I thought, but Frank's look turned serious as he said to me, "Let's save the grand tour for later. As long as Cynthia and her architect are tied up talking business, why don't you and your mycologist talk mushrooms?"

"Sure. Good idea." I'd nearly forgotten the point of the evening's mission. "You've been cracking the books then?"

He nodded. "And I have some findings to report. Another drink first?"

"Yeah, great." My arm needed no twisting—the shift of topic left me feeling that I might really need the security of alcohol at hand.

Frank refilled everyone's glass, then Neil and Cynthia hunkered at the coffee table, where Neil began unfurling his drawings. Before the first squeal had escaped Cynthia's lips, Frank suggested, "Let's go to my study."

Following him through a hall, I caught glimpses of other rooms, concluding that the entire house was similarly decorated, consistently tasteful—I could well understand how Neil and Cynthia had clicked. Frank turned into a room, and I stepped inside after him.

His study was truly a working office, not just a showy den of wood and leather. An entire wall housed rows of books—well-worn textbooks and reference works, not gilt-spined editions of unread master-pieces. His desk was more utilitarian than pretentious, covered with notes, rosters, syllabi, computer printouts, and open books. A battered toy microscope sat displayed on a shelf, perhaps the boyhood Christmas gift that had inspired the course of his career. On the floor, a bulging briefcase showed years of rugged service in lugging heavy classwork, not genteel contracts. Rumpled cushions on a sofa suggested that he liked to lie and read there. "Get comfortable, Mark."

As I sat on the sofa, the room's only seating other than Frank's desk chair, he retrieved some notes and a book from a stack on his desk, then joined me on the sofa, sitting next to me. I sipped my drink, set it on an end table, and told him, "I can't thank you enough for digging into this, for getting involved."

"Hey, my pleasure." He sipped his Scotch and set it aside. "I share your concern for Thad, and besides, the coroner's theory presented an intriguing intellectual challenge. Basically, I had to reverse his thought processes as a test of whether I could reach the same conclusion. He began the process by asking himself, 'What caused Jason's death?' I began by asking, 'Could mushroom poisoning have been responsible for Jason's death?' Tricky stuff."

Clearly, he enjoyed the challenge and the process, while I simply wanted an answer. And the answer I wanted was, no, mushroom poisoning was not the likely cause of Jason's death. However, Frank had told me in the theater parking lot on Sunday afternoon that the mushroom theory no longer struck him as half-baked. With a wary smile, I asked, "Reach any conclusions?"

He nodded, tapping his notes. "I was skeptical on Saturday and unsure on Sunday, but now I think that, yes, Formhals may be on the right track. It's arguable, certainly conceivable, that Jason Thrush was poisoned by fly agaric." He smiled, proud of his research, no doubt.

"Sorry?" I must have seem distracted. Not only had he given me the answer I did not want, but he was touching upon particulars beyond my realm of knowledge.

"Fly agaric," he repeated. "Its scientific name is *Amanita muscaria;* its common name derives from its use to kill flies. The fly agaric is not so highly toxic as its notorious cousins, the death cap and the destroying angel, but under certain circumstances, it can indeed prove deadly."

"And it grows around here?"

"You bet. During summer, you'll find them along the roadside or at the edge of fields or in pine groves. In mixed woods, they often grow in arcs, sometimes called fairy rings."

"Cute." I lifted my glass and drank.

"Actually, they *are* cute—the fly agaric, I mean." He opened the book he'd brought from the desk and showed me a notched page. "This field guide has some great pictures. See? It looks like something out of a storybook."

Glancing at the photo, I nearly choked on my vodka. Setting the glass aside, I leaned forward for a closer look.

Frank was accurate in his description of the fly agaric. The pretty mushroom in the photograph belonged in a children's animated fairy tale. It had a white stalk with a red, dome-shaped cap, spotted white. It was easy to imagine the thing popping out of the ground and doing a little dance. It was also, unmistakably, one of the mushroom species I'd noticed only an hour earlier, stored in a jar—seemingly hidden behind the fronds of a schefflera—in Thad's bedroom.

Trying to focus my thoughts, I asked, "But it's not always deadly?"

He put down the book. "Only rarely. The fly agaric's toxins usually cause only nausea or delirium, which passes within twenty-four hours. But if the victim was already weakened by an illness, the effects could be much more serious. Significantly, its symptoms include copious mucus and closing of the throat. Jason had been ill with a cold, and he exhibited those very symptoms."

I sat back, drawing the apparent conclusion: "That's it, then." I didn't want to even consider the implications of Thad's stash.

Frank shook his head. "This theory is far from airtight, Mark. For starters, fly agaric poisons quickly, within a half hour to three hours after ingestion. So the mushrooms should have been found in Jason's stomach, unless he vomited."

"No," I recalled with a measure of relief, "Dr. Formhals specifically told us—at *lunch*—that Jason had not vomited."

"Then we have a dilemma. As an added complication, the mushrooms would have to be consumed in large quantities in order to prove fatal. We don't know if Jason even *liked* mushrooms. If not, how could he be tricked into eating a sufficient quantity to kill him?" Frank concluded, "The theory presents an interesting possibility, but it has too many holes."

"Well, at least *that's* heartening. While I'm eager, for Thad's sake, to get this wrapped up, I'd prefer that the answer did *not* involve mushrooms."

Frank laughed. "I hear you. Virtually anyone in Thad's mushroom club would have sufficient knowledge to harvest the fly agaric and put it to use. If someone did, that's probably the end of Fungus Amongus."

Mention of the club brought someone to mind, someone I'd been growing curious about. I asked Frank, "What do you know about Tommy Morales?"

"Tommy? Why do you ask?"

I shifted on the sofa to face Frank better. "Neil and I were looking at a yearbook photo, and as far as we could tell, the only one in the mushroom group also involved with the Players Guild is Tommy—and Thad, of course. Am I right?"

He thought for a moment, as if comparing the two rosters in his head. He nodded. "Right, I can't think of anyone else."

"I'm not jumping to conclusions, mind you. Hell, we don't even know if Jason was murdered, and if he was, we don't know that mushrooms had anything to do with it. Still, Tommy knows mushrooms, and Tommy understudied Jason."

"Okay, I see what you're driving at. But Tommy's a sweet kid. I can't imagine either Tommy *or* Thad having any complicity in Jason's death."

I backtracked. "You said that Tommy comes from a big family, right?"

"Yeah. Five kids, I think. Their means are, well . . . modest, but there's been no lack of love or nurturing. He's a quiet, hard worker. Ambitious."

"He was quiet Wednesday night," I recalled, "when I first saw him at rehearsal, but by Saturday night, it seemed he'd really blossomed."

Considering this, Frank reached for his Scotch and soda, then sipped. "Let's just say that Tommy got a much needed emotional boost from stepping into the role of Dawson. I've started driving him to and from the theater, and we've had a chance to talk a bit. Yes, Dawson truly is the role he wanted all along, and he's glad to have it. At the same time, he seems to fully appreciate the tragedy of Jason's death. I don't think there's a connection, Mark."

I recalled a comment made by Tommy at the cast party—he said he'd do *anything* to make theater "happen" for him. I asked Frank, "Were Tommy and Jason friendly?"

Without hesitation, Frank answered flatly, "No. They went to different schools, so they didn't even know each other till this summer. Even then, the two never quite meshed—'different sides of the track,' that kind of thing."

"Did Tommy resent Jason's affluence?"

"Maybe. For whatever it's worth, he's never seemed to resent *Thad's* affluence; they've always gotten along well, both at school and at the theater."

"I may be prejudiced, Frank, but Jason invited resentment. Thad, as far as I know, has never flaunted his own privileged background."

Cynthia popped into the room. "Have Holmes and Watson solved the riddle yet?" She made a beeline for Frank and kissed the top of his head.

Standing, he told her, "Not yet, I'm afraid. I've brought Mark up to speed on fly agaric, but the theory seems to raise as many questions as it answers."

"Fly what?" asked Neil, entering the room.

Frank ran him through our earlier discussion and showed him the photo in the book. Neil regarded it with interest but with no apparent alarm—he'd paid no attention to Thad's mushroom collection when we'd visited his bedroom. Frank summed up, "If Jason died of poisoning from *Amanita,* he must have been a glutton for mushrooms, or someone slipped him quite a recipe."

"Oh!" said Cynthia, sipping her wine. "Speaking of recipes, I found a fabulous first course to serve tonight. It's a tad experimental—hope you don't mind, my guinea pigs."

I quipped, "You're serving guinea pigs?"

"*You're* the guinea pigs," she explained. "The *appetizer* is oyster mushrooms Mornay. It's a nice, light dish to start the meal—shrimp, pasta, pea pods, and of course the oyster mushrooms."

"Don't tell me," I said, deadpan. "You found the mushrooms out back and harvested them yourself." Had the whole world gone mad?

"Exactly. Last week's drenching rain was enough to produce a beautiful cluster on a poplar log that fell behind the garage. *Pleurotus ostreatus* is an easy species to cultivate, so I'll be sure to keep that log well watered now."

I smiled. "Who wouldn't?"

Neil flashed me a behave-yourself. He told Cynthia, "It seems Frank's interest in fungi has rubbed off a bit."

She nodded. "I told you, this doll taught me *everything*."

Growing a bit weary of her doting (to say nothing of all the mushroom chat), I changed the topic, asking her, "Did Neil sell you on his plans for the pavilion?"

"*Oh*, my *God*, yes! That's what we came in to tell you. Frank, Neil has simply outdone himself. Why don't we all take a stroll outdoors and study the site before the sun sets?" As she said this, I noticed that the daylight had turned amber, slanting through the west windows of the study at a low angle.

The four of us left the study with our drinks, retracing our steps to the living room, where Neil picked up his perspective drawing from the coffee table. Cynthia opened the French doors to the backyard, and we followed her outside.

Evening was edging toward dusk. Sunlight still burned the treetops at the far side of the property, but the grounds themselves had slipped into shadow. The warm breeze drifted silently through a clear sky. Birds hushed, preparing for night. A planet or two appeared.

We stood silently at the lawn's edge, paying our respects to the departed day, duly awed by this clockwork of nature. Underfoot, I felt the turning of Earth itself.

Frank nudged my shoulder with his. "Look," he said, barely above a whisper, "*there's* one." The ice in his glass rattled as he pointed across the grass to the fringe of surrounding woods.

I stared, but saw nothing. I whispered, "What?"

"A fairy ring."

Cynthia squealed, *"Really?"*

Neil asked, "Fairy ring?"

Leading us through the grass, Frank explained, "I was telling Mark about them earlier—certain species of mushroom sometimes grow in arcs, or fairy rings, centered on trees where hardwoods mix with pines. This is a beauty."

We stepped inside the ring, walking softly, as if entering hallowed ground. The mushrooms swung in a precise arc from the base of an old oak at the border of the mowed lawn. "They're *beautiful*," said Neil, squatting for a closer look. "Are they the 'magic' variety?"

Frank laughed. "No, psilocybin mushrooms aren't especially pretty—though they may *seem* pretty to someone who's hallucinating."

I looked closer. Noting the dark, rosy cap, I asked, "These aren't . . . ?"

Frank finished my sentence, "*Amanita?* No, they're a form of bolete—and probably quite tasty. There's neither magic nor poison in these little guys."

"But there's magic in this *night*," said Cynthia, flinging her arms wide. "Can't you just *feel* it?" And she twirled across the grass, blessing the turf with a spray of wine from her glass. Hopping outside the fairy ring, she stopped, facing us. "It's midsummer night."

"It *is?*" asked Neil.

Cynthia dropped her wistful tone. "Well, close enough. It depends who you ask. In merry old England, they celebrated it on June twenty-fourth, which baffles me. Others, more logically, peg midsummer in the 'middle of summer,' midway between the June solstice and the September equinox. In other words, right now, a week into August. Tonight, tomorrow, Wednesday—close enough."

Her discourse, while not entirely serious, struck me as both entertaining and appealing. There was something wonderfully pagan about all this—gawking at mushrooms in the woods, calculating the balance of solstice and equinox, finding magic in the night, spicing it with a dash of madness. Not one inclined to revere any form of mysticism, I had to admit that Cynthia's sprightly outlook brought an unexpected dimension to the evening.

Frank said to her, "Show me what you and Neil are cooking up."

She led the way across the yard to an area where Neil, on a previous visit, had roughly sited the new construction. Wooden stakes represented the corners of the building; string stretching between them represented its walls. Cynthia led us around to the far side, where we could look back at it, facing the house from the same angle that Neil had chosen for his perspective drawing.

Neil held up one side of the drawing, and Cynthia held the other, displaying it for Frank and me. Sure enough, there on paper was a precise depiction of the house we saw in reality. In front of it, in reality, was a staked patch of ground; on paper loomed Neil's fanciful pavilion.

Frank said quietly, "Gosh, Neil, I can see why Cynthia was so excited. This is marvelous. Truly, I'm dazzled by your talents."

"So am I," I told Neil, reaching to squeeze his arm.

Cynthia dropped her end of the drawing. "Here's the door," she said, stepping around to the side nearest the house. "And *this*," she said, stepping inside the staked string, "is Frank's new spa."

We followed, but none of us bothered using the door as Cynthia had—we walked right through the walls. Frank asked her, "My spa?"

"I get to enjoy it," she conceded, "but you're the master here. You're the one with magic in his fingers."

Again the magic. With a chuckle, I asked, "What's magic about his fingers?"

"Hasn't Neil told you?" asked Cynthia. "Frank is a highly skilled masseur."

Again I noticed his large hands; even in the twilight, they looked beautifully veined and muscled. Then—hold on—this conversation had a familiar ring to it. And I suddenly recalled Neil's debt of honor, his Sunday-morning promise of a fantasy experience with an erotic masseur, his plan to surprise me with the who, where, and when. Could he possibly have meant . . . ?

"Cynthia exaggerates," Frank was saying. "I'm a rank amateur. I just enjoy it."

"Not half as much as *I* do!" she assured us, laughing.

I stared at Neil, as if to ask, Is Frank . . . ?

But Neil wouldn't let me catch his eye. He told Cynthia, "You two can wrangle over who enjoys it more, but I'm just happy knowing you'll enjoy this new space together. I'd say you're both very lucky."

"That we are," said Frank, wrapping one of those big hands around Cynthia's shoulders and squeezing her tight.

Trying to forget Neil's debt of honor and to focus on the current conversation, I said, "Neil tells me that you already have a nicely equipped spa in the house."

"True," said Cynthia, "but it pales in comparison to Neil's plan."

"Would you like to see it?" Frank offered. "It's getting dark anyway." The moon had begun to rise above the roof of the house.

"And I seem to be out of wine," said Cynthia, examining the glass she'd spilled on the lawn. "I need to check on things in the kitchen, so Frank can give the tour, and I'll meet you in the spa."

As the four of us began trudging toward the house, I wondered if this was all an elaborate ruse. Was Cynthia excusing herself in order to leave Neil and me alone with Frank for a while? Was she lending us her handsome husband—the one with magic in his fingers—to help make good on Neil's debt of honor? Were the Geldens that open-minded? Were *we*? In a bizarre concession to wishful thinking, I was thankful for whatever prescience had motivated me to shower that evening. Then I recalled—the second shower had been Neil's suggestion. Was this really happening?

Once inside, exactly as planned, Cynthia excused herself, took a turn into the kitchen, and began rattling pans. It sounded fake, a sure sign of a setup.

Neil set his drawing with the other plans on the table. Frank refilled our drinks and led us onward through the house, talking and laughing about something, looking uncommonly studly now. Was that strut of his intended to get me in the mood for . . . for whatever they had planned? "Here we are," he announced, opening a door and stepping back to let us pass. Neil also stepped aside. He'd seen the house many times already, and besides, this tour was being staged for my benefit.

Entering the spa, I momentarily forgot these speculations about the evening's presumed ulterior purpose, as the room itself had captured my interest. Neil had described it as Frank and Cynthia's "adult playroom," and I now saw what he meant. Though the square footage was not particularly generous, its appointments were; nothing had been spared in equipping these sybaritic quarters. There was the obligatory whirlpool bath, as well as a variety of gleaming chrome workout equipment (which Frank clearly put to good use) and a closet-size sauna behind a heavy door of cedar planks. A separate tiled shower room had its own changing area, where shelves were stacked with plump terry towels; oversize wooden hooks awaited clothes and robes. Along the walls of the main room, shelving and glass-doored cupboards displayed an array of unctions and paraphernalia intended to relax and soothe the body: oils and extracts of every description, bottles of scented witch hazel and other cooling astringents, canisters of herbs and sea salt, jugs of gels and mud, baskets heaped with sponges and loofahs. Atop a counter sat a curious item, one of those big, white-enameled roasters favored by aunts for their holiday turkeys. The entire room was gently washed by light that spread upward from sconces and downward from recesses in the ceiling. Soft music (New Age, of course, featuring a solo oboe) pampered the ear while fostering a woozy mood.

The room's most riveting feature, though, sat dead center, in the middle of the floor. Under a coved ceiling painted with a blue sky and wispy clouds, a professional massage table loomed huge and conspicuous in the aura created by a cluster of pin-beam spotlights, bringing to mind a surgical theater. Thin, black leather cushions padded the top of the table; below, an outlandish configuration of cranks, levers, and armatures allowed adjustment of height and angle. At one end of the table, an oval nest awaited someone's head, while at the opposite end, a rolled towel would be used to prop someone's feet. Was I to be that someone?

Frank was lecturing, "Most everyone enjoys Swedish massage, and that was the basis of my training; it relaxes the body and stimulates circulation. More popular of late is deep-tissue massage, which helps rid the body of tension while releasing tightness and reducing muscle pain, but I wouldn't recommend it for a first-time treatment. Aromatherapy is a light, gentle massage utilizing the power of essential oils . . ."

Was I supposed to choose? He sounded as if he were reading me a menu, and it all sounded pretty good. The tingle of arousal began to heat my khakis. How on earth had Neil arranged this? And how was *he* to fit in? Would I appear overeager if I began to undress?

". . . since reflexology is applied to the soles of the feet, some people simply don't like it, while shiatsu is applied to acupressure points that run along the body's meridian lines, enhancing energy flow. Then there's holistic massage, which I think is great; it incorporates the whole range of massage techniques—effleurage, petrissage, and tapotement."

"Has he told you about his hot rocks?" asked Cynthia, appearing in the doorway with a full glass of chardonnay.

Neil and I turned to her, looking a bit stunned. What was *she* doing here? And what in God's name was she talking about?

"Not yet," Frank told her. "I was saving the hot rocks for last."

Had I totally lost my mind?

With an uncertain laugh, Neil asked, "Hot rocks?"

"Here." Frank patted the lid of his turkey roaster. "Cynthia and I were at a wonderful resort on Hawaii—the Big Island—last winter, and the spa there was experimenting with a technique I'd never seen before." He lifted the lid, letting Neil and me peer inside. "Smooth, flat rocks gathered from the beach are heated in oil, then used as part of the treatment."

"It's *fabulous*," Cynthia told us, grinning.

Frank explained, "Two similar rocks are removed from the oil, one in each hand, then used to massage the subject's back. They're then left in place at symmetrical pressure points, and two more rocks are used for massage. Eventually, the back is nearly covered with rocks, some of them still quite hot, others beginning to cool."

"It's *fabulous*," Cynthia repeated. Was she trying to sell me on the technique?

Now I was doubly confused. If I'd been uncertain how Neil was to fit into my fantasy massage, I was downright perplexed about Cynthia's role, and I was suddenly uneasy about the direction this had taken. Reminding myself that it was Cynthia who had first promoted to Neil the idea of our friendship, "couple to couple," I lost that warm tingle in my khakis. If it got down to erotic forays, Frank I could handle—sure, anytime, as long as Neil was somehow involved—but not Cynthia.

Neil said, "You really ought to go professional, Frank, and open a massage service. Since you truly enjoy it, it might make a nice sideline. I'm sure you'd attract a loyal clientele."

"He'd better *not*," said Cynthia with a good-natured shake of her fist.

Frank walked over to her and put an arm around her. "Nah," he told Neil. "I have only one client—and I like it that way."

Then I knew without doubt: I'd been way off base about ulterior purposes that evening. My fantasy had been exactly that. It wasn't gonna happen.

Cynthia gestured to our surroundings. "This is our own private world. Thanks to you, Neil, we'll soon be trading up to a much more lavish little world, but the point is, this is *our* special pleasure."

"What happens here," said Frank, "is sort of the glue of our marriage." He gave Cynthia a soft kiss.

She purred. "It's better than sex, honest to God. Hell, I'm forty-three; my clock's stopped. This is what's left, and I love it." She returned his soft kiss.

I was beginning to feel like something of a voyeur—we didn't know these people *that* well, in spite of our mutual desire to foster a friendship.

"But *you* get all the fun," Neil razzed Cynthia.

"Nope," said Frank, shaking his head. "I get plenty out of it. It's a fair exchange. Cynthia provides the setting, buys the equipment, and keeps up with the supplies"—he gestured toward the luxurious inventory of lotions and oils—"while I get to hone my skills on a loving partner. What's wrong with that?"

"Not a thing," I told them, smiling, genuinely warmed by the knowledge that they shared such pleasure in the life they'd built together. Though they had no way of knowing, I also felt genuinely ashamed for having entertained notions of invading their sanctuary.

Frank continued, "And once the pavilion is built, things will be even better."

Cynthia agreed, telling Neil, "The new spa is an absolute knockout."

"But the best part," said Frank, "is the home office. Cynthia should be able to spend more time here."

"God, I hope so," she said with a wistful laugh. "This Tuesday-through-Friday schedule in Green Bay is getting to be a real drag. I finally took an apartment there, but I can't wait to get rid of it." She tweaked Frank's earlobe. "I hope you won't be feeling too abandoned again tomorrow."

"Not at all," he assured her. Then he told us, "During the school year, the goofy schedule is no problem—I'm busy during the week at Woodlands, often on campus in the evening. Summers can get lonely, though. That's why I got involved with the Players Guild."

Neil said, "And now *that's* wrapping up. *Teen Play* closes next weekend."

"Yeah," Frank conceded, "things'll quiet down now. There's a pickup rehearsal on Wednesday night, but otherwise, my week's wide open."

I offered, "Join us at the house some night. Do you mind dinner *en famille?*"

"Not at all. That sounds great."

Neil suggested, "How about Thursday?"

"Perfect."

Cynthia said, "You guys are too sweet, looking after dollface for me." She pinched his nose. "But right now, I need to check on *tonight's* dinner."

"Can we give you a hand?" offered Neil.

"Everything's under control, but sure—it's always a bit of a rush, getting things to the table."

So the four of us adjourned to the kitchen, where we all pitched in with the last-minute tasks of staging our meal. Cynthia fussed with her mushroom dish; Frank tended to the crown roast of lamb (the Margaux we had brought would complement it beautifully); I whisked a vinaigrette for the salad; Neil rearranged flowers and took charge of the table's final setting. When Cynthia decreed that her concoction, oyster mushrooms Mornay, was ready to serve, we moved the party to the dining room.

We had plenty of elbow room. The table could have seated eight, ten in a pinch, so Neil's setting didn't skimp on the side plates, stemware, or silver. He'd split the flowers into two low arrangements and placed them at the ends of the table, allowing the four of us to huddle in the middle, with the Geldens on one side, us facing them. Neil had scattered perhaps a dozen votive candles about the table, giving it a casual air and a festive glow.

Since Cynthia was already well into the chardonnay, the rest of us joined her in this choice to accompany the Mornay, which contained shrimp—as well as the oyster mushrooms she'd found on a wet log behind the garage. To my surprise, I found her recipe thoroughly delicious. The earthy, robust texture of the mushrooms combined with the crunch of shrimp and the snap of pea pods in a delightful mélange with creamy, garlicky pasta.

Sampling my first forkful, I swallowed, dabbed my mouth with the corner of a giant linen napkin, and said, "Cynthia, I'm amazed. I was skeptical, but your Mornay is wonderful."

She accepted my compliment with a nod, lifting her wineglass. After sipping, she told me, "I just *knew* you'd like it—but why were you skeptical?"

I glanced at Neil first, then sheepishly answered, "Well, the mushrooms. It seems everyone around here is 'into' them. Mushrooming is a great hobby, I guess, but I've always been wary of it. Where I was brought up, mushrooms came from supermarkets and restaurants, not the backyard."

The others laughed, Cynthia the most heartily. "I know where you're coming from, Mark. Before I married Frank, my idea of harvesting mushrooms was limited to the challenge of prying Saran Wrap off the package. I wonder why people get so 'funny' about wild mushrooms."

Neil answered bluntly, "Fear of an agonizing death."

"Oh, sure, *that*," said Frank with comic nonchalance, dismissing the issue with a flick of his hand. Then he put down his fork. "Seriously, mycophobia is a typically English trait that seems to have been inherited by America and dispersed through the melting pot. There's really nothing to fear, though. Any well-trained mushroom hunter knows enough basic mycology to distinguish between edible and poisonous mushrooms—and he knows never to gamble when he's not sure. The basic tool is a good field guide. Beyond that, spore tests provide the most reliable method of identification. Sometimes, the spore color can be identified by the use of light and dark papers used as contrasting backgrounds; other times, a microscope is required."

I was tempted to ask, Why bother? Don't pick mushrooms; buy them.

Frank continued, "Fear of mushrooms seems to be giving way to a wave of interest, with mushroom clubs popping up everywhere now. Fungus Amongus, Thad's club at Central High, is a good example; its membership has risen steadily every year I've served as adviser. We try to combine rigorous textbook training with the fun of the hunt, and the kids love it. What's more, we add practical lessons by outside lecturers."

Cynthia said, "Like Nancy, right?"

"Sure, Nancy Sanderson, owner of First Avenue Grill." Frank turned to us. "You know her, don't you, guys?"

"We're there all the time," said Neil.

I asked, "What does Nancy teach the club?"

Cynthia said, "Recipes, of course—what else? In fact, Nancy and I have exchanged any number of mushroom recipes over the years. She's a great gal."

Frank clarified, "Nancy doesn't exactly use her time at the club to swap recipes. She visits once each year to lecture on the do's and don'ts of cooking with local wild mushrooms. She's very thorough. Passionate too."

Tentatively, I asked, "Does she cover bad mushrooms as well as edible ones?"

"Certainly, that's an essential part of the drill. I'll be the first to concede, though, that mushrooming wasn't always so 'scientific' as it is today. Much of what used to pass as knowledge was essentially folklore. I remember when I was little, my grandfather thought his testing method was state-of-the-art. Get this: he kept an old silver dollar to throw into the pot whenever he boiled mushrooms."

"Huh?" asked Neil and I.

"Whatever for?" asked Cynthia, turning to face Frank.

"If the silver tarnished, the mushrooms were exposed as toadstools and thrown out."

We all chuckled at this, but Cynthia stopped short, telling Frank, "That makes a certain amount of sense though. If your grandfather's coin tarnished, it was probably due to an interaction between the silver and hydrogen cyanide or sulfide, which are components of many mushroom toxins."

How, I wondered, did Cynthia know that? I understood that she'd learned mushrooming from Frank, but her grasp of these particulars of chemistry struck me as beyond the realm of a mere enthusiast.

"Yes," Frank was saying, "but the test wasn't foolproof. Silver can react that way with some good mushrooms as well as many bad ones; conversely, some deadly mushrooms would produce no chemical interaction with silver."

"True," said Cynthia, nodding, "but still, the test had *some* scientific basis."

"Excuse me," I said, intruding on their academic discourse, "but I have to tell you, Cynthia, I'm impressed. You knew *nothing* about mushrooms when you met Frank, and now you're talking like Mr. Wizard."

"But, Mark," she said, breaking into laughter, "I'm a molecular biologist."

Neil asked, "You *are?*"

Then Cynthia and Frank leaned together. Wagging their heads in unison, they singsonged, "Birds of a feather!" The routine looked well practiced.

Neil said, "I thought you worked for a cell-phone company."

"Neil!" she scolded through a laugh. "BayCell Industries is a biotech company. We develop bioengineering and DNA technologies that have many applications in industry. You thought I sold *phones?*"

Neil echoed her laughter. "God, Cynthia, I'm sorry. I guess we never discussed your work."

Frank explained, "That's what brought us together. Not quite nine years ago, I put a call in to BayCell, asking if they could provide a guest lecturer to discuss some of the practical applications of molecular biology. They sent Cynthia to visit my class at Woodlands."

She looked at him with goo-goo eyes, a fawning smile.

"And the rest," she told us, "is history."

Tuesday, August 7

Sometime after midnight, closer to one, Neil and I arrived home, switched out a few lights that had been left on, and climbed the stairs together.

Our evening with the Geldens had been thoroughly enjoyable. We'd lingered for hours at the table—through the mushroom course, the meat course, the salad, dessert, then coffee. The meal was splendid, conversation nonstop, laughter frequent. I was glad they had invited us; not only did Neil and I discover strong potential for our future friendship with them, but I'd gleaned some immediate rewards as well.

I now knew, for instance, that if Jason Thrush had been poisoned by mushrooms, the fatal fungus was most likely fly agaric. I also knew that any student member of Fungus Amongus would have sufficient knowledge to harvest the fly agaric and put it to use—including Tommy Morales, who resented the victim's affluence and coveted his role in a small-town theatrical production. What's more, I'd learned that restaurateur Nancy Sanderson, who apparently harbored animosity toward the victim, was considered an expert in the do's and don'ts of preparing local wild mushrooms for consumption. And on a different note entirely, I'd figured out that Neil's cryptic promise of a fantasy masseur had been inspired by Frank Gelden's hobby of pleasuring his wife.

These were all, in a sense, promising developments, but they could not outweigh my mounting concern for Thad. In the three days since Jason's death, my nephew had come under heavy suspicion, and his friend Kwynn had clued me that my fears were well-founded: though

Thad was still attempting to maintain a facade of indifference, the speculation and gossip of his peers had clearly gotten to him. The possibility of severe emotional damage seemed very real. Even worse, I now had to wonder if there was any possibility that Thad might face arrest. There was nothing imaginary about the tide that was turning against him. The ugly, prank phone call was proof enough for me, and the attack by a vengeful gang of jock thugs was proof enough for Thad—he was in a real predicament. This mess was not simply going to "go away," and in fact, it was getting worse.

On top of everything else, there was the stash of fly agaric I'd spotted in his bedroom. Surely there was an innocent explanation—a class project, no doubt. Surely the hidden jar of poisonous mushrooms was not what it implied.

Though it was late, and though a busy day awaited me at the *Register*, I had more than enough on my mind to keep me up and thinking for a few hours.

"All in all," said Neil as we reached the top of the stairs, "I'd say the evening was a total success."

Stepping from the hall into our bedroom, I forced myself to dismiss my vexations and told him, "Any evening I spend with you is a total success. What more do I need?"

"God, you're full of it." He laughed softly, closing the door. Stepping near, he gave me a hug and a kiss—a friendly kiss, nothing passionate.

"In terms of your architectural practice, the evening was decidedly successful. Cynthia bought your plans, right?"

"Hook, line, and sinker. The design phase is complete, and she gave me the go-ahead to send the project out for bids."

"Must be exciting for you."

"Every project is, but this one in particular. The pavilion has—what?—sort of a fantasy element about it. Clients like Cynthia, who are open to such expressive design, don't come along every day."

I sat on the bed to remove my shoes. "Speaking of fantasy, I became suddenly aware this evening of what inspired your promised payback."

Coyly, he asked, "Are you referring to my debt of honor?"

"I am. 'Fantasy masseur,' indeed. It seems you've had Frank on your mind."

"*I'll* say," he confessed without shame.

"I have to admit, he gives a certain kind of guy—guys like us—plenty to think about." I stood, removing my shirt. With a laugh, I told

Neil, "In fact, at one point tonight, I was convinced that Frank was my fantasy masseur, that you'd somehow managed to deliver him as your surprise payback."

"*Mark!*" said Neil with a loud laugh, flabbergasted. "That's nuts."

"Well," I said lamely, "all the pieces seemed to fall into place." As Neil was still laughing, and it was late, I shushed him.

"No one can hear," he reminded me. "Thad's room is across the hall, at the back of the house, and Barb is in her quarters behind the kitchen. We can hoot and holler all night." He slipped out of his loafers, bent, and picked them up.

"Maybe *you* can," I told him, heading for the dressing room (more precisely, a large closet), "but I've got a long day tomorrow."

"Party pooper," he pouted.

Our banter continued, none of it important, as we prepared for bed. We yakked in the closet, yakked in the bathroom, yakked as we passed each other, setting out clothes for the morning. Our backchat petered out as I made a last visit to the bath, needing to pick something from my teeth that I'd missed while brushing. Neil was in the dressing room, rattling hangers, sliding drawers.

Standing at the sink in a comfortable old pair of linen lounge shorts (I have always worn something—shorts, robe, whatever—during the transitions between daytime dress and bedtime nudity and back again), I watched the offending gray fleck of gristle swirl down the drain. Finally, I switched off the light and returned to the bedroom.

Neil was still fussing in the closet, so I checked the clock radio's alarm and, finding it properly set, switched off the lamps, except the one on my nightstand. Stepping out of my shorts, I tossed them onto a nearby chair, then lay on the bed. With arms crossed behind my head, I watched the shadows cast by Neil in the dressing room, and I waited.

After a few moments of dead silence, Neil appeared in the doorway, and contrary to my assumption, he was not ready for bed. Softly, he said, "Surprise."

Backlit by the closet's yellow glow, he wore all white—a tight T-shirt that showed every gym-honed feature of his torso, a crisp pair of pleated tennis shorts with cuffs that hugged his upper thighs, ribbed cotton crew socks folded down to his ankles, and a spotless pair of all-white leather low-tops, fresh from the box. He knew my every little fetish, and there he stood, punching buttons even I had forgotten. With a smallish work-out towel slung around his neck, he looked like a tennis pro heading out for a match. No, more precisely, he looked like a masseur—an erotic, hunky fantasy of a masseur—arriving for duty at my bedside.

"Payback time?" I asked with a grin.

Smiling, he nodded, once.

"Right here?" I meant the bed. I was ready to roll over.

Still smiling, he gently shook his head.

Okay, I got it—he wasn't going to speak. "Where, then?"

He turned, switched off the closet light, and moved across the room, where he opened one of the doors leading to the sunporch. He come-hithered with a tilt of his head.

The sight of him, the anticipation of what was to follow, had already aroused me, and he smiled at the sight of it as I rose from the bed, turned off the last lamp, and crossed the room to the sunporch. He stepped aside so I could enter first, then followed, closing the door behind us.

The scene was set. Earlier that day, I don't know when, he had carefully arranged everything for this dreamlike encounter. The low bench in front of the sofa would serve as his massage table; its cushions were draped and tucked with a smooth white sheet, devoid of the slightest crease or wrinkle. Several rolled white towels would serve as pillows and props, as needed. A stack of huge, folded, white bath towels also stood at the ready, for later. On a little table near the bench, a tray held an assortment of oils and lotions. Had I staged this event, I would doubtless have added music and candles, but Neil had conspicuously nixed these elements, preferring the simple serenity of night. Warm air drifted through the outside wall of screens, as did an oblique shaft of cool moonlight, casting tree-dappled shadows on the white-sheeted bench. I would like to think that this last detail had also been planned by Neil, almanac in hand, but in all likelihood, this bit of astronomical mood-lighting was the product of happy happenstance.

The total effect left me momentarily breathless, and I paused to kiss Neil before we began. With his face in my hands, I touched my lips to his mouth. He returned the kiss tenderly, but again there was no passion in it—he knew that if we opened the door to lovemaking just then, his long-plotted plan would be scuttled by quick rapture. Stepping back from me, he gestured that I should lie down.

Stepping to the bench, I asked, "Face up or down first?"

He pointed down.

And I complied. It was a little awkward getting settled, as I rarely lie flat on my stomach, but Neil waited silently as I adjusted myself, the most crucial adjustment being the position of my nearly erect penis—it ended up pointing down between my legs, not up against my belly. With that conundrum solved, he took one of the rolled towels and positioned it under my head, facing me toward the screens, where I could see the moonlit lawn under a black sky, but sideways.

I also saw Neil's legs as he stepped to the side table, where his tray of unguents awaited. I heard the gentle pop of a bottle's plastic cap. He squeezed a small puddle of oil into one palm, then rubbed his hands together for several long seconds, distributing and warming the oil. Stepping back to my head, he faced my body lengthwise.

He spread his feet slightly, and I saw one foot at the corner of my vision. I saw the shoe he'd bought to please me, the exacting crisscross of its laces. I saw his shin, the muscled calf behind it, and the sparse, silky nap of hair that shone silver in the bluish light.

Then I felt his touch as he leaned and placed his fingertips on my neck behind my ears. He began slowly, moving his fingers in tiny circles that barely touched my skin. While doing this, he bent close and blew his warm, soft breath into my hair. His lips grazed the stubble of my neck; the tip of his nose slid between my shoulders; then he lifted his head.

The circles traced by his fingers now grew wider, till his hands had worked their way down my neck, under my chin. With both hands at my throat, he lifted my head from its nest and gently flexed it. My head seemed to bob on a placid sea. The trees beyond the screen swung lazily, as if suspended from a slow pendulum, till my head was again set to rest on its makeshift pillow. The trees stopped swinging. The tensions of the previous week—something to do with mushrooms?—ebbed from my muscles and my mind. My eyes stared blankly at the backyard.

Neil moved around me to pour more oil on his hands, which he again spread and warmed between his palms before returning to my head. Standing wider now (I saw the angle of one leg), he touched my shoulders, then slid his palms down my spine, working the oil across my entire back. For a moment, the wetness of my skin felt cold, but it was soon warmed by the friction of Neil's hands, kneading my back with long, forceful, steady strokes.

This could go on forever, I thought, and indeed, it seemed to. Neil was breathing harder, and I could tell he was starting to sweat—his pores projected the scent of Vetiver, which hung over my head like a mist. The pungent smell, the sliding pressure on my back, my lover's touch, the dreamy view of trees and moonlight, all converged to lull me into a dreamlike state, a waking trance. Time stopped. My life could be measured only in terms of the sensations that enveloped my body.

I wasn't even aware that Neil had moved around to my side, the side away from my outdoor view. His foot had left the corner of my vision, though, and the sound of his breathing no longer came from overhead. He was working his way down my back, past my buttocks, toward my legs. Another pause allowed him to replenish the oil in his hands, then he began working a thigh with long, brisk strokes toward my knee. He repeated this routine on my other leg, continuing with the calf, toward my foot. He switched legs again, and when both had been fully oiled and pampered, he focused his soothing toil on my feet. Each toe received his attention, followed by a brisk stimulation of the soles. I may have moaned. I felt drool moisten the towel under my head.

One at a time, he lifted each of my legs, resting a foot on his shoulder so he could massage each shin, stopping at the knee. Then he finished off my legs with long strokes, working back up to my hips. During our travels together, we had frequently indulged in spa treatments when visiting better hotels, and so far, Neil was doing a credible job of re-creating the mood and movements of a professional massage. At this point, however, his performance took a distinctive turn.

With both hands, he began to rock my hips slowly, inching upward to the mounds of my buttocks. This continued uninterrupted for some time, and I felt a woozy smile twist my mouth as I vacantly watched the tranquil scene beyond the wall of screens. With his thumbs, he kneaded each cheek more forcefully, circling nearer the crack. As his oiled fingers neared their target, my penis (which had relaxed with the rest of me) became suddenly alert, growing hot between my legs. Neil had apparently been watching for this sign, for I instantly felt a warm, slippery finger trace the length of my penis—or was I feeling the tip of his tongue? I could not see his movements, only the scene outdoors, which grew steadily more surreal.

When I felt his finger slide the length of my crack, whisking over the rim of my anus, I gasped—not out of fear or surprise, but as an involuntary reflex of pleasure. Suddenly fingers were at play around and in me, with my penis and testicles getting the full treatment as well. It seemed he had acquired an extra pair of hands, but I dismissed any curiosity about the dextrous mechanics Neil was employing to accomplish this feat—I was too swept away to care, lost in a warm, slippery ecstasy. Bleary-eyed, I gazed at the midsummer night. Under the moonlight, mushrooms danced in rings around the base of every tree. They chattered and giggled, playing leapfrog. I moaned loudly, transported to a fantasy world rooted in Neil's fingers.

Then I saw his face. Neil had moved around the bench, and his smile was aimed squarely at my eyes. With a blink of recognition, I smiled back, and he nodded, once. I knew his meaning. We weren't finished. Hardly. It was time for me to roll over onto my back.

As I had relaxed to the point of weakness, he helped lift and turn me, settling my head in the towel nest he plumped for me. With eyes now aimed straight up, I saw the angled ceiling of the porch. Then I saw Neil lean over my head as he began to oil my shoulders and my chest. I didn't know how many minutes had passed since I'd first lain down, but Neil had been working hard, and I saw that he had worked up a sweat. His T-shirt, which clung so beautifully to the body I worshiped, was wet, and even in the semidarkness, I could easily distinguish the brown circles of his nipples beneath the white cotton. As he began to work the oil farther down my chest, his crotch began to nudge the top of my head. I was looking right into the radiating wrinkles of his shorts; his bulge grazed my forehead.

I begged softly, "Please."

He stopped, looking down at me with a questioning gaze.

"Take off those shorts."

He smiled—my wish was his command. With a single, sure gesture, he unsnapped and unzipped his skimpy white uniform. Leaning back for a moment, he let the shorts drop and kicked them from his feet. Then he was back, assuming his previous position, leaning forward over me as his hands swirled oil around my belly. This time, however, his cock hung in my face, bobbing with his every move.

Is it possible to explain the goofy rapture of such a sight, the unexpected breathlessness of such a moment? In the telling, it sounds so silly or dirty. But the moment—and all it represented—was exquisite. He stood there sweating, busy at a task he loved, and my only role that night was to remain purely passive, to allow him the pleasure of creating pleasure for me. I could not resist, of course, taking a slurp or two at the meaty fruit that swung above me, but that was gratuitous, and I understood that my instincts were at odds with the slow, disciplined ritual Neil was performing for me. So I relaxed, watched, and left him in command.

He proceeded as before, when I had lain facedown. Moving around the table, he massaged my chest, stomach, thighs, legs, and feet. Then, getting up on the bench, kneeling between my legs, he again moved steadily toward my groin. The sight of him at work on me was in itself enough to induce another trance of dancing mushrooms, but by now my arousal was so extreme, the room's entire energy was focused in a searing pinpoint between my legs—no nodding off *now*.

Neil placed my ankles on his shoulders and bent forward; the finale had begun. With hands and mouth, he manipulated and probed me, front and back. Groaning, sensing something powerful building within me, I let my head fall back, needing air.

"*Watch this*," he told me in an urgent whisper, the first words he'd uttered since announcing his surprise payback.

I lifted my head in time to lock eyes with him. We both broke into wide smiles as my orgasm ripped through his hand and arched above us, barely missing his face. It came in three pulses, the last being the strongest, shooting higher than a foot, maybe two—though it felt like yards.

Before I could catch my breath or utter a sound, Neil drew one foot onto the bench and shifted his oily ministrations to himself. He was ready. Within mere seconds, his body convulsed. From deep within, a guttural sound escaped his mouth; his fist sprayed a thick backlog of hot semen. It landed on my chest, mingling with my own.

I held out my arms for him—the first voluntary movement I had made since lying down. He stretched out on top of me, his wet T-shirt spreading the gobs of our mixed orgasms against my bare skin. It leaked from the sides, trickling cold against my ribs. I laughed as our lips met.

"I love you," we said.

He asked, "It was adequate, then?"

"Paid in full."

He pulled back an inch or two. "It doesn't have to be over, you know."

"You bet, kiddo." We had managed to rekindle something we had lost, and I knew that neither one of us would let go of it again.

He rolled off me and stood. "God, what a mess." He laughed, peeling the sweaty, cum-smeared T-shirt from his chest.

Standing, I told him, "Look at *me*." I gestured at my entire body, greased and oiled from hair to toenails.

He raised a hand to his mouth, suppressing a laugh. "Sorry 'bout that." And he grabbed two of the oversize bath towels, handing me one. "Let me help swab you down, matey." And we went to work, trying to get the oil off me, but without much success.

"I think we both need a quick, soapy shower."

"Care to share?" he asked as he pried his shoes off.

I wrapped an arm around him as we walked toward the bedroom. "Good idea."

We were running late for breakfast Tuesday morning. Monday night's dinner party at the Geldens' country home, topped off by Neil's inventive frolic on the sunporch, had kept us up till the not-so-wee hours. Although we greeted dawn with less than enthusiasm, switching off the clock radio for another half hour, we both savored an unmistakable afterglow that would fuel our day more efficiently than sleep or coffee could. After showering again (by my count, we had done this three times within the last twelve hours, excessive even for us obsessive types) and dressing, we headed downstairs together, hungry from the rigors of our nocturnal workout.

Arriving in the kitchen, we were surprised to find not Barb, the housekeeper, but Pierce, the sheriff, rummaging for a carton of milk in the refrigerator. "Morning, Doug," I told him. "Make yourself at home."

He turned to us. "Oh—hi, guys. Where have you been? It's late."

Neil simply explained, "Late night last night." He winked at me while carrying the full pot of coffee from the counter to the table, where mugs were set out with Barb's bagels and Pierce's kringle.

"Where's Barb?" I asked, sitting.

Pierce shrugged. "She said she had some 'chores' to get busy with." He sat and cut large wedges of kringle for the three of us.

Pouring coffee, Neil asked, "She said 'chores'?"

Pierce nodded while feeding himself.

I mentioned to Neil, "We need to tell her there'll be a dinner guest Thursday."

Neil nodded, taking his first sip of coffee.

Pierce swallowed. "Anyone I know?"

I laughed. "Join us, Doug—no need for subtlety."

He shook his head, also laughing. "Sorry, I didn't mean it that way. I've got a public-safety committee meeting that night, but thanks for the invitation."

Neil told him, "Frank Gelden is coming over. His wife will be out of town again this week. There's a rehearsal on Wednesday night, but Thursday is quiet for all of us."

Pierce recalled, "Oh, yeah—you were out at their place last night. How was it?"

I asked, "You mean, dinner?"

"Well, sure—but *everything*. Wasn't he going to research mushroom toxins?"

"Correct. He found the coroner's mushroom theory plausible, but not airtight. He identified fly agaric as being the likely culprit—*if* mushrooms poisoned Jason—but those toxins act very quickly, so the mushrooms themselves should have been found in Jason's stomach."

"And they weren't," added Pierce.

"Right. So that whole angle is chancy at best."

He reminded me, "The whole 'unnatural causes' angle is still chancy. The coroner hasn't issued his final report yet."

Neil asked, "Do you know when to expect it?"

"Soon. Formhals managed to get a rush on the toxicology tests; the DA has started pressuring *him* as well. Results normally take weeks, but he expects to have them anytime now."

"Well," I said, after swallowing coffee, "at least we're seeing some progress."

Pierce continued, "Depending on the results, if Jason died of natural causes, the case will be closed; if not, I'll be launching a murder investigation." A sobering comment, it produced a lull in our conversation. Pierce poured a glass of milk, then drank some.

Neil leaned back in his chair. "Suppose Formhals does determine that the death was a homicide. Where do you start, Doug?"

"We'll review the possible suspects."

"Okay." I leaned forward. "Let's do a dry run."

Pierce chuckled, telling me, "You seem to have a few ideas already, Mark. Who's on your list?"

I ticked off, "Mica and Burton Thrush, Tommy Morales, and Denny Diggins. And—" I was about to add Nancy Sanderson to my list when Neil interrupted.

"I hate to mention the unthinkable, but what about Thad?"

Good question. Recalling the stash of fly agaric in Thad's room, I forced myself to wonder if his involvement was still unthinkable. I waited to see how Pierce would react.

He told us offhandedly, "Sure, Thad's on my list—I have to keep an open mind about this. But aside from the threat, which was purely coincidental, what could link him to the murder of Jason Thrush?"

Dryly, I mentioned, "Mushrooms. And the starring role on opening night. Sorry to say, a lot of people think it adds up." I pushed away my half-eaten pastry.

"Okay," Pierce conceded, "the threat has a logical link to opening night, but still, that's sheer coincidence. As far as mushrooms are concerned, that angle isn't public knowledge yet. Thad may be headed for an emotional crisis with all this, but we'd need a *lot* more evidence before he faced arrest."

God. We were actually discussing the possibility of arrest. What, I wondered, would Pierce consider sufficient "evidence"—the stash of fly agaric? I'd lost any taste for my coffee—there was a knot in my stomach.

Neil leaned into the conversation. "As long as we're exploring the mushroom angle, let's not forget Tommy Morales."

Pierce asked, "The little kid in the play with Thad?"

"Yeah," I said. "I don't know what to make of him. He's seemingly nice enough. But"—I raised a finger—"he stepped into a major role in *Teen Play* because of Jason's demise. Frank told me that Tommy wanted the Dawson role all along *and* was resentful of Jason's wealth. Plus, I myself heard him express his ambitions at the party last Saturday night."

"But the corker," added Neil, "is the fact that Tommy is the only member of Fungus Amongus who's also involved in the play—other than Thad, of course."

To make sure Pierce was connecting the dots, I explained, "Frank is fairly certain that any member of the mushroom club would be savvy enough to identify and harvest the deadly fly agaric."

"Wow." Pierce shook his head, pulling a pad from the inside pocket of his summer-weight linen blazer. "I'd better start taking notes." He clicked a ballpoint pen and began writing.

We'd all stopped eating, so Neil rose from his chair and carried the pastry and bagels to the counter. Over his shoulder, he said, "Whether mushrooms were involved or not, Mark thinks that both Mica Thrush and her father make appealing suspects."

"I agree," said Pierce. "They're at the top of my list." Proving his point, he flashed us the list. "Burton Thrush had a ten-million-dollar life-insurance policy on his son, and his business is on the skids— enough said. As for Mica, well . . ."

"As for Mica," I finished his thought, "she is one spooky girl. I don't know *where* she's coming from, but her bizarre behavior with her brother's corpse on Friday night gave me the chills. She's obviously into the whole 'gothic' mind-set, fascinated by death." Recalling the grisly fate of her neighbor's cat, I concluded, "When it comes to Mica, nothing would surprise me."

Neil returned to the table and sat, grinning. "She surprised you with that bombshell about Jason being gay."

"That she did." Fingering my coffee cup, I told Pierce. "Like you, Doug, I was inclined not to believe her. But Neil thinks it might be an important lead."

Neil asked, "Didn't she suggest that Jason was having a lovers' spat?"

Pierce nodded. "In so many words, yes. She also suggested that the 'other man' was none other than Denny Diggins."

I asked Pierce, "Did you ever get the computer log of Jason's phone records?"

"Late yesterday. Unfortunately, it gives us too *much* information—every call in or out of the Thrush residence during the week prior to Jason's death. They have several lines, and there were hundreds of calls, but I saw no discernible pattern. Sure, there were conversations here and there with other people involved with the play; you'd expect that. But there was no preponderance of calls to or from any one person, and—get this—there wasn't a single call we could trace to Denny Diggins."

"Hmm." I drummed my fingers on the table. "Mica suggested that Jason had something going on with Denny, and Denny himself told me he'd phoned Jason repeatedly on Friday. Where was he calling from—a phone booth?"

Pierce shook his head. "First thing we checked. No pay-phone calls."

"It just doesn't make sense. I could understand if Denny had been phoning Jason and lied about *not* making the calls, but why would he say he *had* called when he hadn't?"

"Hey," said Neil, enlightened. "He might have told everyone that he'd been desperately trying to reach Jason in order to establish how 'worried' he was, when in fact, he knew all along that Jason was at home, in his bedroom, dying."

Pierce and I glanced at each other. Pierce said the very words I was thinking: "That would fit."

I asked anyone, "What do we really *know* about Denny Diggins?"

Neil shrugged. "Local radio host. Phony accent. Highly conceited. Bachelor."

Pierce nodded. "That sums him up pretty well." He paused before adding, "I hate to sound stupid, but do we actually *know* that Denny is gay?"

Neil glibly answered, *"I've* never slept with him."

I laughed. "Denny's fruity as they come, and it's a reasonable assumption, but I have no direct knowledge that he's gay. Maybe he's closeted. Or just plain affected." Turning to Pierce, I noted, "You've lived here far longer than we have. What's the scuttlebutt?"

"I was deep in the closet myself till last year. If Denny's had an active sexual history in this town, I was never privy to it."

I thought for a moment, then told Pierce, "I'm beginning to feel we should talk to Denny sooner rather than later. This confusion over the phone calls is troubling; it lends a shred of credibility to Mica's offbeat story."

"I agree," said Pierce, "but remember, I'm not investigating a murder yet. If I haul him in and think he's guilty, I've got nothing to book him on. Maybe *you* could devise some reason to question him."

I nodded, pondering this—it wouldn't be the first time I'd called someone down to the newspaper on a spurious pretext.

Neil snapped his fingers. "Glee Savage. *Teen Play* will be running for another weekend; assign Glee to write a follow-up feature on the play and its director. Denny is such a publicity hound, he could easily be lured down to the *Register* for an interview. Once you've got him, ask him anything you want."

Standing, I kissed Neil's forehead. "Thanks, kiddo. You're brilliant as well as beautiful."

He told Pierce under his breath, "Mark married me for my brains, you know."

"I believe it," said Pierce with a laugh, throwing his hands in the air, recognizing a no-win debate. He stood and carried his cup and a plate to the sink. "That's the plan, Mark?"

"That's the plan. I'll discuss it with Glee as soon as I get downtown. And you'll let me know if you hear anything from Formhals?"

"Absolutely." Pierce moved to the back door. "I thought I'd drop by the paper later this morning anyway. You'll be around?"

"All morning. See you later, Doug."

"Bye, Doug," Neil told him as he left the house with a wave.

I began rinsing a few things, putting them in the dishwasher. Neil cleared the table, returning the milk to the refrigerator. I asked him, "Want more coffee?"

"No, thanks—all tanked up." He brought the pot from the table and dumped it in the sink, then handed it to me.

While giving the glass pot a good rinse, I said, "It seems the mystery of Jason's death has been as heavily on your mind as on mine."

"Well, *sure*. This isn't 'just another news story'—it hits pretty close to home."

I nodded. "Did you notice? When we discussed Thad with Doug, he dismissed the likelihood of 'arrest'—but he did broach the subject, and he did say the word."

"Yeah, I caught that. Thank God Thad didn't surprise us with another early mushroom hunt. If he'd popped into the kitchen and heard that, he'd have been devastated."

I walked back to the table, looking toward the hall doorway, hoping Thad slept soundly upstairs. "I'm afraid he's already on shaky ground, emotionally I mean. We've *got* to put this behind him." Turning to Neil, I said, "That was a great suggestion, by the way, about Denny's follow-up interview."

He crossed to me from the sink. "Just doing my bit."

I put my hands on his shoulders. Softly I told him, "In case I neglected to mention it, you were spectacular last night."

Grinning, he repeated, "Just doing my bit."

He placed his hands around my waist, and we stood together, looking at each other for several long, silent seconds.

Then the soft, breathy notes of a clarinet drifted through the house and met our ears. Instinctively, we turned toward the hall, listening. After a few practice scales, the sounds took on the structure of music. I recognized a phrase or two from the melody I'd heard Barb practicing on Sunday morning, now sounding much more polished.

"She's been busy," said Neil.

Nodding, I told him, "She's really good—surprisingly good."

The piece had odd rhythms, an eerie quietude, and frequent little trills suggestive of birds. It seemed plaintive and vulnerable, yet agitated by an underlying turbulence.

Neil cocked his head. "It's not quite 'pretty,' but it certainly has a beauty about it. Do you know the piece?"

"It's familiar, but I can't place it. I know this much, though: it's modern, and it's extremely difficult. Barb may be a bit rusty, but she's a highly skilled player." Her clarinet drifted through measure after measure of the piece, exploring a sensitive range of dynamics while evoking unseen colors and teetering, uncertain emotions.

Then, with a sad, quiet trill, it ended.

A small bird, I felt, had died.

Glee Savage grinned. "Why do I get the feeling that your interest in Denny Diggins runs deeper than theater?"

We were seated in the conference area outside my office at the *Register*. It was sometime after nine that morning. I answered her question with one of my own: "Has anyone ever told you that you're as astute as you are stylish?"

"*Often.*" She smiled through those big red lips.

"Here's the deal—"

Lifting a finger, she asked me to wait as she retrieved a steno pad from her huge, flat purse (this one was adorned with a bouncy calypso-themed pattern of dancing lemons, limes, and oranges—a palette that was repeated in the eye-searing solids of her jacket, blouse, and skirt). Clicking her pen, she was ready for shorthand. With a nod, she told me, "Shoot, boss."

I brought her up to speed. "As you can probably guess, this relates to the death of Jason Thrush. His sister, Mica, told Sheriff Pierce and me that Jason was gay, and she implied that he was having an affair with Denny Diggins, also claiming that they were recently on the outs. Last Friday, when Jason failed to appear at the theater on time for his six-thirty call, Denny was out in the parking lot wringing his hands, telling everyone, myself included, that he'd been trying desperately all afternoon to reach Jason by phone. Now we have phone records for the Thrush residence, and there were *no* calls from Denny that day."

Glee looked up from her note-taking. "My, that *is* intriguing."

"Uh-huh. So we need to quiz him on several matters—"

"All in the context of publicity for his play." Glee's tone had turned coy.

"Precisely." I smiled. "If anyone can pull this off, you can, Glee. You're a pro to your bones." She was. Having been on the *Register*'s staff for thirty years, she knew everyone in town—which fostered another idea. "How well do you know Denny Diggins?"

She thought. "Not very. And that's sort of odd, isn't it? For decades, we've both worked for the local media. Guess we don't mingle in the same circles."

"And you're both single. Is he gay?"

"I always *thought* so. I've never known him to date women."

"We need to try to pin that down. Also, let's see if he changes his story about the phone calls. And another important detail: How extensive is his knowledge of mushrooms?"

Glee removed her reading glasses, eyeing me skeptically.

I explained, "The coroner is working on a theory."

She nodded—say no more.

"Do you think you can devise enough 'intelligent' questions to keep him off base for a while?"

"Of *course.*" She looked playfully affronted. "As long as I'm bothering, I do plan to get a decent feature out of this—regardless of whether you end up with a page-one headline."

Dear, driven Glee. Ever so practical. I suggested, "You may want to conduct the interview right here. There's more room, and—"

"—and that puts you in a convenient position to 'drop in' at the appropriate moment."

Yes, we'd done this before.

"I'll phone him right away," she continued, "and set up the interview."

I was about to get up and return to my desk when Lucille Haring stepped in from the newsroom. "Got a minute, Mark?"

"Sure, Lucy. Glee and I just finished. Join us."

Carrying a folder, she walked into the room and sat in the chair next to Glee's. Lucy wore one of her typical olive-drab pantsuits, a jarring contrast to Glee's over-the-edge ensemble. Patting the folder, she said dryly, "The plot thickens."

Both Glee and I perked up. I asked, "What have you got?"

"Another possible motive."

I uncapped my Montblanc, ready for notes; Glee's pen was already poised.

Lucy elaborated, "We already know that Burton Thrush, the victim's father, carried a sizable life-insurance policy on his son. Turns out, he's not the only one. Mica Thrush, the kid's snotty sister, had also insured Jason's life."

I nodded. "Interesting . . ."

"*Very* interesting. Jason's death was worth a cool two million to the charming Miss Thrush."

Glee tisked. "Why, that little . . ." Glee's oaths didn't get much stronger.

"So," I said, "two million for Mica and ten for Daddy. It seems we have more motives than we know what to do with."

"Right. We've got motives"—Lucy grinned—"but the Thrushes have zilch, so far. Both Mica and Burton have retained lawyers to help rush their claims, but the insurance companies are balking over cause-of-death issues."

"And I don't blame them." Glee sounded genuinely steamed at the whole situation. "You'd think the boy's family, of *all* people, would have the decency—or at least the curiosity—to let the truth be discovered before clamoring for the loot." She crossed her arms.

Lucy countered, "It doesn't seem that decency—or patience—is a Thrush-family trait. Not only have both Burton and Mica tried, through their lawyers, to rush their insurance claims, but I have reason to believe that Burton is now attempting to influence a quick, favorable ruling from Dr. Formhals by exerting pressure through Harley Kaiser."

Something had told me that name was about to pop up. "What's our hot-dog DA got to do with this?"

"I checked the records. Kaiser has been the recipient of generous campaign contributions from Thrush. According to Kaiser's secretary, Thrush paid a closed-door visit to Kaiser's courthouse office late yesterday. She's sure it was Thrush—the old guy looked like he needed oxygen."

"Yes," I mused, "that would be he."

Glee stood, smoothing wrinkles from the front of her skirt. "It really is appalling how the scent of cash seems to bring out the very worst in people."

Lucy added, "Especially people who *need* the cash—like Burton Thrush."

Glee moved toward the door. "It's unthinkable, though. His own son."

I reminded them both, "We don't know for certain that Jason was killed, and if he was, the circumstances point to any number of suspects."

"One of whom," said Glee, "will make a fascinating subject for a features interview." Then she turned and left my office to phone Denny Diggins.

Opening her folder, Lucy told me, "That field of suspects seems to have grown by one. You asked me for some background on Nancy Sanderson."

I turned to a fresh page of my notebook. "And?"

"And I've pieced together a bit of history that does indeed link Nancy to the Thrushes. Nancy was married to Leonard Sanderson, but twelve years ago, he died while still in his forties, leaving Nancy a middle-aged widow; they had no children. When Leonard died, he was in the employ of—guess who—Burton Thrush, and by most accounts, he had helped build Thrush Typo-Tech during its heyday. By the time Leonard died, though, the business was in its early years of decline. What's more, the terms of Leonard's employment contract with Thrush were either vague or outdated. The bottom line is that Thrush screwed Nancy out of a proper death settlement. With no other means of support, she had to fend for herself, and that's when she opened the restaurant."

I sighed. "And all along, I just assumed that Nancy liked to cook; I thought the Grill was sort of a lark. I had no idea that she'd been forced to earn a living. It probably happened at about the time when she and Leonard were entertaining their first thoughts of retirement."

Lucy nodded. "Sounds like grounds for a grudge."

"Sure. But is it grounds for murder?"

"Probably not—if the trouble had ended there, twelve years ago— but it didn't."

I sat back. "There's a chapter two?"

"Oh, yes. Two years ago this fall, Jason Thrush and some of his friends got frisky at the Grill one night and did some substantial damage."

"Do tell? Doug told me about the incident, but he didn't specifically mention that it happened at the Grill. Somehow, Thrush managed to keep the entire story out of the *Register*."

"Indeed he did." Lucy displayed the contents of her folder. "This didn't come from *our* files. Investigating Nancy's background, I traced *this* information from police records. As I understand it, Jason's father wrote a check for the damages, but never compensated Nancy for two weeks' lost business during repairs. If you ask me, Nancy should have sued the bastard, but she didn't."

I reasoned. "Instead, Nancy chalked off the experience as another encounter with 'bad blood' in the Thrush family."

"Possibly." Lucy closed the file on her lap. "Or she may have waited, deciding to exact her own brand of justice."

Later that morning, Thad visited my office with Kwynn Wyman, his theater chum. He had told me that she was involved with the school newspaper and interested in journalism but had never seen "the real thing," so I gladly invited them downtown for a tour, suggesting we all have lunch afterward.

As I walked them through the offices and the plant, Thad did most of the talking, and I was surprised by the accuracy with which he recalled so many details from his few previous visits. Kwynn gawked wide-eyed at the flicker of dozens of computer terminals in the newsroom, at the hustle of the circulation and advertising departments, at the huge, silent presses that would roar through the middle of the night. Along the way, I stopped to introduce her to reporters and photographers; she seemed amazed to learn that there were real, breathing people behind their familiar bylines.

Retracing our steps to the second-floor newsroom, Kwynn gushed superlatives about her morning's adventure, and I recalled the old spark that had drawn me to journalism in the first place—its romance, its youthful pace, its high ideals of truth and freedom. These wistful thoughts were nipped, though, by the sight of Sheriff Pierce waiting in my outer office. Assuming he had come to discuss developments on the Jason Thrush case, I asked Lucille Haring if she could spend a few minutes with Thad and Kwynn, hoping to keep the kids distanced from a disturbing topic. Lucy easily read my intentions and began an extemporaneous lecture on recent technical developments in electronic newsgathering. I slipped into my office.

Pierce didn't see me enter; he was paging through the morning paper. "Hi, Doug," I greeted him, my voice inexplicably hushed. "What happened?"

He looked up at me and shrugged. "Nothin'. I told you I'd be dropping by this morning—I thought you might want to have lunch."

I laughed at my own jumpiness. "Sorry, Doug. Sure, *now* I remember. Thad's here with Kwynn Wyman; I'm taking them over to the Grill. Care to join us?"

He stood. "I'm not intruding?"

"Of course not. Neil can't make it—he has another meeting out at Quatro Press—so we're a foursome." Lowering my voice again, I asked tentatively, "Any word from Dr. Formhals regarding toxicology?"

Pierce shook his head. "Not yet. I checked with him just before I came over here."

I glanced at my watch. "Well, then—time to eat."

Pierce and I walked out to the city room, where I rescued Thad and Kwynn from Lucy's learned discourse. I gave her a wink of thanks and farewell; then the kids, Pierce, and I headed downstairs to the lobby. Connie, our receptionist, waved from behind her glass cage, saying, "Enjoy your lunch, Mr. Manning." I saw her check a box on a form, denoting I was out.

Out on First Avenue, Pierce and I walked behind Thad and Kwynn, whose brisk pace seemed too energetic for the midday heat. They chattered all the way. As they passed Neil's office, I noticed Thad point out the sign to Kwynn. Several steps behind, Pierce and I speculated about the timing of the coroner's report.

"Do you think he'll wrap it up today?" I asked.

"It all depends on toxicology. I think we're getting close though. Vernon said he'd page me as soon as he has something, but it won't be earlier than one o'clock."

I instinctively looked at my watch as we stepped up behind Thad and Kwynn at the curb, waiting to cross the street. Thad was directly in front of me, inches away, and I realized that my eyes were level with the top of his ears—he was almost exactly my height. When did *that* happen?

Thad turned to ask me, "Where's Neil today?"

"Quatro Press. Another meeting about the plant expansion."

Kwynn said, "I've never seen an *architect's* office, Mr. Manning. Would Mr. Waite mind if I stopped in sometime? I mean, when he's not too busy?" She carried a bag—not exactly a purse, not quite a backpack, sort of a canvas tote bag with shoulder straps, which appeared to be heavy. As we waited at the crosswalk, she moved the straps to her other shoulder.

"I'm sure Neil wouldn't mind at all." I smiled. "Just call first."

She nodded with enthusiasm, then fell back into conversation with Thad.

The light changed, and we all crossed the intersection toward the restaurant, which lay ahead on the next block. Pierce was saying something, nothing important—in truth, I wasn't listening. I was focused on Thad again, and Kwynn too. Thad, I realized, didn't look like a kid anymore, and neither did Kwynn. They looked like young adults. What's more, they looked like a couple. This impression was made all the more vivid when we stepped under the Grill's awning and Thad paused to open the door for Kwynn. He held it for Pierce and me as well—quite the little gentleman. Except, he wasn't little.

Entering the restaurant, I was welcomed by the usual rush of air-conditioning, the mixed aromas of serious cooking, the clatter of lunchtime activity. These sensory perceptions, though, remained in the background, diffuse and muted and unremarkable—like wallpaper—as my mind was still locked on the notion that Thad had grown up.

Nancy greeted us with an effusiveness not natural to her. It was the first time she'd seen Thad since the previous Saturday's performance of *Teen Play*, which she'd attended, and she was lavish in her praise of Thad's acting, again making no mention of *the* hot topic, the death of Jason Thrush. She also recognized Kwynn from her smaller role in the play, hailing her performance as one of the evening's special highlights. Both Thad and Kwynn were made to feel like visiting celebrities, and as Nancy finished seating us at my usual table, she turned back to tell us with a wink, "Dessert's on me today."

I glanced at Pierce with arched brows, mirroring his. Thad and Kwynn lapped up the attention, beaming with toothy smiles.

Eventually we ordered and fell into conversation, all four of us sharing lighthearted patter about the weather, the newspaper tour, the coming school year, and the play, but we managed to avoid *the* hot topic, at least for a while.

At a pause in the meal between courses, Kwynn finally sighed, her face pinched with worry. "It's not true, is it, Sheriff, that Thad might be arrested? Some of the kids are saying that if—"

"*Kwynn*," Pierce stopped her, "there's no reason for your friends to say such things."

Though he gave the right answer, the question itself had already produced the predictable effect—Thad's breezy manner was instantly quelled by the unexpected mention of arrest. I don't know if the possibility had yet crossed his mind, but now, there it was, openly discussed at lunch by his best friend and the county sheriff.

Berta, our waitress, bustled over to clear salad plates, leaving the glass boat of iced relishes. I helped myself to a slice of pickle, eating with a show of nonchalance till she left the table.

Thad listened, stunned, as Kwynn continued, "It's just that what happened to Jason is so *much* like the play itself. Just this morning, I met Thad at the house before we toured the *Register*, and he got the most awful phone call—some dunce calling him a 'killer boy toy' or whatever."

So Sunday's prank call was not an isolated instance. Though I'd managed to shield Thad from that first one, another had gotten through to him. Had there been others? He wilted even further as Kwynn recounted it.

She shook her head. "I *know* Thad didn't have anything to do with what happened, but some of the kids are saying that he *must* have. Even Mr. Diggins has been—" She stopped short.

While I was grateful that she at last understood how disturbing Thad found her words, she had raised a topic that interested me greatly. Since the door was already open, I decided to venture in. I asked quietly, "What *about* Mr. Diggins?"

She turned to Thad briefly, apologetically, then answered, "He's been talking about, um"—she searched for the word—" 'contingencies,' he calls them, contingencies for this weekend's run of the play."

"Huh?" said Thad, now looking more confused than upset.

With a soft laugh, I explained, "Contingencies are options or alternatives when there's a possible problem."

With a soft laugh of his own, Thad said, "And the possible problem is, like, me—in jail." Eyeing the relishes, he helped himself to a pickle.

Pierce assured him, "If you didn't kill Jason, that's not going to happen, Thad."

Though I was pleased to hear it from Pierce's lips, my worst apprehensions about Thad's stature in the microsociety of the theater troupe had now been borne out, and I again feared the emotional toll this would exact from him. Even the play's director, the pompous Mr. Diggins, was preparing for Thad's demise. Was Denny simply looking out for the show's best interests? Or was he moving forward with a more sinister agenda? I told Thad, "I'm sure that Mr. Diggins just wants all the bases covered. If, for some reason—*any* reason—you couldn't go on this weekend, who'd take over for you?"

Thad shrugged. "I don't have an understudy, not anymore. I guess Tommy would step up, if he could memorize the role fast enough."

Listening to this, Kwynn nodded. "He's a quick study." She picked up a long, thin slice of carrot and munched the end of it.

"Meaning," Pierce asked her, "Tommy learns lines quickly?"

She swallowed. "Uh-huh. There were a couple of times at school when Mrs. Osborne had to make late casting changes, and Tommy always came through. I think he'd get better roles in the first place if he wasn't so short; maybe that's why he tries so hard. Anyway, when I was back at Unity High during my freshman year, there was a flu bug or something going around during the spring production. Our director had to make lots of last-minute cast changes, and *nobody* could handle it; the show turned out a mess." Kwynn shook her head, lamenting the fiasco. "We could have really used Tommy, but he's always gone to Central."

I'd forgotten—if I'd known at all—that Kwynn had attended both of Dumont's high schools. "When did you start attending Central, Kwynn?"

"Sophomore year. We moved to a new house, in town."

She was referring to the geographical distribution of the two schools' students. Dumont Central was located near downtown and served the city school district; Unity High was located just beyond the city line and served several outlying county districts. She continued, "I could have stayed at Unity because I started there, but since Central has a better theater program, I made the switch." She turned to Thad, smiling. "Glad I did too."

It dawned on me that Kwynn was doubtless a good "source" regarding who's who—she'd been a student at both high schools, and she'd been involved with theater two years longer than Thad. I asked, "Did you know Jason back at Unity?"

"Sure, Mr. Manning. We were in the same class, and we were both in a couple of plays that year."

Pierce figured out why I'd asked. He leaned forward on his elbows. "How well did you know him, Kwynn?" Tentatively, he added, "Did you ever . . . date?"

She laughed. "Not as *freshmen*, Sheriff. Besides"—she and Thad briefly turned to each other, sharing a grin—"Jason didn't exactly 'date.' "

Pierce and I turned to each other, sharing a grin of our own. I crossed my arms, asking both Kwynn and Thad, "Level with me—was Jason Thrush gay?"

They looked at each other and exchanged a shrug. Turning to me, they both nodded matter-of-factly. Thad qualified his nod: "Jason never actually said so."

Kwynn told me, "He put up a good act, but everybody knew Jason liked boys." À la Seinfeld, she quickly added, "Not that there's anything wrong with that."

Pierce laughed.

I slapped a palm to my forehead. "Jeez, guys, why didn't you ever *mention* this?"

"You never asked," said Thad, taking another pickle.

"And everybody *knew*," Kwynn repeated.

Had times changed that much? An attractive, outgoing high school athlete/scholar/actor from a prominent family was generally known to be gay, and no one bothered to *talk* about it? Somehow, I couldn't quite believe that the gay subculture had been that successfully mainstreamed out here in the middle of Middle America. Though Wisconsin could boast a proud tradition of tolerance and progressive attitudes, the Jason Thrush story struck me—any way you sliced it—as hot gossip-fodder.

I laughed quietly, shaking my head at the irony of the situation. "If Jason was gay, his put-down of Thad at last Wednesday's rehearsal was not only mean-spirited, but the height of hypocrisy."

Pierce snorted. "Yeah—the pot calling the kettle black."

Thad and Kwynn looked at each other, not quite getting it.

I explained to Thad, "When Jason called you a 'boy toy,' he implied that you were gay, and he meant it as an insult. Knowing what you knew about him, why didn't you just shoot the insult right back at him?"

"Because"—Thad hesitated—"you and Neil were there. How could I put Jason down for being gay?" He smiled at me. "Not much of an insult, not in my book."

My jaw sagged. A lump came to my throat. I couldn't respond.

Kwynn leaned forward. "I hope you weren't offended, Mr. Manning, when I razzed Jason about his 'cheap perfume.' As soon as I'd said it, I wished I could take it back."

"Hey," I managed to tell both of them, coughing past the lump, "you guys are *way* too sensitive. But believe me"—I rose from my chair, stepped between them, and hugged both their shoulders—"I appreciate it." Laughing, I added, "Jason very nearly heard far worse from *me*. I'm glad you both spoke up when you did." Sheepishly, I returned to my seat.

Even Pierce was moved by these tender emotions—he fidgeted with the knot of his tie and wiped a fleck of something from the corner of his eye. Taking a stalk of celery from the relish boat, he bit off the end, breaking our momentary silence. After swallowing, he said to Kwynn, "You mentioned that everyone at school knew that Jason liked boys, but you said he 'put up a good act.' I'm sort of surprised that he got so involved with theater. I mean, theater's great, but in the jock mentality, isn't it a bit . . . suspect?"

Kwynn rolled her eyes. "Maybe, but Jason couldn't have cared less. He had this whole *macho* thing—the sports, the big talk, even the way he walked."

She'd noticed too, huh? I could still envision Jason's butch swagger. I asked, "But he didn't date?"

"Well," she qualified her previous statement, "he didn't 'date' date, if you know what I mean. He occasionally went out with girls, but as far as I know, that was just 'public' stuff."

"Like school dances?"

She nodded. "Exactly. Do you know who Nicole Winkler is—from the play?"

Indeed I did. "I've met her mother. Nice woman. Nicole seems a bit—what?—emotional, I guess. Was she friendly with Jason?" I was playing dumb, of course, hoping to hear the story from a perspective other than Burton Thrush's or Mica's.

Thad suppressed a laugh.

Pierce, also playing dumb, looked from face to face, asking, "What'd I miss?"

Thad said, "Nothing, Sheriff. I'm sorry. It's just that Jason and Nicole were sort of an item. *Sort* of."

Kwynn amplified, "At least *she* thought so. This goes back a couple of years. I had already transferred to Central High, but you keep your friends, and friends talk. Nicole is a year older than Jason was, but they got acquainted while working on a school play. She apparently bought the macho act and fell for him, dismissing all the rumors. I guess *he* figured Nicole made a good 'cover,' so they went to dances and stuff together. They looked good together too."

I said, "Jason's father mentioned that they were on the homecoming court."

"Yup," said Kwynn, "last fall. That's when Nicole assumed things were getting serious, and I guess that's when Jason decided it was time to back off. In certain ways, they seemed like the perfect couple, but what was he gonna do—*marry* her? So no one was surprised when Jason dumped Nicole."

Pierce asked, "No one was surprised—except Nicole?"

Kwynn shuddered. "*That's* putting it mildly. She just didn't accept it. What do you call that—denial? And from what I hear, her mom wasn't much better. That's the only reason Nicole got involved with summer theater—to be near *Jason.* And that's also why her mom got involved with the costuming—to be near *Nicole.*"

I recalled, "Nicole leaves town this fall for college, right?"

Kwynn nodded. "As far as I know. She graduated in June."

"Wow," said Thad, who'd been listening quietly, "next year, that's *us.*"

He was referring to graduation and college, and his voice carried an unmistakable verve, suggesting he was eager to get on with his life. Was he truly focusing on the future, as I would expect of any bright seventeen-year-old, or was he merely yearning to escape the mess that now surrounded him in Dumont?

Berta appeared again to serve the main course of our lunch, depositing plates in front of us with efficient flicks of her wrist. Only Thad had opted for that day's special, Nancy's renowned mushroom strudel. This unique creation, something of a signature dish, I'd sampled many times and enjoyed. Today, though, it struck me as wrong for the warm weather, and besides, I'd grown squeamish of late about fungi, even the most benign button variety.

While we ate, we continued to converse, shifting to topics less emotionally fraught than Jason's sex life or Nicole's unrequited crush. Our talk drifted back to school, and it was clear that both Thad and Kwynn were now ready to put *Teen Play* behind them and get back to the "real world" of hitting the books. Not that either of them was all that scholarly, but both of them, naturally, looked forward to ruling the roost next year with their fellow seniors. The word *college* kept popping up as well, and it became apparent that they'd both been giving their options considerable thought. What I had not realized, though, was that they'd been making these plans *together*.

Thad nudged his plate aside, leaning forward to tell me, "Kwynn's parents have decided that if she wants to major in theater, she can. Isn't that great?"

Truly, I didn't know how to answer. It was important to *enjoy* college, of course, but it was also important to learn disciplines useful in later life. Objectively, Kwynn's chances of actually becoming "someone" in the theatrical world were slim. There were, after all, countless kids with stars in their eyes, heroes of their local drama clubs, dedicated, determined, and talented. But few would ever achieve anything professionally; most would end up waiting tables while waiting for the big break, broke. Their hopes could be dashed by *anything*—a fickle casting director, a favor owed someone else, even the color of their eyes. Only minutes ago, Kwynn herself had said that Tommy Morales could never get a decent role because he was a few inches too short. How, I wondered, could would-be actors willingly, eagerly subject themselves to the desperate competition, superficial standards, and cold scrutiny of the profession they sought to enter?

Thad, Neil, and I had already had this discussion with regard to

Thad's intentions. He wanted to study theater; we were grateful for his enthusiasm, but gave him the hard-knocks lecture; still, his ardor was undampened. Privately, Neil and I ultimately conceded that with the Quatrain family fortune left in trust to Thad by his mother (he'd collect nothing till he turned twenty-five), he was in the enviable position of not needing to worry much about his "next meal" after college. Why *shouldn't* he devote his education to something he loved? And—who knew?—he might just be the one to beat the odds and achieve stardom.

Kwynn, though, was another matter. I barely knew her parents and had no awareness of their financial circumstances. It might well behoove her to devote her college years to honing skills more predictably marketable than acting.

"Isn't that great?" repeated Thad.

Tentatively, I directed my answer to Kwynn. "Well, it's a bit risky, you know."

She laughed, but it carried warmth. "You sound like my *dad*, Mr. Manning."

"Dads worry. It's our nature."

Kwynn and Thad pattered on, but I was stuck on the comment I'd just made—I'd referred to myself as a dad, and it had rolled off my tongue as naturally as tomorrow morning's headline. This was something of a watershed moment, and I had no way of sharing its significance.

Pierce seemed to understand that I was "dealing with something," so he helped carry the conversation, asking questions about the colleges Thad and Kwynn mentioned. Their answers reinforced that they were in this together, and in my mind's eye, I saw them sitting there, talking, a few years down the road, married, with a baby. A *baby?* I'd barely gotten comfortable with the notion of *myself* as a father—now this quick, precipitous leap into grandfatherhood.

"It's in California," Kwynn was saying to Pierce as she handed him a pamphlet that she'd pulled out of her purse. (Bag? Tote? Rucksack? God, I felt old—even my vocabulary was failing.)

Thad said, "Mrs. Osborne, our director at Central, told us about it. It's a brand-new arts college, not even built yet. It opens *next* fall, after we graduate."

California? I knew that Thad would soon begin applying to colleges, and I assumed that he'd want to get away from home. Since he was serious about theater, I figured, Northwestern has a fine program. Maybe the Goodman School of Drama in Chicago. Either way, he could still drive home for a weekend whenever he wanted. If he needed a bit more distance, well, Yale is hard to beat. Sure, he could go Ivy League—if they'd have him. But California? It's two thousand miles away. He couldn't *get* any farther within the contiguous forty-eight.

"Oh, yeah," said Pierce, pushing back from the table to look at the brochure. "Desert Arts College. I've read something about this. Glenn Yeats, the computer-software tycoon, apparently thought it was time to 'give back' to society. Dipping into his billions, he's building, from scratch, a complete college campus dedicated to the arts. It's already under construction in the Palm Springs area, near one of his homes. The facility itself will be first-class, and money is no object when it comes to raiding top faculty from other schools."

Kwynn dabbed her lips, having finished her lunch. "That's why Mrs. Osborne told us about it. This really important director has just agreed to move out there from New York—from *Broadway*—to be in charge of the new theater program when it opens a year from now."

"Who is he?" asked Pierce.

I wasn't really listening. I didn't really care. I was sure there were better theater schools—established schools with long-earned reputations for excellence—much closer to home.

"It's not a *he*," said Kwynn with a laugh. "The director is a woman."

That caught my attention. Could it possibly—?

Thad told Pierce, "Mrs. Osborne says she's the very best. Ugh, what's her name? It's short. Something like . . . like . . ."

"Claire Gray?" I asked.

"That's it!" both Thad and Kwynn responded.

"Of *course*," said Pierce, "she's a playwright too. A few years back, she wrote *Traders*—it was a hit on Broadway and became a hot movie."

Thad asked me, "Then you already know about her?"

"Sure, I know about her. I also happen to *know* her. She was in Chicago a couple of years ago and attended the housewarming party that Neil and I gave at our loft. In fact"—I paused for effect, *dramatic* effect—"I danced with her."

Kwynn was wide-eyed. "*Really*, Mr. Manning?" Thad seemed no less surprised. Pierce cocked his head skeptically.

"Yes, *really*." I laughed. "Just because none of you have ever seen me dance with a woman doesn't mean I can't do it." Sitting back, I added, "Claire thought I was pretty good."

Pierce asked, "So it's 'Claire,' huh? You're on a first-name basis."

"We are," I stated flatly.

"Hey"—Thad thought of something. "You could write our letters of recommendation, Mark. Kwynn and I would be *sure* to get in."

"Hold on," I said, suddenly not so smug. "We don't know *anything* about this school—it isn't even *built* yet. And it's halfway around the world."

From the side of his mouth, Pierce reminded me, "It's four hours by plane."

Thad said, "You too, Sheriff. Can we count on you for letters?"

Pierce was obviously flattered, but he took his cue from my reticence. "Once everyone's decided on the schools where you should apply—of course, I'd be happy to recommend you. Both of you."

Both Thad and Kwynn were getting googly over these prospects when Nancy came to the table with Berta. Nancy lilted, "I hope everyone saved room for you know *wha-aat*," as Berta began clearing dishes.

Great, I thought. Just what the kids needed. Get a little sugar in them, and they'd be bouncing off the walls.

Dessert, it turned out, was a sensible concoction of mixed berries, heavy cream, and a drizzle of booze, so the fructose was blunted by the alcohol. By the time we left the restaurant, Thad and Kwynn were still bubbly, but short of hyper. Out on the street, they thanked me for lunch and the earlier office tour, then took off together to check on weekend reservations at the theater office, leaving Pierce and me to walk back to the *Register*.

Along the way, Pierce asked, "Was it just my imagination, or is there something going on between Kwynn and Thad?"

I shrugged. I sighed. "Beats me. It seems they're closer than I thought. Whether it's friendship or romance, I can't tell."

Pierce laughed softly. "Chances are, neither can they."

"God. They're talking about going off to *college* together. I wonder if Neil has picked up on that." We were walking past his office, and I could see that he had not yet returned from his lunch meeting. My question would have to wait.

Pierce and I continued voicing these idle speculations, but as we approached the door to the *Register*'s lobby, he stopped speaking in the middle of a thought, reached inside his jacket, and unclipped the pager from his belt. Peering at it, shading it from the sunlight with his hand, he told me, "It's Vernon. I can call him from my car, or we could go up to your office."

"Let's go upstairs." I opened the door for him. Entering, I waved to Connie, and we climbed the stairs.

Leading Pierce across the newsroom, I headed straight for my office without greeting staff or snooping at the city desk. Glancing up, Lucy noted my rushed entrance, and deducing correctly that there was a development on the Jason Thrush story, she followed Pierce to my office.

I waved her in. "The coroner just paged Doug—toxicology, I assume."

Pierce was already dialing from my desk. A few seconds later, he said, "Yes, Vernon. What have you got?"

Pierce listened, nodding, then said, "Hold on a moment, Vernon. I'd better take notes." So he sat at my desk, clicked his pen, and began writing on a pad that I kept near the phone.

Lucy and I glanced at each other, antsy for information, while Pierce scribbled, occasionally asking for spellings. His half of the conversation revealed little, though, consisting mainly of mumbled uh-huhs and okays. At last he said, "Thanks for putting a rush on it, Vernon. I'll see you later this afternoon." And he hung up the phone.

Lucy and I both stared at him with an expression that asked, Well . . . ?

He looked over his notes briefly, then summarized, "Toxicology tests have revealed the presence of choline and muscarine in Jason's remains, pointing to poisoning by the mushroom known as"—he squinted at his writing—"fly agaric."

I tossed my hands in the air. "Frank Gelden was right on the mark. Just last night, he told me that if Jason died from mushrooms, it was probably fly agaric."

Pierce continued, "Since fatalities from this species are rare, and since the mushrooms themselves were not found in the victim's stomach, the circumstances are deemed highly suspicious. Vernon will issue his final report later today."

"Unless I'm mistaken," said Lucy, "the Jason Thrush case has moved up a notch."

"Yes, indeed." Pierce stood. "Jason's routine postmortem has just launched a murder investigation."

PART THREE

Midsummer Night

DEADLY MUSHROOMS

Toxicology tests suggest foul play in mysterious death of Jason Thrush

By CHARLES OAKLAND
Staff Reporter, Dumont Daily Register

Aug. 8, DUMONT WI—In a report issued late yesterday, Dumont County coroner Vernon Formhals concluded that Jason Thrush, 17, died last Friday as the result of mushroom poisoning. Circumstances surrounding the tragic death point to foul play.

Dr. Formhals told the *Register*, "The mechanism of death was respiratory failure. Toxicology revealed the presence of choline and muscarine in the boy's body, which produced deadly complications to a common cold."

The toxins are associated with a species of mushroom known as fly agaric *(Amanita muscaria)*, which is found locally at this time of year. However, a large amount of these mushrooms would have to be ingested to prove deadly, and under analysis, the victim's stomach contents did not include mushrooms.

"Because these particular toxins act quickly," explained Formhals, "the mushrooms would still have been in the boy's stomach had he accidentally eaten them. The presence of these toxins, then, is highly suspicious. As there is no circumstantial evidence suggesting suicide, we can only conclude that the manner of death was homicide."

Dumont County sheriff Douglas Pierce is leading the police investigation, which is already under way. He told the *Register*, "Several leads are being actively pursued, but there are currently no firm suspects."

Pierce cited the perplexing biology of the boy's death as a formidable hurdle to unraveling the mystery. "We've isolated the telltale toxins," he said, "but they left no sign of the mushrooms themselves. How, then, was Jason Thrush poisoned?"

The victim was a student, athlete, and actor who would have entered his senior year at Unity High this fall. His death on Friday occurred a mere two hours before he was to appear in *Teen Play*, the current production of the Dumont Players Guild. ❑

Wednesday, August 8

I awoke to a noise, not startled, but simply aware that I was no longer sleeping. Though my mind was not fully alert, my brain tried to analyze what I'd heard while assuring me that its source was benign. A flushed toilet? A distant car? A single, light cough or snore from Neil? Then I heard it again, but more distant. Smiling with the satisfaction of a mystery solved, I knew that the morning paper had landed on my porch, then another copy had landed next door. The *Dumont Daily Register* was peppering the town.

Rolling onto my back, I saw that it was not yet dawn. Beyond the French doors on the far wall of our bedroom, the sunporch was washed with a gentle bluish light, not from the sun, but still from the moon.

Close your eyes, I told myself. Go back to sleep.

But my sleep that night had been restless at best. It was now official: Dumont had a murder on its hands. A killer was at large, and due to the timing of an adolescent spat, a number of locals believed that the killer was Thad. When the town awoke today and read my own front-page story detailing the coroner's report that Jason Thrush had in fact been murdered—and that the bizarre weapon was poisonous mushrooms—fuel would be added to the smoldering suspicion that already whorled around Thad, suspicion that could well ignite into an ugly public outcry.

Close your eyes, I told myself. Such fretting is neither logical nor warranted, at least not yet. Go back to sleep.

But sleep was now impossible. At best, I could simply try to rest, to store a bit of energy for a day that promised to be difficult. And there was no point in disturbing Neil. Glancing to my side, I saw him in the dim, ambient moonlight, sprawled under the sheet, one leg fetchingly exposed. I stifled the tremor of a gentle, silent laugh, recalling his performance the night before, out on the sunporch. Making good on his promise to surprise me with a gift of ecstasy, my "fantasy masseur" had done that and more—he had reminded me that everything I wanted, I already had.

These pleasant thoughts, I knew, could not erase the vexing Jason-and-Thad issue, but they did provide a respite from my worries, and I must have dozed. Minutes escaped me, and my head rolled on the pillow. A lazy eye drifted open, aimed at the doors to the sunporch. Still no daylight. Still only moonlight. Still, it seemed, a midsummer night. Somewhere in that netherworld between waking and sleeping, between thinking and dreaming, I relived the pleasures of the previous night, when mushrooms had danced.

Neil appeared—buffed and ready and crisply dressed in white. Announcing his payback, he said no more. With a gesture, he invited me to the sunporch, where he'd arranged a bench like an altar for the purpose of physical, manual worship. Oiling his hands, he touched my body, starting with my head, exploring every inch. He both lulled and excited me. Relaxed and stimulated, I rode waves of emotion that stemmed as much from the mind as from the groin. Ultimately, though, it was indeed the groin that was the focus of his attentions, the focus of my waning consciousness. The orgasm, when at last it came, was both eerie and wonderful—eerie because it seemed to draw life itself from me, yet wonderful because I surrendered it so fully and willingly to Neil. He watched with a woozy smile as I thrashed beneath his hands. A moment later, he thrilled me with the sight of his own ejaculation. Then we kissed. It seemed like hours. But finally, my erotic massage was over.

And the cleanup began. Neil was drenched with sweat, my entire body was an oily mess, and we were both splattered with semen so thick, it was gummy. We laughed at ourselves; Neil even apologized for my unctuous condition as we both attempted to towel me off, but with little success. I needed a shower, but even that left a slippery sheen on my skin—oil and water don't mix. While Neil had acquitted himself superbly at mimicking the ministrations of a professional masseur, this last detail, in truth, fell short.

"What's so funny?"

I blinked. The ceiling reflected the soft glow of early daylight. Neil's whisper had cut through my dream.

"You were laughing in your sleep," he told me through his own quiet laugh.

I rolled my head on the pillow to look at him. "Morning, gorgeous. Sorry I woke you."

He propped himself on one elbow. "You sounded happy."

"Ecstatic. I was reliving one of the best nights of my life."

He grinned. "Was I there?"

"Uh-huh."

"What was I doing?"

I tossed back the sheet to give him a gander. "*That.*"

He stretched to look at the clock radio over my shoulder. "Officially, we don't wake up for another twenty minutes."

I rolled toward him and burrowed into him. "Twenty minutes ought to do it."

"In a pinch."

And together, we made a bit of spontaneous, free-form magic.

Once again, mushrooms danced.

Once again, Neil and I were a few minutes late for breakfast, arriving in the kitchen together, still enjoying some afterglow.

Once again, Pierce had already arrived and was arranging things on the table in our absence. Barb puttered at the sink.

"Morning," I announced brightly, hanging my sport coat on the back of my usual chair.

"Yeah," said Barb—she was running water, perhaps scrubbing vegetables.

"*Well* now," said Pierce, looking up from the bagged kringle he was ripping open. "Did you guys have another late night?"

"No," Neil answered innocently, "just a little slow this morning." As he sat at the table, he caught my eye, and we both grinned, telegraphing the cause of our tardiness.

Pierce shook his head, suppressing a laugh. "You guys . . ."

Moving to the counter to get the coffeepot, I glanced over to the sink. Barb was indeed cleaning vegetables—a pile of them—potatoes and green beans, plus the raw beginnings of an extravagant salad. This struck me as an odd sort of kitchen duty for seven-something in the morning. With a laugh, I asked, "What's all that?"

"Just working ahead," she told me without looking at me. "You've got a dinner guest tomorrow night."

I shrugged. "I appreciate the effort, Barb, but don't knock yourself out. It's just a casual family meal, plus one."

She nodded. "That's what your note said. Who is it, if I might ask?"

I'd been rushed yesterday morning, and my note, I realized, lacked detail. "Sorry, I wasn't trying to be mysterious. Frank Gelden is coming over."

She shut off the water and turned to me. "Frank?"

"Yes, Frank." I crossed to the table and began pouring coffee. Over my shoulder, I asked, "Why, do you mind?"

"No, of course not." She primped her hair, tucked in her polo shirt—you'd have thought Frank was arriving in thirty-six seconds, not thirty-six hours. "Where's wifey-poo?"

Neil reminded Barb, "Her name's *Cynthia*. She often works in Green Bay during the middle of the week. Frank's Thursday was open, so we asked him over."

I sat down next to Pierce, telling him, "The invitation's still open, Doug, if you'd like to join us."

He shook his head. "Thanks, but I can't. That committee meeting—public safety. It starts early and always runs late."

Barb said, "Then come for dessert. We'll save you a spot." This implied, of course, that she'd be dining with us that night, as was her habit. She went to the refrigerator, popped a can of diet cola, and joined us at the breakfast table.

"We'll see." Pierce's reticent tone signaled other things—more important things—on his mind. That morning's *Register* lay there on the table, folded to my page-one article about the coroner's report.

I said what we were all thinking: "By now, the whole town knows that Jason was actually murdered. Before, we were working with theories, but now, we're faced with the elusive realities of a vexing crime. The pressure's on."

"Tell me," said Pierce. "Harley Kaiser, our esteemed district attorney, was already feeling pressure from Burton Thrush to push the coroner for his report. Now Kaiser is pressuring *me* for an arrest—he phoned me at home last night. Jeez, the official murder investigation is less than a day old." Pierce slurped some coffee, pushing away his Danish, having apparently lost taste for it.

Neil asked him, "Where do you start?"

"Back at the Thrush residence. When in doubt, start with the family. Both Burton and Mica had the most to gain from Jason's death. They're also the two people who can give us the most intimate background on the victim, if they're willing. All of our other leads are highly speculative at this point." Pierce turned to me. "But that's where *you* could do some effective digging, Mark."

"I'll be at it all day." Reaching behind me to the jacket I'd hung on my chair, I fished my notebook from a pocket, opened it, and reviewed my plans aloud. "First thing this morning, Denny Diggins is coming down to the office for that 'features interview' with Glee. Depending on what he says, I may need to explore other leads. In any event, I want to meet with Dr. Formhals and try to get a better handle on the biology involved. It's also time for a heart-to-heart with Nancy Sanderson at First Avenue Grill; I need to explore the history of bad blood between her and the Thrushes. By the way"—I looked up from my notes with a wry smile—"I wish you'd told me that the restaurant trashed by Jason and his pals was the Grill. I've found Nancy's behavior suspicious since Saturday night, but I couldn't imagine what might have motivated her apparent antagonism toward Jason."

Grinning, Pierce countered, "If you'd clued me that you'd found Nancy suspicious, I'd have supplied you with a motive."

Neil suppressed a laugh.

With a shrug, I conceded the point. Uncapping my pen, I made a new note, telling Pierce, "Even though you've already questioned the entire cast of the play, I'm beginning to think I should have a talk with Nicole Winkler, the girl Jason dumped last year. Ditto for Tommy Morales—if there's time."

Pierce nodded, impressed with my plans. "You'll be busy today."

"I *have* to be, Doug. There are already enough people convinced that Thad killed Jason, making good on the very public threat he made last Wednesday night. Now that the word is out that Jason was indeed murdered—with mushrooms, no less—it won't take long for word to spread that Thad is an apt, avid student of mycology." I wasn't about to mention the jar of fly agaric I'd found in his bedroom, so I concluded, "Thad's interest in mushrooms is just another nail in his coffin."

Barb choked on her soda. *"That's* a morbid metaphor."

I laughed lamely. "Sorry."

Pierce laughed with me. "Let's hope it doesn't come to that."

Though I appreciated his sentiments, I'd have been all the more grateful if he'd said, It *won't* come to that.

Neil brought the discussion back to basics. "The surest way to clear Thad is to expose the actual killer."

"You make it sound so simple," Pierce joshed. Then he pushed back his chair and stood, telling me, "I've got work to do, and the sooner the better. Call me if you learn anything, okay, Mark?"

"Absolutely."

I made a move to get up, but Pierce gestured that we should all stay seated. We exchanged a round of good-byes and good-lucks; then Pierce left the kitchen through the back door.

Neil, Barb, and I continued discussing the past day's developments on the case, but it soon became apparent that the answer to the central question—whodunit?—was simply beyond our grasp.

Barb stifled a belch, picked up her soda can and a plate bearing the remains of a bagel, and carried them to the sink. Pitching her trash in a waste bin under the counter, she turned over her shoulder, musing, "So Frank's coming to dinner . . ."

I grinned at Neil, then told Barb, "*That* was an unusual segue; we were talking about murder. It seems tomorrow night's dinner has captured your imagination."

"Obviously." She smirked. "So Frank's coming to dinner . . . without Cindy." She turned on the water, then ran the garbage disposal, which roared as it ground up something. At a subliminal level, was Barb watching Cynthia Dunne-Gelden swirl down the drain, feet first, screaming?

Neil ventured, "It seems you still carry something of a torch for the guy."

Barb shut off the disposal and turned to us with a blank look. "Excuse me?"

I laughed. "God, Barb, could you *be* more transparent?"

She stepped halfway to the table, hands on hips. "What *are* you talking about?" She looked me in the eye, then Neil, then me again.

I explained, "You've perked up every time we've mentioned Frank's name. When we first talked about him last Thursday morning, you remembered him from high school as a nerd, and you were intrigued by Doug's statement that he'd matured into an attractive man. Then when you *met* Frank at Saturday night's party, your eyes nearly sprang out of your head."

"I admit," she said, crossing the remaining steps to the table, standing between Neil and me, "Frank is a much better-looking man than the kid I knew in school."

"Uh-huh." Neil nodded knowingly. "But then Cynthia arrived in the kitchen, and when you learned she was Frank's wife, you seemed stunned. Face it, Barb, you've got the hots for Frank." Under his breath, he added, "Not that I blame you."

"Listen, smart-ass." Barb sat in the chair between us, leaning toward Neil. "If I seemed stunned when I met wifey-poo, it was *not* 'cause I used to think Frank was a dweeb—which he was. No, the wife blew me away 'cause I used to think Frank was *gay*. We all did."

Her words came as a jolt to both Neil and me. I recalled meeting Frank the previous Wednesday night—my gaydar had gone on full alert. But then I saw his wedding ring, which spoke volumes more than our housekeeper's high school gossip. Neil lectured Barb, "Just goes to show how wrong you were."

She shook her head, clucking, then singsonged, "I'm not so su-uure."

"Barb," I said, leaning forward on the table, "why not just admit you were wrong and give Frank the benefit of the doubt. He's married."

Neil added, "Eight happy years."

"You *guys*." Barb rolled her eyes, laughing. "Haven't you ever heard of a marriage of convenience?"

"I'm familiar with the term," I assured her, "but there's not a reason in the world to think that Frank and Cynthia's marriage is anything less than genuine, loving, and committed."

Neil nodded once—so there.

But Barb wouldn't let up. She asked rotely, "Who's older—Frank or Cindy?"

Neil answered, "Cynthia is forty-three, three years older than Frank. So what?"

"Who makes more money—Frank or Cindy?"

Neil conceded, "Cynthia does *very* well, yes. Frank's a teacher."

Barb had another question: "Who's prettier—Frank or Cindy?"

There was a pause as Neil and I looked at each other. I answered, "I don't mean to sound cruel, but objectively speaking, Frank is far better-looking."

Barb nodded. "I'm stabbing at this one, but who's the better cook?"

My sense memory of Frank's crown roast of lamb still made my mouth water. I told Barb, "Don't be ridiculous."

She shrugged. "Can't win 'em all. Still, I trust I've made my point." She rose from the table, picked up everything but our coffee, and took the dishes to the sink.

Neil lolled back in his chair, finishing his coffee, looking slightly perplexed. I reached across the table, refilled his cup from the pot, then sat back, mirroring his languid position. I mirrored his perplexed expression as well. We looked at each other, silently asking, Could Barb be right?

Oddly, when I'd first met Frank, I'd *hoped* he was gay. Now, with someone *telling* me he was gay, I was reluctant to believe it. I didn't even *want* to believe it. We'd visited the Geldens' home and had already become a small part of their lives. This whiff of sexual intrigue became an oddball variable in the equation of our couple-to-couple friendship, an unsettling unknown, just at the time when I'd happily (and lustily) reaffirmed my "couplehood" with Neil. I'd finally learned to rein my roving eye. The last thing I needed to confront right now was temptation of the flesh—Frank's flesh.

Barb finished cleaning the coffeemaker and loading the dishwasher. Wiping her hands, she told us, "It's all set to go. Just load your cups and push the button."

Neil asked her, "Headed out on errands already? It's early."

"Nah. Thought I'd go upstairs and do some practicing—if it won't disturb you."

"Not at all," I told her as I rose from the table, crossing to the sink with my old *Chicago Journal* mug and the coffeemaker's glass pot. "Have you started the clarinet lessons yet?"

She grimaced. "Tonight. It's all set up. Thanks for introducing me to Whitney Greer. Nice man, very engaging—he took a real interest in my background as a money manager. He was also very helpful—found me a teacher from the orchestra."

Neil said, "We heard you practicing yesterday. You're *good*, Barb."

"I *was* good, years ago. It's gonna be a long road back."

"That piece," I said, "the piece you were playing yesterday—what was it? It was hauntingly beautiful, but I couldn't quite place it. It sounded modern. And French, right?" I rinsed the coffeepot, swirling hot water in it.

"Yup. Olivier Messiaen. It's from the third movement of his *Quartet for the End of Time*."

"How cheery," said Neil. He rose and joined us at the sink, rinsing his cup.

She explained dryly, "The composer wrote it from a German prison camp in 1941—he was having a bad day."

Feeling chastised, Neil told her, "Sorry. Didn't mean to be glib." He put our cups in the dishwasher and turned it on.

I said, "The melancholy running through the music was unmistakable. But I thought I heard bird sounds as well."

"Very *good.*" Barbs pasted an imaginary gold star on my forehead. "The third movement—highly unusual, being a long clarinet solo—is titled '*Abîme des Oiseaux,*' or 'Abyss of the Birds.' Later, Messiaen would frequently mimic birdsong in his music, but this was the first instance. I've got my work cut out for me; it's a difficult piece." She folded and hung the dish towel she'd been using.

I nodded. "Keep pluggin', Barb. I'm impressed that you can play it at *all.*"

"Thanks." Her smile verged on a grin. She wasn't the type to take a compliment with grace, but when it came to her music, she clearly appreciated my praise, accepting it without a snappy comeback. She told us simply, "Time to practice," and left the kitchen, heading toward the front stairs.

Neil told me, "You've got to admire her—chucking a lucrative career at forty and pursuing another interest, just for the love of it."

I thought of Thad and his eagerness to pursue theater in college, "just for the love of it," as Neil had said. I asked him, "Do you think that Barb actually intends to *pursue* music—I mean, as a career?"

He shrugged. "With Barb, who knows?" He picked up a shopping list from the counter, moved to the table, and sat, adding a few items to the list, presumably for dinner the next night with Frank Gelden.

Joining Neil at the table, I asked him, "What'd you think of Barb's theory—that the Geldens have a marriage of convenience?"

He paused, looking up from the list. "Barb made some interesting points. Certain aspects of Frank and Cynthia's relationship do seem a bit offbeat, at least collectively. Still, there's no reason to suspect that their marriage is anything other than 'real.' Even if kids in school *did* think that Frank was gay, that doesn't mean anything—maybe he was just 'different.' In any event, he's been committed to Cynthia for eight years, so even if he *was* gay, he's made some difficult decisions, which we need to respect. Case closed."

I nodded. There was nothing else to be said on this topic; there was no point in weighing the what-ifs. As I mulled this, a clarinet interrupted my thoughts. Barb was practicing some warm-up scales, which bounced through the silence of the house like bubbles of sound.

"Actually," said Neil, "there's *another* relationship that concerns me much more right now."

Uh-oh. *Our* relationship? Was something wrong?

He answered my unspoken question: "Roxanne and Carl."

"*Oh,*" I said, sounding too relieved. "What about their relationship?"

"Exactly—what's going on? Rox left here in a dither on Monday morning, and we haven't heard a peep since. I'm getting the uneasy feeling that she may be waffling about her move-in with Carl. I'm going to phone her today."

"Good idea. You ought to be able to catch her at the office."

Neil perused the amended shopping list, but the wrinkles of a frown confirmed that his thoughts were occupied by Roxanne, not groceries.

"Hi, guys."

Neil and I looked up. Thad had just entered the kitchen from the hall. He was barefoot, wearing fleece workout shorts and a huge T-shirt. His hair was a tangle, as if he'd just rolled out of bed and grabbed anything handy to wear downstairs.

"Morning, Thad." My chipper tone masked suspicion that something was wrong.

Neil laughed softly. "A bit early for *you*, isn't it? Did Barb's clarinet wake you?"

Thad shook his head and answered quietly, "I was already awake. I had trouble sleeping, so I thought I might as well get up." He crossed the room to the refrigerator, opened it, and took out a carton of milk.

Neil and I glanced at each other, concerned. I told Thad, "Barb wrapped up some bagels for you; they're in the cupboard. Or would you like some toast?"

He shook his head, poured a glass of milk, and brought it to the table.

Neil said, "You seemed sort of quiet at dinner last night. What's wrong?"

Barb finished her scales. There was a pause. Then she began playing the baleful opening measures of the Messiaen solo.

Thad told us, "When Kwynn and I went over to the theater after lunch yesterday, Mr. Diggins was there, onstage with Tommy Morales. He was running Tommy through Ryan's blocking."

I wasn't quite sure what this meant, but it didn't sound good for

Thad. On the other hand, it sounded promising indeed for the ambitious little Tommy Morales.

Neil asked Thad, mainly for my benefit, "You mean, Tommy was getting the stage directions for your role?"

Thad nodded. "When Mr. Diggins saw me there with Kwynn, he got real nervous. He told me not to worry. He said that nothing was changed, that everything would be normal at tonight's pickup rehearsal. Just to be on the safe side, though, he'd asked Tommy to start learning my part. He called it a . . . what?"

"Contingency," I reminded him.

Barb's clarinet stuttered on the pained song of a blackbird—a blackbird calling from an abyss.

"Yeah," said Thad. "Contingency."

I couldn't help marveling at—and mourning—Thad's transformation since Tuesday's lunch, when he and Kwynn had nearly bounced out of their chairs anticipating the adventures of their theatrical pursuits in college. Minutes later, when they'd visited the Dumont Playhouse, Thad's future hopes had been put on hold while Denny Diggins and Tommy Morales weighed their contingencies. Now, it seemed, just as I had dreaded, Thad felt the full impact of the situation that whorled around him, worsening day by day. I feared that he feared arrest, despite our shaky assurances that that could never happen. Worse, I feared that this whole experience would sour him on theater—that he would revert to the brooding indifference that had marred his earlier years of adolescence—that he would grow into adulthood without direction or passion.

Denny Diggins, a man whom I had never liked, played a role in all this, but the extent of his role was unclear to me. So on Wednesday morning, waiting for Glee Savage to interview Denny for a trumped-up midrun feature on *Teen Play*, my emotions were thoroughly mixed. Was Denny friend or foe?

Friend: he had written a play, had given my nephew an opportunity to gain valuable experience and exposure starring in it, had himself been victimized by the opening-night loss of a leading actor, and was now struggling to hold the show together while the police attempted to solve the crime.

Or foe: he had been partner to a secret, soured tryst with Jason

Thrush, had himself murdered the boy, had somehow colluded with another young actor, the scheming Tommy Morales, and they were both now attempting to scapegoat Thad.

Mulling these polar possibilities, I looked up from my desk to see the subject of my thoughts, Denny Diggins himself, being escorted across the newsroom by the *Register*'s features editor, Glee Savage. Though the morning was warm, promising a return to oppressive August heat, Denny wore a navy, double-breasted blazer, charcoal wool slacks, and a white, button-down shirt, collar open—very correct, very theatrical— he lacked only a paisley silk ascot. Not to be outdone, Glee wore yet another of her fashion-forward ensembles, bright and summery, which included both a purse *and* a hat—a bloodred straw hat with a huge, flat, round brim. She looked for all the world like a cardinal (not a bird, but a prince of the church) in procession through the newsroom.

According to plan, she breezed by my outer office, stopping in the doorway to announce, "Denny Diggins is here, Mark. He's kindly consented to an interview for a follow-up feature I'm planning about his play."

"Hello, Denny." I showed barely enough interest to look up from my desk.

He nodded prissily. "Mahk."

I returned my attention to the pile of proofs on my desk.

"Uh, Mark," Glee continued, exactly as scripted, "I really hate to disturb you, but the regular conference room is booked, and my own office is cramped. Might I impose upon you to use your outer office?"

With a why-not shrug and a be-my-guest gesture, I admitted them. Step into my parlor, I thought smugly.

Glee took one of the stuffed chairs around the low table, positioning herself so that Denny would sit where I could see him squarely from my desk. She set down her purse (but left her hat on—it was a "statement," after all) and arranged a folder of notes and clippings, along with her pen, pad, and tape recorder, on the table in front of her. Denny waited, crossing his legs, lolling, spindling a lock of his dyed-auburn hair around an index finger.

"Shall we begin?" asked Glee with a pert smile, snapping on her tape recorder.

"Of course. I was flattered to receive your call, Glee."

"In some ways, I imagine, *Teen Play* has been successful beyond your wildest dreams. With the opening weekend behind you, are there any thoughts you'd like to share regarding the intense public interest generated by this production?"

He considered his words before answering. "I'd *like* to say that the acclaim for *Teen Play* is simply based on the show's own merits." He laughed quietly. "However, as we all know, *other* factors have lent an unexpected element of notoriety to the production." As he said this, his glance moved from Glee to me, meeting my eyes as I watched.

Glee said, "You're referring, I presume, to the tragic death of Jason Thrush."

"Certainly." Denny bowed his head, shaking it. "A dreadful, inexplicable loss."

Glee glanced at me before telling Denny, "It's no longer inexplicable. The coroner says it was murder."

Denny looked up. "Really? Is it official?"

"Yes, indeed. Dr. Formhals issued his report late yesterday, and there was a front-page piece in this morning's *Register*."

"Oh." He squirmed some. "I haven't seen today's paper." Then he added, doubtless for my benefit, "I don't subscribe."

Feeling I'd just been invited into the conversation, I said from my desk, "I should think you'd want to stay on top of this story, Denny. Here's the scoop: Jason was murdered. He was poisoned. With mushrooms, if you can imagine."

"*Mushrooms?*" Denny twisted in his chair to face me directly. "You can't be *serious*, Mahk."

I stood, asking flatly, "Do you think I'd joke about such a thing?"

He raised his hands delicately in a mollifying gesture. "Of course not. But you must admit, it all sounds rather . . . unlikely. I mean, how does one poison one with mushrooms—bake nasty little toadstools in a crusty little ramekin and leave it at one's doorstep?" He snorted at the intended absurdity of his question.

"We don't *know* how one does it," I answered, aping his prim syntax. Stepping out of my office and into the conference area, I added, "There were no mushrooms in Jason's stomach. We don't know how the toxins were ingested."

Denny raised a hand to his mouth. "Ugh. Such a grisly business—dissection and such. Poor Jason. Such a beautiful, *mah*-velous young man. To think that he's been . . . *butchered* in the search for mere 'evidence.' "

Glee jumped in, soothingly. "You were close, you and Jason?"

Denny looked at her, astounded. "Well, *yes*. He was my star, my leading man."

Glee noted, "So is Thad Quatrain. Do you feel close to Thad?"

Wary of the question, Denny watched Glee for a moment, then looked at me, explaining, "Yes, I *do* feel close to Thad. He's a wonderful young man—intelligent, talented, dedicated to the show. I respect Thad a great deal. He's been a pleasure to work with."

I had to ask, "Is that why you've been coaching Tommy Morales to take over Thad's role?"

Denny sighed. "Mahk, I fell *terrible* that Thad caught me 'in the act' yesterday afternoon. Please understand—I'm simply taking precautionary measures, looking out for the best interests of the show—that's my job. The sad truth is, I'm not fully confident of Thad's ability to carry the last three performances."

"Why? Because he might be arrested?"

"Heavens *no*," Denny replied without hesitation. "Thad was *mah*-velous Friday night, as he had been throughout rehearsals. But the whole business of Jason's death has clearly gotten to him. You saw Saturday's performance—he slipped terribly. And Sunday was worse. I'll have to see how things go at tonight's pickup rehearsal. I'm hoping that with a few days' rest, Thad will bounce back tonight. If not . . . well, I'll face some very difficult decisions."

As much as I hated to admit it, Denny's words made sense, and he seemed genuinely distraught at the prospect of replacing Thad in the cast. "Okay," I said, "I appreciate your respect for Thad, and I believe your statement that you feel close to him. Is it the same sort of closeness that you felt for Jason Thrush?"

Denny hesitated. "This is not intended to disparage Thad in the least, but I always felt there was something special about Jason. I can't define it. I don't understand it. He had a certain magnetism, a star quality." Denny paused, indulging in his memory of the boy.

Without implication, I asked quietly, directly, "Did you love him?"

Denny nodded, exhaling a soft laugh. "Yes, I suppose I did. Jason . . . *demanded* love, didn't he? Like a beautiful horse, or a dog, a pet. It seemed he *existed* to be loved; his role in the world was to be loved. He was golden. Did I love him? Of course I did . . ." His voice trailed off with emotion.

I stepped around the furniture and closed the door to the newsroom;

our space became suddenly hushed. Crossing to Glee's chair, standing behind her, I asked Denny, "Were you and Jason lovers?"

His head was bent, and it froze in that position for a moment, as if he hadn't heard me, as if he had died. But then he slowly looked up, his eyes meeting mine. His features twisted with an emotion I couldn't peg—fear, dismay, repugnance? His lips stretched and his mouth opened to voice a single syllable: *"What?"*

Glee touched my leg, signaling that I shouldn't speak. She told Denny, "You've told us that you loved Jason. Did you express that love through a physical relationship with him?"

"Good *God,*" Denny muttered as his face fell to his hands. Then he simply, openly broke into tears. Through childish sobs, he told us, "You people are *sick.*"

Glee and I looked at each other, uncertain what to make of the situation. She got up, moving to the chair next to Denny. I also sat down next to him, opposite Glee. She leaned to him, patting his knee. "What do you mean, Denny? Why are we 'sick'?"

With a petulant sneer, he looked at me, swiping tears from his cheek with the back of his hand. He turned and told Glee, "You people are always ready to assume that love is sex, or *repressed* sex, or dirty. My God, you're both mature and savvy. Can't you appreciate that I truly loved Jason without thinking of him *that way?* Must it always boil down to *fucking?*" And again Denny wept.

If this was an act, it was a good one. I felt ashamed and embarrassed in the face of such naked emotion. "Denny . . . ," I began.

"*You,* Mahk, surely *you* understand the depth of feeling that such a boy can nurture. But I did *not* lust for him. If that were the basis of my love for him, do you think I'd dare hope that Jason could love *me?*" Denny vaguely gestured to himself with both open palms, looking vulnerable and pathetic.

I sighed, unsure what to tell him. "Jason's sister, Mica—"

"Oh, please. Gag me." He rolled his reddened eyes.

I laughed, grateful to find even a shred of humor in our conversation. "Jason's sister surprised Sheriff Pierce and me with something she said on Monday. She told us that Jason was gay."

Denny shrugged. "I think he was, yes. So?"

I plunged ahead. "She suggested that you and Jason had been having an extended affair, which had soured. She claimed to have heard Jason fighting with you on the phone, and—"

"My *God*," Denny nearly shrieked. "You think that I'm the *killer?*"

Glee to the rescue. "No, Denny, of course not. It's just that certain aspects of Mica's story seemed to add up: Jason was gay, and he'd been working with you on the play, and—"

Denny shrieked. "You think that I'm *gay?*"

Glee looked at me; my blank expression told her that she was on her own. She answered Denny, "Well . . . *yes.* Aren't you?"

I was tempted to add, Not that there's anything wrong with that.

"*No,*" he insisted, sitting upright, hands on hips.

I borrowed his previous line: "Oh, please. Gag me."

He turned to me, looking a mite steamed. "Mahk," he minced, "you, of all people, should be sensitive to the dangers of stereotyping. The way I dress, walk, or e-*nun*-ci-ate is no accurate barometer of my psychosexual makeup. Your stud-muffin charade"—he pronounced it with a French twist, *sha-ROD*—"is certainly no barometer of *yours.*" Harrumph.

I lifted a hand to my forehead. Glee stifled a laugh. I asked him flatly, "Are you seriously asking us to believe that you're straight?"

"Mr. Manning"—he eyed me coldly—"I don't give a shit *what* you believe."

"Yeah, Mr. Diggins? My readers might give a—"

Again, Glee to the rescue. "I think what Mark is trying to say is that public opinion can be extremely volatile, especially in a small town. The circumstances of Jason's death seem to have everyone on edge. When word gets around—as it surely will—that there may have been a sexual angle to the murder, people will start to see you in a suspicious light. Your best strategy is preemptive, Denny. Why not just clear the air on this issue?"

Glee deserved a raise. Come Friday, she'd notice a blip on her stub.

Denny nodded, weighing all this. "It's really no one's business, but the truth of the matter is that I'm—God, I hate the word—asexual."

I glanced at Glee for help, but saw that I was on my own. "You mean . . . you're, uh, sterile?"

He tisked. "I *mean,* sex just doesn't interest me. I don't, in the parlance, 'swing' *either* way. I'm a virgin at forty-eight, okay? Satisfied? Go ahead—laugh it up."

I wasn't laughing. Though I suddenly saw Denny as a self-deceptive, sexually confused, and tormented middle-aged man, I found it unlikely, given the enormity of his ego, that these humiliating admissions were lies. In short, I believed his contention that he was not actively gay. There was a further consideration: Denny had clearly been stressed on Friday evening when his play's leading actor failed to appear for the opening performance. These two factors led me to believe, with a measure of disappointment, that Denny was not the culprit. Mica Thrush, the victim's sister, was seemingly wrong. Had she merely invented the whole story of her brother's liaison with Denny as a means of diverting suspicion from herself? Or was she somehow mistaken on the details?

I rose from the chair without comment, stepping to the window wall that separated my offices from the newsroom. Facing out, I watched the midmorning activity through the huge pane of plate glass. Behind me, Denny breathed heavily, his emotions spent. Glee riffled through her notes.

Then the rustle of paper stopped. "The phone calls," said Glee.

I turned. Denny looked up at me, then over to Glee.

She said to Denny, "You've told a number of people that you repeatedly tried phoning Jason on Friday afternoon, concerned about his recovery from his cold."

Denny nodded, affirming, "I was nervous as a cat that day—with good reason."

"But"—I stepped near him—"the police have checked the computerized phone records, and there were no calls traceable to you that afternoon, in or out, on any of the several lines that serve the Thrush residence."

He shook his head, stating flatly, "That's impossible. I phoned at least six or eight times from noon onward, leaving messages on the machine."

Glee suggested, "Or on voice mail."

"Whatever," he snapped. "What's the difference?"

"Denny," I said, sitting on the arm of the chair next to him, "it's pointless to lie about this. The records are clear-cut. The police can check your own phone records as well, which'll only prove—"

Glee interrupted with a new thought. "What number did you phone, Denny?"

With a put-upon sigh, he fished a classic "little black book" from the inside pocket of his blazer. He noisily flipped its tiny, gilt-edged pages. "Thrush, Jason," he said; then he read us the phone number.

Glee and I looked at each other, my pinched features mirroring hers.

"That exchange doesn't sound right," she said, having worked at the paper for decades. "In fact, it's not familiar as a local exchange at all."

I guessed, "Maybe it's a cell phone." Sitting in the chair, I reached for the speakerphone and slid it near me on the low table. When I punched a button, we all heard the dial tone. "That number again, Denny?"

He repeated; I dialed; a line rang. After several rings, there was a telltale shift of ring pattern as the voice mail kicked in.

Then a disembodied, digitized voice spoke to us, as if from the grave: "Hey, it's Jason. You know the drill. Talk to me." Beep.

With a jittery finger, I punched a button, disconnecting the call.

The color had drained from Denny's face. He stared at the phone, speechless.

Glee bounced the tip of her pen against her glossy red lips. "Interesting."

I nodded. "Could you phone Sheriff Pierce, give him that number, and ask him to run a history?" I stood, stepping into my office to grab my jacket.

Glee smiled. "Dashing off?"

Feeling inside my pockets for notebook and fountain pen, I told her, "I'm overdue for a visit with Mica Thrush." And I took off toward the newsroom.

Remembering my manners, I paused in the doorway and turned back. "Thanks for coming in, Denny. Have a great day."

Mica was in the driveway of her big dumb house, hosing her brutish new Mustang. Was it merely the slant of my own gay disrelish, or do babes with hot cars *always* seem a tad vulgar? Picture this:

Mica's jet-black muscle car lurched at a rakish angle on the blacktop, as if ready to pounce, intending to devour its mistress. Mica herself wore the skimpiest of black bikinis, a garment consisting of little more than string and pasties. Her toenails, I noticed, were lacquered black to match her fingernails and lips. She frolicked with a black bucket of white suds, stretching to sponge the car with one leg pricking the air. Her other hand held a sputtering black rubber hose, which twisted and jerked around her body like a hungry, venomous mamba. She giggled and dripped in the hot August sun, pampering her hot rod with languid inefficiency. This spectacle could doubtless provide a testosterone goose for some, but not, alas, for me. To each his own.

As I parked at the curb and got out of my car, Mica pretended not to notice my arrival, swirling a gob of suds in one of the Mustang's front wheel wells, as if cleaning its ears. She squatted on the slick pavement with her back to me, knees splayed, the string of her thong consumed by her crack. As I walked up the driveway, she tried to steal an unnoticed glimpse of me while adjusting the nozzle to rinse her beefy Pirelli tires.

So I stepped on her hose.

She twisted the nozzle, banged it on the pavement, then looked it in the eye, mystified by its limp performance.

I was tempted to move my foot and let her have it, but I resisted. "Morning, Mica. What's seems to be the problem?"

She sprang to her feet, aping surprise. "Oh, hi, Mr. Manning. The water . . ." She wagged her flaccid hose, still bewildered by the problem.

Struggling not to laugh, I summoned an air of sternness. "We need to talk."

"Your cute friend was here already, and *we* talked. You know, the cop."

"Sheriff Pierce is beginning a difficult investigation. I hope you helped him all you could."

She shrugged. "He went over all the same old stuff with Daddy and me."

"Where's 'Daddy' now?"

"He went back to bed. The sheriff was boring."

"Well, I have a few *new* questions. Maybe you'll find them more interesting."

"I'm kinda busy right now." She dropped the hose, sloshed the sponge in her bucket, and slathered some suds on the Mustang's side windows.

"New car?"

She nodded. "Just got it. Just last night."

Uh-huh. Once the coroner ruled out suicide, she and Daddy must have figured the insurance checks were in the mail. Getting to the point of my visit, I asked, "Did Jason have a cell phone?"

"Sure." She was working toward the rear window. "Jason was wireless."

Frustrated, stepping toward her, I asked, "Well, why in hell—?" But my question was interrupted by the hiss and spray of the hose, which jerked across the driveway, dousing my shoes. "Christ," I muttered, stooping to grab the nozzle, screwing it shut.

Mica's tongue hung out as she panted her lifeless laugh.

Kicking water off my feet, I finished my question: "Why in hell didn't you mention Jason's cell phone when we were here on Monday? You *knew* we needed to trace your brother's last phone calls, didn't you?"

"Well, *sorry*." She looked at me as if I were nuts. "You were asking about the number of lines in the house and the voice mail and all—we weren't talking wireless." She plopped her sponge in the bucket.

Shaking my head, I thought aloud, "I should have figured it out yesterday, as soon as Doug reported that there were no calls from Denny on the phone log."

"Denny Diggins? Definitely—he and Jason talked all the time—I heard them. Like I told you, they were . . . involved." She tittered. "Can't imagine what Jason saw in *him*."

"Mica," I said flatly, "you've been making things up, and I want to know why."

She put her hands on her hips, striking a defiant pose—quite a sight, considering her near nudity. "*What* have I been making up?"

"The whole business about your brother being gay and his on-the-rocks love affair with Denny Diggins." There was now good reason to suspect that Jason had indeed been gay, but I was trying to put Mica on the spot. Would she back down and admit that Monday's revelations were mere speculation? Or would she get defensive, reaffirming the whole story?

She got defensive. With an uncharacteristic touch of fire, she assured me, "Jason *was* gay. He told me things; I saw things; I heard things. And I know that he was involved with that old guy. Sometimes Jason was away all afternoon with him, sometimes all night. They were together. They were having sex. And lately, they were fighting about it. I *know*—because I heard Jason on the phone." Having made her speech, she reached behind her head, flicked her long, straight mane of black hair to the side, and picked up the hose.

Watching her attempt to rinse the sun-dried soap from her car, I weighed two possibilities: either Denny had lied about his asexuality during our emotional encounter earlier that morning, or Mica was lying to me now. Somehow, I still trusted Denny's soul-baring on this touchy matter. But if Denny had never even broached intimacy with Jason, why would Mica so stridently assert the story of a soured tryst? I could think of only one clear motive for such a lie.

I asked her, just loudly enough to be heard over the spray of the hose, "Why did you take out a life-insurance policy on your brother?"

She twisted the nozzle, dropped the hose, and turned to face me. "Why? Because it was cheap."

I might have predicted any number of answers, but this was not one of them. Stupidly, I asked, "What?"

"I'm twenty-one, Mr. Manning." She suddenly sounded mature, worldly, and shrewd; I wondered if her bimbo routine had been an act all along. "Mom's dead, Dad's sick, and his business is failing. School's not my thing. Success, in my book, is a fast car and a place in Aspen. No one's going to hand it to me, so I've learned to look out for myself. I live well enough here, for now. What money I have, I invest."

"In life insurance?"

"Exactly. It's a waiting game, but I'm young—and as I've said, Dad's sick. I've assumed all along that the business would go to Jason, so I had to insure Dad's life to make sure I'd get something substantial when he dies. Trouble is, Dad's a bad health risk, and the insurance is expensive."

I offered mock consolation. "What a shame."

With a fuck-you sneer, she squatted at the bucket, wringing her sponge. "*Anyway,* while exploring all this, I discovered that it was dirt cheap to insure Jason's life—he was young and healthy, with excellent actuarials. So I figured, What the hell? For a few extra bucks I could give myself a nice extra cushion. Now, lo and behold, Jason is dead, and I get two million dollars." Standing, she tossed the sponge aside, lifted the bucket, and carried it to the curb.

Following her, I asked, "Has it occurred to you that many people might find the circumstances of your brother's policy suspicious?"

She threw the dirty water into the street, then turned to me. "I got lucky," she said with a shrug, "that's all."

Neil and I met for lunch at First Avenue Grill, and I reported on my meetings with Denny and Mica.

He, in turn, reported on his attempt that morning to phone Roxanne at her Chicago law office. "They said she'd gone down to Springfield for a few days—can you imagine? I wonder what *that's* all about."

"Carl. Obviously."

"Obviously—I can't quite see Rox visiting Lincoln's tomb. But what *about* Carl? Did she go to confront him, to 'talk,' or just to spend some time with him?"

I shook my head. "Only she can answer that. We'll have to wait to hear from her." In truth, I didn't really care, not just then. As a friend, I owed Roxanne at least a sympathetic ear in her ongoing saga of romance-versus-commitment, but that Wednesday afternoon, I had weightier concerns on my mind.

Finishing lunch, I told Neil, "I have a meeting scheduled with Dr. Formhals later, down at the Public Safety Building. I need a refresher on the medical aspects of Jason's death. But I have some spare time first—"

"Time to kill?" cracked Neil.

I smiled, but let it slide. "I think I'll linger here at the Grill for a while. When the lunch crowd thins out, I want to talk to Nancy."

"Be gentle," he told me, grinning. "No rubber hose."

"Not yet," I assured him, returning his grin. My smirk, however, was triggered not by the image of Nancy Sanderson sweating out a brutal interrogation, but by my recent memory of Mica Thrush wound up in wet black tubing.

Neil stayed for an extra glass of iced tea while I had coffee, but he kept checking his watch. "Sorry, I need to get back. I'm sending Cynthia's pavilion project out for bids today, and there's a lot to wrap up this afternoon."

We clasped hands over the table. I told him, "No need to keep me company. Get your work done. We'll catch up tonight."

He stood. "Early dinner, remember. Thad has rehearsal."

I nodded. "I'll give you a call if anything develops."

We winked as a substitute for a kiss, then I watched him leave, never bored by the sight of him in motion.

Some twenty minutes later, the last of the other patrons had left the restaurant, and Nancy noticed that I alone remained. She crossed to my table with a tentative smile, asking, "Is everything all right, Mr. Manning? Is there something you need—more coffee, your check?" She whisked an imaginary fleck of lint from the sleeve of her neat silk suit.

I smiled. "Everything's fine, thank you, Nancy. I was hoping, if you had a few minutes, we could talk awhile."

Clearly, my request was unexpected, but after only a moment's thought, Nancy bobbed her head. "Of course, Mr. Manning. My pleasure." She added, "As long as it's 'just us,' may I offer you a chilled glass of Lillet? I just might join you."

Laughing, I replied, "How could I refuse such an offer?"

So she got the bottle and a pair of small glasses, then joined me at the table. As she poured a few ounces for each of us, she told me through a wan smile, "It seems very strange to be sitting with you."

"I hope it's not unpleasant."

"Heavens *no*, Mr. Manning." She recapped the bottle of Lillet. "I merely meant that you've dined here hundreds of times since your arrival in Dumont, and it's always been my pleasure to *serve* you."

"I understood what you meant." Since she had offered the liquor and poured it, I expected her to signal that we should drink it—perhaps a casual toast—but her hands had left the table, resting demurely in her lap. So I took charge. Fingering the little glass (it resembled a juice glass, but was more delicate), I raised it slightly and told her, "After all this time, it's a pleasure to get better acquainted."

"It is indeed." Her right hand left her lap, lifted her glass, and touched it to mine. We both sipped the blond, sweet, syrupy vermouth. She swallowed, then dabbed her lips. "Was there something in particular you wished to discuss?"

I nodded—the topic was difficult, and there was no point in dancing around it. "The death of Jason Thrush."

"Ah." She sat back a fraction of an inch. "I understand your concern."

"You do?"

"Well"—her gaze wandered from mine as she searched for the words—"I understand there are circumstances that, in the eyes of some, might appear to implicate your nephew." Quietly, she added, "I'm sorry, Mr. Manning."

"I presume, then, you've read about the coroner's report."

"Certainly. I saw it in this morning's paper. The very notion of mushroom poisoning seems terribly bizarre, don't you think?"

"Yes, I do." Shaking my head, I added, "It makes me wish that mushrooming was *not* among Thad's various interests."

She leaned toward me. "That's precisely my point. Thad's avid interest in mycology is rather well-known, and deservedly so. I've lectured many a year to the mushroom club at Central High, and he's one of the brightest pupils I've encountered—to say nothing of his infectious enthusiasm for the subject." She smiled. "I'm sure you're very proud of him."

I laughed at the irony. "I *would* be, of course. Unfortunately, this particular area of expertise only adds to the suspicions of those who already feel Thad had some sort of vendetta against Jason."

Nancy lowered her eyes. "Yes, I heard about the, uh . . . threat." She was doubtless tempted to add, It's the talk of the town, but she spared me that insight.

I exhaled noisily, gathering my thoughts. "Nancy," I began, uncertain how to broach this remark, "you seem to be fond of Thad, but I get the impression—from some things I've heard—that you disliked Jason Thrush."

She sipped her Lillet before telling me, with no apparent emotion, "That's correct. As you may know, I have something of a history with the Thrush family, and it has not been cordial."

I nodded. "I'm aware of two painful incidents, one of them twelve years ago, the other more recent. I learned this only yesterday, and I was especially sorry to hear the circumstances of your husband's death."

"Thank you, Mr. Manning. My husband—his name was Leonard—had worked with Burton Thrush since the founding days of Typo-Tech. He was a chemical engineer and was largely responsible for developing some of the processes that enabled the business to capture the early market in phototypesetting. There was a computer team as well, of course, and Burton himself was a chemist, but it was ultimately Leonard who cinched the key formulas and processes. His contributions and loyalty were such that many people assumed he and Burton were partners in the business, but in fact, Leonard was simply a paid employee. He was very *well* paid, and the terms of his contract were generous, but he had no real stake in the business itself."

"Burton had always been the sole owner, correct?" Flipping open a steno pad and uncapping my pen, I began to make a few notes.

She nodded once. "Yes. Burton's ownership was never in dispute."

"What *was* in dispute?"

She thumped her fingers on the table. "Issues of decency, honor, simple justice. That sounds rather vague, I'm sure. Specifically at issue were the terms of Leonard's contract—after he died."

"He died too young, I know. But how? Was it related to his work?"

Her head wobbled. "We don't really know. He was forty-six; I was forty-five. He took gravely ill with a liver condition that was untreatable, at least back then. There was talk of a transplant, but the disease progressed too quickly, and Leonard died within a month of the diagnosis. He had a family history of late-life liver problems, so he was prone to the condition, but his lab work with experimental chemistry may well have triggered the final sclerosis. If you're asking whether I *blame* Burton for Leonard's death, no, I don't. But I do blame Burton for making *my* life a living hell after Leonard died."

I paused in my note-taking to sip the Lillet. "There was supposed to be some sort of death settlement?"

"Yes, from the very beginning, but it turned out there had been some legalistic oversights in Leonard's initial employment contract with Burton, and since the company was entering a period of decline, Burton took full advantage of those loopholes. Leonard had devoted himself heart and soul to that business, but when he died, despite his considerable 'sweat equity,' I got virtually nothing."

"Did you take Burton to court?"

"You bet. But he had good lawyers, and the written contract was faulty, and he just plain lied about his verbal agreements with Leonard. I lost—not only the lawsuit, but a comfortable future as well. With no children to lean on, I had to enter the workforce." She drank the last of the Lillet in her glass, then tapped the bottle, as if to ask me, More?

I accepted with a nod, and she poured a bit more for both of us.

"I had never much *liked* Burton, but after the showdown in court, I must confess, I hated the man. Two years later, when his wife, Patricia, died in a car accident, I was sorry for her, but I found great joy in his misery. His failing health has also brightened my spirits."

"And the death of his son?"

She smiled. "You're too perceptive, Mr. Manning." She raised her glass, toasting destiny: "What goes around, comes around."

Though my mouth felt dry, I could not quite bring myself to join her as she drank. Instead, I sat back, watching her. "Unless I'm mistaken, the justice you find in Jason's death is sort of a double payback."

"Yes," she confirmed flatly, "it is." She leaned forward on the table, resting her weight on her elbows, and I realized she had begun to feel the alcohol. "Did you hear what happened? It was shortly before you took over the *Register.*"

I nodded. "Jason did some damage here at the Grill."

She snorted. "*That's* an understatement. It was two years ago, come October. Late one evening, Jason and some teammates came in. They had been carousing and were already drunk, needing food. I was inclined not to serve them, but in truth, we were afraid to refuse, given their condition. On top of which, I figured, a good hot meal would take the edge off their drunkenness, so they were served. As soon as the meal was under way, though, Jason demanded liquor, and then the others did as well. My staff and I naturally refused—not only because the boys were already far too drunk, but because they were clearly underage."

"And then they got . . . rowdy?"

"Rowdy? With Jason as their ringleader, they practically *destroyed* the place. I was shut down for two weeks for repairs. Burton would barely admit that his son was in any way to blame; he claimed I was falsely accusing Jason out of spite for our own previous run-in. Ultimately, grudgingly, Burton did pay for the repairs, but he *refused* to make any restitution for those two weeks of lost business."

I shook my head. "Nice guy. You should have sued him, Nancy."

"Yes, I probably should have. The sad truth, though, is that I feared losing to him in court again. I had thought I'd easily win the case over Leonard's death settlement, but I didn't. I was drained of all confidence in confronting Burton. It was easier to cut my losses."

"Exactly as he wanted."

She nodded, then lifted her glass and drank.

I leaned forward on the table. "So when Jason died, you shed no tears."

"Please." She laughed. "I'm not the least bit sorry that Jason is dead, and I'm delighted to watch Burton suffer through yet another tragedy that has befallen the house of Thrush. But"—she leaned within inches of me and spoke with slow, deliberate resolve—"I. Did. Not. Kill. Jason."

Unprepared for this statement, which seemed to both read my mind and counter my unspoken thoughts, I stammered guiltily, "No one ever meant, uh . . . *I* never meant to accuse . . ."

"Mr. Manning." Her flat inflection was candid and unemotional. "I have never made a secret of my intense dislike for the Thrushes. Objectively speaking, I'd have had a strong motive to kill Jason, and many people know it. When I read this morning that Jason was the apparent victim of mushroom poisoning, I realized at once that suspicion could begin to focus on me, much as it has focused on your nephew, Thad; this is borne out by your invitation today, for the first time ever, to sit and talk with you. Your reasoning in these suspicions is solid. My affection for local mushrooms and their culinary purposes is, I daresay, legendary. The flip side of ingesting wild mushrooms is avoiding the poisonous ones, so it's only logical to assume that I am well acquainted with the fly agaric and the entire *Amanita* family—which indeed I am. If you'd care to step outside, I can point out specimens growing within a hundred yards of the door, right downtown."

I cleared my throat. "That won't be necessary, Nancy. I trust your expertise."

Still leaning near me, she picked up her glass and drank the last of her Lillet; I did likewise. Swallowing, she breathed heavily, then told me, "I had a motive to kill Jason, and I had a working knowledge of the mushrooms that killed him—but so did Thad. You seem eager to believe that Thad could not have committed this crime. I'm asking you to believe that I too am a gudgeon of circumstance." Having stated her case, she again breathed heavily, then sat back in her chair, watching me.

I remained propped on my elbows, leaning over our empty glasses. The calm features of my face surely gave no hint that my mind was in a spin. These dizzying thoughts were not the result of alcohol, nor were they caused by Nancy's words. No, a scent hung there at the table, sweet and flowery, which at first I assumed to be that of the liquor, perhaps carried on Nancy's breath or even my own.

No, I realized, what I smelled was Nancy's perfume. It was saccharine, feminine, and cloying—much like the fragrance that lingered in Jason's room after his death. Once again, the smell triggered a vague memory from many years back.

But I just couldn't place it.

By the time I left First Avenue Grill, I was nearly late for my meeting with Coroner Formhals, so I hopped into my car and drove the few blocks to the Public Safety Building, which also housed the sheriff's department. As luck would have it, just as I arrived, someone pulled out of a space not far from the front entrance. I parked at the curb and trotted from the car to the door, glancing at my watch. It was exactly two o'clock; I was on time.

I checked in at the dispatch booth, telling one of the officers on duty at a switchboard that Dr. Formhals was expecting me. The deputy greeted me by name, recognizing me from previous visits to Sheriff Pierce. She asked, "Do you know how to find the coroner's office?"

I replied that I did, then asked, "Does the sheriff happen to be in now?" If Pierce was free, I reasoned, he might want to sit in on the meeting with Formhals.

Checking a logbook, the deputy shook her head. "Sorry. He's out on a call."

Thanking her, I headed down one of several wide hallways that radiated from the dispatch booth. The heels of my shoes (they had dried from that morning's encounter with Mica's frisky hose) snapped on the hard, gray terrazzo floor. I turned down a narrower hallway, where white walls reflected the sterile glow of too much fluorescent light. Stepping to a door bearing an engraved-plastic sign, CORONER, I turned the knob and stepped inside.

The dreary little outer office had a desk where a clerk normally sat, but not today. Opposite the desk were a few extra chairs along a windowless wall. Reaching above the chairs, I straightened a faded print of a tranquil country landscape that hung askew in a cheesy plastic frame. My fussing did little to improve the general air of civil-service shabbiness.

"Is that you, Mark?" called the doctor's deep voice from around a corner. In the breezy tones of his handsome speech, I thought I detected the hint of a Caribbean patois, but as Formhals had worked in Dumont far longer than I, I knew nothing of his roots.

"Yes, Vernon. Anybody home?"

He stepped out of his office and extended his hand. "Just me today, I'm afraid. I've been expecting you. Welcome." His manner, as always, was cordial enough, but I'd always found his bearing stiff, his air professorial. A crisp white lab coat did nothing to soften this image. His half smile seemed to say with a chortle, This won't hurt a bit. Instead, he asked pleasantly, "How can I be of help?" And he escorted me around the corner, into his office.

The office was far more inviting than the waiting room. The space was larger and more comfortable, dominated by a massive wooden desk. In addition to the expected books, files, and medical charts, the office bore various personal touches of its occupant, accumulated over the years—diplomas, certificates, photographs, sporting memorabilia, travel knickknacks, a child's finger painting, a maple-based desk lamp that had been retired from home use. Behind the desk, he settled into a creaky chair with worn leather upholstery. In front of the desk, I took a more spartan seat of county issue, opened my notebook, and readied my pen.

I told him, "Before you issued your report on Jason Thrush yesterday, concluding that the manner of death was homicide, Sheriff Pierce welcomed my investigation into the matter, as the grounds for an official police investigation were limited."

Formhals nodded. "I'm aware of that, Mark, and Douglas has asked me to continue to assist you."

"Excellent. Thank you." I gathered my thoughts. "The search for Jason's killer has so far been focused on motivation, which has broadened the field of suspects instead of limiting it. In other words, I've found that plenty of people, to varying degrees, had reason to want Jason dead." I glanced at my list of possible suspects: greedy Burton and Mica Thrush, vengeful Nancy Sanderson, sexually confused Denny Diggins, ambitious Tommy Morales, jilted Nicole Winkler, and finally, Thad.

I continued, "I'm essentially back at square one, Vernon. Instead of focusing on motives, I should probably take a closer look at the killer's method, which has been a point of confusion all along."

Freshening the dimple in the knot of his tie, he asked patiently, "What confuses you?"

I tossed my hands. "Everything." Reviewing my notes, I said, "You've determined that the cause of death was mushroom poisoning. This was first suspected on the basis of the victim's symptoms and later confirmed by toxicology tests. Choline and muscarine were the specific toxins detected, and these poisons are associated with the mushroom known as fly agaric, which grows here at this time of year."

"Bravo." Formhals smiled. "A fine summation. Keep going."

I tapped my notes. "Here's where I get confused. Fly agaric is rarely lethal unless consumed in large quantities, and its toxins act quickly, within three hours of ingestion. That's not long enough for the mushrooms themselves to be digested and passed through the intestines. What's more, Jason hadn't vomited, so there should have been mushrooms in his stomach—but there weren't." I looked up at Formhals. "How can you reconcile this disparity?"

He sat forward in his chair, exhaling a sigh. "I don't have *the* answer, Mark. The pathology takes us only so far; the rest is a matter of detection. Still, there are a number of ways that the poisoning could have occurred, ways that are consistent with the known facts of the case."

I scribbled a few Palmer loops to get my pen running. "Meaning, Jason didn't necessarily eat a heap of fly agaric, then keel over."

"Correct. In fact, we know that he ate no mushrooms whatever."

I asked my key question: "Then how did the poison get *into* Jason?"

As if it were obvious, he responded with a shrug, "By first taking the poison *out* of the mushrooms."

I paused as if slapped. Looking him in the eye, I asked, "You can *do* that?"

"Of *course.*" He laughed. "I do apologize, Mark, but these technicalities seem second nature to me. Let me qualify my 'of course.' Actually, it would take a bit of lab know-how, but certainly, the choline and muscarine could be extracted from fly agaric. Once that's done, there are any number of ways to poison the victim, who wouldn't need to ingest a single mushroom. Offhand, I can think of at least three possibilities."

I smiled. "My pen is poised, Doctor."

He cleared his throat, preparing to lecture. "First, the extracted toxins could be added in strong doses to virtually any food or liquid, then fed to the victim—the classic method of administering poison. Second, the extracted toxins could be suspended or dissolved in alcohol, creating a tincture; if the infected alcohol was then spilled on the victim, the toxins could be efficiently absorbed through the skin, with deadly consequences. Third, the extracted toxins could simply be injected into the victim, with very fast results."

I looked up from my notes. "But that would leave a needle mark, right?"

"Right. During my physical examination of the victim, I scrutinized every square centimeter of the body, finding no evidence of injection—but a killer will sometimes resort to fiendish measures to disguise needle marks."

I didn't want to ask.

"An additional possibility," Formhals rambled on, "is that the two telltale toxins could have been combined from sources other than mushrooms, then used to kill the victim, giving the *appearance* of mushroom poisoning. This method would of course send the investigation down a false path, focusing on innocent suspects along the way . . ."

He continued to weigh the finer points of his theory, giving examples of how the mushroom toxins could be replicated, but I tuned out, having already learned the crucial detail that would steer my investigation in a new direction. I now knew that Jason had not actually eaten mushrooms; he'd simply been poisoned—by whatever method—with toxins either extracted from mushrooms or combined to mimic mushrooms. Something Formhals had said still rang in my ear: "it would take a bit of lab know-how" for the killer to pull this off. As Formhals lectured onward, I scratched at my notes, drawing a series of empty boxes, borrowing Lucy's grid technique.

Gazing at the list of names, I recalled with relief that Thad had been a miserable chemistry student during his junior year; no one could argue that he had sufficient skill to pull off any of the scenarios suggested by the coroner. I inked a thick X over Thad's box on the grid.

But, I wondered, what about Tommy Morales? I knew nothing of his academic record—was he perhaps a chemistry wiz? An enticing question mark snaked through his box.

Then I focused on the Thrushes. Mica was a total ditz who wouldn't know a centrifuge from a Bunsen burner—she got a quick X—but her father, Burton Thrush, was another matter. I'd learned just an hour ago from Nancy Sanderson that Burton, like Nancy's late husband, Leonard, was a chemist. Now *there* was a promising angle, explaining how the sickly Mr. Thrush could pump new life into his ailing business with an enormous and badly needed insurance payoff. I darkened Burton's box so forcefully, my pen nearly tore the paper.

And what about Nancy herself? Might her masterful kitchen techniques be matched by devilish lab skills? Her own husband, after all, was something of a test-tube genius whose experimentation may have triggered his untimely death. Had Nancy picked up a few tricks of her own along the way, techniques that would allow her to exact grim revenge on the family that had, in her own words, made her life "a living hell"? A question mark now adorned Nancy's square on the grid.

Denny Diggins—I doodled around his square. Where, if at all, did he fit into this? His only accuser was the lamebrained Mica Thrush, who claimed that Denny had been in the throes of a tempestuous sexual relationship with her brother. It didn't add up, I felt. Denny himself had asked, "Do you think I'd dare hope that Jason could love *me?*" Even Mica had echoed that question. Still, she stood by her story, and the story was appealing because it led back to the Players Guild.

Everything about Jason and his death seemed so . . . well, *theatrical.* He was a hunky young heartthrob, a teenage actor tragically downed in his prime (by poisonous mushrooms, no less) on the very evening he was to debut the starring role in an original play. The dramatic overtones of his murder had escaped no one, and for this very reason, Thad was seen by many as the prime suspect.

Though my list included several people who had gained some form of satisfaction from Jason's death—Nancy Sanderson, Mica Thrush, and her father, Burton—these names were not associated with the Players Guild, which is where my instincts pointed. Among those involved with *Teen Play*, Thad was never a real suspect in my eyes, while the others—Denny Diggins, Tommy Morales, and Nicole Winkler—were suspicious only by virtue of mere conjecture.

Mulling over the coroner's new angle that the killer would need a good deal of lab savvy, I realized that I was lucky to have a valuable resource at my disposal. Frank Gelden, who had so willingly offered his know-how in exploring the coroner's initial theory, had since underscored his friendship to Neil and me and would doubtless be willing to help again. He had accurately deduced that Dr. Formhals had targeted fly agaric. As an experienced researcher, Frank was surely familiar with the techniques now described by Formhals. Perhaps Frank could be of help in identifying others who might share this background—others who had some involvement with the Players Guild.

"Excuse me, Vernon."

The coroner's extended scientific monologue clipped to a halt as he reacted to the sound of my voice. From behind his desk, he looked at me as if he'd forgotten my presence. With a jolt of recognition, he asked, "Yes, Mark?"

Leafing to the back of my notebook, I said, "I wonder if I might use your phone. Something just occurred to me."

"Of course." He turned the desk phone in my direction. "Be my guest."

I found the Geldens listed among several other recent acquaintances. Closing my notebook, I lifted the receiver. I explained to Formhals while dialing, "I have a biologist friend who's knowledgeable about mushrooms, and he happens to be tech director at the Dumont Playhouse. I'm hoping he'll be able to steer me—" I raised a finger, as the other phone had begun ringing.

After four rings without an answer, my call transferred to voice mail. "Hi," gushed a breathy voice, Cynthia's. "You've reached the Dunne-Gelden residence, but neither Frank nor Cynthia is available at the moment. Please leave a message, and we'll get back in two winks." Beep.

Shaking my head, I hung up—two winks, indeed.

Formhals asked tentatively, "Is something . . . funny?"

"Not very. It was just the phone message, promising to get back 'in two winks.' "

"How precious." Formhals gave me a big, exaggerated wink, bursting into laughter. I couldn't recall having seen him indulge in an expression of mirth more forceful than a low chortle, so this reaction was tantamount to an outburst.

Getting in the spirit, I reminded him, "That was *two* winks—you owe me one."

So he supplied the other wink, laughing all the louder.

To my mind, it wasn't all that funny, but he was clearly enjoying himself, so I chuckled along, waiting for his laughing jag to pass. It didn't though. Instead, his hilarity seemed to snowball, and soon he was pounding the desk, gasping for air. "My God . . . two winks!" Which of course proved infectious. Before long, I was whooping away with him.

And then, I almost gagged on my own laughter. All this talk of "two winks" had led me to recall that there was not just one Winkler, but two, the pretty Nicole and her mother, Joyce. I'd been focusing on Nicole, Jason's jilted armpiece, but I hadn't given her mom a second thought. I now realized that she too had an ax to grind. Joyce was one of the first people I'd met at the previous Wednesday's dress rehearsal—the costume mistress who'd volunteered for the show in order to do some bonding with her despondent daughter. When she'd complained about having to juggle night shifts on her "real job," Denny had explained, "Joyce is a lab technician at the hospital."

"Mark?" said Formhals, swiping a tear from his face. "What's wrong?" His jollity had subsided, done in by my own sudden seriousness.

"Nothing's wrong, but something may be falling together here. Tell me, Vernon, would a hospital lab technician be likely to have knowledge and skills sufficient to extract the mushroom toxins in the manner you've described?"

He paused in thought, eyes to the ceiling. "Depends on the specific job, but sure, anyone employed in hospital tech work should have some fairly advanced lab skills." His gaze returned to me. "Why? Who is it?"

"It's someone in the theater group who may have had a vendetta against Jason—in other words, a *motive* for murder. Now I know she also had the *means* to extract mushroom toxins, the apparent murder weapon."

Formhals arched his brows. "You're getting close then."

I frowned, idly flapping my notepad, as if expecting answers to spill from its pages. "What I don't know—at least not yet—is whether she had the *opportunity* to poison Jason."

Thad was despondent at dinner, so I offered to drive him to the mid-week pickup rehearsal. In truth, I'd been scheming since my afternoon meeting with the coroner, trying to come up with an excuse to go to the theater that evening, so Thad's mood proved opportune. Pushing food around his plate, he accepted my offer with a listless "Whatever."

Driving downtown a few minutes before seven, I asked Thad, in the guise of idle conversation, "Fly agaric—ever heard of it?"

With a sour grin, he asked back, "You mean, *before* this morning's news?"

"Yeah. I had no idea that honest-to-God poisonous mushrooms were growing in the wild around here. Did you learn about them in school?"

"Well, *sure*." He turned to me, showing a bit of life, a spark of genuine interest. "We cover the bad mushrooms with the good in Fungus Amongus—that's the whole point of the club."

"Makes sense, I guess. Fly agaric—it even *sounds* nasty. Are they ugly?"

"Not at all. In fact, fly agaric is among the more beautiful of the local species. Later tonight, I'll show you some—I've got a jarful in my room."

"Really? What are you doing with something like that?"

He shrugged, as if the answer were obvious. "They're left over from the field exam we had at the end of the semester."

"Ah." With a satisfied smile, I understood that Thad's "secret stash" was, as I'd hoped, nothing the least bit sinister or incriminating. I could now dismiss the nagging suspicion that had vexed me since Monday evening and focus squarely in the direction suggested by Dr. Formhals that afternoon.

Turning onto First Avenue, I asked, "Mind if I hang around the theater awhile? Just want to see how it's going."

"No problem." He smiled faintly, having read my concern, if not my intention. "You can watch the whole show if you like."

"Well, I'm always up for a bit of good theater."

He laughed quietly. "Don't count on it." I was afraid he meant that he anticipated giving a lousy performance, but he explained, "Pickup rehearsals are always on the sloppy side. There's no makeup or costumes—it's just a refresher for lines and tech cues."

"Ah." Still, I'd stay. I wasn't interested so much in watching the play as in observing the dynamics of the cast and crew. My plan was not to be entertained, but to unmask a killer.

Pulling into the parking lot near the stage door, I saw that most of the troupe had already arrived; many of the cars had begun to look familiar to me. I locked up my own car and crossed the lot with Thad. The stage door had been propped wide open, and I assumed that the theater had heated up again during the week. Though the days had begun to shorten and the sun hung low in the midsummer sky, it was going to be a hot night.

Inside, cast and crew milled together around the stage and in the auditorium. Because of the heat, almost everyone wore shorts and a T-shirt; I recalled Thad telling me that this rehearsal would not be in costume, which gave me a sudden worry: Would Joyce Winkler, the show's costumer, be there that night? After all, she wasn't needed. But then I noticed Joyce sitting with her daughter Nicole on the far side of the stage. Nicole looked bereft, as she had since Jason's death, and Joyce spoke to her softly, stroking the girl's honey-colored tresses.

Thad spotted Kwynn Wyman, who was busy at a folding table checking paperwork against a list (advance ticket sales, possibly), and walked over to join her. I descended a short stairway from the stage apron to the auditorium floor. Banks of lights flashed in sequence as circuits were tested from the control booth. Tommy Morales sat off by himself with his nose planted, as usual, in a script, readying himself to step into yet another new role—that of Ryan, Thad's character. Walking up the center aisle, I passed the makeshift director's table in the fifth row. Denny Diggins acknowledged me with a quiet, neutral "Mahk," and I returned the scant greeting with an equally limp "Denny."

I took a seat about two-thirds back and checked my watch; it was several minutes past seven. The upper rows of the auditorium were stifling, and I knew that I was in for a long, sticky evening. I had on the same dress slacks I'd worn to the office, as well as the same shirt, collar open, arms rolled up a few turns. I wished I'd had sense enough to wear something more comfortable. In the dim, warm light that glowed from the stage, I opened three more buttons below my collar.

"People!" said Denny, thwacking his hands. "Listen up. We're running a bit late already, so gather round. I have a few announcements." He picked up his clipboard and glanced through several pages of notes, waiting for his "people."

As the cast and crew converged from scattered areas of the theater, I couldn't help noting how the tone of things had changed in a week. The previous Wednesday at dress rehearsal, everyone had shared an upbeat mood of anticipation, itching to open the show. Tonight, though, the entire company seemed sullen and demoralized, wanting only to be done with it. What's more, I noticed with dismay that the group was now clearly divided into factions, forming two clumps as they approached Denny's table. On the one side were Thad, Kwynn, and a handful of other kids; on the other were Tommy Morales and everyone else.

"All right," said Denny. "Let me begin by telling all of you how proud I am—of you, and of the show. We opened under taxing, tragic circumstances, and you rose to the challenge like pros. We've enjoyed good press and great audiences, and we're assured of three more sellout crowds this weekend. It's only natural to feel a bit of a midrun slump, so we all need to focus tonight, get back in the groove, and remember what we're here for."

When he paused for breath, a hand shot up, and a girl in the cast asked, "Mr. Diggins? If Tommy takes over as Ryan, who'll play Dawson?" And the whole group broke into animated discussion. Thad, naturally, looked stunned.

So did Denny. "*Melissa,*" he scolded above the yammering, "nothing's been said about a cast change."

"But," said someone else, a guy on the running crew, "what about the . . . you know, the contingencies?"

Denny managed to shush everyone. "I *know* we've had some difficulties, and I *know* there have been rumors of a cast change, but that's pure speculation—at this point. There's nothing to it."

" 'At *this* point,' " someone repeated skeptically.

"Tonight," said Denny, "we're running the show exactly as before. Try to keep the pacing up, and let's try to recapture some of that lost energy."

Kwynn spoke up. "Don't worry, Mr. Diggins. The show's in good shape. Once we're up and running again, we'll look better than ever." Pointedly, she added, "All of us."

Thad squeezed her wrist, mouthing, Thanks.

Denny beamed. "Now *that's* the attitude." Flipping a page of his notes, he said, "There's no 'good' time to talk about this, so I might as well mention it before we begin. As you may have heard, now that the coroner has issued his report, Jason's body has been released for burial. The family announced this afternoon that the funeral will be held this Saturday morning. There'll be a huge turnout, of course, and I assume everyone here plans to attend. I think it'd be a nice gesture if all of us from the Players Guild attended as a group—*en masse*, as it were."

Couldn't Denny have predicted the effect this little speech would have on the troupe? Certainly, there was no "good" time to make funeral plans for a murdered colleague—but *now?* With Kwynn's help, he had just succeeded in psyching up the cast to put the past behind them and pull together for a rough rehearsal, but now his mention of "the coroner" and "Jason's body" had brought the group back to the grim reality of what had happened.

A wave of chattering swept over the kids, punctuated by a chorus of moans. Nicole broke into loud sobs; Joyce hugged her daughter's shoulders, looking off into space with a steely expression. Someone from Tommy's faction started to say, "There wouldn't be a funeral at all if—" but he stopped short of saying Thad's name. A girl from Tommy's crowd shouted over the noise to Denny, "I don't think it's right for *all* of us to be there," meaning Thad was not welcome. Thad rested his forehead in one hand; Kwynn patted his hair and whispered something in his ear. Denny watched with a disapproving glare, waiting for the ruckus to fizzle out.

When the kids finally calmed down, Denny had sense enough to drop the topic he had so imprudently raised. "We're here to rehearse," he reminded everyone. "Places, please. And let's give it some pizazz."

As instructed, the cast disappeared backstage, the crew took their posts. The work lights onstage flicked out, the houselights dimmed, and after a few moments' blackout, the stage lights rose and the scene was set. I heard the familiar opening lines of dialogue before Thad would make his entrance as Ryan. Everything was the same as at the two performances I'd attended, except for the mishmash of street clothes worn by the young actors.

Thad entered, and as soon as he opened his mouth, I knew he was in trouble. The events of the past week, coupled with the near unanimous hostility vented only minutes earlier by the rest of the cast, had taken their toll. Thad's movements looked unsure and clumsy; his vocal delivery lacked projection and realism. Worst of all, he began to flub lines, and without the assistance of other cast members who should have fed him cues, he broke character during several agonizing silences.

Tommy Morales—need I mention?—was superb in his performance as Dawson. He was thoroughly in control and growing into the role, easily stealing the show. Watching Tommy's interaction with Thad, I was grateful not to be responsible for the decision that Denny Diggins was surely weighing.

Thad was dragging the whole show down. Even I could tell that the pacing was off by a mile or two; act one was running many minutes longer than it should have. At last, though, the action arrived at the fight scene, the finale before intermission. Thad's weeks of rehearsing the precisely choreographed climax were for naught. I could barely watch as he stumbled about the stage with Tommy, who did his best to give the scene a measure of dramatic tension and realism. Finally—mercifully—the phone started ringing, the lamp crashed from the table, Tommy recited Dawson's threat, and upon his exit, the lights blacked out.

I recalled, a week earlier at dress rehearsal, Denny leaping to his feet at this point, shouting, "*Mah*-velous!"

Not tonight. "All right," he said dryly as the houselights rose, "that was a bit rough. However, that's the reason we rehearse—thank God there wasn't an audience." He glanced at his pile of notes and checked his watch. "Look, we're running way late. Take a short break—ten minutes, please—then we'll run act two. Notes at the end." He sat back thinking, shaking his head.

The cast hopped down from the stage, stepping out of character. They mingled, chatted, and gulped soda, conspicuously avoiding Thad. Kwynn stuck by him though, ever cheery, trying to draw him into conversation with whoever was near. The theater seemed even hotter than before, and everyone was sweating. Thad was drenched from the rigors of the fight scene.

Though I had no idea what to say, I needed to offer Thad a few words of encouragement, so I rose from my seat and stepped down the aisle toward the front of the auditorium. Watching Thad and Kwynn, I noticed Tommy veer near them as he edged through the yakking little crowd. He was sweating even worse than Thad, and I chuckled at his bedraggled appearance.

Kwynn nabbed Tommy and managed to engage him in a bit of discussion with Thad. As I drew nearer, Kwynn was saying something, but stopped short, breaking into laughter. Staring bug-eyed at Tommy, she wafted her hands near him. "God, Tommy, when did *you* start wearing that cheap perfume?"

Hearing this comment, Nicole Winkler turned and whispered something to her mother.

Tommy shrugged off Kwynn's question, excusing himself to go get a can of pop. As he brushed past me, I got a good whiff, and sure enough, Kwynn was right—he wore the same fruity fragrance I'd smelled in Jason's room when the body was found, and it definitely wasn't Vetiver. Tommy skittered away from me, and I cocked my head, watching, again associating that fragrance with some long-ago boyhood memory. What *was* that?

And suddenly, I knew. Everything began to make sense. Within a moment, the whole riddle seemed plain to me.

By now, Thad had noticed my approach and doubtless wondered what I'd have to say. As I now had some urgent business to attend to, I simply gave Thad a big smile and a thumbs-up, as if he'd just given the performance of his young career—he must have thought I was nuts. Then I spun on my heel and approached Denny at his director's table.

"My!" he cooed. "Aren't *we* looking rakish?"

I'd forgotten that most of my shirt was open. Fastening the lower buttons, I sat in the seat next to him and said, "Something's happening, Denny. Could you do me a favor? After rehearsal, when you give your notes, could you ask Thad and Tommy to stay a few minutes late, then excuse the others?"

He gave me a sidelong glance. "It's hot, Mahk. We're running late as it is."

"I know." I put a hand on his shoulder. "It's important, Denny."

With a woebegone sigh, he told me, "Oh . . . very well."

Speaking low, I told him, "One more thing. After you've established with everyone that Thad and Tommy are staying late, pretend you've had an afterthought and ask Joyce Winkler to stay as well."

He propped himself on one elbow, removed his glasses, and asked, "You want me to . . . 'pretend'?"

"Yeah, pretend. You know—*acting.*"

"I presume you have a *very* good reason for this."

"Denny, I'm in no mood for games either. Of *course* there's a good reason."

He paused—dramatically—then nodded his assent, dismissing me with a wave as he returned his attention to his notes.

For once, his cavalier attitude didn't bother me in the least. Having gotten what I wanted, I stood, returned to the aisle, and bounded up to the back of the auditorium, where I slipped through the double doors to the lobby.

I recalled seeing a pay phone somewhere and spotted it near the glass doors to the street. My footfalls echoed as I crossed the ornately tiled lobby—its Moorish design seemed all the more exotic and mysterious in the semidarkness. Massive iron-framed chandeliers and wall lanterns hung black and bleak. The only indoor light came from a gaudy popcorn machine at the concession stand. Near the front doors, a diagonal slash of orange light angled in from the streetlamps and snaked across the contours of the phone. The coins rang loudly as I dropped them through the slots; then I punched in a number I had come to know well.

"Hello?"

"Hi, Doug. Sorry to bother you at home."

"Always a pleasure, Mark. Besides, the law—like the press—never rests."

"Glad to hear it. Finished with dinner?"

Pierce laughed. "Why?"

"I'm downtown at the theater, and I think you'll want to join me."

"Hm. Good show?"

"It's only a rehearsal, and the first act, to quote the esteemed director/playwright, was 'a bit rough.' I have an inkling, though, that the evening is about to get considerably more interesting."

"Oh?"

"Pardon the cliché, but at the end of act two, we should be ready to lower the curtain on the mystery of Jason's death."

Pacing the lobby, I waited for Pierce to arrive, thinking through everything I'd learned in the five days since Jason Thrush's unexpected death. We'd come to understand that the boy was murdered—puzzle enough—but the most daunting challenge still lay ahead: to prove beyond doubt the identity of his killer. On the phone, I'd offered Pierce no specifics of my just-evolved theory, nor had I needed to. Without pressing for details, he'd offered to come down to the theater at once.

I'd told him not to use the stage door; I would unlock the front entrance for him.

I could hear that the rehearsal had resumed inside the auditorium, so I attempted to muffle my steps as I crossed the tiled floor again to the front of the lobby, where I stopped and waited, watching the street through the row of plate-glass doors. First Avenue was quiet; it seemed that nothing moved in the eerie, palpable heat of the midsummer night. Double shadows, cast by warm lamplight and icy moonlight, added a disjointed, dreamy edginess to the surreal streetscape.

As the sheriff's tan sedan rolled into view and parked at the curb, I turned the dead bolt on one of the doors and stepped out to meet Pierce under the marquee, preferring not to speak inside the lobby. The thud of his car door seemed to reverberate up and down the street, as did the amplified scrape of his soles on the cement as he walked toward me, offering the unspoken greeting of his handshake. "What happened?" he asked.

I began explaining, "I met with the coroner at his office this afternoon."

Pierce nodded. "I heard that you'd been in the building. Was Vernon helpful?"

"Very. He offered a number of plausible explanations as to how Jason could have been poisoned by mushrooms without having actually eaten mushrooms. One of those possibilities seems suddenly relevant."

"Okay"—Pierce smiled, his cheeks shining with sweat—"clue me in."

"I learned that it would be possible to extract the two toxins— choline and muscarine—from fly agaric and to suspend them in alcohol, creating a tincture."

"You mean . . . like a Mickey?"

I shook my head. "You wouldn't have to *drink* the stuff. If you got enough of it on your skin, the toxins could be absorbed through the flesh, having the same effect as if the mushrooms themselves had been ingested."

"Whew. That would explain why there were no mushrooms in Jason's stomach. But where does *that* leave us?"

"I had no idea"—I grinned—"until tonight. Let me back up. Last Wednesday at dress rehearsal, when Jason and Thad had their set-to, I had noticed a sweet, fruity fragrance in the theater, and later, Kwynn

Wyman wisecracked that Jason was wearing 'cheap perfume.' On Friday night when we responded to your page to the Thrush residence, I noticed the same smell in Jason's bedroom, probably on his body; I assumed he had again overdone it with some cheap aftershave. On Monday, though, when you and I again visited his bedroom, I found that Jason didn't use aftershave, but a pricey men's cologne, Vetiver, which has a scent totally different from the one Kwynn and I had noticed."

Pierce was listening patiently but looked skeptical. "Intriguing, yes. So . . . ?"

"So tonight"—I paused—"Tommy Morales was sweating at intermission, and he reeked of the same 'cheap perfume' that Jason was wearing when he died."

"God," said Pierce, stunned. Barely above a whisper, he asked, "You mean that Tommy's *aftershave* was used as a deadly tincture to kill Jason? Could Tommy be clever enough—or scheming enough—to commit such a crime?"

I answered merely, "We'll soon find out." Then I explained that the rehearsal's second act was already in progress and that, at its conclusion, Denny Diggins had agreed to ask Thad, Tommy, and Joyce Winkler to remain after the others.

"Why Joyce Winkler?" asked Pierce.

"All in due time."

We entered the lobby, I locked the door behind us, and then we slipped into the auditorium, where we took seats in the shadows of one of the back rows, watching the remainder of the rehearsal.

Thad's performance deteriorated further, and the pacing of the second act was even worse than that of the first. Thad's slump infected the entire cast, who now seemed resigned to the futility of their efforts— save Tommy Morales, a consummate trouper, oblivious to the slipshod dramatics that surrounded him. Had the scenery begun crashing to the floor, the performance would have been no worse, and in fact, a bit of unscripted commotion might have added a much needed spark to the floundering theatrics.

When at last the show was over—the action never climaxed as intended, but simply petered out—Denny called everyone to gather around for notes. There was none of the usual gabbing or horsing around as the kids came down from the stage. They already knew they'd done badly; their sole uncertainty was the extent to which Denny would vent his wrath.

He surprised everyone, though, by telling them calmly, "There's not much need for specific notes on tonight's weak spots. There were far too many, and you're already aware of them." He set aside his clipboard, its clamp bulging thick with notes. "And that's my point: you've performed this show perfectly in the past, so you're well aware of how it should look, sound, and feel. Tonight's pickup was meant to remind and refresh; I only hope it hasn't done more harm than good. I trust you've gotten the lethargy out of your systems—on Friday night, there'll be a living, paying audience filling these seats, and if you fail to bring this show back to its previous high level, you'll embarrass only yourselves."

The cast hung their heads as he glanced from face to face. "It's after ten already. I don't need to tell you that your pacing was abysmal. So we won't protract this sorry evening. Go home—go directly home, go to bed—and get some rest. Between now and Friday, review your blocking and run your lines. Friday night, you have the usual six-thirty call, curtain at eight. Any questions?"

They would barely look up at him. A few shook their heads. One of the girls in the cast was sniffling, dabbing tears and snot from her face with a Kleenex—their bungling had been that profound.

"You can be going, then, except for Tommy and Thad. May I ask you to stay, please? There's something I need to discuss with both of you."

Suddenly everyone seemed alert, attentive, and inquisitive. As they stood and prepared to leave, their heads wagged at each other, mouthing questions, wondering if this was "it." Surfacing from this flurry of speculation was the obvious assumption that Thad was getting axed and that Tommy would step into the leading role of Ryan. For all I knew, this was exactly Denny's intention. Had he forgotten that it was my request that he ask the boys to remain?

Nicole Winkler, looking as pretty and distraught as ever, again whispered something into her mother's ear, but this time there seemed to be considerable urgency to her message. Other kids conversed in low tones, smiling or frowning in response to the presumed shake-up. One guy gave Tommy a discreet, congratulatory nudge with his elbow.

Kwynn, visibly saddened by the prospect of Thad's ouster, gave him a big, sympathetic hug. Then she moved away from him and headed backstage toward the door, as did most of the cast and crew.

"Oh!" said Denny, clunking his forehead (he was acting). "I just had a thought. Joyce? Joyce Winkler, could you also remain behind for a few minutes, please?"

This only reinforced the others' assumption that Tommy was taking over Thad's role—Denny was asking the costume mistress to stay late for a quick refitting. Heads turned in search of her; several people called her name. Someone said, "I think she left, Mr. Diggins. She and Nicole seemed to be in a hurry."

"Ah, very well," he responded with his dismissive, well-practiced wrist flick. Shuffling papers on his table, he turned and looked for me in the dark back rows of the auditorium, offering a shrug of apology for Joyce's departure. He couldn't see me though—his gesture was directed to the wrong side of the aisle.

Sitting next to me in the shadows beneath the balcony, Pierce whispered, "She's gone. Is that a problem?"

"Maybe not. We'll see."

Within a couple of minutes, everyone had cleared out, except for Thad and Tommy, who now sat next to each other in seats near Denny's table. The theater had grown quiet, except for the sounds of some routine puttering up in the control booth—Frank Gelden was shutting down after the rehearsal, or perhaps he was just busying himself while waiting for Tommy, who needed a ride home. Both Thad and Denny could assume that I was still there somewhere, though they couldn't see me. No one was aware that Pierce was also present.

"Mr. Diggins?" said Thad, willing to take the lead in a difficult discussion. "I know I've been a disappointment, and I'm sorry."

Denny told him, "You did beautifully—in both roles, Ryan and Dawson—all through rehearsal. And your opening night as Ryan was an absolute triumph."

Thad nodded lamely. "Thanks, Mr. Diggins. But after that, things got . . . well, messed up for me. I've had a lot on my mind, and I know I've let you down." Thad turned to the boy next to him. "Tommy, you really *should* play Ryan this weekend. You deserve it. I'll just leave—it's best for the show."

"Now hold on," said Denny through a soft, apprehensive laugh. "That would leave us in the lurch, Thad. Even if Tommy could pick up the role that fast, who'd play Dawson? I'd happily step into the part myself—I wrote it, after all—but I doubt if the audience would be quite that willing to 'suspend disbelief.' " With a blurt of laughter, he added, "*Me*, a virile adolescent?"

Tentatively, both Thad and Tommy joined in laughing at the image Denny had conjured. Tommy turned to Thad, telling him, "No one wants you out of the show—at least *I* don't."

"And neither do I," Denny added.

Thad looked relieved but, understandably, confused. He told Denny, "That's, uh, *great*. But then why did you ask Tommy and me to stay late tonight?"

"Well," said Denny, unable to mask his own confusion, "that's a very good question. You see, I . . . er . . ."

I had already stood and started down the center aisle. Emerging from the shadows into the pool of light near the front of the stage, I explained, "Denny asked you guys to stay tonight in order to help me with something."

Denny rose from his table. "*There* you are, Mahk. Thank God."

"Hi, Mark," said Thad, who had turned at the sound of my voice. A gentle smile conveyed that he was simply glad to see me, and I knew how important had been my efforts of the past five days. "What's up?"

I stepped in front of the stage apron and turned to face Thad, who was seated in the front row with Tommy. Denny now stood near them in the center aisle. I told all three, "The one thing that would assure the success of this weekend's run of *Teen Play* would be a resolution to the mystery of Jason's death. If we could prove that Thad had nothing to do with the murder, he could concentrate on his acting and the rest of the cast could pull together again. Right?"

"Sure," they answered, nodding. "Yeah." "Of course."

"Well, I think I've got it figured out." With a chuckle, I added, "Thad had nothing to do with it."

Tommy asked, "Who did it, Mr. Manning?"

Denny said, "Yes, Mahk. You're sounding terribly sure of yourself tonight, whereas this morning, you were grasping at straws. Do tell us, if you truly can: Who murdered Jason Thrush? And how?"

I raised a finger, nodding. "The how is really the crux of this riddle; the who flows naturally from it."

"For God's sake," said Denny, losing patience, "now *you're* talking in riddles."

"Sorry." I slipped my hands into my pockets, taking a pace or two forward. "Let me explain. This afternoon, I learned from the coroner that Jason wasn't *fed* poisonous mushrooms; the killer's methods were far more sophisticated. What probably happened is this: someone who had a reason to want Jason dead was clever enough to extract the poisons from a local, lethal mushroom—fly agaric— and suspend them in a solution of alcohol, creating a deadly tincture. If this tincture was splashed over a large area of Jason's skin, the poisons could be absorbed through his flesh, killing him, leaving the confusing evidence that he had died of mushroom poisoning when no mushrooms had been eaten."

Denny tisked. "It's theoretically *possible,* I suppose—I really wouldn't know—but in practical terms, how would the culprit get a sufficient splash of the infected liquid onto enough of Jason's skin?" He folded his arms smugly.

"That's exactly the question I struggled with all afternoon. The answer occurred to me this evening. It might have clicked earlier, but it was buried in a boyhood memory."

Denny shook his head. "Again the riddles."

Under his breath, Thad clued me, "He's right, Mark."

"Okay"—I laughed softly—"let me back up. Last Wednesday at dress rehearsal, Kwynn made a crack about Jason's 'cheap perfume.' I had noticed it earlier that night. Sweet and fruity, it *did* smell like cheap perfume. Sorry, Denny—my first thought was that perhaps you'd overdone it with the aftershave that evening."

"Well, *really.*"

"But thanks to Kwynn's comment, I realized that Jason was wearing it. Then, Friday night, when I went with Sheriff Pierce to the Thrush home, where Jason was found dead on his bed, I noticed the same distinctive fragrance there in his room. A few days later, though, I learned that Jason's preferred cologne was something with an entirely different smell, crisp and woody."

Tommy looked up at me quizzically. "Meaning . . . ?"

"Meaning that the fragrance, the 'cheap perfume,' was not his own." I paused. "Did he get it from you, Tommy?"

Thad and Denny turned to look at him, astounded. In turn, little Tommy Morales looked back at me wide-eyed, his mouth agape.

I told him, "Kwynn noticed it again tonight—on you. She asked, 'When did *you* start wearing that cheap perfume?' "

"Mr. Manning," Tommy stammered, "I . . . I don't even *shave* yet . . . I mean, not today . . ."

"But you *are* wearing it. I can still smell it—we all can."

"Hey!" said a voice through uncertain laughter, interrupting us. Frank Gelden had finished his tasks in the balcony control booth and now trotted down the aisle from the back of the theater. "What's going on down here? Something sounds fairly intense." He wore loose-fitting shorts and a tight gray T-shirt that was seductively darkened by the pattern of his sweat. Though I'd spent an evening with him only two nights earlier, I was once again surprised by the depth of my gut-level attraction to him.

I said, "Yes, Frank, this is 'fairly intense.' We're close to solving a murder."

He stopped as he entered our circle of light. "Jason's?"

From where Denny stood in the aisle, he answered for me, "Mahk has some cockamamy theory that Jason was poisoned with 'cheap perfume.' "

"Actually," I told Frank, "it's the coroner's theory again, not mine." I ran him through the particulars I had discussed with Dr. Formhals that afternoon, concluding, "Perfume or aftershave is largely alcohol, which would make a convenient vehicle for the toxic tincture."

Weighing all this as I spoke, Frank nodded, then told me, "I must admit, it makes sense. The culprit would really have to know what he—or she—was doing, but once the toxins were in the aftershave, the victim would end up dousing *himself* with the poison. Pretty slick."

Tommy, near tears, blurted, "He thinks *I* did it, Mr. Gelden."

Frank looked at Tommy in stunned silence, then turned to me. Dismayed, he said, "You can't be serious, Mark. Tommy's a wonderful kid. Sure, I suppose he 'gained something' from Jason's death, and sure, he did resent—"

"*Smell* him," I told Frank. "Isn't it obvious? He fairly reeks of the same sweet, fruity scent that Jason Thrush was wearing at last Wednesday's dress rehearsal. Friday night, I smelled the same scent on Jason's poisoned, lifeless body."

"Mr. Gelden," Tommy pleaded, now crying openly, "*help* me. I promised I wouldn't tell, but—" He cut himself off, breaking down in a full-blown bawl, burying his head in his hands. As he heaved with sobs, Thad, though confused, stretched an arm around Tommy's shoulders, offering comfort.

Frank froze speechless, as if horrified by the intensity of Tommy's breakdown.

"Frank," I said quietly, "what did Tommy promise not to tell?"

Frank turned to look at me as if he couldn't fathom my words.

I repeated, "What did Tommy promise not to tell? Did you treat him to an erotic massage this afternoon—out at your house, with your wife out of town—the same routine you used to enjoy with Jason Thrush?"

Frank closed his eyes, unable to answer. His shoulders slumped; he looked as if he might topple. There in the center aisle, he slowly lowered himself, sitting on the carpeting that covered the bottom step. Denny and Thad watched silently, astounded. Tommy's tears stopped; he looked humiliated, betrayed, and outraged, all at once. Doug Pierce had risen from his seat in the darkness and now walked down the aisle, stopping next to Denny, behind Frank. As everyone was still absorbing the full impact of the question I had posed to Frank, no one even raised an eyebrow at the sheriff's unexpected appearance.

Frank shook his head, clearing his thoughts. "Mark," he began tentatively, "that's nuts. I would never—"

"You did *too*," yelled Tommy, rising from his seat and stepping in front of Frank. "You said I was 'special' and 'so mature.' But *Jason?* He got the same routine? *Answer me!*"

"Of *course* not," said Frank, himself near tears.

"Frank," I cautioned, "don't deny something that's so easily proven. By tomorrow, we should have the computer records of calls to and from Jason's cell phone; your number will be all over that list. And everything else fits."

Mustering a cynical laugh, he asked, *"What* fits?"

I collected my thoughts, then began proposing a script for murder: "Jason's sister, Mica, told Doug and me that Jason was gay and had been having an extended affair with someone from the theater group, someone 'older' who she assumed to be Denny. What's more, she knew that the relationship had recently soured because she'd heard Jason fighting with the guy on the phone. It had never occurred to me that Jason might be gay, but recalling last Wednesday night, Neil found it strange that Jason had accused Thad of being our 'boy toy,' an unlikely term for a het seventeen-year-old to pull out of thin air—unless, perhaps, he himself was someone's boy toy.

"Meanwhile, Frank, I got to know you and Cynthia through Neil. This past Monday night, we visited your home, and I saw your well-equipped spa, noting its many amenities and supplies, learning that your knowledge of massage techniques rivals that of any pro. I also learned, just this morning from our housekeeper, Barb Bilsten, that you were presumed gay during your high school years. I won't embarrass you, Frank, by detailing our reasoning, but Neil and I concluded that you might indeed be gay and that your relationship with Cynthia might be a marriage of convenience."

Frank looked me in the eye. "How *dare* you?"

"You're right to be offended, and I apologize. Any understanding you may or may not have with your wife is no one else's business—unless it sheds light on a murder plot."

"*What* murder plot? All you've said is that Jason may have been gay and that you suspect me of being gay too. It sounds as if you've been doing some wishful thinking, Mark. It does *not* sound as if you can tie me to Jason's death."

Pierce cleared his throat. "Mark, that *is* a bit of a stretch."

"Patience," I told them. "There's more. The critical link here is the 'cheap perfume,' the fragrance we noticed on Jason and now on Tommy, which we've presumed to be aftershave. All along, the scent seemed familiar, triggering some long-ago memory, but I couldn't place it till this evening, when I realized that the smell wasn't aftershave, but something else, something with a very specific use."

Tommy sniffed himself, looking confused.

"Recently, I myself happened to enjoy a relaxing massage"—my listeners needed no details regarding the circumstances or the purpose of Neil's delightful payback—"but at its conclusion, I found it difficult to remove all the oil. Neither toweling nor showering did a satisfactory job, and I recall thinking that oil and water don't mix. What my masseur had failed to provide was the typical finishing rubdown with an astringent that would cut the oil and cool the skin. Plain old rubbing alcohol would do the trick, as would witch hazel, which is mostly alcohol—and is often scented with a sweet, fruity fragrance that I now remember from my youth. It was routinely used in neighborhood barbershops, back in the dark ages before salons and stylists. At the end of a haircut, witch hazel was splashed on the back of the neck to soothe it after being shaved. It's still used by some masseurs at the conclusion of a treatment. And in fact, I noticed scented witch hazel among the many products stocked in the Geldens' home spa."

Still sitting in the aisle, Frank leaned back against the first row of seats. He had listened, grinning. "Boyhood memories of barbershops—big deal. Witch hazel in my home spa—big deal. Mark, this adds up to nothing."

"Hardly," I told everyone. "As I said before, everything fits. And here's how. Here's a detailed chain of events that can explain how Jason died:

"Frank was gay, but he married Cynthia some eight years ago. It was a classic marriage of convenience, made all the *more* convenient for Frank by Cynthia's work schedule in Green Bay. In recent weeks, she's been out of town every Tuesday through Friday. Frank got involved with the Players Guild this summer, and Jason Thrush entered his life.

"The physical attraction was mutual, and Frank wasted little time luring his hot young friend out to the country house, to the spa, where he treated Jason to the first of many long, lazy, sensual massages—treatments that surely reached an energetic climax for Frank as well as Jason. Frank routinely finished off each session by cleaning the oil off Jason's entire body, rubbing him down with liberal amounts of witch hazel. They had one of their sessions last Wednesday afternoon, and that evening at dress rehearsal, the smell of the scented witch hazel was conspicuous on Jason when he began sweating in the hot theater.

"This arrangement was heaven for both Frank and Jason, for a while. But something went wrong; the relationship soured; perhaps Jason made threats of exposing Frank. A professor of molecular biology and a knowledgeable mycologist, Frank found it an easy feat to extract choline and muscarine from fly agaric. Suspending these toxins in witch hazel, he created a tincture that Jason, already weakened by a bad summer cold, would find deadly—within three hours of its application. So on Friday afternoon, Frank treated his boy toy to one last doozy of a hot massage, capped off by the tainted witch hazel. Jason went home to get ready for that night's opening performance, but he succumbed to the toxins before leaving the house.

"With Jason gone, Frank saw an opportunity to nurture a *new* boy toy, an even younger one. Barely old enough to drive, he hadn't a clue, when his car broke down and Frank offered to give him rides to and from the theater, that he would become an innocent young victim of middle-age lechery. But sure enough, tonight Tommy sweated through a hot rehearsal, branded as Frank's prey by the smell of witch hazel.

"Minutes ago, Tommy's own words condemned you, Frank, as a child molester. When I asked if you had given him an erotic massage, you denied it, but he yelled, 'You did too.' Tomorrow, when Jason's cell-phone records reveal, as they surely will, that you had numerous, long conversations with him—at all hours, day and night—will there be any doubt whatever that you lived out your fantasies with Jason, at home, in the spa? With that established, will our hot-dog prosecutor, Harley Kaiser, have any doubt whatever that these circumstances supply every missing piece of the puzzle described in the coroner's report?"

Listening to all this, Frank had slumped forward, legs folded in front of him, head down. There on the floor, in his shorts and T-shirt, he looked like a little boy who'd sat down for a cry, scolded for stealing cookies. The real accusations, both spoken and implied, were of course infinitely more grave.

Tommy was first to speak, and his voice now carried not anger, but fear. "Am I going to die, Mr. Gelden? Were you trying to kill *me* too?"

Frank looked up, tears falling from his face, turning black as they hit the gray cotton of his shirt. "*No*, Tommy—I'd *never* hurt you."

Thad rose from his seat and approached me, needing my touch, needing to connect with his family, to which I was the sole remaining blood link. I closed the last step between us and gave him a full embrace, saying into his ear, "It's okay now. It's over."

Though Thad's crisis had passed, Frank's had just begun. Pierce touched his fingers to Frank's shoulder and softly recited the Miranda formula.

Frank nodded, then looked up at the sheriff. "I need to explain what happened."

Pierce said, "You're in deep trouble, Frank, but the more you admit now, the better. Cooperate, and the DA may show some leniency."

Thad and I stepped forward to listen, joining Pierce, Tommy, and Denny. We stood in a circle, with Frank sitting at our feet.

Frank breathed a long, mournful sigh, then wiped his cheeks with both hands. With a vacant look that seemed to stare through my knees, he told us, "Jason Thrush was the most beautiful young man I've ever seen—I never thought of him as a 'boy.' "

Pierce reminded him, "The age of consent is eighteen in Wisconsin. Jason was seventeen; he was a boy."

Frank laughed at this detail as if it didn't matter. "You couldn't pos-sibly understand. Neither could Cynthia, which is why she could never know about Jason. Yes, our marriage is unconventional, but it suits both our needs. It's an arrangement we can both live with; we're happy. By and large, it works. But when I met Jason earlier this summer, it was as if destiny had conspired to bring us together. Not only was he beautiful, but he said I was beautiful too. He *wanted* to know me; he *wanted* our special friendship; he *wanted* to see me at the house while Cynthia was out of town. And her schedule proved all too convenient. Naturally, I offered to Jason the private gift of my own massage skills. Those sessions were nothing short of magic; they were addictive, for both of us. Our afternoons together were sublime. Our occasional evenings were pure rapture." He paused with his memories.

Pierce asked, "But something went wrong?"

"Yes." Bitterness colored Frank's voice as he spoke to the floor. "Jason, you see, was not only beautiful, but he knew it. There was a certain arrogance about him, and for a while, I chalked it off as something of a birthright, the price of his beauty. It didn't stop at arrogance, though. He was petty as well. And when arrogance is combined with pettiness, it produces vindictiveness, a mean streak."

I couldn't help marvel that it had taken Frank all summer to discover this; the darker side of Jason Thrush was apparent to me the first night I'd seen him. But then, I hadn't been blinded by lust.

"After a point," Frank continued, "our relationship became strained, at least from his perspective. I don't know why—perhaps he got bored, perhaps he was ready to find something 'better.' In any event, he threatened, just for the hell of it, to expose the whole affair. It goes without saying, that would spell the end of both my marriage and my teaching career, so I got panicky."

I said, "And that's when you concocted the deadly tincture of fly agaric and witch hazel."

He looked up and told me flatly, calmly, "No. I did no such thing. I confess, I *thought* about the possibility of killing Jason, but I never acted on it because, ultimately, I just couldn't—I loved him."

Pierce asked, "Do you deny giving Jason Thrush a massage last Friday?"

Frank answered without emotion, without squirming, "As a matter of fact, I *did* give Jason a massage on Friday afternoon, finishing it off with witch hazel. I asked him to the house that day in hopes of effecting a reconciliation. I also thought that a long, soothing massage and sauna might help get him in shape for that night's performance. But it was *not* my intent to kill him, and the witch hazel had *not* been tainted by mushrooms—or anything else. I was surprised as anyone to learn later that night that Jason was dead."

Pierce scratched behind his ear. "Do you expect us to believe that, Frank? All the circumstances clearly, logically line up against you."

Frank threw his hands in the air. "I gave Tommy the same massage today, the same rubdown with witch hazel. He's fine."

"Get up, Frank. You're under arrest."

Frank stood. "For *what*, for God's sake?"

"Criminal sexual conduct, multiple counts." Pierce produced a pair of handcuffs. "And suspicion of murder."

Thursday, August 9

B arb turned to me from the sink with the coffeepot. "Whataya *mean*, 'Frank won't be coming to dinner tonight'? I've busted my ass."

Neil didn't say a word. He'd heard the whole story in bed after I'd returned late from the theater. Now, preparing for a rushed breakfast, he buttered toast. Thad was still in bed. Doug Pierce was probably at the gym for his morning workout, but he would not be paying his usual visit to the house on Prairie Street; he was meeting me at the *Register*'s offices promptly at eight. The Thursday paper lay there on the kitchen table, carrying not a word about the events of the previous night; I had left the theater well after the front-page deadline, and besides, even now, the story was incomplete.

Succinctly, I explained to Barb, "Frank's in jail."

"*Huh?*"

"Let's just say I should have listened to you yesterday—about the marriage of convenience. You were right. Frank's gay."

Barb beaded me with a sly stare, seating herself next to me at the table. "They don't lock people up for being gay, Mark, at least not in Wisconsin, last I heard."

Neil broke his silence with a laugh, then buttered more toast.

"Look, this is not for public consumption, at least not yet." I paused—the whole mess was embarrassingly sordid. "It seems Frank has something of a history of intimacy with underage boys, behind his wife's back, of course. One of those boys was Jason Thrush."

Barb's eyes widened with interest as she poured coffee for Neil and me.

242

I continued, "There was sufficient circumstantial evidence for Doug to arrest Frank on suspicion of murder. He was held overnight, and the DA is still reviewing the case, deciding if he wants to permit bail."

Barb whistled, mulling this turn of events. "What'd wifey-poo say?"

Neil ate toast.

After a quick slurp of coffee, I answered, "Cynthia was on the job in Green Bay, but Doug and I managed to track down her apartment. Sometime after midnight, we reached her there by phone." Unnecessarily, I added, "She wasn't happy."

"I'll bet. Where is she now?"

"She should be back in Dumont by now. She was shocked, of course—angry and confused. Even if bail is allowed, she threatened not to post it. As a courtesy to a friend, I offered to keep everything out of today's paper; in truth, it was already too late to run anything. I suggested that she come to my office this morning so we could discuss the paper's handling of the story."

Barb's brows arched. "That was big of you."

Neil ate more toast.

"It was the least I could do. It's one of those 'sensitive' stories—bound to be inflammatory—and both Cynthia and Frank have been generous with their friendship. So we booked a meeting for eight-fifteen."

Neil swallowed. "She's always punctual."

Drinking more coffee, I checked my watch. "Yeah, I'd better run. I need to meet with Doug first; he'll be at my office in ten minutes." I rose.

Barb also got up from the table. Moving to the refrigerator to grab a diet soda, she paused, suggesting, "If Cindy has no dinner plans, ask her over."

Though it was just past eight o'clock when I climbed the stairs from the lobby, activity in the *Register*'s newsroom was already in full swing. I'd phoned Lucy overnight to tell her the situation with Frank, and she had suggested extra staffing that morning as the story continued to break. Our readers wouldn't learn the details for another twenty-four hours, but when they did, we wanted them fully informed.

I could see that Doug Pierce had already arrived; he sat with Lucy inside the glass wall of my outer office. Crossing the newsroom, I noticed them hunkering over something on the low table that anchored the several upholstered chairs. Entering, I laughed upon discovering the object of their attention.

"Morning, Mark," said Lucy. "Prune!"

Pierce was sitting with his back to me. Turning, he said with a smile, "Hey, Mark. Kringle?"

I asked skeptically, "Prune?"

"Yeah." He licked frosting from a finger. "Thought I'd try it—it's good."

"Great with coffee," confirmed Lucy. A pot with several stacked mugs sat there on a tray. She poured for me.

"Thanks." I sat between them. Deigning to try a small slice of the brown-smeared Danish, I admitted, "Not bad."

Lucy flipped open a folder and ran over her notes. "Cynthia Dunne-Gelden arrives at eight-fifteen, correct?"

I nodded, glancing at my watch. "She's habitually prompt—she'll be here in ten minutes." I grabbed a steno pad from the side table and removed from a pocket my pet pen, the antique Montblanc. "Have you prepared a list of interview questions?"

"A few," said Lucy. "Once we get rolling, I assume we'll just wing it."

"A reasonable assumption," I agreed.

Pierce clapped crumbs from his hands. "My phone call—it'll get through?"

Lucy nodded, grabbing the phone on the conference table. "I'll make sure." She punched zero, then waited a few seconds. "Hi, Connie. Two things. First, we're up in Mark's outer office with Sheriff Pierce. A woman is coming in shortly, Cynthia Dunne-Gelden. She has a meeting with Mark, so let me know when she arrives, and I'll come down for her. Second, the sheriff is expecting an important call"—Lucy paused, checking her notes—"shortly after eight-thirty. Be sure to put it through to this extension, but no other interruptions. Okay? . . . Thanks, Connie." Lucy hung up the phone and crossed her arms.

"Great," I said, "we're ready. Let's run over some of those questions."

As Lucy and I reviewed the interview points she'd prepared, Pierce listened quietly, cutting a few more slices of kringle.

Mere seconds past eight-fifteen, Connie phoned up to tell us that Cynthia had arrived. Lucy excused herself, heading down to the lobby. Pierce and I waited, and within the minute, I saw Lucy's crop of red hair bobbing up the stairway at the front of the newsroom. Cynthia followed, and I could tell, even from a distance, that she had been awake all night. The shattering news of her husband's infidelity and arrest, the bizarre scheme of infecting witch hazel with mushroom toxins, the unplanned wee-hours drive home from Green Bay, all these factors had taken their toll. Normally the very picture of self-assurance, impeccable grooming, and tasteful attire, Cynthia now looked like hell. She needed sleep, she needed makeup, and she needed to change out of yesterday's clothes.

Lucy escorted her through the newsroom and into my office. Pierce and I rose. I stepped to meet her at the doorway. "My God, Cynthia," I said while giving her a hug, "I'm so sorry about everything. You must be crushed."

She nodded, managing a slight smile. "Thank you, Mark. You've become such a dear friend. At times like these—" She broke off, raising a hand to her lips, stifling a whimper.

I asked, "You've met Sheriff Douglas Pierce, haven't you?"

"Of course. Good morning, Sheriff." She extended her hand.

"Morning, Cynthia. Mark invited me to sit in on this, in case any procedural questions come up. I couldn't be sorrier about the . . . circumstances."

She assured Pierce, "Neither could I."

Lucy suggested, "Why don't we all sit down." We grouped around the table, Pierce and Cynthia across from each other, Lucy across from me.

Settling in, fingering my pen, I made a few preambular remarks, but Cynthia seemed more focused on the pastry than on my words. "I'm sorry," I told her. "Coffee? Prune Danish?"

"Thanks," she said, nodding, "I'm starved. Forgot to eat." Lucy poured the coffee; Pierce stacked a few slices of kringle on a napkin and passed it to her.

I continued, "Since news of all this won't break in the *Register* till tomorrow morning's edition, I wanted to discuss with you our treatment of the story. First, you have my assurance that we'll do nothing to sensationalize the more . . . well, 'sensational' aspects of what's transpired."

"*Thank* you, Mark." Cynthia slurped her coffee, broke off a bit of pastry.

"In exchange for this consideration, if it's not asking too much, we'd like to run an exclusive interview with you. From our perspective, it's good, solid journalism. From your perspective, it's a chance to spin the story any way you wish. Fair enough?" I uncapped my pen; Lucy switched on her tape recorder.

Cynthia nodded, swallowing. "Of course, Mark. I appreciate this opportunity."

"Excellent. Lucy has a few prepared questions to get us started."

Lucy glanced at her notes. "What was your first reaction, Cynthia, when you learned that Frank had been arrested on suspicion of murdering Jason Thrush?"

"I was stunned, of course—I still am. The revelation of Frank and Jason's apparent relationship is particularly distressful, as I'm sure you can understand. Regarding the murder, though . . . well, I just can't believe it."

I asked, "Are you saying generally that news of the murder was unexpected, or are you saying specifically that you don't believe Frank is the killer?"

She paused, thinking through my dual question. "Both. Obviously, the Thrush boy's murder came as a great shock to *everyone*. As for Frank, even though the circumstances seem damning, he just *couldn't* be responsible—I know him far too well."

Lucy asked, "Did you know he was gay?"

Cynthia closed her eyes, exhaling. "I knew he had a past." After a moment's thought, she opened her eyes. "May I speak off-the-record, Mark? I'd like to tell you some background."

"Please do." I capped my pen and set it down, but Lucy made no move to stop her tape recorder.

Cynthia leaned back in her chair. "When Frank and I first met, when I guest-lectured to his class at Woodlands, we clicked instantly. Sure, we shared the same background in molecular biology, but we also *liked* each other. We made each other laugh. We became friends. And I hardly need add that I found Frank achingly attractive—who'd blame me? Yes, I knew from the start that the attraction, the *physical* attraction, wasn't mutual, but we both seemed to understand that *that* didn't really matter. After all, I brought *other* things to the relationship. Things, you might ask, like success and affluence? Sure. Did that make me feel 'used' or 'bought'? Not in the least. I felt blessed, I felt *lucky* to land a man like that, a man wanted by many other women, a man they could never have."

I asked, "When you married Frank eight years ago, did you have a specific understanding that he would 'give up' his gay life?"

"Yes. That was part of the bargain, if you will. But we didn't phrase our understanding in terms of gay versus straight. We simply agreed that our marriage vows would be taken literally and seriously—we promised to remain faithful to each other, excluding all others."

"Cynthia," I said tentatively, "forgive me if this gets too personal, but it does seem to shed some light on what's happened. When Neil and I visited your home on Monday night, while we were touring the spa, you implied that there was no sex in your marriage. You said you were forty-three; you alluded to menopause. Then, referring to the spa as your 'private world,' you said, 'This is what's left, and I love it.' You said that it was better than sex."

A wan smile crossed her face. She gave a tiny shrug. "I can't deny it, and why should I? Yes, Frank and I have had a sexless marriage. So what? Many 'conventional' marriages evolve into that anyway. And *those* folks don't have our private world to fall back on, our retreat, our sanctuary. *Those* folks don't have the magic of Frank's fingers to get them through their lonely nights."

I nodded, recalling, "On Monday, when Neil suggested that Frank should open a massage service, you shook your fist, telling us, 'He'd better *not*.' Then Frank assured everyone—you and us—that he had 'only one client.' He called the spa the 'glue' of your marriage. Just now, you called the spa your 'sanctuary.' You do indeed think of it as a sanctuary, a holy place, don't you, Cynthia?"

Through a wistful, far-off look, she answered, "I do indeed."

I asked, "So it *angers* you to know that Frank has violated that sanctuary?"

"You better believe it," she told me without hesitation.

"Did it also anger you when you first figured it out?"

Now she hesitated. "I'm not sure what you're asking, Mark. I first found out about it last night—when Sheriff Pierce phoned."

"Sorry, but I doubt that." I didn't need my notes. I didn't need my pen. But I did feel like having another bite of prune Danish. So I put Cynthia through the agony of waiting several seconds while I fed myself, before telling her, "Sometime earlier this summer, you figured out that Frank was fooling around. Then you figured out a way to kill his lover. And the beauty, the supreme irony, of your plan is that your victim died at the hands of Frank himself, making your husband not only an unwitting accomplice, but also the apparent culprit." Reaching for my coffee, I asked, "Essentially, that's it, right?"

Her gaunt stare now made her appear even more haggard than when she'd arrived. Breaking eye contact with me, she shook her head fiercely. "*No*, I had no *idea* this was happening. For God's sake, I was out of *town* when the boy was killed."

"Sure," I said, "and that's what makes it all so slick. Everything points to Frank. And while Frank admits to giving Jason an erotic massage on the day he died, Frank also insists that he did not infect witch hazel with the mushroom toxins that killed the boy. Minutes ago, you yourself said that Frank couldn't be the killer, and on that point, I agree with you. But if Frank didn't do it, Cynthia, it had to be you."

"You're out of your mind." She sat back, now more angry than defensive.

"Doug doubted me too, when I started piecing this together last night after he'd arrested Frank. But Doug hadn't visited your spa on Monday, when I got the grand tour. I noticed some scented witch hazel among the other massage supplies, and that's what eventually led me to suspect Frank. Later last night, though, I recalled something else that was said during my tour. Frank mentioned how much he enjoyed honing his massage skills on a loving partner, and in return, 'Cynthia provides the setting, buys the equipment, and keeps up with the supplies.'"

Though the implication was clear enough, Cynthia bluffed, "So?"

I detailed the likely sequence of events: "So sometime this summer, probably a few weeks ago, you checked the supplies and noticed that they were being used much more quickly than before. Since you were supposedly Frank's one and only massage client, you drew the obvious conclusion that he was indulging in frequent midweek sessions with someone else during your absences. Your knowledge of mushrooms is equal to Frank's, as are your lab skills, so you had ample savvy to create a toxic tincture of witch hazel, leaving it for Frank to use on his secret lover during your stay in Green Bay last week. Returning on Saturday, you simply switched the infected astringent with a fresh bottle. Over the weekend, you doubtless enjoyed several loving treatments under Frank's magic hands, secure in the knowledge that he'd used those same hands to scrag your competition—without even knowing it."

Cynthia looked from me to the sheriff, then to Lucy, then back to me. "That's ridiculous," she said flatly. "Prove it."

I checked my watch. "We're working on it."

Pierce checked his watch. "Cynthia, at Mark's urging, I've secured warrants to search for any evidence linking you to the tainted witch hazel—fly agaric mushrooms, any form of the toxins choline and muscarine, or the infected alcohol itself. Confident that you'd arrive here promptly at eight-fifteen this morning, we arranged to execute the warrants at eight-thirty precisely. One minute from now, police officers in Green Bay and my own deputies here in Dumont will begin searching your office, lab, and apartment in Green Bay, as well as your Dumont home and your car. If we turn up the evidence we think we'll find, I'll be informed with a phone call—very soon—and you will be arrested, charged with murder, and prosecuted to the fullest. If, however, in the few seconds remaining, you choose to cooperate with this investigation and assist us in solving the crime, you may find the whole ordeal a bit easier." Pierce checked his watch again. "It's eight-thirty. Well, Cynthia?"

Both Lucy and I had our pens poised. The tape was rolling. The metaphorical clock was ticking. Cynthia stared numbly at the speakerphone in the center of the table. A full minute passed, feeling like ten. No one spoke.

The phone rang.

Pierce reached, then paused to repeat, "Well, Cynthia?"

She raised her head to eye him defiantly. Was she clinging to some last-ditch hope that he might be bluffing?

He was not. The phone rang again, and he punched the flashing button. "This is Pierce."

"Hi, Sheriff. Jim Johnson." I recognized the name and voice of the deputy who'd met us at the Thrush residence on Friday night. "I think we've got—"

"*Wait.*"

"Hold on," Pierce told his deputy. Turning, he asked, "Yes, Cynthia?"

She knew that further denials would be futile, further stalling was pointless. Through dry, sticky lips, she said weakly, "It's . . . in the car . . . the witch hazel, the suspension of mushroom toxins. The bottle's in the trunk of my car, parked in front of this building." Then she seemed to wither in her chair.

Pierce turned to the phone. "Did you get that, Jim?"

"Yes, Sheriff. We found it."

"Handle with care. That's the murder weapon. Send it out for analysis. Thanks, Jim." Pierce punched another button, disconnecting.

Cynthia had begun murmuring something.

Pierce asked, "What's that, Cynthia?"

She looked up at us with swollen eyes. "I didn't mean to *kill* him, I swear to God. I didn't even know who it was. I assumed it was a man, but I didn't even know that, not for sure. I wanted to make him sick, to teach them both a lesson. It was meant to be a . . . a 'dirty trick,' that's all. Poisoning from fly agaric is rarely lethal—how was I to know it was just a kid, a kid with a bad cold?" She broke down, weeping into her hands.

Pierce, Lucy, and I exchanged a silent round of troubled looks, resigned to what would follow.

Pierce cleared his throat, recited Cynthia's rights, then stood. "Come on, Cynthia. Let's go now. You need some rest—and a good lawyer."

Nodding, she stood.

Lucy and I rose as well. We followed as Pierce escorted Cynthia out of my office and began leading her through the newsroom. At a high sign from Lucy, one of our staff photographers stepped forward and, with strobe flashing, captured the dramatic exit that would grace tomorrow's front page.

Though my promise not to sensationalize the story was merely part of a ruse, intended to trap a killer, I still felt compelled to honor it. The Geldens and the Thrushes would suffer only the humiliation they had brought upon themselves. The *Register* would stick to the facts.

I grinned. There was no way to tame this story. It didn't need trumped-up headlines, cheap innuendo, or other tabloid tricks.

Tomorrow's front page would be, in a word, sensational.

EPILOGUE

One Week Later

OUR TOWN'S PAIN

*Moving beyond a recent tragedy, we can
learn lessons of tolerance*

By MARK MANNING
Publisher, Dumont Daily Register

Aug. 16, DUMONT WI—The death of Jason Thrush two Fridays ago and the revelation of sordid circumstances leading to the tragedy have deeply bruised the public psyche of the town we call home. Though these emotional wounds are still fresh, it is time to place these events within a broader perspective.

Pedophilia is not a "gay perversion." Such behavior, prohibited by both instinct and law, is no more common among homosexuals than among heterosexuals. The gay community, in fact, is especially quick to condemn any infraction of this taboo.

Which makes recent events all the more distressing. There is no defense for Frank Gelden's violation of public trust. As a teacher, a mentor of youth, he has not only harmed his young victims; he has besmirched the gay community and betrayed Dumont at large.

Still, a measure of understanding is in order. Gelden's actions with Jason Thrush were motivated by no intent to harm the boy. To the contrary, Gelden was motivated by misplaced passions confused with love. Similarly, when Cynthia Dunne-Gelden discovered her husband's illicit affair and plotted her now well-known revenge, she too acted out of passion, neither knowing her victim nor intending to kill.

Sadly, though, one boy is now dead. One man is now disgraced, with his career abruptly ended and his future uncertain before the law. And one woman's happy life is now consumed by day-to-day remorse as she awaits trial on manslaughter charges.

As a fair-minded community, can we judge these individuals? In this instance, judge we must.

The chain of events that led to the ruin of these lives was rooted not in Frank's gayness, as some might conclude, but in Frank and Cynthia's faulty attempt to sublimate his true nature in a contrived but "acceptable" marriage of convenience, a relationship that ultimately bred deceit and deadly retaliation. ❏

Thursday, August 16

T he humdrum routine of the dog days of summer never felt better. Two weeks earlier, I had lamented the quiet pace of life in Dumont as an obstacle to putting out a daily newspaper. I'd gone so far as to wish for "a modicum of mayhem." Would that other wishes, more benignly focused, were so promptly granted. Now, though, that week of midsummer mayhem was fully a week past, as was the crisis that had so profoundly affected our household on Prairie Street.

Thad was in bed, dreaming sweet nothings, growing another inch.

Barb fussed with something at the sink, gabbing and grousing.

Neil and I sat at the kitchen table, dressed for the day, lingering over breakfast, content in the maturity of our relationship. That contentment was reflected in the shared afterglow of another spontaneous, early-morning experiment in our ongoing quest for fresh romance. Details of that morning's experiment need not be shared. The particulars would merely provide gratuitous titillation—containing no clues related to crime-solving. Suffice it to say, the experiment was highly successful, so our quest has continued.

Neil set down that morning's *Register*, folded open to the opinion page. "Good editorial," he told me, giving my arm a squeeze of approval. "Good point."

Too modestly, I averred, "Nobody reads that stuff." I was fishing.

Barb took the bait. "*Sure* they do," she said, turning to us. "Lots of people flip to the editorial page—first thing. It's the heart of the newspaper."

"Heart *and* soul," I agreed. "Did you read it, Barb?"

"Every word." She turned off the water—she must have been cleaning mushrooms, the bounty of an early hunt. Wiping her hands, she approached the table. "If you ask me, Cindy's getting off too easy. Manslaughter—what's up with that?" Barb sat with us, refilling our coffee mugs from the pot on the table.

I explained, "Cynthia claims that she assumed the tainted witch hazel would not be deadly, and Harley Kaiser, our duly elected DA, believes her. She's agreed to cooperate and plead guilty to the lesser charge. She'll still do time."

"Good." Harrumph. "Any way you slice it, she killed that kid. Besides, the whole situation was of *her* making. She was the one itching to play wifey-poo. Cindy thought she could change Frank—everyone knows that's a fag-hag mission that *never* works."

Neil choked with a spurt of laughter while trying to swallow some coffee. After wiping his mouth, he reminded Barb, "Frank said 'I do.' He agreed to play house with Cynthia. Now they've *both* filed for divorce. What a mess."

"Yeah, well . . ."

I added, "Life will be no picnic for Frank either. With considerable fanfare, he's been dumped from the Woodlands faculty—he'll never teach again. He's never lived anywhere but Dumont, and his reputation here is down the crapper. He'll need to build a completely new life somewhere else."

"You mean, after prison?" asked Barb.

With a shrug, I explained, "That's up in the air. He's out on bail right now, and the DA still hasn't figured out what charges to bring against him. No one's come forward with claims that Frank molested anyone *before* Jason, and the ailing Burton Thrush has no desire to press charges that would put him center stage at a very sordid, very public trial. The DA could still hand down charges against Frank on the simple merits of the case, but he'll think twice before crossing Burton, who helped elect him. Besides, Kaiser's a hot dog; chances are, he'd rather focus on Cynthia's trial. It's far less messy, and he'll still reap a nice political spin."

Neil asked, "Tommy Morales has been left out of it, right?"

"Right." I breathed a sigh of relief, shamed by my previous suspicions of the boy, who was neither a killer nor a conspirator, but, ultimately, a victim. Feeling I owed him something, I decided to have his car repaired—one less thing for him to fret over while he focused on school and his theatrical ambitions.

Answering Neil's question, I elaborated, "On the night when Doug arrested Frank at the theater, Tommy *begged* us not to make known what had happened that afternoon—he'd be in for a real hammering from friends and family alike. Doug pitied the kid, so Tommy's been spared the emotional trauma of being dragged into the scandal."

"Thank God. Doug's a pal. He's—"

"Any coffee left?" asked Pierce himself, poking his head through the back door.

I laughed. "Sure, Doug. Come on in. We were just talking about you."

Neil added, "*Most* of it was complimentary."

"Glad to hear it," said Pierce as he approached the table.

Barb stood. "Morning, Doug. Have a seat." Vacating the chair, she crossed the kitchen to fetch a cup for him.

Sitting down, Pierce said sheepishly, "Sorry I'm empty-handed. I ran late at the gym, and I've got an early appointment at the department, so I didn't have time to swing past the bakery."

"No need to apologize," Neil assured him. "A little less Danish and a lot more running seem to be in order." He patted his flat stomach as if he were woefully flabby; in fact, he'd never looked better.

Barb brought the extra cup to the table. "Here you go, Doug. Help yourself."

"Thanks," he said, pouring. "Can't stay long. Just wanted to say hi, really."

She told him, "Thad will be sorry he missed you again. He's been wanting to thank you for attending the play *again* last weekend." The four of us had seen the show together on Saturday night.

Pierce said, "I should thank *him*—it was great."

"Yeah, it was, wasn't it?" Barb sat in the remaining chair. "The second weekend, he was even better than he'd been on opening night. He's got some real talent, that kid."

Her observation was apt. With the mystery of Jason Thrush's death resolved, Thad had been completely exonerated in the eyes of his peers—no more prank phone calls, no more back-alley scuffles. With his emotions cleared, he'd excelled in the final three performances of *Teen Play.* I told everyone, "Denny Diggins was elated. He says he can't wait to try his hand at another play."

"You're kidding," said Neil. "After all the ups and downs with that production, I wouldn't be surprised if Denny never set foot in a theater again."

I grinned. "Well, he did mention that his second play will feature a small cast of adults—no kids."

Neil said, "I'm just glad his first play is behind us. All's well that ends well."

"Yup," I summarized, "the curtain has fallen, the villains have been unmasked, and justice has triumphed."

Pierce snorted. "Those villains gave us a good runaround. In the end, though, it was most accommodating of Cynthia to leave the poisoned tincture in the trunk of her car for us. We'd have pieced the evidence together eventually, but that bottle of witch hazel brought the whole investigation to a quick, definitive close."

"Yeah," said Neil, "I was wondering about that. Why would Cynthia hang on to such incriminating evidence? Why not dump it right away?"

Barb offered, "Maybe 'cause she's *stupid?*"

I laughed. "No, Cynthia's anything but stupid. Even though she may not have intended to kill Jason, when she learned what had happened, she must have taken a measure of perverse pride in it. By keeping the evidence—a sort of trophy—and storing it in her trunk, she was, in effect, gloating. She thought she'd gotten away with murder."

"She damn near did," Pierce reminded us, no humor in his voice.

I told Neil, "Good thing she paid you fast for the pavilion design. Her future's shaky now, to say the least—I doubt if she'll proceed with construction."

"Tell me." Neil shook his head. "The pavilion's dead, I'm sure. I'm glad I got paid, but what I *really* wanted was to see the place built."

I reached a hand to his shoulder. On impulse, I suggested, "Let's build it."

"No." His tone was pensive. "It was a custom project, designed for *them*, for *their* land, for *their* life together. It's gone." This observation produced a lull in our discourse as we mulled the tragic disintegration of the Geldens' lives.

Pierce broke the silence. "I've been meaning to ask you, Mark. Last Wednesday, when you called me down to the theater during intermission, you mentioned that Denny had agreed to ask Thad, Tommy, and Joyce Winkler to remain that night after the others. But Joyce and her daughter Nicole slipped out as soon as the rehearsal was over. What was that all about?"

I nodded, grinning, having wondered when he'd ask me to clarify that detail. "Earlier that day, my suspicions began to focus on Joyce because her daughter had been jilted by Jason and because Joyce, a hospital lab tech, could probably have pulled off the tainted-tincture scenario newly suggested by the coroner. During intermission, when Kwynn questioned Tommy about his 'cheap perfume,' Joyce and Nicole began whispering to each other, further raising my suspicions. In the next moment, though, the whole witch-hazel angle clicked for me, and at that point, my suspicions shifted firmly to Frank."

"Okay . . . ," Pierce said tentatively. "So why did you want Joyce to stay?"

"First, I felt there was still a *chance* she might be the culprit. But more important, I wanted *Frank* to think that I suspected her. He was up in the control booth, so I knew he'd see me when I confronted the others after rehearsal. If Frank knew I suspected *him*, I was afraid he might bolt, get violent, or who knows? But if he thought the crime was about to be pinned on *Joyce*, I hoped he would be lured down to help support my accusations. As it turned out, Joyce had left, my fears proved groundless, and Frank came down from the booth to find Tommy, who'd planned to ride home with him. The whole setup worked fine without Joyce."

Pierce fingered the rim of his cup, nodding. "And I suppose we'll just never know what Joyce and Nicole's 'suspicious' whispering was all about. Doesn't matter now, I guess."

"Uh"—I laughed—"as a matter of fact, I've since gotten the whole story. Denny asked Joyce about the whispering and the rush to leave, and he later shared the details. The theater was especially hot that night, and at intermission, everyone was sweating. That's when Kwynn barbed Tommy about the 'cheap perfume.' Hearing this comment, the pretty, vain Nicole realized that she had neglected to use antiperspirant that evening. She was afraid that the heat might expose this grievous lapse of personal hygiene, and she was anxious for Joyce to take her home. Mystery solved."

Neil laughed heartily. "What a ditz."

With a derisive snort, Barb added, "I can understand why Jason dumped her."

Philosophically, Pierce observed, "And thus three nefarious suspects—Denny, Joyce, and Nicole—have ceased to warrant scrutiny."

I reminded him, "There were others. And I don't mean Thad."

"Indeed there were. Burton and Mica Thrush were at the top of *my* list all along. Due to those whopper insurance policies, both Burton and Mica had *the* classic motive to want Jason dead. Greed."

I nodded. "Though neither the father nor the sister proved to be a murderer, the more I've learned about them, the more I'm appalled by their unvarnished avarice. Burton, who supposedly insured his son's life to guarantee the future viability of Thrush Typo-Tech, has now announced the closing of his company; for the few years he has left, he'll live high off the death benefit. Mica, of course, never made a pretense of lofty motives for her own policy. Right after her brother's funeral on Saturday, she headed west in her new Mustang, planning to do some condo-shopping in Aspen. She had the gall to tell me last Wednesday that she 'got lucky, that's all'—and from her warped perspective, I guess she was right."

Barb whistled. "Too bad the killer *wasn't* one of those two. There'd be a certain joy in nailing people like that."

Neil said, "There'd have been no joy in nailing Mark's *other* suspect."

Barb and Pierce looked at him quizzically.

"Neil raises a good point," I told them with a soft laugh. "If Nancy Sanderson's blood feud with the Thrushes had proven her guilty of murder, First Avenue Grill would now be padlocked and shuttered. *Then* where would we be?"

"Someplace *else* for lunch," Neil answered, feigning a shudder.

With a thoughtful, serious tone, Pierce wondered, "Do you suppose Nancy really does take comfort in Burton's suffering? Sure, she herself has suffered due to Burton's insensitivity and egotism, but she's always struck me as a good, decent person. Could she really be that spiteful?"

I shrugged. "I heard Nancy talking to another woman in the theater lobby about Jason's death. She said, 'Sometimes destiny doles out its own harsh justice.' Can't argue with that—not in *your* line of work, Doug." I smiled.

"No, guess I can't." Checking his watch, he said, "Gosh, gotta run." He stood. "Thanks for the coffee. Tomorrow—kringle, I promise."

The rest of us stood. Stepping to Pierce, I put an arm around his shoulder. "Pastry or not, you're always welcome here, Doug."

Barb piped in, "You might bring bagels now and then."

"Don't start," I told her.

She showed me the tip of her tongue. She didn't expect to see mine displayed in return, and when she did, she howled with laughter.

Neil gave Pierce a farewell hug, we said a round of good-byes, then Pierce left through the back door. Barb offered to make more coffee, but Neil and I declined; our cups were nearly full, and we'd already drunk more than usual.

As we sat again at the table, Barb carried the pot to the sink and began rinsing it. "Did you see yesterday's mail?" She jerked her head toward a stack of envelopes and catalogs tucked next to the wall at the end of the counter. "No bills—I checked."

Absentmindedly, I got up, grabbed the mail, returned, and sat, putting the stack on the table between Neil and me. We routinely handled so much paper at each of our offices, opening mail seemed more and more like work—besides, it rarely brought anything other than credit offers, charity pitches, and politicians' beg letters. We both ignored the pile.

Neil asked Barb, "How are the clarinet lessons going?"

While drying the pot and reassembling the coffeemaker, she told him, "Terrific. Last night I had my second lesson. I like my teacher, and I've been working on some of my old disciplines. It feels good."

"It's been *sounding* good," I assured her, "the Messiaen piece. I'm glad we were able to get you connected with Whitney Greer."

"Me too." She stepped near the table. "He *phoned* me yesterday afternoon."

"Yeah? What for?" The community orchestra's manager had helped Barb find a teacher, but why the follow-up?

"Do you guys have a minute? I need to ask you about something."

Neil and I exchanged a quick, wary glance. "Sure, Barb. Sit down."

She did. *"Well,"* she explained, wide-eyed, "when Mr. Greer met me here at the cast party, he seemed very interested in my background as a money manager, and yesterday, I found out why. There's a vacant position on the orchestra's board of directors, and they've been needing someone with solid financial expertise, and I *am* an MBA—so he met with the board, they all talked it over, and they'd like to have me join. On the *executive* committee, if you can believe it—they need a new treasurer." She sat back, grinning.

"That's wonderful," said Neil.

"Congratulations." I told her. "Go for it. But what did you need to ask us about? I thought—" Actually, I wasn't sure *what* I had thought, but she'd made it sound so ominous.

"They have meetings, you see, and they're at night. There's a monthly board meeting, and another monthly meeting of the finance committee, which would involve me. So I'd need to be away from the house on certain evenings, if that's no problem."

"Of *course* it's no problem," I told her. "We'll muddle through when we have to—we've done it before, God knows."

"Besides," added Neil, "you'll be making a real contribution to the quality of life in Dumont."

She nodded. "That's what I figured, but I thought I'd better check. Thanks, guys." She stood. "I'll clean up after you leave. Right now, I'd like to go upstairs and get in a bit of practicing."

"Enjoy," I told her, and she left the kitchen, headed for the front stairs.

Neil sighed. "Well, we can't put it off any longer."

"What?" I'd begun flipping through the stack of mail.

"Work." He laughed, pushing back his chair. "Might as well get going."

Vacantly, I agreed, "Uh-huh." An envelope had caught my attention, addressed by hand to Messrs. Waite and Manning.

Neil leaned to look at it. "What's so interesting?"

"It's addressed to us—you first—from a hotel in Boston." As I handed him the letter, my eye fell to the next envelope, addressed to Thad, typewritten.

Barb's clarinet sounded a few warm-up tootles and scales.

Neil's face wrinkled with curiosity. Working his finger under the envelope's flap, he opened it and removed a two-page letter written on Ritz-Carlton stationery. Flipping to the end, he said, "It's from Roxanne! What the hell has she been . . . ?" He'd begun skimming from the top, then stopped. "My God," he said flatly, "you won't believe this." He positioned the letter squarely between us on the table.

It was dated Monday, three days earlier. Together, we read it:

Hi, boys!

Sorry I've been out of touch. I know you've tried to reach me, Neil, but Carl and I have been sequestered (that's the lawyer in me talking), examining options for our future. As you know, the plan to move in with him, to say nothing of the deeper issue of commitment, has weighed heavily on me. I needed some "time out," so Carl suggested a retreat to his place in Springfield, where we spent most of last week.

It's a small apartment, and both of us had managed to cut ourselves loose from office duties, so we spent a lot of time together in close quarters—a good test. And I'm happy to report that we both passed with flying colors. Have I ever actually mentioned to you that I _love_ Carl? There, surprise, I've said it. Here's another surprise:

Last Friday, Carl suggested that we consider marriage, and I tendered revocable consent (the lawyer in me again). We've set a target date of about a year for the i-dotting and t-crossing. That should be plenty of time for planning, for testing the living arrangement—and for me to back out! So I guess we're "engaged." Carl wanted to celebrate with a trip to Boston, a city he's always loved, and here we are, enjoying a prehoneymoon.

We return to Chicago this weekend. I'll phone, and we can really talk. But I wanted to warn you first by letter, hoping you won't be too shocked. You're the first to know, by the way. And here's something to think about: Would both of you, Neil and Mark, consent to stand as witnesses at our wedding? I promise, no jokes about "bridesmaids"— we need two witnesses, and we'd be honored if they were you.

Carl was married before, of course, and the whole marriage thing makes me a tad uncomfortable anyway, so the wedding itself will be very simple, very civil. In fact, we might even want to have it up there. But I'm getting ahead of myself. Let's talk. I'll phone this coming Saturday.

I miss you guys. I think of you often. And believe it or not, I'm one ridiculously happy woman.

Love, Roxanne

PS: How's everything with Thad? I assume they haven't locked him up, or you'd have managed to get through to me.

By the time we finished reading, Barb had finished practicing scales and moved on to real music, not the Messiaen solo, but a new piece, lighter in tone, more whimsical in spirit. The sounds of her clarinet drifted softly through the house as Neil and I stared speechless at Roxanne's missive.

At last, Neil broke the spell, shaking his head in disbelief. "*Engaged?*"

With a chuckle, I told him, "It happens. It's a surprise—but I'm happy for her."

"I know this sounds silly, but I feel as if we're 'losing' her."

Reaching to hold his hand, I coyly reminded him, "You had your chance. Roxanne was hot for you long before she was hot for me, which was long before she met Carl. You could have been playing house with her all these years."

He smirked. "Like Frank and Cynthia, huh? Point taken." He stood, stepped behind my chair, and placed his hands on my shoulders. "I'm much better off right here, with you—and Thad. Still, the thought of Rox getting married gives me an icky feeling that she's . . . drifting away from us."

I lifted one hand to grasp his fingertips. "Speaking of 'drifting away,' look at this." With my other hand, I raised the next envelope for him to see, the one addressed to Thad.

"Oh, God," Neil moaned, slumping behind me to rest his chin on my shoulder. "He's getting ready to fly the nest."

The envelope was from the registrar's office at Desert Arts College in California. It contained the application materials Thad had phoned for earlier in the week, after talking through his dreams, goals, and intentions with Neil and me. *Teen Play* had just closed, he'd taken his theatrical achievements to a new level, and he was dead serious about applying to study with the illustrious Claire Gray on a new campus near Palm Springs, a school that wasn't even built yet. Neil and I had ultimately agreed that if plans for the school passed muster with Claire Gray, it must be reputable, and if Thad could beat the competition to enter her program, he'd be studying with the best. With our blessing, then, he'd phoned to get the application process rolling.

I told Neil, "College is still a year away. But he needs to start applying."

"That year will go so fast though."

I stood, faced Neil, and held him in a loose embrace. Laughing at the odd turns our shared life had taken, I asked, "When you met me, did it ever cross your mind that one day we'd find ourselves in the unexpected role of parents, pining over the future of our kid?"

Looking into my eyes, Neil smiled and shook his head. "Never."

"In the time we have left with Thad, we can make every second count."

Neil nodded.

"Meanwhile," I reminded him, "you and I have all the time in the world."

As Neil kissed me, Barb's wistful clarinet sang in the distance, upstairs on Prairie Street. ❑